T0380386

PRAISE FOR THE NOVELS OF JOANNA WYLDE

"A really good bad-boy biker book! Exactly what I've been looking to read."

—*Maryse's Book Blog*

"Joanna Wylde's writing has a way of sucking the reader into the Reaper's MC world, with quirky characters and an enthralling plot that took on a personality of its own . . . I would highly, highly recommend this book to readers who love romance, but are also looking for something different. This was a very enjoyable book, and trust me when I say, you will not be disappointed."

—*The Little Black Book Blog*

"It's hot, explosive, intense, and will leave you tingling in all the right places . . . For fans of true biker books, this is one not to be missed."

—*Under the Covers Book Blog*

"*Reaper's Property* was a perfect mix: edgy, sexy, and fun. I love that Joanna Wylde really did her research with this book. She didn't just write a love story and throw in some hot bikers."

—*The Book List Reviews*

"Dying for more books in this series."

—*Smexy Books*

PRAISE FOR THE NOVELS OF JOANNA WYLDE

"[illegible] exactly what I've been looking for [illegible] to read." —[illegible]

"Joanna Wylde's [illegible] of sucking the reader into the Reaper's MC world, with quirky characters and an endearing [illegible] that [illegible] of its own [illegible] I would [illegible] highly [illegible] this book to readers who love romance, [illegible] something different. This was a very enjoyable [illegible] and trust me when I say you will not be disappointed."

—[illegible]

"It's hot [illegible] will leave [illegible] in the right places [illegible] Her fans [illegible] missed." —[illegible]

"Reaper's Property [illegible] edgy [illegible] and [illegible] that Joanna Wylde really did her [illegible] this book. [illegible] and [illegible] some [illegible]."

—[illegible]

"[illegible]" —[illegible]

REAPER'S LEGACY

JOANNA WYLDE

BERKLEY BOOKS, NEW YORK

THE BERKLEY PUBLISHING GROUP
Published by the Penguin Group
Penguin Group (USA) LLC
375 Hudson Street, New York, New York 10014

USA • Canada • UK • Ireland • Australia • New Zealand • India • South Africa • China

penguin.com

A Penguin Random House Company

REAPER'S LEGACY

This book is an original publication of The Berkley Publishing Group.

Copyright © 2014 by Joanna Wylde.
Penguin supports copyright. Copyright fuels creativity, encourages diverse voices, promotes free speech, and creates a vibrant culture. Thank you for buying an authorized edition of this book and for complying with copyright laws by not reproducing, scanning, or distributing any part of it in any form without permission. You are supporting writers and allowing Penguin to continue to publish books for every reader.

BERKLEY® is a registered trademark of Penguin Group (USA) LLC.
The "B" design is a trademark of Penguin Group (USA) LLC.

Berkley trade paperback ISBN: 978-0-425-27234-3

An application to register this book for cataloging has been submitted to the Library of Congress.

PUBLISHING HISTORY
Berkley trade paperback edition / February 2014

Cover art by Tony Mauro.
Cover design by George Long.
Interior text design by Kristin del Rosario.

This is a work of fiction. Names, characters, places, and incidents either are the product of the author's imagination or are used fictitiously, and any resemblance to actual persons, living or dead, business establishments, events, or locales is entirely coincidental.

The publisher does not have any control over and does not assume any responsibility for author or third-party websites or their content.

146028962

ACKNOWLEDGMENTS

Special thanks to Kristin Hannah, an amazing author who took time out of her own busy life to change mine. You'll never know how much it meant to me, Kristin. Thanks also to Amy Tannenbaum, Cindy Hwang, and Uncle Ray for making this possible.

I also want to thank my online community—you are truly amazing people. Love and appreciation to Maryse (SQUEEE!), Jenny, Gitte, Angie, Lisa, Paige, Sali, Sparky, Cara, Hang, the Triple M, and the ladies of Kristin Ashley Anonymous. Special thanks to Backyard for all her support.

My writing friends are fabulous, too—I love you, Raelene Gorlinsky, Cara Carnes, Katy Evans, Renee Carlino, Kim Jones, Kim Karr, Mia Asher, and my evil sister, Kylie Scott. (Watch your back. Those koalas can't protect you forever.)

Last but not least, thanks to my husband for not killing me during the writing of this book. No jury would have convicted you.

AUTHOR'S NOTE

After writing *Reaper's Property* (the first book in this series, although *Reaper's Legacy* stands alone), the most common questions I heard from readers were about my research and the characters' names. Specifically, how accurate are the books, and why do some of the names sound almost silly? The answer is that I started my career in journalism and researched outlaw motorcycle club culture extensively for my stories. This included talking to people in club life, many of whom answered questions for me throughout the writing process. The *Reaper's Legacy* manuscript was reviewed and corrected by a woman attached to an outlaw MC.

Many readers have questioned the accuracy of the road names I chose, feeling that they aren't fierce or intimidating enough (Horse, Picnic, Bam Bam, etc.). Some have suggested that no real badass would be called "Picnic," but they don't realize that road names are often whimsical or flat-out funny. Not every biker has a name like "Ripper" or "Killer." The "Picnic" in my book is named after a real man—although his name wasn't just "Picnic." It was actually "Picnic Table." The majority of the names in my book were taken from real life.

Ultimately, this book is a romantic fantasy, which means I didn't let the reality of MC culture get in the way of the story I wanted to tell. If you are interested in learning more about real women living in MCs, I highly recommend the book *Biker Chicks: The Magnetic*

Attraction of Women to Bad Boys and Motorbikes by Arthur Veno and Edward Winterhalder. The book explores stereotypes about women and motorcycle clubs by allowing real women to tell their own stories, rather than drawing conclusions based on secondary information provided by male sources.

REAPER'S LEGACY

PROLOGUE

EIGHT YEARS AGO
COEUR D'ALENE, IDAHO
SOPHIE

"I'm gonna stick it in now."

Zach's voice was rough and full of urgent need.

I smelled him all around me, sweaty and hungry and so beautiful I could die. After tonight he'd be mine for real. His hand reached down between us, guiding the round, rubbery head of his penis as it nudged my opening. It felt weird. He pushed at me and I guess he missed, because it hit me too high and—

"Ouch! Shit, Zach, that hurts. I think you're doing it wrong."

He stopped immediately and grinned down at me, the gap between his front teeth teasing. Holy crap, I loved that grin. I'd had the biggest crush on Zach since we were freshmen, but he never noticed me, not until a couple of months ago. My folks didn't let me out much, but in July I'd managed to get permission to stay with Lyssa for a night and we'd snuck out to a party. Zach had homed in, and we'd been a couple ever since.

I'd gotten really good at sneaking out.

"Sorry, babe," he murmured, leaning down to kiss me. I softened immediately, loving the feel of his lips ghosting across mine. He adjusted himself and started sliding into me again, slow and steady. This time he didn't miss, and I stiffened as he stretched me open wide.

Then he hit a barrier and paused.

I opened my eyes and looked up at him. He looked back down at me and I knew right then and there I'd never love anyone half so much as I loved Zachary Barrett.

"Ready?" he whispered. I nodded.

He shoved into me and I squealed, pain ripping between my legs. Zach kept me pinned with his hips as I gasped, shocked. Then he pulled out and I tried to catch my breath. Before I could, though, he'd thrust back into me. Hard. *Ouch.*

"Holy shit, you're tight," he muttered. He pushed himself up on his hands, throwing his head back as he pumped into my body, over and over, eyes closed and face straining with hunger.

I don't know what I'd expected.

I mean, I wasn't stupid. I knew it wouldn't be perfect the first time, no matter what the romance books said. And it didn't hurt *that* much. But it sure as shit didn't feel good, either.

Zach moved faster, and I turned my head on the couch to look across the small apartment. His brother's, apparently. We had it for the night—it was supposed to be our special, perfect time together. I'd expected flowers or soft music and wine or something. Stupid. Zach had pizza and some beer from his brother's fridge.

"Ouch," I muttered again as he paused, face twisting.

"Shit, I'm gonna come," he gasped. I felt his penis throb deep inside, almost twitching. It was weird. Really weird. And nothing like I'd seen in movies—not even a little bit.

Was that it?

Huh . . .

"Oh, *fuck* that's good."

The apartment door opened as Zach collapsed between my legs, oblivious to the world. I couldn't do anything but watch in horror as a man walked in.

I didn't know him, but he couldn't have been Zach's brother. He didn't look anything like Zach, who was taller than me, but not by a whole lot. This guy was *really* tall, and muscular in the way men who work with their hands get from heavy lifting on the job.

He wore a black leather vest with patches over a ratty T-shirt and jeans that had streaks of dark motor oil or grease or something. A half rack of beer dangled from one hand. His hair was short and dark. Almost military. His lip was pierced and he wore two rings in his left ear and one in his right, like a pirate. Eyebrow was pierced, too. His features were bluntly handsome, but nobody would ever call him pretty. Big black boots covered his feet, and the chain from his wallet hung low across his hip. One of his arms had a full-sleeve tattoo. The other had a skull with crossed blades behind it.

He stopped in the doorway and looked us over, slowly shaking his head.

"I told you what I'd do if you broke into my place again," he said quietly. Zach popped up and his face went white. His entire body—with one notable exception—stiffened. I felt that exception slither out of me, along with some fluid, and realized we hadn't even bothered to put a towel down or anything.

Ewww.

But how was I supposed to know we'd need a towel?

"Shit," Zach said, his voice a tight squeak. "Ruger, I can explain—"

"Don't fuckin' explain," Ruger said, pushing forward into the room. He slammed the door shut behind him and walked over to the couch. I tried to hide my head in Zach's chest, more ashamed and embarrassed than I'd ever been in my life.

Flowers. Were flowers too much to ask?

"Jesus Christ, what is she? Twelve?" Ruger asked, giving the couch a kick. It shuddered under me, and Zach sat up, pulling away from my body. I shrieked and pushed my hands down between us, trying to cover myself from his brother's gaze.

Shit. SHIT.

Then it got worse.

The brother—*Rooger?* whatever the hell kind of name *that* was—looked right at me as he leaned across my body, grabbing a folded blanket from the back of the couch.

He tossed it over my crotch.

I moaned and died a little inside. My legs were still spread wide, my skirt up high around my waist. He'd seen everything. *Everything.* This was supposed to be the most romantic night of my life and now I just wanted to go home and cry.

"I'm takin' a shower and by the time I'm done, you need to be gone," Ruger said, getting in Zach's face. My boyfriend flinched. "And stay the fuck outta my apartment."

With that, he walked down the hall to the bathroom, banging the door shut. Seconds later I heard the shower come on. Zach jumped up, muttering.

"Asshole. He's such a goddamn asshole."

"Was that your brother?"

"Yeah. He's a prick."

I sat up and straightened my shirt. Thank God I hadn't taken it off. Zach loved to touch my breasts, but we'd actually moved pretty fast once we got started. I managed to get to my feet, holding the blanket in front of me while I pulled down my skirt. I had no idea where my panties had gone, but a quick look around didn't reveal them. I leaned over the couch, digging in the pillows, hunting. No luck, but I managed to stick my hand in the disgusting wet spot we'd left behind.

I felt like such a whore.

"Fuck!" Zach yelled behind me. My head jerked up—how could

things possibly get any worse? "Holy fuck, I cannot fucking believe this!"

"What's wrong?"

"The condom broke," he said, eyes wide. "*The fucking condom broke.* This has got to be the worst night of my life. You better not be pregnant."

The air froze in my lungs. Apparently things *could* get worse.

Zach held the broken rubber out toward me. I stared down at the nasty thing, not quite believing my bad luck.

"Did you do it wrong?" I whispered. He shrugged, not answering.

"It's probably okay," I said after another long pause. "I mean, my period just ended. You can't get pregnant that soon after your period, right?"

"Um, yeah, probably," he said, flushing and looking away. "I didn't really pay attention to that shit in class. I mean, I always use a condom. Always. They never break, not even—"

My breath caught and I felt hot tears well up in my eyes.

"You told me you'd only done it once before," I said softly. He winced.

"I've never done it with anyone I loved before," he said, dropping the broken rubber and grabbing for my hand. I tried to tug away. The mess on his fingers grossed me out, but when he pulled me in tight and wrapped his arms around me, I caved.

"Hey, it's gonna be okay," he muttered, rubbing my back as I snuffled against his shirt. "It'll be fine. We're fine. And I'm sorry I wasn't honest with you. I was afraid you wouldn't stick with me if you knew I'd been stupid before. I don't care about any other girls and I never will. I just want to be with you."

"Okay," I said, pulling myself together. He shouldn't have lied, but at least he owned up to it. Mature couples worked through hard stuff all the time, right? "Um, we should probably get out of here. Your brother looked pretty pissed. I thought he gave you a key?"

"My stepmom has an emergency key," he said, shrugging. "I took it. He was supposed to be out of town. Grab the pizza."

"Should we leave some for your brother?"

"Screw him. And he's my stepbrother. We're not even really related."

Oookay.

I found my shoes and slipped them on, then got my purse and the pizza. I still didn't know where my panties were, but just then I heard the shower stop.

We needed to get *out*.

Zach glanced over at the bathroom, then winked at me as he grabbed the half rack off the counter.

"C'mon," he said, taking my hand and pulling me toward the door.

"You're stealing his beer?" I asked, feeling a little sick. "Seriously?"

"Fuck him," Zach said, narrowing his eyes at me. "He's a total dick, thinks he's better than everyone else. Him and his stupid fucking motorcycle club. They're all assholes and criminals, and he is, too. Probably stole it in the first place. And he can buy more anytime he wants, not like us. We'll take it to Kimber's. Her parents are in Mexico."

We jogged down the apartment complex stairs, then crossed the parking lot to his truck. It was kind of old, but at least the full-size Ford's king cab had plenty of room. We'd take it out sometimes, just the two of us, and spend hours lying in the bed under the stars, kissing and laughing. Other times we packed three or four couples in, all sitting on each other's laps.

Zach hadn't done such a great job tonight, but that wasn't his fault. Sometimes life just didn't follow the plan. I was still crazy about him, though.

"Hey," I said, stopping him as he opened the driver's-side door.

I turned him around and popped up onto my toes, kissing him long and slow. "I love you."

"I love you, too, babe," Zach said, smoothing my hair back behind my ear. I melted when he did that—made me feel all safe and protected. "Now let's go kill some of those beers. Shit, fuckin' crazy night. My brother is such a dick."

I rolled my eyes and laughed as I hauled ass around the truck.

So losing my virginity hadn't been perfect and beautiful and all that. But at least it was over and Zach loved me.

Too bad about the panties, though.

I'd bought them special and everything.

EIGHT MONTHS LATER
RUGER

"Fuck, it's my mom. I gotta grab that," Ruger yelled across the table at Mary Jo, holding up his cell. The band hadn't started yet, but the place was still packed, and he couldn't hear a damned thing. He didn't get out much since he'd started prospecting the Reapers. Earning a place in the club was a full-time job by itself, and he pulled shifts at the pawnshop, too.

Ma knew that, and she wouldn't have called if it wasn't important.

"Hey, lemme get outside," he said loudly into the phone, walking toward the door with long strides. People got the fuck out of his way, and he bit back a smile. He'd always been a big guy, but now that he wore an MC cut?

Fuckers practically dove under the tables when they saw the club patches on his vest.

"'Kay, I'm outside," he said, moving away from the crowd in front of the Ironhorse.

"Jesse, Sophie needs you," his mom said.

"What do you mean?" he asked, peering at his bike, parked down the street. Was that guy getting close to it? *Oh, not gonna happen . . .*

"So, are you going?" she said. Shit. She'd been talking.

"Fuck, sorry, Ma. Missed what you said."

"I just got a panicked phone call from Sophie," his mom repeated. "Stupid kids. She went to a kegger with your brother and now she thinks she might be in labor. He's too drunk to drive her and she's having contractions, so she can't drive herself. I'm gonna kill him. I can't believe he'd take her somewhere like that, especially now."

"Are you fuckin' kidding me?"

"Jesse, don't use that language with me," she snapped. "Can you help her or not? I'm in Spokane and it'll take at least an hour to get there. I'll start making more phone calls if you can't do it."

"Wait, isn't it too early?"

"A little too early, yes," she replied, her voice tense. "I wanted to call an ambulance but she insists it's just Braxton Hicks. Ambulance rides cost a fortune, you know, and she's scared of the bills. She wants to go home but I think she might need the hospital. Can you get her or not? I can meet you there as soon as I hit town. I've got a real bad feeling about this, Jess. Didn't sound like Braxton Hicks to me."

"Yeah, of course," he replied, wondering what the hell "Braxton Hicks" were. He saw Mary Jo come out of the bar, smiling at him ruefully. She knew all about sudden phone calls and changes in plans. "Where are they?"

He got the information, then hung up, walking over to his date and shrugging his shoulders. This sucked. He wanted to get laid, and not at the clubhouse. Some fuckin' privacy would be nice for once, and Mary Jo was wild as they got.

"Club business?" she asked lightly. Thank fuck she wasn't a drama queen.

"Nope, family," he replied. "My asshole stepbrother knocked up his girlfriend and now she's going into labor. Needs a ride to the hospital. I'm gonna go get her."

Mary Jo's eyes widened.

"You should leave," she said quickly. "I'll take a cab home. Shit, that sucks . . . How old is she?"

"Just turned seventeen."

"Damn," she said, shivering with genuine horror. "I can't imagine having a kid that young. Call me later, okay?"

He gave her a fast but hard kiss. She reached down and offered his cock a quick squeeze. Ruger groaned, feeling himself stiffen. He *really* needed to get laid . . .

Instead, he pulled away and walked over to his bike.

The party was halfway to Athol, off in some field that he vaguely remembered visiting when he was in high school. He found Zach's truck easy enough. Sophie stood next to it, looking scared in the summer twilight. Then her face tightened and she hunched over her giant belly, groaning. Now she looked terrified.

Ruger parked his bike and realized he'd have to leave it in the field—no way she could ride with him. Fucking great. Asshat little shits would probably run over it or something. Sophie's face was white with strain, though. No room to fuck around. She needed to go in the truck, and clearly she needed to go *now*. Ruger shook his head, glancing around for his brother.

He still couldn't figure out why a smart, beautiful girl like her would pick Zach, of all people. Sophie had long, reddish-brown hair, beautiful green eyes, and a way about her that screamed feminine softness—a softness he'd spent more than one night imagining with his dick in his hand. Even pregnant in the middle of a field party, she was still gorgeous.

Way the fuck too young, though.

She saw him and winced, reaching around to put one hand against her back, stretching as the contraction ended. Ruger knew she didn't like him, and he didn't blame her. They hadn't met under the best of circumstances, and things between him and Zach went further to shit every day. Ruger hated the way he treated their mom and hated the way he lived his life. More than anything else, he hated the way the little fuck was already running around on Sophie behind her back.

Cocksucker didn't deserve a girl like her, and their kid sure as hell hadn't won the lottery when it came to his future daddy.

"How you doing?" he asked, coming up to Sophie and hunkering down so he could see her face. Her eyes were full of panic.

"My water broke," she said, her voice a hoarse whisper. "The contractions are coming really fast. Way too fast. It's supposed to be slow with your first baby, it never happens this fast. I need to get to the hospital, Ruger. I shouldn't have come here."

"Oh, fuck me," he muttered. "You got the keys?"

She shook her head.

"Zach does. He's over by the bonfire. Maybe we should call an ambulance? Oh . . ." she groaned, leaning over.

"Hang in there," he said. "I'll get Zach. I can drive you to the hospital faster than an ambulance at this point."

She groaned again and leaned back against the truck. Ruger took off toward the bonfire, finding Zach half passed out on the ground.

"On your feet, asshole," Ruger demanded, grabbing him by the shirt and dragging him upright. "Keys. Now."

Zach looked at him blankly. Was that barf on his shirt? High school kids stood around watching them, eyes wide as they clutched their big red Solo cups of cheap beer.

"Fuck me," Ruger muttered again, digging down into his brother's pants pocket, hoping like hell he hadn't lost them. This was closer to Zach's dick than he ever needed his hand to be. He pulled out the keys, dropping Zach back onto the dirt.

"You wanna see your kid gettin' born, get your ass in the truck now," Ruger told him. "I'm not waiting for you."

With that he took off toward the Ford, wrenching open the door and lifting Sophie into the backseat. He heard a thudding noise and saw Zach climb into the truck bed out of the corner of his eye.

Little prick.

Ruger turned on the engine and popped the truck into gear, ready to go. Then he slammed it back into park, jumped out, and ran over to his bike. He had a little first aid kit in there. Nothing fancy, but at this rate they might need it. He climbed back in the truck, pulled out of the field, and started toward the highway, watching Sophie anxiously in the rearview mirror. She was panting hard and then she screamed.

Every hair on the back of his neck stood up.

"Holy shit, I feel like I need to push," she cried. "Oh, God, it hurts. It hurts so bad. I've never felt anything like this. Drive faster—we need to get there fast . . ."

Her voice trailed off as she groaned again. Ruger drove faster, wondering if Zach had something to hold on to. He couldn't see him back there. Maybe he'd passed out in the bed.

Hell, maybe he'd bounced out. Ruger didn't care either way.

They'd almost made it to the highway when Sophie started shouting.

"Stop! Stop the truck."

Ruger stopped, hoping to hell that didn't mean what he thought it did. He threw on the parking brake and turned to see her, eyes closed, face almost purple and full of agony. She was crouching forward, moaning.

"Ambulance," he said, his voice grim. She nodded tightly. He made the call, giving the operator the details of their situation. Afterward, he put the phone on speaker, dropping it to the seat. Then he got out and opened the back door, leaning in.

"I'm here with you, Sophie," the 911 operator told them. "Hold on. The paramedics only have to come up from Hayden. You'll see them soon."

Sophie groaned through another contraction.

"I have to push."

"The ambulance is ten minutes out," the operator said. "Can you hold on until they reach you? They have everything they need to help you with this."

"FUCK!" Sophie screamed, squeezing Ruger's hands so hard his fingers went numb.

"All right. It's unlikely the baby will be born before they arrive, but I want you to get ready, Ruger," the operator said, her voice so calm she sounded stoned. How did she do that? He felt about thirty seconds away from a heart attack. "Sophie needs you now. The good news is that childbirth is natural and her body knows what to do. A baby born this fast usually means a very smooth delivery. Do you have a way to wash your hands?"

"Yeah," Ruger muttered. "You gotta let go for a sec, Sophie."

She shook her head, but he pried his hands free. He ripped into the first aid kit, pulling out a couple of ridiculously small sanitary wipe packets. Then he attacked his hands and tried to go after hers.

She screamed and punched his face.

Holy shit, girl had some power behind her. Ruger shook his head, then pulled it together, his cheekbone throbbing.

Another contraction.

"It's too early," Sophie gasped. "I can't stop it. I have to push *now.*"

"When is she due?" the operator asked as Sophie moaned long and low.

"About a month," Ruger told her. "It's too early."

"All right. The most important thing is to make sure the baby is breathing. Don't let it fall on the ground if it's born before the EMTs arrive. You'll have to catch it. Now don't panic—it can take hours to push out a baby, especially the first one. But just as a precaution, I want you to find something warm to wrap around the child if Sophie delivers. You'll check the baby's breathing. If it's good, you'll lay him on the mother's bare chest, facedown, skin to skin. Then put whatever you have over him. Don't tug on the cord, cut it, tie it off, or anything. Keep your hands away from the birth canal. If the afterbirth comes out, wrap it with the child."

That's when it hit him.

Sophie was going to have her baby right here on the side of the road. His nephew.

Right now.

Holy shit, she needed to get her pants off first.

She wore leggings and he tried to pull them down with her still inside the cab. It didn't work, and she couldn't seem to find a comfortable position, either.

"We have to get you out of here," he said. She shook her head, teeth gritted, but he picked her up and set her feet on the ground anyway. Then he pulled down her sopping wet leggings and panties in one smooth move, lifting one foot and then the other to free her legs from the clinging fabric.

Now what?

Sophie cried out again, face tight as she bore down next to him, falling into a squat beside the truck.

Fuck, he needed something to keep the baby warm.

Ruger glanced around frantically, finding exactly nothing, so he pulled off his cut and tossed it into the truck. Then he ripped his T-shirt over his head. It wasn't the best, but it was relatively clean. He'd showered and put on a fresh one before meeting Mary Jo.

Sophie pushed for an eternity, crouched down and digging her fingers deep into his shoulders. He'd have bruises there in the morning. Probably cuts from her nails, too. Whatever. The 911 operator's calm voice encouraged them, saying the ambulance was only five minutes out. Sophie ignored her, lost in her own world of pain and urgency, giving loud, low groans with every contraction.

"Can you see the baby's head?" the operator asked. Ruger froze.

"You want me to look?"

"Yes."

He was pretty damned sure he didn't want to look. Fuck. Sophie needed him, though. The kid needed him, too. Ruger dropped down to peer between her legs.

That's when he saw it.

A tiny head, coming out of her body, covered with dark black hair. Holy crap.

Sophie sucked in a deep breath and gripped his shoulders even harder. She let out one loud, long moan as she pushed again.

Then it happened.

Ruger reached down—almost in a trance—as the world's most perfect little human slid right out of her and into his hands. Sophie started crying with relief as blood streaked her thighs.

"What's happening?" the operator asked. He heard a siren in the distance.

"The baby just came out," Ruger muttered, awed. He'd seen a calf born, but that had nothing on this. "I'm holding it."

"Is it breathing?"

He watched as the newborn opened its little eyes for the first time and looked right at him. They were blue and round and confused and fucking gorgeous. They closed again as the baby screwed up its tiny mouth, sucked in a deep breath and let out a piercing wail.

"Yeah. Fuck. The kid is fine."

Ruger looked up at Sophie as he raised the baby between them. She smiled hesitantly and reached for her child. Her exhausted, tear-streaked yet radiant face was the second-most beautiful thing he'd ever seen in his life.

Right after those tiny blue eyes.

"You did good, babe," he whispered to Sophie.

"Yeah," she whispered back. "I did, didn't I?"

She kissed the boy's head softly.

"Hey, Noah . . . It's Mommy," she said. "I'm gonna take such good care of you. I promise. Always."

CHAPTER ONE

SEVEN YEARS LATER
SEATTLE, WASHINGTON
SOPHIE

Our last night in Seattle didn't go so great.

My babysitter, my emergency backup sitter, and my second emergency backup sitter all had the flu. I'd have been screwed if one of my new neighbors hadn't volunteered to keep an eye on Noah. I didn't really know her, but we'd been living next to each other for a month and no red flags. Not the best, I know.

You do what you have to when you're a single mom.

Then Dick yelled at me for coming in late for my shift.

I didn't tell him I'd nearly missed work altogether because of Noah. And no, I'm not just calling him Dick because he's actually a dick (although he is). It's his real name.

That night I truly understood why he was in such a bad mood, because of the six girls who were supposed to be on, only two showed. Two had the flu (genuine—half the city had it) and two had dates. Or I'm assuming they had dates. Their official stories were a dead grandmother (her fifth) and an infected tattoo.

Apparently none of the drug stores in her neighborhood carried Bacitracin.

Either way, things fell to shit fast. We had a band, which put the customers in a good mood, but the live music and drunken dancing made it even harder to keep up with my tables. Also made us busier than usual. We would've been stretched even with a full staff. To make things perfect, it was a local band and most of their fans were college students, which meant crappy tips.

By eleven I was already tired and needed to pee in a bad way, so I ducked into the bathroom. Out of toilet paper already (of course), and I knew damned well nobody had time to restock. I pulled out my phone, doing a quick check for messages, and saw two. One from Miranda, my babysitter, and a second from Ruger, the world's scariest almost-in-law.

Shit.

Miranda first. I held it to my ear and listened, hoping to hell everything was all right. No way Dick would let me off early, even for an emergency. Ruger could wait.

"Mom, I'm scared," Noah said.

I froze.

"I took Miranda's phone and I'm hiding in the closet," he continued. "There's a bad guy here and he's smoking inside and he wanted me to smoke, too, and they kept laughing at me. He tried to tickle me and make me sit on his lap. Now they're watching a movie that has naked people in it and I don't like it. I don't want to be here and I want to go home. I want *you* to come home. I really need you. *Right now.*"

I heard his breath hitch, like he was crying but didn't want me to know, and then the message cut out.

I took a couple of deep breaths, trying to control my surge of adrenaline. I checked the time on the message—almost forty-five minutes ago. My stomach twisted and for a second I thought I might puke. Then I pulled it together and left the bathroom. I managed to walk back into the bar and have Brett, the bartender, unlock the drawer where we kept our purses.

"I need to get home, my kid's in trouble. Tell Dick."

With that I headed toward the door, pushing through drunken frat boys. I was almost out when someone grabbed my arm, spinning me around. My boss stood there, glaring.

"Where the hell do you think you're going, Williams?"

"There's an emergency," I told him. "I need to go home."

"You leave me now with a crowd like this, don't come back," Dick growled. I leaned forward and stared him down, which was pretty easy considering the guy was hardly more than five feet tall. On good days I thought of him as a hobbit.

Tonight he was just a troll.

"I need to take care of my son," I said coldly, using my deadliest troll-killing voice. "Let go of my arm. Now. I'm leaving."

Driving home took at least a year.

I kept trying to call Miranda, but nobody answered. When I reached our ancient apartment building, I tore up the wooden stairs to the top floor, shaking with a weird mixture of rage and fear. Miranda's place was right across from my little studio, and while my thighs and calves hated the climb, I'd loved how we were the only residents up here. Until now.

Tonight it felt remote and scary.

I heard music and grunting as I pounded on the door. No answer. I pounded harder and wondered if I'd have to break in. Then the door flew open. A tall guy with unbuttoned pants and no shirt blocked the entry. He had the start of a gut and bloodshot eyes. I smelled pot and booze.

"Yeah?" he asked, swaying. I tried looking around him, but he blocked me.

"My son, Noah, is here," I said, struggling to stay calm and focus on what really counted. I could kill this asshole later. "I'm here to pick him up."

"Oh, yeah. Forgot about him. C'mon in."

He stepped aside and I ducked past him. Miranda's place was a studio just like ours, so I should've seen Noah right away. Instead I spotted my useless neighbor on the couch, collapsed on her back with her eyes glazed and a dreamy smile on her face. Her clothes were rumpled, her long hippie skirt shoved up above her splayed knees. The phone lay on the coffee table in front of her, next to a bong made out of plastic pens, foil, and a Mountain Dew bottle. Empties surrounded it, because apparently weed wasn't enough to keep her entertained while she failed to babysit my seven-year-old child.

"Miranda, where's Noah?" I demanded. She looked at me blankly.

"How should I know?" she slurred.

"Maybe he went outside," the guy muttered, turning away from me as he reached into the fridge for another beer.

I caught my breath.

Across his back was a giant tattoo that looked kind of like Ruger's, only it said Devil's Jacks instead of Reapers. Motorcycle club. Bad news. *Always* bad, despite what Ruger insisted.

I'd think about that later. *Focus.* I needed to find Noah.

"Mama?"

His voice was soft and trembling. I looked around frantically, then saw him climbing in through an open window facing the street. *Oh my God.* I moved toward him, forcing myself to approach oh-so-carefully. Four flights above the ground and my boy was clinging to a windowsill. If I wasn't damned careful, I'd knock him off the ledge.

I reached out and clamped my hands around his upper arms, pulling him in and clutching him close. He wrapped around me like a little monkey. I rubbed my hand up and down his back, whispering how much I loved him and promising never to leave him alone like that again.

"I don't get what you're so upset about," Miranda muttered, pulling herself up to make room for her asshole boyfriend. "There's a fire escape out there and it's not like it's cold. It's August. Kid was fine."

I took a deep breath, closed my eyes, and forced myself to stay calm. Then I opened them and looked past her.

That's when I saw the porn on the TV.

My eyes skittered away from the sight of a silicone woman screwing four guys simultaneously. Something terrible took fire in my heart.

Stupid bitch. Miranda would pay for this.

"What's your problem, anyway?" she slurred.

I didn't bother answering. I just needed to get my boy out of there and home safe. I'd deal with my neighbor tomorrow.

Maybe by then I'd have calmed down enough not to end her miserable life.

I carried Noah out of the apartment and across the hallway to my own door. Somehow I managed to get it open without dropping him, fingers trembling from suppressed rage and a healthy dose of guilt.

I'd failed him.

My baby needed me, and instead of protecting him, I'd left him parked with a druggie who could've gotten him killed. Being a single mom sucked.

It took a warm bath, an hour of snuggles, and four books to get Noah to sleep.

Me? I wasn't sure I'd ever sleep again.

The summer heat didn't help—I swear, the place had zero air-flow. After an hour of sweating in the darkness, watching his little chest rise and fall, I gave up. I popped a beer and sat down on our couch, a thousand plans running through my head. First, I'd kill Miranda. Then either I needed to find a new place to live or she did. I also pondered whether to call the cops.

I liked the idea of throwing her and her stoner boyfriend to the wolves. They deserved a friendly visit from the boys in blue.

But since her man was in a motorcycle club, calling the cops might not be the smartest move. Guys in MCs generally weren't fond of the police, a perspective he and his club brothers might feel the need to share with me once he made bail. Not to mention Child Protective Services would get involved, which could also get pretty ugly.

I loved Noah and would do anything for him. I was a damned good mother. When other girls my age were out partying and having fun, I was taking him to the park and reading him stories. I spent my twenty-first birthday holding him while he puked from stomach flu instead of hitting the bars. No matter how rough things got, I spent time with Noah every day and made sure he felt loved.

But I didn't look so good on paper.

Single mom. Dad out of the picture. No family around, crappy studio apartment. Probably unemployed after tonight . . . What would CPS make of that? Would they blame me for leaving him with Miranda in the first place?

I had no idea what to do. I took a long pull on the beer and then turned on my phone, where Ruger's message glowed at me accusingly. Crap. I hated calling him. No matter how much time he spent with us (and he made a point of seeing Noah regularly), I just couldn't relax around him. Ruger didn't like me and I knew it. I think he blamed me for destroying his relationship with Zach. God knows, I played my part. I pushed that memory away.

I *always* pushed that memory away.

If only I unnerved him, too, but apparently that was too much to ask. Instead he just looked right through me, hardly bothering to acknowledge my existence.

Even more frustrating? Ruger had to be the hottest guy I'd ever met. He was all danger and hard muscles, with his tattoos and piercings and that goddamned black Harley of his. When he walked into a room he owned it, because it only took one look to see he was a fucking badass, the type who takes what he wants and never says he's sorry.

I'd been nursing a hell of a crush on him for longer than I cared to acknowledge, something he'd failed to notice despite his apparent fascination with every other woman under the age of forty within five hundred miles. Well, failed to notice all but once, and that hadn't exactly ended well.

At least he never brought any of his club whores around (which I greatly appreciated), but that didn't change the fact that he was one of the biggest sluts in north Idaho.

So that's where we stood.

Presented with my nonthreatening charms, the panhandle's sexiest, most prolific man-whore still preferred hanging with my seven-year-old child during his visits.

I sighed and hit the play button.

"Sophie, answer your fucking phone," he said, his voice cold and unyielding, like usual. "I just got a call from Noah. I talked to him for a while and tried to keep him calm, but then some bitch started yellin' and took the phone away. Nobody answered when I called back. I don't know what the fuck you're thinking, but your kid needs you. Get off your ass and go get him. Now. I swear, if anything happens to him . . . You don't wanna go there, Sophie. Just fucking call me when you find him. No excuses."

I dropped the phone and leaned forward on my knees, rubbing my temples with the tips of my fingers.

In addition to everything else, now I had to deal with Mr. Being-a-Biker-Isn't-a-Crime losing his shit on me. Which he would do, I had no doubt. Ruger was scary enough in a good mood. The one time I'd seen him truly enraged still gave me nightmares, and that's not a figure of speech. Unfortunately, he had a point. When my son needed me, I hadn't answered the phone. Thank God Ruger had been there for Noah. But still . . . I really didn't want to deal with him right now, either.

I couldn't leave him hanging, though, worried about Noah all night. He'd called me a bitch the last time I'd seen him, and maybe he had a point, but I wasn't a big enough bitch to torture him like that. I hit the callback button.

"He all right?" Ruger demanded, not bothering with a hello.

"I've got him and he's fine," I said. "I couldn't hear the phone ring at work, but I found his message and left about forty-five minutes later. He's okay. We got lucky and nothing happened, not that I can tell."

"You sure that asshole didn't touch him?" Ruger asked.

"Noah said he tried to tickle him and make him sit on his lap, but he ran away. They were completely cross-faded. I don't think they even noticed when he took off. He was hiding outside on the fire escape."

"Fuck . . ." Ruger said. He didn't sound happy. "How high up was he?"

"Four stories," I replied, closing my eyes in shame. "It's a miracle he didn't fall."

"Okay, I'm driving. I'll talk to you later. Don't fucking leave him alone again, or you'll answer to me. You got that?"

"Yeah," I whispered. I hung up the phone and set it down on the table. The room felt stifling and I couldn't get enough air, so I crept softly across the floor to the window. The splintery wooden sash slid up with a groan and I leaned out, looking down at the street, sucking in the cool breeze. The bars had just emptied and people laughed outside, walking along like everything was fine and dandy.

What if I hadn't checked the voice mail? Would any of these happy drunks have looked up and seen a little boy clinging to the fire escape? What if he'd fallen asleep out there?

Noah could be dead on that pavement right now.

I finished my beer and grabbed a second one, then sat on my ratty couch and pounded it. The last time I checked the clock, it said three a.m.

A noise in the predawn darkness woke me.

Noah?

A hand covered my mouth as a large body came down over mine, pinning me to the couch. Adrenaline poured through me too late—no matter how I struggled, bucking my entire body against his, my attacker held me trapped. All I could think about was Noah, sleeping right across the room. I needed to fight and survive for my son, but I couldn't move and I couldn't see a damned thing in the darkness.

"You scared?" a rough, dark voice whispered in my ear. "Wondering if you'll live through the night? What about your kid? I could rape and kill you and then sell him to some sick pedophile fuck. You couldn't do a goddamned thing to stop me, now could you? How you gonna protect him livin' in a place like this, Sophie?"

Fuck. I knew that voice.

Ruger.

He wouldn't hurt me. *Asshole.*

"I didn't even have to break through the fuckin' pathetic lock you have on this shithole," he continued, shifting his hips over mine, emphasizing how little control I held. "Your window's open and so is the window in the hallway. I just stepped out on the fire escape and walked right over, which means *anyone else could, too.* Including that sick fuck who messed with our boy earlier. That bastard still in the building? I want him, Sophie. Nod your head if you'll stay quiet, and I'll let you talk. Don't scare Noah."

I nodded my head as best I could, trying to calm the racing of my heart, torn between the remains of fear and my building anger.

How *dare* he judge me?

"You scream, you'll pay."

I jerked my head. He pulled his hand away and I took several deep breaths, blinking rapidly, trying to decide if lunging at him with my teeth would be worth it. Probably not . . . Ruger was heavy and he covered my entire body, his legs clamping down across mine, my arms trapped deep in the couch. I couldn't remember him ever voluntarily touching me before—not for four years, at least. That was a good thing, because something about Ruger turned off my brain in a bad way, leaving my body in charge.

I got knocked up the last time I left my body in charge.

I'd never regret my son, but that didn't mean I should let my libido do the thinking for me again. After I finally got shot of Zach, I'd only gone out with very safe, very boring men. I'd had three lovers total in my life, and numbers two through three were nice and tame. I didn't need a complication like my son's biker uncle . . . But I'd caught his familiar scent now—gun oil and a hint of male sweat—which led to an annoyingly predictable response down below.

Even angry, I wanted Ruger.

In fact, I usually wanted him *more* when I was angry. This was unfortunate, because he had a gift for pissing me off. Life would be so much simpler if I could just hate him. The man was truly an asshole.

He just happened to be an asshole who loved the hell out of my kid.

So now he lay on top of me and I wanted to head-butt him or something, but I also felt embarrassing heat pool between my legs. He was big and hard and *right there* and I didn't know how to handle that. Ruger always kept his distance from me. I expected him to let me up now that he'd made his point in the least constructive way possible, but that didn't happen. Instead he shifted again, leaning up on his elbows on either side of me, holding me trapped.

His legs moved, one coming to rest between mine. Way too intimate. I tried to close my knees, but he narrowed his eyes and slid his hips into the cradle of my pelvis.

Wrong. So wrong . . . And unfair, too, because clenching him between my legs didn't exactly make my brain work better. I squirmed, needing him to be far away from me. Immediately. Yet I couldn't help wondering whether I could reach down between us and open his fly.

The man was like heroin—seductive, addictive, and a damned good way to wake up dead.

"Hold still," he whispered, voice strained. "The fact that my dick's in its happy place is probably saving your life. Trust me when I say I'm seriously considerin' strangling you, Sophie. Thinking about fuckin' you helps balance that out."

I froze.

I couldn't believe he'd just said that. We had an agreement. We'd never discussed it, but we both followed it scrupulously. Sure enough, though, he pressed his hips into mine again and I felt his hard length growing against my stomach. My inner muscles clenched, sending a wave of need wrenching through me. This was cheating. The infatuation went one way—I lusted after him, he ignored me, and we pretended nothing had ever happened between us.

I licked my lips and his eyes followed the small movement, unfathomable in the dim light starting to filter through the windows.

"You don't mean that," I whispered. He narrowed his eyes, studying me like a lion scoping out the slowest gazelle. Wait, did lions eat gazelles? Was this really happening?

Think.

"This isn't you, Ruger," I told him. "Think about what you just said. Let me up and we'll talk."

"I fucking mean every word," he replied, harsh and angry. "I hear my kid is in trouble and his mom's nowhere to be found. I spend hours driving across the state, scared shitless that someone's molesting or murdering our boy, and when I finally get here I find you in a total shithole with a broken lock on the downstairs door and easy access to your apartment through an open window. I crawl in and find you passed out on the couch half naked and smellin' like beer."

He dropped his head down, scenting me and twisting his hips into mine. Shit, that felt good. I actually ached between my legs, it felt so good.

"I could've taken him away from you, easy as fuck," he continued, raising his head, eyes burning through me. "And if I could, so could anyone else, which is not fuckin' okay. So you'll just have to sit tight and wait for me to cool down a little because right now I'm not feeling particularly reasonable. Until then, I'd suggest you *not* tell me what I mean, you got that?"

I nodded my head, eyes wide. I believed every word he said. Ruger held my gaze as he shifted his legs again and then both were between mine and I felt every inch of his dick right up against my crotch. He surrounded me completely, overwhelming me with his strength, and I had a sudden, crazy flashback to that night I'd lost my virginity to Zach in Ruger's apartment.

Me sprawled on a couch, legs spread, watching my life fall to shit.

Full circle.

Adrenaline still raced through me, and he wasn't the only one who needed to cool down a bit. He'd *scared* me, damn it, and now the bastard was turning me on, a sensation that mixed disturbingly well with the anger and fear already overwhelming my system. I really couldn't move, either. Ruger dropped his head down next to mine and groaned, grinding his hips into me. A swirl of tingling, tightening, traitorous desire twisted up along my spine from my pelvis. I moaned as he pressed hard against my clit. This felt good. Too good.

My inner slut suggested a surefire way to burn off tension . . .

As if reading my mind, Ruger's breath caught. Then he pushed into me harder, rubbing his length back and forth against the thin layer of cotton covering my center. Neither of us said anything but I tilted my hips up to feel him better and he stiffened.

This is a bad idea, I thought, arching into him, closing my eyes. I'd wanted him for years. Every time I saw him, I secretly wondered what he'd feel like inside me.

Of course, if we did this, I'd still have to look at his smug, smirking face. He wouldn't even be embarrassed, the stupid jerk. We had to stop immediately. But he felt fucking incredible. His scent surrounded me, the hard strength of his body pinning and spreading me like a captured butterfly. His nose brushed the curve of my ear and then he dropped lower, giving my neck a slow, sucking kiss, lips dragging across my skin until I had to bite my own to stay quiet. I twisted underneath him and acknowledged the truth. I wanted him deep inside. Now.

I didn't care that captured butterflies die when they're pinned.

"Mama?"

Shit.

I tried to speak but nothing came out. I cleared my throat and tried again, the heat of Ruger's breath playing across my cheek. My entire body throbbed, and he shifted, slowly dragging his hips across mine again, deliberately taunting me.

Bastard.

"Hey, baby," I called to Noah, my voice unsteady. "Um, give me a sec, okay? We have company."

"Is it Uncle Ruger?"

Ruger thrust against me one last time before jackknifing up. I sat up unsteadily, rubbing my hands up and down my arms. Noah's voice should've been cold water on my libido, but no such luck. I still felt Ruger's delicious hardness between my legs.

"I'm here, little man," Ruger said, standing and running his hands across his head. I studied him in the dim morning light, wishing with all my heart he looked more like my former boss, Dick. No such luck. Ruger was over six feet tall, roped with muscle and annoyingly handsome in an I'm-probably-a-murderer-but-I've-got-dimples-and-a-tight-ass-so-you'll-still-lust-after-me kind of way. Sometimes he wore a mohawk, but the last few months he'd taken to wearing the same buzz cut he'd had when we first met, the slightly longer hair on top dark and thick.

Combined with his size, his piercings, his black leather club vest, and the tattooed sleeves on both arms, he belonged on a "Wanted" poster. Noah should've been terrified of him. But he didn't seem to notice how scary his uncle was. He never had.

"I promised I'd come get you, didn't I?" Ruger said softly. Noah crawled out of bed and stumbled over to Ruger, reaching his arms up for a hug. Ruger caught my boy and swung him high, meeting his gaze eye-to-eye, man-to-man. Ruger always did that—he took Noah seriously.

"You okay, bud?"

Noah nodded, wrapping his arms around his uncle's neck and clutching him close. He worshipped Ruger, and the feeling was mutual. The sight was heartbreaking.

I always thought Zach would be Noah's hero. Obviously, my instincts were shit.

"I'm proud of you, little man," Ruger told him. I stood, planning to join them, but Ruger turned away. So he wanted some privacy. I wasn't going to argue if it made Noah feel safe, but I still strained to hear the conversation as he carried my boy back to bed.

"You did good callin' for help," I heard him say faintly. "You ever get in a situation like that again, you call me. Call your mama. You can call the cops, too. You remember how to do that?"

"Nine one one," Noah muttered, his voice sleepy and thick. A giant yawn caught him off guard and he slumped against Ruger's shoulder. "But I'm only supposed to do that in an emergency and I wasn't sure if I'd get in trouble."

"A bad man touches you, that's an emergency," Ruger murmured. "But you did your best, you did what I said. You hid and that was real good, little man. I want you to lie down and go back to sleep, okay? In the morning I'm taking you to my house and you'll never have to see those people or this place again. But you can't come with me if you're too tired."

I caught my breath. What the hell?

I watched as he tucked Noah in, my mood far from mellow. Seconds later my kiddo was out again, clearly still exhausted. I pulled on a robe and waited for Ruger to come back, crossing my arms and bracing for battle.

He cocked a brow at me, deliberately checking me out. Was he trying to use sex to bully me? That might explain his little seduction-on-the-couch game . . .

"You forget the part about not pissin' me off?"

"Why did you tell Noah he's going to your house? You can't make promises like that."

"I'm taking him home to Coeur d'Alene with me," Ruger replied, his voice matter-of-fact. He tilted his head to the side, waiting for the fight he had to know was coming. His neck was thick with muscles and his biceps flexed as he crossed his arms, matching my stance. It really wasn't fair. A man this frustrating should be short and fat, with hairy ears or something. But it didn't matter how sexy he was this time, I wouldn't cave—he wasn't Noah's dad and he could step the fuck *off.* "I'm betting you'll want to come with us, and that's great. But he's not stayin' in this shithole another night."

I shook my head slowly and deliberately. I felt the same way about our apartment—it didn't feel safe anymore—but I wasn't going to let him just swoop in and take over. I'd find us a new place. I wasn't quite sure how, but I'd do it.

I'd spent the last seven years honing my survival skills.

"You don't get to make that decision. He's not your son, Ruger."

"Decision's made," Ruger replied. "And he may not be my son, but he's definitely my kid. I claimed him the minute he was born, and you damned well know it's true. I didn't like how you took him so far from me, but I respect why you did it. Things have changed now. Mom's dead, Zach's gone, and this"—he gestured around the ratty little studio—"this isn't good enough. What the fuck do you need in your life that's more important than giving Noah a safe place to live?"

I glared at him.

"What's *that* supposed to mean?"

"Keep it down," Ruger told me, stepping forward into my space, pushing me back. It was a power play, pure physical intimidation. I'll bet it usually worked for him, too, because when he loomed over me like that, every survival instinct I had told me to roll over and follow his orders. Something quivered down below . . . Stupid body.

"It means exactly what it sounds like," he continued. "What the fuck are you spending your child support on? Because it sure as shit isn't this hellhole. And why the fuck did you move out of your other place? It wasn't great, but it was okay, and it had that little park and playground. When you told me you were moving, I thought that meant you found something nicer."

"I'm here because I got evicted for not paying my rent."

His jaw tightened convulsively. His expression darkened, something impossible to read filling his eyes.

"You wanna tell me why—exactly—I'm just hearin' about this situation?"

"No," I replied honestly. "I don't want to tell you anything. It's none of your business."

He stilled, taking a series of deep breaths. Long seconds passed, and I realized he was consciously forcing himself to calm down. I thought he'd been angry before, but the cold fury that came off of him now was a whole new level . . . I shivered. That was one of the many problems with Ruger. Sometimes he scared me. And the guys in his club?

Even scarier.

Ruger was poison to a woman in my situation, no matter how sweet he was to Noah or how badly my body craved his touch.

"Noah is my business," he finally said, each word slow and deliberate. "*Everything that touches him is my business.* You don't get it, that's your problem, but it ends tonight. I'm taking him home where it's safe so I won't ever get another fucking phone call like that one again. Jesus, you haven't even done the basics to secure this place. Don't you ever listen to me? I told you to get some of those little alarms for the windows until I could come over and wire the place up right."

I steeled my spine and held fast.

"One, you don't get to take him anywhere," I said, trying very hard not to flinch or let my voice tremble. I couldn't afford to show any weakness, despite the fact that I was perilously close to peeing myself. "And two, your asshole brother hasn't paid me any child support for nearly a year now. Health and Welfare can't find a trace of him, either. I did my best, but I couldn't keep up the rent on the other place. I can afford the rent here, so we moved. You have no right to judge me—I'd like to see you raise a child on what I earn. They don't just give out those window alarms for free, Ruger."

His jaw twitched.

"Zach's working the oil fields in North Dakota," he said slowly. "Makin' damned good money. I talked to him two months ago, about Mom's estate. He said everything was okay between you two."

"He *lied*," I said forcefully. "That's what he *does*, Ruger. This isn't news. Are you really surprised?"

I felt suddenly tired—thinking about Zach always made me tired, but sleep wasn't the answer. He waited for me in my dreams, too. I always woke up screaming.

Ruger turned and walked over to the window, leaning on the sill and looking outside thoughtfully. Thank God, he seemed to be calming down. If he didn't look so deceptively attractive silhouetted in my window, my world would make sense again.

"I guess I shouldn't be," he said after a long pause. "We both know he's a fuckin' loser. But you should've told me. I wouldn't have let this happen."

"It wasn't your problem," I replied softly. "We were doing fine, at least until tonight. My regular sitters all have that flu that's going around. I made a mistake. I won't make it again."

"No, you won't," Ruger said, turning to face me. He tilted his head to the side, eyes boring through me. He looked a little different, I realized. He'd lost a bunch of his piercings. Too bad it hadn't softened him up even a little bit, because his expression was pure steel. "I won't let you. It's time to admit you can't do it all on your own. Club's full of women who love kids. They'll help out. We're a family, and family doesn't stand by when someone's in trouble."

I'd opened my mouth to argue when I heard a light knock on the door. Ruger pushed off the window and strode over to open it.

A giant of a man walked in, taller even than Ruger, which was saying something. He wore faded jeans, a dark shirt, and a black leather vest covered with patches, just like Ruger's, including his name and a little red diamond with a 1% symbol on it.

All the Reapers had them, and my old friend Kimber had told me it meant they were outlaws—*that* I had no trouble believing.

This new guy had shoulder-length, darkish hair and a face so perfectly handsome he could've been a movie star. Under one arm he held a stack of broken-down cardboard boxes, tied together with what looked like baling wire.

In the other he held an aluminum baseball bat and a roll of duct tape.

I swallowed and nearly fainted. My hands actually started sweating, because I'm cliché like that. My nemesis hadn't just come to rescue us, he'd brought along one of his accomplices. That was the biggest problem with Ruger—he was a package deal. You bought one Reaper, you bought them all.

Well, all of them who weren't currently serving time.

"This is one of my brothers, Horse," Ruger said, closing the door behind him. "He's gonna help us move your shit. Stay quiet, but start packing whatever you want to bring. You'll be staying in the basement at my place. Don't think you've seen my new property," he added pointedly, which I knew was a dig at me for refusing his offer of a room at the beginning of the summer when we visited Coeur d'Alene. "But it's got a daylight basement with a kitchen and everything, and you'll have your own little patio. There's tons of space for Noah to run around, too. It's furnished, so only bring what you really care about. The rest of this shit can stay."

He glanced around the room, judging my furniture. I saw his point. Most of it had been scrounged off curbs next to Dumpsters. The finer pieces came from thrift stores.

"How's the kid?" Horse asked softly, setting the boxes down and leaning them against the wall. Then he hefted the bat, giving it a little toss and catching it with his other hand. I couldn't help but notice how thick his arms were. Apparently club life wasn't all drinking and whoring, because Ruger and his friend obviously did some serious weight lifting. "Did the bastard touch him? What're we dealing with?"

"Noah's fine," I said quickly. I eyed the tape, which Horse had failed to deposit next to the folded boxes. "He was scared, but it's over now. And we really don't need your help, because we aren't going back to Coeur d'Alene."

Horse ignored me, glancing toward Ruger.

"The guy still here?"

"Dunno yet," Ruger replied. He looked to me. "Sophie, show us which apartment they're in."

"What are you going to do?" I asked, glancing between them.

Their faces were completely blank. "You can't actually kill him. You know that, right?"

"We don't kill people," Ruger said, his voice calm and almost soothing. "But sometimes assholes like him have accidents when they aren't careful. Can't control that—it's a fact of life. Show us where he is."

I looked at Horse's big, strong hands holding his baseball bat and the roll of duct tape, one thumb caressing the silver surface.

Then I thought about Noah clinging to a fire escape, four stories high, hiding from a "bad man" who wanted him to sit on his lap so he could tickle him.

I thought about the booze and the pot and the porn.

Then I walked to the door, opened it, and pointed across the hall toward Miranda's studio.

"They're in there."

CHAPTER TWO

Ten minutes later, I couldn't stop wondering what Ruger meant by the word "accident."

Were they planning a *fatal* "accident"?

I told myself it wasn't my problem. Miranda's fate was set the moment Noah called Ruger, crying and begging for help—totally beyond my control. Telling myself that worked for about half an hour, and then my conscience kicked in.

If Ruger and Horse weren't planning to kill someone, why did they need a bat and duct tape? Those weren't constructive-discussion-about-what-you-did-wrong supplies. Those were killing-someone-and-hiding-the-body supplies. The only thing missing was a box of big black garbage bags. I'd seen *Dexter.* I knew these things.

Miranda deserved serious payback for Noah, but she didn't deserve to die. I didn't need that kind of karma.

I called Ruger's cell. He didn't answer.

Then I crept across the hall and knocked on the door. There

weren't any screams or anything coming from inside. Good sign or bad? Hard to tell—this was my first felony and I didn't know the proper procedure. I heard boots crossing the creaky wooden floor.

"It's me," I said, pitching my voice low. "Can you come out for a sec? I really need to talk, Ruger."

"Ruger's busy," Horse replied through the door. "We'll be done here soon. Go get packed and take care of your boy. We got this."

I tried the knob. Locked.

"Seriously, Sophie, go back to your place."

I backed away from the door. Now what?

The open window at the end of the hall caught my eye. The fire escape. Ruger had used it to get into my apartment, and Miranda's place was a mirror of mine. Maybe I could get in that way to make sure everything was all right?

I ducked back into my studio for a quick check on Noah, closing and locking my own window while I was at it. Thankfully, he was still totally out. Not a surprise, given the night we'd had. I slipped through the door and locked it, then walked over to the hall window and stuck my head out to scope the situation.

Sure enough, the narrow iron landing stretched from my window and across the hallway before stopping under hers. I put my leg through cautiously and stepped onto the platform, making it creak. I glanced down and swallowed.

Never been a huge fan of heights.

I held the rail with one hand, trailing the other along the brick wall until I reached her closed window. I crouched low, peeking through. Miranda wasn't much of a decorator, so she didn't have real blinds, just a filmy, translucent scarf she'd tacked over the pane. Details might be a little fuzzy, but I could still see clearly enough.

Her boyfriend lay facedown on the floor, hands bound tightly behind his back with duct tape. They'd wrapped his feet, too, with more tape around his head—like they'd decided to shut his mouth and just kept going. Blood trailed from a cut on his forehead and dripped out of his nose. Bruises were forming along his ribs. He seemed to be unconscious.

Ruger stood over him, aluminum bat in one hand, cell phone in the other.

Miranda knelt in the middle of the room, hands taped tight just like her man's. More duct tape covered her mouth and she wore a sleazy nightgown that was probably supposed to look sexy. Horse lounged casually across from her, leaning against the wall. He seemed bored.

I sighed with relief. I'd been crazy to think they'd actually butcher two people in cold blood. That didn't happen in real life. Sure, whatever was going on in there didn't look fun, but I could live with that.

Ruger hung up his phone and shoved it into his pocket. He said something to Horse. Horse shrugged and must've cracked some sort of joke, because Ruger laughed. Then the big man walked over to Miranda, knelt down, and ripped the strip of silver off her face. Her lips quivered as she asked him a question. He shook his head as he replied, and she started trembling so hard I could see it from across the room and through the curtain.

Then things got bad.

Horse reached around and pulled an ugly black handgun out of the back of his jeans. I watched in frozen horror as he cocked the slider-thingy on top, clearly preparing to shoot. Then he said something else to Miranda.

Tears ran down her face as she slowly opened her mouth.

Horse nudged her lips wider with the barrel of his gun, pushing it in.

Holy fuck. HOLY FUCK.

I jumped up and pounded on the window with both hands, screaming at them to stop.

Ruger spun around, moving so fast I couldn't follow. Within seconds he'd ripped open the window and jerked me into the room.

The sash crashed down again as he wrapped his arms around me, pinning me to the front of his body, my back to his stomach. I tried to scream again, but his hand slammed across my mouth.

The bat clattered as it rolled across the wooden floor.

Miranda's eyes darted toward me, full of desperate hope that quickly melted when neither man moved. Then Horse spoke.

"Time's up, sugar. Usually people close their eyes. Your call."

Miranda moaned, shutting her eyes tight and visibly bracing her body.

Horse glanced up, smiled, and blew me a kiss.

Then he pulled the trigger.

RUGER

Sophie exploded in his arms, thrashing furiously. Her bitch of a neighbor screamed and fell back on the floor, flopping around dramatically.

Neither seemed to notice the fucking gun hadn't been loaded.

Ruger fought to control the banshee in his arms, hating Horse because the bastard just stood there, smirking at him like the smug, cocksucking asshole he'd always been. Seriously, a goddamned kiss? Sick fuck. One of Sophie's heels lashed back and caught him in the shin. When he grunted, she kicked the same spot again. Savagely.

"Fifty bucks says your baby mama could take you in a fair fight," Horse taunted.

Miranda's shrieking suddenly stopped and she froze, opening her eyes to look around in stunned confusion.

Finally, dumbass had noticed she wasn't dead.

Sophie stilled and Ruger's aching shin rejoiced.

"Feel like I'm repeatin' myself here," he muttered in her ear. "But if I move my hand, you better keep quiet. Got me?"

She nodded her head tightly.

Ruger let go and Sophie jerked away. Fast as a snake, her hand flashed out and slapped him across the face, which fucking *hurt.*

Damn.

"You bastard," she hissed. "You scared the crap out of me! What kind of sadist pulls shit like this?"

"The kind interested in making a lasting impression?" Ruger asked, cocking his head at her. "Jesus, did you *want* us to kill her?"

Sophie's face twisted and her mouth opened, but before anything came out, the bitch on the floor started crying. Loud. Ruger had come to realize Miranda did *everything* loud. Horse leaned forward and caught Miranda's arms, jerking her up and onto her knees. He caught her chin, forcing her to meet his gaze.

"We do this again, a bullet comes out and pulps your brain. Got me?"

She nodded frantically, her sobs even noisier than before. How was that even possible? Then Ruger caught the unmistakable smell of piss and sighed. Sure enough, she'd left a puddle.

"Every fuckin' time," he muttered. Horse snorted.

"Pussy."

"I can't believe you guys," Sophie said, clenching and unclenching her hands, shaking with adrenaline. She was so angry she'd forgotten to be afraid. He actually liked that about her—Sophie had grit. But right now she was getting on his nerves. They had a lot to do and limited time before the Jacks showed up. "I thought you were killing her. *She* thought you were killing her. How can you do this?"

"We wanted to catch her attention," Ruger replied, temper fraying. "Near-death experiences tend to stick with a person. Next time she'll make better choices."

Sophie opened her mouth, then snapped it shut and glared.

The sound of tape ripping cut the air as Horse covered Miranda's mouth again. Thank fuck for that. Ruger was tired of her noise, he was exhausted from driving all night, and he was hungry.

"Go back next door, Sophie," he said, rubbing a hand through his short hair. He caught a whiff of his own scent when he raised his arm. Nasty. He'd have to shower at her place before they left for Coeur d'Alene. "We won't go crazy, I promise. But don't forget, Noah spent more than an hour hiding on the fire escape last night. Four stories up, Sophie. Your babysitter's man is a registered sex offender, by the way. Bitch knew it, too. She still invited him over while she had a kid at her place. Don't feel sorry for either of them."

Sophie's eyes widened.

"How do you know all that?"

Horse answered.

"They told us."

"I wouldn't think sex offenders go around sharing that kind of information," she said, suddenly wary.

"We're very persuasive people," Ruger told her. "You just gotta ask the questions right. Go home, Soph. We need to finish up here and get you moved out. I'm tired, honey."

"This is all wrong. I feel like an accomplice," Sophie replied, shaking her head. "I don't like it."

For fuck's sake . . . She hadn't been too worried about being an "accomplice" when she pointed out Miranda's place earlier. Little late to be complaining at this point in the game.

Enough.

"Really? You don't *like* it? Personally, I don't *like* the idea of the next kid getting raped just because he isn't smart enough to hide on the fire escape," Ruger said, stepping slowly into her space and backing her toward the wall. "How 'bout this? You go ahead and feel guilty about being an accomplice, and I'll go ahead and keep doing your dirty work so you don't break a fuckin' nail or something. Then tonight we'll open a bottle of wine and talk about how today made us feel. Maybe eat some chocolate while we're at it, then watch *The Notebook* together. That work for you?"

She hit the wall and he leaned forward, slapping his hands flat on either side of her head. Ruger dropped his face into hers, eyes blazing.

"Shit, Sophie—I think I'm showin' extreme patience, all things considered. This is not a fuckin' joke. Noah made it through last night because he stayed awake and alert on that fire escape, not because either of these fucks lifted a finger to help him. *They terrorized a little boy and laughed about it.* Now it's their turn. Don't expect me to feel bad about that. Go. Home."

Sophie swallowed, eyes wide. She stayed quiet as she slowly slid down and out from under the barrier of his arms, skirting the edge of the room until she reached the door. She slipped through, closing it behind her very softly.

Ruger glanced over at Horse, who raised a brow. Great. Now he'd catch shit from him, too.

"Your baby mama's kinda hot when she's pissed," Horse said helpfully.

"Jesus, Horse. You got no sense of boundaries, you know that?"

"Yup," he replied, and Ruger seriously considered taking the bat and smashing the bastard's face in. Of course, then he'd have Horse's old lady to deal with . . . Bitch was a damned good shot.

Miranda fell over with a thump, eyes wide. They looked down at her.

"What should we do with this one?" Horse asked. "I want her out of our faces, but I gotta say, don't like the idea of leaving her here for the Jacks when they come to pick up their problem child." He jerked his chin toward the still-unconscious man on the floor.

"Let her go right before we take off?" Ruger suggested. He walked over and nudged her with his foot. "Hey, Miranda. We cut that tape off in a couple hours, we need to worry about you sharing this little adventure with anyone? 'Cause that would put me in a real bad mood."

She shook her head violently.

"You sure?" Horse asked. "If it's a problem, we'll figure out something else for you. Saw an empty lot not too far from here. Wonder how long it'll take before some construction worker digs up your body."

Miranda grunted, eyes wide.

"I'm gonna assume that means you'll keep your mouth shut," Ruger said, sighing and rubbing the back of his neck. Muscles were way too tight back there. "Oh, somethin' else you should know. It's not just us you'd be dealing with if you talk. There's a hundred and thirty-four brothers in the club. Generally, I'm considered one of the nicer ones."

"True story," Horse chimed in. "Fuck with us, we'll fuck you back. Harder. Always."

She nodded frantically.

"Sounds like a plan," Horse said. He glanced over at the man on the floor and then caught Ruger's eye. "Might wanna tell your baby mama that the next time she has a run-in with a guy from another club, she should give us a heads-up before we go in. This could've been ugly."

"She doesn't get it—not ink, not cuts, nothing. She may have seen his tats, but she didn't know what they meant. Tape," Ruger said. Horse tossed it over and Ruger crouched down next to the woman. "Legs together, bitch. It'll be a new experience for you."

She obeyed, and he started wrapping tape tight around her ankles.

"You were still in Afghanistan when Sophie and Zach's shit went down," Ruger told Horse. "But trust me, it got ugly, and we didn't exactly socialize after that. She hates me, she hates the club, and the only reason she puts up with the situation is that she loves

Noah too much to take away the only man in his life. Sucks for him, but I'm the best he's got."

"Sounds like she's a bitch," Horse said. "Rumor is, you saved her ass. Fuckin' knight in shining armor. Might wanna trade your bike in for a pretty pink unicorn to ride, seein' as you're such a special snowflake and all."

"Shut the fuck up, asshole," Ruger replied. "I saved her, but I also lost my shit on her in a big way, at a time she couldn't handle it. Not that it matters now. Long story short, she knows jack about club colors or how we live. She didn't mention the back patch because she's fuckin' clueless."

"If I could offer a suggestion?" Horse asked.

"No."

"You gotta tell her what to expect, help her understand club life before she fucks up again," he said. "Save yourself an assload of trouble down the line. Trust me on this, bro. Breaking in a civilian like Sophie as your old lady is rough enough. Don't make it harder than it needs to be. Also, she's got a helluva mouth on her. What happens in private is one thing, but she can't pull that kind of shit at the Armory. You know it's true."

Ruger snorted, dropping the tape as he finished wrapping Miranda's legs. Why had he brought Horse? Anyone would've been less annoying . . . even Painter, despite the fact the kid probably couldn't find his own dick in the shower, let alone pin down a woman.

Unfortunately, only Horse had been both sober and stupid enough to answer his phone in the middle of the night.

"This'll be hard for your tiny little brain to process, so listen carefully," Ruger said, rising to his feet and tossing the tape onto the couch. "One, she's not my baby mama, so stop calling her that. Only funny the first fifty times. Two, I'm not plannin' to make her my property. I'm helpin' out because she's Noah's mom and for all practical purposes he's my son. I'll keep an eye on her for his sake, but she's a free agent. I doubt she'll ever set foot in the Armory, no matter what I tell her."

"Bullshit."

"Not bullshit," Ruger snapped. "She doesn't want me, asshole. Trust me, I have reason to know this. Our history is fuckin' complicated—way too complicated for a dumbass cocksucker like you to understand."

"You struck out," Horse declared, a slow grin stealing across his face. "And you're still drivin' across the state in the middle of the night so you can set her up in your house? You are well and truly screwed, brother."

"I didn't strike out," Ruger replied, eyes narrow. "It wasn't like that. And I don't think of her that way."

"Here's a suggestion for future reference, then," Horse said. "Try jerking off before answering the door if you want me to believe you don't think of her *that way*. Wood like you were sportin' usually implies the opposite. Unless it was for me? If that's the case, I'm genuinely flattered. No judgments."

"Why hasn't Marie shot you yet?"

"Because I'm not in denial about what my cock wants," Horse replied. "I piss her off, I get no pussy. Watch and learn. Now let's get them locked down and start hauling your girl's shit out to the truck. Jacks'll be here in a couple more hours, and I don't particularly care to stay and discuss techniques for removing dumbasses' ink with them. What kind of suicidal idiot doesn't black out his tats when his club cuts him loose?"

"Well, he joined the Devil's Jacks in the first place," Ruger replied, shrugging. "That doesn't say much for his intelligence. Hope he has health insurance. Probably gonna need it."

"Only if he's lucky. So tell me, brother. How many times you seen *The Notebook*? 'Cause that's information the boys back home are gonna need to know."

"Asshole."

SOPHIE

Noah slurped down his cereal, hopping in his chair like a bouncy ball.

"We're going to Uncle Ruger's today, right? Do you think he has Skylanders?"

"Yup, we're going to Uncle Ruger's. No idea about the Skylanders, but I wouldn't get your hopes up," I replied. My rush of adrenaline had died down, making it harder to sustain any real anger. Instead I surveyed my studio and finally admitted the truth.

The place was a total shithole. Not only that, I had no excuse for not putting on the window alarms. They sold them at the Dollar Store, for God's sake.

I didn't like letting Ruger win, but reality was on his side. I was broke, I'd lost my job, and I couldn't protect my own child. Waiting tables hadn't paid enough to support us anyway, and I wouldn't have been working there in the first place if I'd had better offers. My folks certainly wouldn't help. I'd been dead to them ever since I refused to "terminate" Noah.

Turning down a safe, free apartment would be insane.

I still wasn't quite ready to forgive Ruger, though. Intellectually that didn't make a whole lot of sense. Sure, he'd been a dick to me. He'd also dropped everything to drive hundreds of miles and save Noah when he'd needed help. The two should probably balance each other out, if I wanted to be fair. Not only that, Ruger had made a point I couldn't shake.

I really *didn't* want to do my own dirty work.

Ruger and Horse had assessed the situation, made a tough call, and fixed things. And that was a huge relief. Ultimately, I'd gotten mad at Ruger for scaring *me*, not for scaring Miranda. Well, that and his bullying.

He could've just talked to me about moving to Coeur d'Alene instead of playing creeper man in the night.

"We have to pack before we leave," I said as Noah finished up his cereal. He carried his bowl carefully to the sink, spoon teetering. "We aren't just going for a visit, we'll be living there for a while. I'm going to get most of your stuff, but I want you to pick out some jammies and clothes to wear tomorrow. Tuck them in your backpack. You should also grab some books to read in the car, okay?"

"Okay," Noah replied, dragging his bag out from under his bed. He didn't seem bothered at the thought, which said a lot about our existence. He'd moved at least once a year his entire life. I shook my head, feeling the familiar weight of guilt settle over me. No matter how hard I tried, I couldn't seem to get it right.

I rinsed out his bowl and put on some coffee. Then I grabbed a box to start packing.

"Want some music?" I asked Noah.

"My pick?"

"Sure," I said, handing him my phone. He plugged it into our little speaker set like an expert. *Here Comes Science* started playing, and after a few minutes we were both singing along about the elements and the elephants. As kid stuff went, it wasn't too bad. Beat the hell out of Disney crap.

We didn't actually own much, so packing wasn't hard. Coffee helped. Three boxes of stuff for Noah. Two boxes for me, plus a suitcase. I had to stand on a chair to take down our big tie-dyed wall hanging. We'd made it together last summer, on one of those glorious days where the sun is so bright and beautiful you don't even consider making your kid go in at bedtime. I used it to wrap the framed family portrait I'd splurged on when Noah was three.

Then I looked around the room—not much left. Just the kitchen and bathroom stuff . . . Packing up two lives should take more than an hour, I thought wistfully. I decided to take a quick shower before clearing out the bathroom.

"Don't open the door unless it's Uncle Ruger or his friend," I told Noah, emptying the coffeepot into my mug. "You cool with that?"

"I'm not a *child*," he replied, offering me a look of genuine disgust. "I'll be in second grade soon."

"Okay, seeing as you're an adult, you go ahead and finish up out here. Make sure I haven't missed something," I replied. "I'll wash up fast."

I shut the door and pulled off my clothes. The room was small, but at least we had a tub. Unfortunately, the hot-water situation wasn't too great—one of the joys of living on the top floor of a building with shared boilers. I showered quickly, grabbing a towel as I stepped out, dripping all over my dirty laundry. I dried off and wrapped the towel around my head before reaching for my clean clothes. They weren't there. I'd already packed them all up without giving it a second thought.

Well, crap.

I heard Ruger's voice in the apartment. Wasn't that just perfect? I grabbed a second towel and wrapped it around my body, opening the door a crack.

"Noah, can you come here?" I called.

"He's downstairs with Horse. Wanted to help load the truck," Ruger answered. He strolled toward the bathroom, all lean and tall and full of controlled strength. A great big killer cat. He stopped outside the door and crossed his muscular arms, eyes dark with something I couldn't interpret. Memories of those arms around me earlier flashed through my head and I flushed . . . *Stupid*. Ruger was a dead end, at least in terms of a relationship, and I sure as hell didn't want a booty call. Okay, that was a lie. I'd love a good booty call. Just not with a guy I'd still have to deal with ten years from now. My hormones needed to find something else to obsess about.

"What's up?" he asked.

"I forgot clean clothes," I told him, considering my strategy. "You mind stepping outside for a sec? I'll get dressed fast."

"You gonna give me crap about coming to Coeur d'Alene?" he asked, raising a brow in challenge. Great. I'd gotten over my snit, but clearly he hadn't.

"No."

"You wanna bitch me out for what happened next door?"

"No."

"That's a fast turnaround."

"I don't have a lot of choice," I admitted, forcing myself not to grit my teeth. "It's not what I'd pick, but it's better than staying here. And you win—I didn't want to do my own dirty work. I'm glad you did it for me. Happy?"

"You say that like it hurts."

It did hurt. The man was like a cheese grater on my skin.

"Just let me grab something to wear, Ruger. You won. Don't rub it in."

He laughed, the sound harsh.

"Glad you figured that out," he said. "Life's easier when you have help, like it or not. I'll dig something out for you. Suitcase?"

"That's okay—" I started, but he'd already turned and grabbed the bag, flopping it on the now-naked bed to unzip it. I swallowed as he began digging around. Not that I had anything to hide, but I didn't like him touching my things. Way too intimate.

"Nice," Ruger said, turning back toward me, dangling a black, lacy push-up bra from one finger. The side of his mouth twitched and those dark eyes warmed. "You should wear this one."

"Put it down, Ruger," I told him. "Just go outside. I'll find what I need."

"I like these ones, too," he said, pulling out a pair of turquoise panties. "They'd go good with the garter belt."

I bit back a groan. I might have a thing for pretty underwear, but I didn't need his input. Jerk. I checked my towel, making sure it was securely tucked in. Then I walked out of the bathroom, determined to get his hands off my panties.

"Just put them down," I repeated as I moved across the floor. He turned toward me, eyes sweeping over my figure and pausing on my breasts. I felt exposed and uncomfortable, which was silly. The towel covered more than most swimsuits. He had a hungry gleam in his eye, though—one I refused to take as a compliment. We'd already established that Ruger found me attractive on a basic, biological level.

Problem was, Ruger found *every* woman attractive on a basic, biological level.

I really didn't like this new dynamic between us. Things were more comfortable when Ruger treated me like a piece of unwanted furniture.

"But I like them," he said, examining the soft fabric with a smirk. I grabbed for the panties but he held them out of my reach.

"I just got done convincing myself I've been unfair to you," I told him, narrowing my eyes. "Don't ruin it."

Ruger didn't say anything for several seconds. Then he stretched the panties between his hands like a rubber band and shot them at my face. I lurched to grab the silky blue missile. That's when the towel slipped and I flashed enough of myself to earn a damned fine collection of Mardi Gras beads.

"Nice rack," Ruger told me. "Checked out the rest of you before, but never those. Usually the other way around, now that I think of it. Tits before—"

"Jesus, you're a pig," I said, cutting him off as I jerked up the towel.

"I'll concede the point," he said, shrugging and stepping away from the suitcase. "But only if you wear that black bra. I liked the girls. They deserve something nice."

"Asshole," I muttered, pissy mood back in full force.

I dug through my bag, pulling out a pair of ratty cutoffs. Then I spotted the super tight, super low-cut "Barbie Is a Slut" tank top my friend Carrie got me two years ago for Halloween, when we stayed with her folks in Olympia. We'd taken Noah out trick-or-treating wearing friendly witch costumes early in the evening. Then we tucked him safely in bed at her mom's place and took ourselves out trick-or-drinking. I made out with three different guys at three different parties . . . using three different names. We finished by eating our weight in chocolate chip pancakes at IHOP as the sun rose.

Best. Night. Ever.

I pulled the tank out with a smile. Ruger wanted to treat me like one of his sluts? I could go there. I'd let him perv on my boobs. All day. Publicly. Maybe I'd flirt a little, too, but not with him. Nope, he could just suck it while I flashed the world. That would teach him to play with my panties.

I hoped his balls turned so blue they froze.

I ignored him as I took the shorts, tank, bra, and panties back to the bathroom and got dressed. I dried my hair and put on full war paint. Then I stepped out to find Horse and Noah were back.

"Hey, Mom—Horse has a dog named Ariel. Can we get a dog, too?" Noah asked the instant he saw me.

"I don't think so," I replied. "A dog's a lot of work. We should start smaller. Maybe a hamster. Let's ask Uncle Ruger if that's okay or if he thinks it's too much."

I smiled at Ruger, whose eyes were glued to my chest. I adjusted my tank, pulling it down just enough to expose the top of the bra he'd requested.

He wanted to break our rules and bully me?

No problem. I was a big girl now, and I could fight back.

"So what do you think, Uncle Ruger?" I asked sweetly. "Is it too much?"

CHAPTER THREE

Despite his earlier breakfast, Noah had no trouble polishing off a full plate of pancakes, two slices of bacon, and a glass of orange juice.

Another growth spurt coming, I realized. That sucked. Seemed like I'd just bought him new clothes a month ago. Every time I caught up, the kid got bigger.

"You done?" I asked him, leaning back in the booth. We'd finished packing an hour ago, at which point Ruger and Horse kicked us out. Apparently we were getting in their way. Ruger handed me two twenties and told me to take Noah out for breakfast down the street, which made sense, given the long car ride ahead of us. I didn't like taking his money but I had to be practical. I couldn't afford to waste cash on something as frivolous as eating out.

"Done," Noah said, grinning at me. God, he was beautiful. His face still held a hint of the softness he'd been born with, but his legs and arms were getting lanky. He liked his hair on the long side, so it hung shaggy around his face and shoulders. Not quite long enough for a ponytail, but close. People told me I should cut it. I figured it should be his choice. When he was older he'd learn all about peer pressure and fitting in. For now I wanted him to enjoy the blissful freedom that comes from not giving a rat's ass about the world's opinions.

His skin was light, with a smattering of freckles across his nose and face. Sometimes I caught glimpses of myself or Zach in him, but not often. Noah was his own person, no question of that.

Kind of took after Ruger that way, I mused.

"Okay, let's go," I said, dropping some money on the table. I tipped the waitress nearly fifty percent—she seemed overworked, and I knew how that felt. Also, it wasn't my money.

I texted Ruger as I left, wondering if we'd killed enough time. He replied, telling me to give him another thirty minutes. We didn't have a park right by our apartment, but there was a lot about three blocks away that Noah liked running around in. I'd heard it used to be a hangout for dealers and users, but a few years back yuppies had started moving into the neighborhood. Now about half of it was a community garden, and the rest was for the kids. Someone had built a wooden swing set. Murals on the sides of the buildings bordering the lot kept the place looking cheerful and bright.

It took us about ten minutes to reach the park, and Noah made the most of his time there. I ran laps with him around the edges, hoping to tire him out. It didn't work, of course. Then we headed back, popping into a used bookstore on the way to pick out something special for the car ride.

We found Horse, Ruger, and two guys I didn't recognize on the sidewalk outside the building. The newcomers wore leather vests that read "Devil's Jacks" across the back. Below that was a picture of a red devil and the word "Nomad." They were both tall guys, one bulky in a muscular way and the other long and lean in his strength. Both had dark hair. One raised his chin in silent greeting.

The men clearly appreciated my Barbie tank top. They were both attractive, but the tall one was actually almost pretty, he was so cute. He had floppy brown hair and hadn't shaved in a couple of days. He wore a battered Flogging Molly T-shirt with his faded jeans and leather boots. Both of them looked about my age.

"Hey," I said, coming up to them, smiling. "You must be Ruger's friends? Nice to meet you. I'm Sophie. This is my boy, Noah."

Ruger's eyes narrowed.

"Go wait in the car," he said, tossing me his keys.

"Those aren't my keys. Introduce me to your friends."

"They're my keys. Blue rig, right over there," he told me, nodding toward a large SUV across the street. "Car. Now. Horse is gonna drive yours back to Coeur d'Alene."

I opened my mouth to argue, just on general principle. Then I caught Horse's eyes, which held a silent warning. He glanced toward Noah, then toward the strangers. That's when I finally caught the tension in the air—their body language was far from friendly.

Oops. This wasn't a happy visit.

"Nice to meet you," I said, taking Noah's hand. I dragged him across the street and climbed into the big SUV waiting for us. Ruger had already installed a booster seat in the back. Noah's backpack sat next to it. I leaned over and stuck the keys in the ignition, then switched on the AC.

Ten minutes later, Ruger came over and climbed into the driver's seat.

"You buckled in, little man?" he asked as he popped the SUV into reverse.

"Uh-huh," Noah replied. "Thanks for grabbing my backpack. I'm excited to see your house. Do you have Skylanders?"

"Got no idea what a Skylander is, kid," he replied. "But I'm sure we can get some."

"Ruger—" I started, but he cut me off.

"Jesus, Sophie," he said, glaring at me. "Now I can't buy the kid a present? Shit, he's had a rough night. If I wanna buy him something, I will."

"Actually, I was going to ask if I could take him upstairs to the bathroom before we leave," I replied, smiling sweetly. "He drank a big glass of juice at breakfast. We aren't going to get far without a pit stop."

Ruger's glare faded.

"That's totally reasonable."

"Yeah, I know. I'm a reasonable person."

"We'll stop at a restaurant or something," he said, pulling out. "I don't want you going back upstairs. Hunter and Skid are up there now."

"Hunter and Skid?" I asked. "Those the guys you were talking to on the sidewalk? Things seemed a little tense. What was that all about?"

"Don't worry about it," he said. "Club business. I'll pull off when I see a good place to stop."

Predictably, Noah started begging for a kid's meal when we stopped at a fast-food place, especially when he saw they were Skylander-themed. He couldn't possibly be hungry, but Ruger ordered two of the overpriced little boxes.

"That's ridiculous," I told him as he carried them back to the car. "The food will go to waste. Noah is stuffed. Not to mention he already ate out earlier. He doesn't need unhealthy junk like that."

"They're for me," Ruger replied. "He can have the toys, I'll take the food. I'm starving."

As we pulled out and onto the freeway, Noah started telling Ruger all about the Skylanders. By now he was totally wired and it was a damned good thing he was belted in—otherwise he might have jumped around until we crashed the car. He talked Skylanders as we cleared the city. He talked Skylanders as we passed North Bend. He talked Skylanders as we started up Snoqualmie Pass.

Poor Ruger. He had no idea how much conversational stamina Noah had . . .

"I'm taking a nap," I said, raising my arms and stretching, chest thrust out. I saw Ruger's eyes flick toward me, and they weren't looking at my face. Good. I wanted his balls so blue they stayed that way, because maybe that would teach him a lesson about changing the rules of our relationship without warning. I still had a crush on him, but he wasn't crushing on me at all.

Nope.

Ruger was just horny.

"Sure," he grunted. Noah rattled on in the background as I leaned my seat back and closed my eyes.

I woke slowly, feeling myself in motion and trying to remember where I was. I heard Noah talking and it came back to me. Ruger. Coeur d'Alene. Packing. Miranda.

"Then the Skylanders realized they needed the Giants if they wanted to defeat Kaos," Noah said to Ruger, his voice earnest.

"You still talking about Skylanders?" I asked sleepily, turning to look at Noah. He was all smiles, clearly excited to have a captive audience.

"Yup. Still talkin' about Skylanders," Ruger said, his voice strained and his expression dark. I bit back a laugh. "Been talkin' about Skylanders nonstop. I think we ran out of new material a while ago, because now he's tellin' me the same shit over again. We're almost to Ellensburg. I want to pull off and buy one of those little DVD players for him to hold on his lap, and some headphones. We got almost three and half more hours. This might kill me."

"Will I get to have it in my room?" Noah asked, his excitement kicking up a notch, voice growing shrill. "I want lots of movies. I want to watch it every night. Mom doesn't let me watch very much TV and—"

"Just for the car," Ruger snapped. Noah's face fell. Ruger glanced back in the mirror and grimaced. "Sorry, little man. Didn't mean to yell at you . . . Uncle Ruger is kinda tired. Think we could keep it quiet until we get to the store? Please?"

The poor man was clearly desperate. I bit my tongue, looking out the passenger-side window, trying not to laugh.

"Shut up, Sophie."

"I didn't say anything."

"I heard you thinkin'."

I started giggling. I couldn't help it. Soon Noah joined in, filling the car with his happy noise.

Ruger stared straight ahead at the road, face grim.

If I were a better woman, I wouldn't have enjoyed it so much.

I had to admit the silence was refreshing.

Noah was a fantastic kid, but his mouth didn't have an off switch. Ruger had gotten him a little DVD player that strapped to the back of the passenger seat and plugged into the car. Combined with Star Wars headphones and four new movies, the trip was already a thousand times more tolerable.

I waited until Ruger's fingers stopped clenching the steering wheel so hard they turned white before I opened the conversation.

"We need to talk."

He glanced toward me.

"Never good words, comin' from a woman."

"I'm sorry if it's not convenient," I replied, rolling my eyes. "But we've got to figure some things out. At least, I need to figure some things out. What's the plan once we're back in Coeur d'Alene?"

"You're moving into my basement," he said. He reached back

and rubbed his shoulder with one hand. "Shit, I'm all knotted up here. That's what I get for driving all goddamned night."

I ignored the comment and pushed ahead.

"I know the basement part," I continued. "But I'm going to have to figure some other things out, too. Noah needs to get registered for school. It starts a week from tomorrow back home. Do you know when it starts in Coeur d'Alene?"

"No idea," he replied.

"Do you know what school he'll be going to?"

"Nope."

"Did you think about schools at all?"

"I didn't think about anything other than getting him safe and hurtin' the fuckers who nearly killed him. That's fixed, so from here on out you're in charge."

"Okay," I muttered, leaning back in my seat. I put my bare feet up on the dashboard, knees bent. I enjoyed not having to drive. Noah and I weren't like most families, where the adults could take turns on a road trip. "I'll take care of that. The next thing to worry about is a job. You have any idea what the market is like right now?"

"Nope," he said again.

"You're not the most helpful person."

"It's not like I planned this, babe," he replied. "I got a phone call last night, I called Horse for backup and we left. That's it. Haven't had time to do a damned thing since then. If I'd known about this shit ahead of time, I would've hurt the fuckers preemptively. I'm doin' this on the fly, Sophie."

I felt my snark die. He was right, which wasn't fair. Again. Ruger was always right. It didn't make any sense, because so far as I could tell he lived life without a second thought for the future. I scrimped and saved and planned and worked, yet I still couldn't get any traction.

"Might be able to arrange something for you with the club."

I looked at him and frowned.

"I appreciate all you've done for me and Noah," I said slowly. "I even appreciate what you and Horse did earlier. I don't care that it was a crime. But that's where I stop, Ruger. I don't want to get involved in any more illegal things. I won't be your drug runner or something."

Ruger burst out laughing.

"Jesus, Sophie," he said. "What the hell do you think I do all day? Fuck, my life's not even close to that interesting."

I had no idea what to say.

"I'm a gunsmith and security expert," he continued, shaking his head. "This should not be a surprise to you, seein' as I've wired up your apartments over and over. I spend most of my time repairing firearms in a perfectly legal shop the club runs. I design and install custom security systems on the side, 'cause I get off on that shit. Lotta rich fuckers with summer homes on the lake. All of 'em need security and I'm more'n happy to take their money."

"Wait—they let a motorcycle gang run a gun shop?" I asked, startled. "I didn't know that part. I'll bet the cops love that."

"First, we're a club, not a gang," he said. "And the store is technically owned by one guy. Slide. Been a brother for fifteen years. But we all pitch in and it's a group effort. Having him hold the deed makes the paperwork easier, given the type of business. I apprenticed with him."

"So this gun shop is one hundred percent above the table?" I asked skeptically. "And people actually pay you to install their security. Aren't they afraid you'll be the one breaking in?"

"I'm damned good at what I do," he replied, smiling. "Not exactly forcing 'em to hire me. You want to see the gun shop, come check it out. Check out any of the businesses."

"You have more than one?"

"Got a strip club, a pawnshop, and a garage," he said. "Lot of the guys work in those, but we got civilian employees, too."

"And what do you see me doing, if I worked for the Reapers?" I asked, considering the strip club.

"I don't know what we need," he said, shrugging. "Not even sure there's an opening. We'll have to check and see. But it'd be good for you. Got health care plans and shit."

"So you guys don't do anything illegal? It's all legitimate?"

"You think I'd tell you if we were doing something illegal?" he asked, sounding genuinely curious.

"Um, no?"

He laughed.

"Exactly. So it doesn't really matter what I tell you anyway, because you wouldn't believe it. Club business is for club members. Seeing as you're not a member, it's not your problem. All you need to know is I'm trying to help you here. If there's a job you're qualified for, it'll be yours. If not, no big deal."

"Ruger, don't take this personally, but I don't want to work for your club at all, even if there's an opening," I replied. "You know I've never wanted anything to do with the Reapers. You and Horse helped me and I appreciate it, but nothing's changed. I don't agree with your lifestyle. I don't want Noah around your friends, either. I don't think it's a good environment for a child."

"You've never even met them. Kinda judgmental, don't you think?"

"Maybe," I said, looking away. "But I'm going to do the best I can for Noah, and hanging out with a bunch of criminals isn't part of that. I don't believe for a minute that there isn't something shady going on with you guys."

Ruger's hands tightened on the steering wheel. Great. Now I'd insulted him.

"Considering your folks haven't talked to you in seven years, your son's father needs a restraining order, and you can't hold down a job or provide for your child, seems to me like you aren't in a position to be calling us anything," he told me, voice tight. Friendly Ruger was gone. "Lotta things happen at the clubhouse. Some of those things run deep, no question. Might scare you. But I'll tell you one thing. When one of our own is in trouble, we don't kick 'em out in the street. More than I can say about your daddy. He's the model citizen and we're the criminals, but shit goes down, I can count on my brothers. You got anyone you can say that about? Besides me? Because deep down in my heart, in my guts, in my fuckin' DNA, I'm a Reaper, Sophie. Still sure we aren't good enough for you?"

I caught my breath, hating how my eyes filled with moisture. Bringing up my folks was a cheap shot. I tried to ignore the tears, refusing to blink and let them fall. Then my nose started running and I sniffed.

"That was low, Ruger."

"That was *true*, Sophie. You wanna be all high and mighty, you need to find another target. Your ass is gettin' saved by me, and behind me stands the club. If you were with the Reapers, Noah'd be surrounded by adults who care about him. Lot of kids in the club, Soph. They go home when things get wild, but lemme tell you—somethin' like this happened in Coeur d'Alene to one of our kids, I'd have to fight my brothers for the privilege of killin' the guy. That's *family*, Sophie. And Noah could use some of that family around him."

"I don't want to talk about this."

"Then don't talk," he replied. "But listen up. I get that you don't want to be part of club life. Don't worry. I'm not gonna force the point, because if you're gonna be a stuck-up bitch I wouldn't want you around them anyway."

"Stop it!"

"Shut the fuck up and listen," he snapped. "This is important.

Love the club, hate the club, you need to be aware of a few things, because they're part of your reality now. The asshole that hurt Noah, you saw the ink on his back, right?"

"Yes," I replied, wishing him straight to hell.

"Called a back patch," he continued. "It's his club colors, right on his skin. Club colors are what we wear on our cuts—our vests, call 'em rags, too—and they say a lot about a man. In this case, those colors said he was part of the Devil's Jacks. Lotta MCs out there, good and bad, but the Jacks are one of the worst. Reapers and Jacks are enemies. Things worked out this time, but you run into a guy with colors like that again, you need to tell me. I'll still go after him, but I'll call in more backup first. This morning it all worked out. Next time it might not. You got me?"

I shrugged, looking away. Ruger growled in frustration.

"I don't think you get me, Soph," he said. "Let me tell you a little story. Got a brother named Deke, down in the Portland chapter. Deke's got a niece named Gracie—his old lady's sister's kid. She had jack shit to do with the Reapers, by the way. So Gracie went off to college down in northern Cali three years ago and started dating a guy who turned out to be a hangaround with the Jacks."

I looked over at him, unnerved. He stared straight ahead, face grim.

"So little Gracie went to a party with him and a bunch of guys raped her, one right after the next," he said. "You ever heard of a train?"

I stared at him and swallowed.

"Believe it or not, some women are down with that," he continued. "Gracie isn't one of them, and they were *not* gentle. They tore her up so bad she'll never have kids. Then they carved a 'DJ' into her forehead and dumped her in a ditch. Deke found out when they sent him pictures they took of her with her own fuckin' phone. Tried to kill herself. She's doin' better now, engaged to one of the brothers in the Portland chapter. Did I mention they aren't nice guys?"

He fell silent. I thought about the two men I'd met earlier, Hunter and Skid.

"What happened to the men who did it?" I asked hesitantly. "Were they . . . were those guys you were talking to . . . ?"

"It was four hangarounds and two Jacks," he told me. "Good news is, they won't be hurtin' any more girls. Hunter and Skid weren't part of that particular mess, which still doesn't qualify them as decent human beings. So let me ask you again—you got me, Soph?"

"Yeah," I whispered, feeling sick.

Silence fell. Noah started laughing at his video in the backseat. Ruger drove, jaw muscle tight, staring straight ahead. Gracie's story played over and over in my head, along with what he'd said earlier.

"I'm not a stuck-up bitch."

"Coulda fooled me."

"I have a right to keep my son away from your club."

"That why you left Coeur d'Alene?"

"You know damned well why I left Coeur d'Alene," I said, hating him. "And that's the second time you've called me a bitch. Don't do it again."

"Or what?"

"I don't know," I replied, frustrated. I crossed my arms. The motion pushed my breasts up high. His eyes caught on them in the rearview mirror and I dropped my arms, tugging up my tank.

What a stupid game I'd been playing that morning.

Ruger wasn't a boy I could tease by dressing like a slut. I didn't want his attention, or to get more involved in his world.

I'd never be more than a toy to him, and the men in his family had a history of breaking their toys.

They just did it in different ways.

• • •

Ruger didn't actually live in Coeur d'Alene. He lived west of town in Post Falls, back in the hills near the Washington border at the end of a private gravel road. We pulled up to his place around five that evening, Horse behind us. The driveway widened into a large parking area behind an L-shaped, two-story cedar house overlooking a small valley. The setting was fantastic. Evergreens surrounded us, and I heard the trickle of a stream somewhere not too far away. A strip of grass ran down the hillside around to the front. It looked like it needed water, and given the yard's condition, I got the impression Ruger liked his landscaping natural.

Noah bounded out of the car, running around the house in excitement. I stretched up high as I stood, pulling the tank up with me, exposing my stomach. I felt Ruger's eyes touch me, cool and speculative, and I quickly pulled it back down.

Really, really stupid idea, that tank.

What the hell had I been thinking? You don't pull a tiger's tail. I'd spent years wishing Ruger would notice me, just once. Now I needed him to *un*notice me and start treating me like furniture again. Life as furniture might not be exciting, but it was definitely safe.

"Your car needs a tune-up," Horse said, walking over to us. He tossed me the keys and I caught them, chest jiggling precariously. Horse eyed me, then smirked at Ruger, who watched us with something like disgust. "I'll help haul your shit in, then I'll head home to Marie. She's startin' school day after tomorrow. Want to enjoy some time with her before she gets all stressed out and bitchy."

Ruger walked to the door, which sat kitty-corner from the three-car garage forming one side of the "L." A narrow band of deck followed the line of the house around to the front. He punched in a code, opened the door, and we went inside. There he put in another code, because apparently one wasn't enough for Mr. Security-Is-Critically-Important.

I walked in and my mouth dropped open.

I fell in love with the house instantly.

Before me was a great room with a giant, prow-shaped bank of windows looking out across the valley. The place wasn't huge, but it was definitely big enough to impress me. To the right was a door that had to lead into the garage. To the left was an open-plan kitchen with a breakfast bar. A separate dining area held a table. Dishes littered the counter, and a smattering of empty beer bottles stood on the bar, which separated the kitchen from the main room. A stone fireplace lined one wall in the living room, and a sweeping staircase snaked upward along the other.

Forgetting all about the men, I walked slowly forward to take in the view. Directly in front of the house was a broad meadow, ringed by evergreens lower on the slope. The valley lay beyond that, stunning and sweeping. Here and there I saw other houses, a mix of high-end, new construction and original farms. I looked up to see that the ceiling vaulted all the way to the second story. Behind me was a loft. A pile of dirty laundry had been shoved against the open railing, and I couldn't help but smile.

Ruger had never been much of a housekeeper.

The living room needed attention, too. The leather couches seemed to be relatively new, as did the rest of the furniture, but for all the care he took to keep things clean it could've been a frat house. There was even an empty pizza box on the coffee table.

I heard a beer top pop and turned to find the men standing in the kitchen.

"Your house is almost as disgusting as the Armory," Horse said to Ruger.

"Like yours used to be?" Ruger asked.

"I don't remember that," Horse replied, his expression innocent.

"Just be glad you have Marie around. Otherwise you'd be livin' this way, too."

"I was never gross like this."

"It's not that bad," I said, smiling at Ruger, my earlier frustration forgotten. I honestly couldn't believe how gorgeous his place was. I had no idea what the basement looked like, but it could be a spider hole and I'd still be thrilled, just for the location. Not to mention the yard for Noah. "But how did you get a house like this? I mean, it had to cost a fortune. How much land do you have?"

"Fifteen acres," he said, a shadow crossing his face. "I bought it in March. Used my share of Mom's estate for the down payment."

I cocked my head, stunned. Ruger's mother, Karen, had been disabled in a car accident a couple years before I met her. She'd been living on disability by the time I came along, pinching every penny. I'd never forget the sacrifices she made when she brought me into her home.

I'd also never forget the betrayal on her face when I moved out after sending her stepson to jail.

"What the hell? Why was she living so poor if she could afford something like this? Why did you let her?"

His expression darkened.

"They finally settled," he said. "After all those years, fuckin' insurance company finally offered us a settlement. Too late. It went into the estate and I used my half to buy this place."

My breath caught.

"When?"

"Just about a year ago."

"And Zach got the other half?" I asked, swaying. "He's got money like this and he still stopped paying his child support?"

"Sounds like it," Ruger replied, his voice tight. "Remember what you asked me earlier? You really surprised by anything Zach does? Mom never thought she'd leave anything but bills. Estate planning wasn't a priority."

"That bastard," I whispered, stunned. "We're starving and he's off spending your mom's money . . . She'd be so pissed."

"Hard to argue with that," he muttered. "Marrying his dad was the stupidest thing she ever did, and I've been payin' for it ever since. Zach's a fuckin' weight around my neck. Everything he touches turns to shit, and then I'm stuck haulin' out his garbage. Again."

I felt like he'd just punched me in the stomach.

"Is that how you feel about me and Noah?"

CHAPTER FOUR

RUGER

Fuck.

He couldn't believe he'd said that. At least Noah hadn't heard it. Sophie, though . . . Jesus.

"I'm gonna start unloading the car," Horse said. Coward.

"No, I don't feel that way, Sophie. Believe me," Ruger said, and he meant it. "You're the only fuckin' thing he ever did that's worth a damn. I'm crazy about Noah, you know that. And we don't always get along, but you're important to him and that makes you pretty fuckin' important to me."

She offered him a quavering smile, and to his horror he saw the glint of tears in her eyes. Not good. Ruger could handle Sophie pissed off, but crying?

No. Fuck no.

"Let me show you your place," he said quickly. "Downstairs. You got your own French doors down there, private entrance. It's pretty. You can use the front door, too, if you like."

"Thanks," she murmured. Ruger walked across the kitchen to the basement door. He opened it, leaning in to turn on the light, holding it open for Sophie. He followed her down the steps, feeling like a dick. Then he felt like a bigger dick, because instead of thinking about ways to make things better, he checked out her rather fine ass.

Damn woman had been driving him crazy all day.

Her tits practically jumped out of that tank of hers, and the cutoffs had to be ten years old, the fabric was so worn and thin. They were tight, too, which matched his theory about their age. Sophie wasn't fat, but she'd put on some weight since high school. In fact, she'd filled out far too nicely for his comfort. Having her in the house would be a living hell. Hell already. He couldn't see her legs without imagining them wrapped around his waist. When she'd propped them up on the dash earlier, he'd almost crashed the goddamned car.

He thought about that morning, on the couch in her apartment. His cock grew bigger with the memory, and he hoped to hell she wouldn't notice, because he'd been right about one thing. Sophie really could be a stuck-up bitch, and he didn't doubt for a minute she'd use his attraction against him. She might want to fuck him—and he knew she did, she'd been as into it as he had—but that didn't mean she thought he was good enough for her.

Fuck, she was probably right about that one.

Screwing her would kick ass. But after that? Things would get weird. Ruger wasn't interested in settling down with any woman, but if he ever did, she'd be different from Sophie. She'd fit in with the club, for one thing. She'd be the kind of girl who knew how to crack a beer at the end of a long day, kick back, and then give him a blow job before bed. She'd love riding on the back of his bike, she'd be blonde, and she'd be tough enough to hold her own in a fight.

Most important, she wouldn't fucking talk back to him. Sophie had a hell of a mouth.

"Wow, it's beautiful," Sophie said, stopping him dead at the bottom of the stairs. He looked at her to find all traces of wistful sorrow gone. Instead she smiled big at him, clearly thrilled with something or other. Damn, woman's moods changed so fucking fast, a man couldn't even begin to keep up. "I can't believe this. How did you get everything ready so quickly?"

He blinked, then looked around, shocked.

What the fuck?

When he'd left that morning, the place had been clean-ish. Not because he'd cleaned it, of course, but because one of the girls from the clubhouse had a few weeks ago for some reason. Trying to hook him for her old man, probably. He'd fucked her and kicked her out, because he'd be damned if he'd let one of those bitches get their claws into him.

It wasn't sort of clean now, though. It fucking sparkled.

This was supposed to be a family room, with a small kitchen built into the back for reasons he'd never bothered to consider. There was a short hallway to the side, with two bedrooms, a bathroom, and a utility room. He used one of the bedrooms for storage, the other as a place for his friends to crash. Never once had it looked or felt like a home.

Someone had come in and fixed all that.

Softy, fuzzy-looking blankets were draped across the couches, and a spiral rag rug full of bright colors covered the center of the beige carpet. There were fresh flowers on the coffee table, right in front of the wall of glass looking out over the valley. French doors opened onto the little patio under the ground-floor deck. Two loungers covered in big, soft pillows sat ready and waiting for use outside, framed on either side by cascading hanging baskets.

They hadn't been there that morning.

There were even more fresh flowers on the pretty blue-checked cloth covering the round table near the kitchen. A goddamn mystery table, because he had no fucking clue where it came from. Even the windows looked different. He studied them, then realized they had new blinds and long, gauzy curtains.

Then he saw the TV. A flat-screen sat on what looked like an old-fashioned wooden radio, which he had to admit was kind of cool and different. Not a huge TV, but plenty big for the space. Sophie darted down the hallway, sadness forgotten. He understood her sudden happiness, because right now the basement looked a lot more comfortable and welcoming than his space upstairs.

"Ruger, I can't believe this!" she said called from one of the rooms. He walked in to find a child's bed, dresser, and bookshelf set up and ready to go, complete with a motorcycle-covered blanket and pillowcase. The walls had been painted light blue and little pictures that matched the blanket edged the ceiling. One wall had a big, black square painted on it, with the words "Noah's Room" written on it in chalk. "Noah is going to love this. Thank you so much!"

Sophie launched herself at him. Ruger wrapped his arms around her automatically, confused as hell. Shit, she felt good. His dick jumped to full-on attention and he sniffed her hair, wondering what it'd feel like wrapped around his fingers while she sucked him off.

Sophie stiffened, obviously feeling his hard cock, and tried to pull away. He slid his hands down to her ass, holding her tight as he studied her face. Her tits pressed tight against his chest and he felt her nipples harden. She wanted this as bad as he did. Fuck, her lips were big and soft and pink.

He wanted to bite them.

"Mom!" Noah called. "Mom, where are you? I can't believe this, there's a stream and a little pool to play in. Ruger's got four-wheelers, too. Horse says they'll take us on a ride sometime!"

Ruger jerked away from Sophie.

"We can't do this," she whispered, eyes wide. "This is breaking the rules."

"Yeah, you're right," he said, which was a goddamn shame. For four years they'd played this game, pretending the other didn't exist. It'd been the right thing to do. Sometimes they'd played it so well he almost believed it. That's what his nephew needed from them, not some sort of bullshit one-night stand ruining things.

Ruger could get laid anytime—Noah only had one mom.

The kid ran in and stopped, eyes wide as he took everything in.

"Is this my room?" he asked.

"Um, yeah," Ruger said. "Looks like it. What do you think?"

"Cool!" Noah said. "I've never had a room like this. Mom, you gotta see the yard!"

He tore off again. Then Horse stuck his head in, offering Ruger a shit-eating grin.

"Nice, ain't it?"

"We should talk," Ruger said to him, jerking his chin toward the living room. Sophie took the opportunity to dart through the door and investigate the second bedroom.

Horse nodded, and Ruger followed him out.

"What the fuck happened here?" Ruger asked, keeping his voice low.

"What do you think?" Horse said. "Marie. She and the girls came over to fix the place up. All of 'em. I asked her to."

"Why the hell did you do that?"

"You want your baby mama and kid to feel good about stayin' here, right?" he asked. "Maybe feel safe and welcome? Chicks need that. Figured it would make life easier. Not only that—made the girls happy to do it."

"A heads-up would've been appreciated."

"You were too busy pretending you don't wanna fuck Sophie," he replied, shrugging. "Someone needed to step in. Marie charged everything, by the way. I told her to leave the receipts for you upstairs, on the counter. You can give me a check now or I'll catch you later."

Ruger froze.

"Fuck, didn't think of that," he said, looking around again, appraising things with new eyes. How much did TVs cost, anyway? He glanced back at Horse, whose shit-eating grin had grown to full-on mockery.

Oh, crap . . .

"You did this on purpose," he said. "You did it just to fuck with me, didn't you? Like you give a flyin' fuck about welcoming Sophie. You know I can't take it back now. How much did Marie spend, asshole?"

"I told her to keep it under three grand," Horse replied innocently. "And I think she got most of the furniture used. You know Marie, never spends money unless she has to. Hell, you don't even have to pay her back, it's not like you told her to do it. I'll cover the bill if you won't. Not every man provides for his family—takes all kinds. I get that . . ."

"You're a cocksucking bastard," Ruger said, advancing on him. Horse laughed.

"You're a cocksucking bastard," Noah repeated like a damned parrot. Ruger turned to find the kid standing in the open patio door, looking proud as hell.

"Oh my god," he heard Sophie gasp. He spun around to find her bracing a hand against the wall at the entrance of the hallway. Fuckin' perfect, because they really needed more to fight about, right? "Ruger, you can't say things like that around Noah."

"Gonna have to work on that mouth of yours, brother," Horse told him. "Don't wanna make Sophie mad. Like I said earlier, pretty sure she could take you in a fair fight. I'd pay to see it, too."

"Get out," Ruger said to him, jerking his head toward the stairs. "Just get the fuck out. Go home before I shoot you."

Sophie opened her mouth. Ruger turned and stopped her with one look. *Enough.*

"This is my house," he said. "I'll talk however the fuck I want, and you'll keep your goddamned mouth shut. Got me?"

She gaped as he turned and stomped back up the stairs. Behind him, he heard Noah chanting, "Fuck. Fuck. Fuck. Fuck."

He needed a beer.

Make that a shot.

SOPHIE

Noah glared at me like an angry leprechaun. He sat in time out on our couch, thanks to repeated use of his new favorite word.

I popped a beer and raised it in a silent toast to the women who'd come to clean, decorate, and fix us food. I'd been serious when I told Ruger I didn't want to spend time with the club, but what they'd done for me was enough to make me reconsider.

At the very least, I'd need to make an appearance to say thanks. They even left me a card and a long welcome letter full of important information, everything from their cell-phone numbers to the address of Noah's new school.

This was particularly important, because school would be starting on Monday, a full week earlier than back in Seattle. In addition to stocking the basics, they'd left me a pan of taco meat and all the fixings, ready to heat and serve. Thank God for that, because there was no way in hell I was going upstairs in search of food.

In fact, I had no intention of going upstairs at all, not without an invitation. I'd use the patio door. Safer that way. Not that I was still mad at Ruger—this was so much better than our old place that not even I could hold a grudge at this point. Nope, by then I was more scared of him, because the rules kept changing and I wasn't sure where we stood.

Drinking one of the beers helpfully stocked in my fridge helped me relax a little.

Most of our stuff was still out in the car. Ruger and Horse had done the heavy lifting at my old place, but I could handle unloading by myself. Not like we owned much anyway. I figured I could start hauling things down tomorrow, feeling pleased that I'd had Noah pack jammies for the road. No pressure to find his clothes tonight.

The one thing I would *not* be doing was asking Ruger for help. Things were weird enough already.

I heated the tacos and grabbed a couple of plates (the kitchen was fully stocked—just Corelle, nothing fancy, but it looked new to me).

"You ready to make good choices?" I asked Noah.

He glowered at me and crossed his arms.

"Okay, I'm going to eat," I told him. I filled my plate, grabbed a second beer, and walked over to the doors, opening them wide and stepping out to one of the loungers. I sat down with crossed legs, setting my plate on the pillow in front of me. Then I took a bite.

Holy shit, that tasted good after a long day.

"This is really yummy!" I called to Noah. "It's your favorite. Lots of cheese and no tomatoes. Too bad you aren't hungry."

Noah didn't respond, but I heard the scrape of a chair on the deck overhead. I looked up to see the shadow of someone above, through the cracks in the decking. I waited for Ruger to say something. He didn't.

Okay.

I finished one taco and considered the second. Noah would be impossible if he didn't eat, but I couldn't let him get away with defying me like that, either. Time for the big guns.

"Noah, you sure you don't want a taco?" I called. "I'm halfway done, and when I finish I'm putting the food away. Nothing but plain bread after that if you get hungry. Not only that, they left pie and ice cream."

Silence.

Then the chair above scraped again, and I heard footsteps as Ruger walked across the deck. Great. I hoped my yelling wasn't pissing him off even more. I couldn't get that garbage comment out of my head. I polished off my beer, bracing myself for battle on two fronts.

"What kind of pie?" Noah asked.

"Looked like berries to me," I replied. "I'm going to warm mine up before I put the ice cream on."

"I'm ready to say I'm sorry," he replied. I allowed myself just a few seconds to gloat before I walked back inside, face stern.

"So?" I asked him.

"I'm sorry," Noah said. "I'll make better choices next time. Can I make my own taco?"

"You can't use bad words like that," I told him seriously. "You say that at school, you'll get in really big trouble."

"Why can Uncle Ruger say them?"

"Because he's not in school."

"That's not fair."

Kid had a point.

"Life isn't fair. Make your taco."

I was digging through the fridge for the milk when I heard a light knock on the outside door.

"Uncle Ruger!" Noah called. "We're eating tacos. Do you want some?"

"Sure," he replied. I straightened and turned toward him, wondering if he was still upset with me. I couldn't quite figure out how he'd been the one to teach Noah to say "fuck," yet I'd gotten in trouble.

Of course, there were all sorts of things I'd never figured out about Ruger.

He came in and I handed him a plate warily, waving toward the food. He didn't smile at me, but he didn't scowl, either. I decided to take it as a positive sign.

"You made all this?" he asked.

"Nope, the girls from your club did," I told him, figuring it was always good to make peace over food. And I definitely wanted peace with him, for both Noah's sake and my own.

Maybe we could just forget today and start over tomorrow?

I decided I liked that idea a lot. I grabbed two more beers and handed him one, smiling hesitantly. "I found it all in the fridge. I still can't believe they pulled everything together in one day. Thank you so much—I had no idea you were planning something like this. I'm blown away."

He grunted, not bothering to look at me. Okay, guess we were back to him treating me like furniture.

Because I'm a perverse bitch, I didn't like it. Stupid, right?

"You want to bring your food upstairs?" he asked us. "I've got a table on the deck. Hell of a view, and we'll be able to watch the sunset."

"Thanks," I said, surprised. Guess he wanted to make peace, too. Thank God for that—neither of us had anything to gain from a cold war. And this really was nicer than any place Noah and I had ever lived. I liked the idea of having access to the deck . . . so long as Ruger didn't turn on me again. Would I ever get to the point where being around him wasn't hard to handle?

Yes, I told myself. I'd force myself to do it. For Noah's sake.

Dinner went better than expected. Noah talked the whole time, which smoothed the way for me and Ruger. I finished my food and then went and grabbed us some more beer, refilling Noah's glass of milk while I was at it. Eventually Noah got bored and headed down the stairs on the side of the deck to run around. By then I'd had enough alcohol to feel slightly less awkward, and Ruger seemed to be in a good place, too. I dragged my chair away from the table to the deck rail, propping my feet up against the railing. He went back into the house and started some music, a mix of old and new stuff.

We each drank another beer as the sun grew low in the sky. I went from feeling good to feeling fucking fantastic all around.

Noah needed bed, so I took him down and gave him a quick shower. Poor kid was dead on his feet, falling asleep before I finished his story. I decided to go back upstairs and sit on the deck awhile longer. I liked a little time away from Noah every day, which had been hard to get in our last couple of apartments. This was different, though. Noah could be safe while I had space.

"Hey," I called as I climbed back up to the deck. "You mind if I sit up here for a while longer?"

"What it's for," Ruger said. He stood at the railing, leaning forward on his elbows and looking out across his kingdom. He must've gone in and taken a shower while I was putting Noah to bed, because his hair was damp. He'd changed into a pair of worn flannel lounge pants that hung low enough to expose his hipbones.

Maybe I was projecting one of my dirtier fantasies, but I was pretty sure he wasn't wearing anything under those pants, either.

They certainly gave me a nice, defined view of his ass.

The look worked for him in a big way. Ruger was all lean and muscular, with a six-pack that tapered down nicely and biceps that were a work of art. Oh, wow. One of his nipples was pierced, too. I'd never seen that before. His pecs were broad and hard, large enough to be hot without venturing into man-boob territory. And his tattoos . . .

I'd always wondered about his tattoos.

His back was all Reapers MC, but his arms and shoulders had ink, too. I wanted to study them up close, but that seemed sort of rude. Also, I couldn't quite get my eyes to focus.

I settled for standing next to him, leaning forward against the rail.

"Want another beer?" he asked. I shook my head.

"I've had enough," I replied. I'd had slightly more than enough, actually. I'd swayed climbing the stairs, and to be honest, I needed to either lean on the rail or sit. I felt my cheeks warm, and then I giggled.

Ruger glanced at me, raising his brows in silent question.

I giggled again.

"What?"

"Pretty buzzed," I admitted, smiling at him. "Guess the beer hit me a little harder than I thought. Been that kind of day. Not enough food, not enough sleep. You know how it goes."

He smiled back at me, and damn, he was beautiful. He'd definitely taken out some of his piercings, though.

"Why do you have less metal in your face now?" I asked, my sense of tact lost along with my sobriety. "It makes you look less scary and more human."

He glanced at me, raising his brows.

"I pulled most of 'em out last winter," he said. "Started boxing, and they aren't so good for that."

Huh. I didn't know what to say about that. My eyes caught on the ring he'd left on the lower left side of his lip. I wondered how it would feel if I kissed him there, maybe sucked it into my mouth. I'd tug on it with my teeth and then attack the rest of his—

"You're cute when you're drunk," he said, startling me.

"I'm not drunk," I told him, indignant. "I'm buzzed. Perfectly okay . . . just . . . happy."

He laughed, then leaned over to whisper in my ear.

"Get much happier, you're gonna pass out. Then imagine what I could do to you."

That was pretty funny, and I found myself giggling harder.

"Are you flirting with me?" I asked, feeling daring. I'd been trying to figure him out all day. Why hadn't I just asked? I'd been afraid to talk about our relationship before now, but I couldn't remember why. "Because I don't understand you, Ruger. Half the time you seem to hate me and then it all changes. Keeps flipping back and forth. It's weird."

He raised his brows. My eye caught on the piercing there, too. I wondered how much that hurt. Of course, it was nothing compared to his tattoos. My eyes dropped back down to his lips. They were full and way too soft for a guy, which I knew for a fact because they'd been all over my neck earlier.

Yup, I'd definitely suck on those, given the chance. I'd suck on them for a good long time.

Then I'd start moving down, trying out that pierced nipple on the way down to his cock. Was it as big and built as the rest of him? I wanted to know, desperately. I swayed again, feeling heat rise up through me, nipples hardening.

"I'm not trying to flirt with you," he said.

Oh. Now *that* was a buzzkill.

"That's too bad," I said, sighing. What a shame. I wanted to sleep with Ruger. I really did. Or hell, anyone, for that matter. My rule about only dating safe guys I could control didn't lead to much in the way of action. Maybe I should revisit those guidelines. . . "I don't get to flirt enough. I spend all my time working and taking care of Noah. It's kind of tiring, Ruger. I'd like to meet someone, you know?"

He didn't respond, looking straight ahead. A little muscle in his jaw clenched. If I'd been just a little braver, I'd have leaned over and licked his jawline. He had just enough of a five o'clock shadow that it'd be nice and rough under my tongue.

"Don't look at me like that," he said, closing his eyes. "Despite what happened this morning, I'm not trying to start something with you, Sophie. You realize how fucked things would get if we started screwing each other? I'm not looking for a relationship and I'm not a one-woman man. We gotta work together for Noah. You know that."

I sighed. I did know it. Stupid beer.

"Yeah, you're right," I said, turning away from him to look out across the valley. He'd really found a hell of a place. I still couldn't believe how great our new home was.

Felt great to really relax, too, let it all out.

"Noah has to come first, we can agree on that one. I just want to get laid, though. Do you think any of the guys in your club are available? I don't want a boyfriend, just a friend with benefits. Someone I can fuck and then ditch, guilt-free, when it gets old."

Ruger made a choking noise and I glanced over at him, concerned.

"You okay?"

"I thought you didn't want anything to do with the club," he said, his voice strained. "How did you go from that to friends with benefits so fast?"

"Actually, I think I might give the club a chance," I replied. Maybe the Reapers would be all right—and the more I considered the whole friend-with-benefits thing, the more I liked the idea. I *never* got to have sex. I was twenty-four years old, for God's sake. I should get to have sex!

"They did some really nice things for me today. Horse left home in the middle of the night to help someone he didn't even know. And those girls . . . They must've worked for hours, getting everything ready for us. Just the furniture is amazing, let alone leaving dinner ready to go. I think the stencils are still wet."

"Jesus fuckin' Christ."

I frowned at him.

"What's that supposed to mean?" I asked. "I thought you *wanted* me to get to know your friends in the club. And seriously—I deserve to get laid. I've earned it!"

Ruger straightened and turned to me, every muscle in his body tense and tightly leashed. His nose flared as he took a deep breath, and my eyes caught on the muscle in his jaw. He'd always been scary, but right now he looked downright lethal. I should've been terrified, but I had my buzz wrapped around me like a nice warm blanket of protection.

I wasn't going to let him bully me anymore.

"I think the girls would be good for you," he said. "At least, some of them. You stick with the old ladies. Don't want you around the others. But this friends-with-benefits shit? Not happenin', Soph. Put that outta your mind, got me?"

"Why not?" I demanded, outraged. "You screw everything that moves. Why can't I?"

"Because you're a mother," he said, his voice almost a growl. "You got no business fuckin' around like that. I'm serious."

"I'm a mother, but I'm not *dead*," I said, rolling my eyes. "Don't worry, I won't let Noah meet someone unless it's serious. But I'm ready for a little fun. Horse is hot, and if any of the other guys in your club are like him—even a little—they'd be perfect for me. Don't give me shit about it, either. I know you guys fuck around. Why shouldn't I?"

"Those are sweetbutts and club whores," he said, his voice hard. "They're trash. No fuckin' way you're gonna be one of them. Not happening, Soph."

"You aren't my boss."

"You sound like a goddamned fourteen-year-old," he replied, eyes narrowing.

"At least I don't sound like an overprotective father," I snapped. "You're not my dad, Ruger."

He reached out and caught me behind the neck, jerking me into his body. Then he dropped his mouth down to my ear, my face so close to his chest I could've licked him.

"Trust me, I'm well aware I'm not your father," he said. His nose traced the curve of my ear, the warmth of his breath sending a shiver through me. "If I was, they'd throw my ass in jail for the shit I think about you."

I raised my hands, sliding them up along his sides, tracing the line of his muscles before bringing them in to graze his nipples. I couldn't help myself—I leaned forward and flicked his piercing with my tongue. Ruger groaned, and his fingers tightened in my hair. His entire body tensed, and then I felt the brush of his cock against my stomach.

Holy hell.

My nipples peaked and the flesh between my legs spasmed. I shifted restlessly. One of his hands slid down my back, past my shorts and panties, to cup my bare ass. His fingers tensed as I licked his nipple again, then sucked the ring into my mouth.

"Jesus . . ." he groaned. "You got two seconds before I lay you over that table and fuck you so hard it breaks. Swear to God, Soph. You wanna tell me how we're gonna explain that to Noah? 'Cause I got shit. I'm not lookin' to marry you and I sure as fuck won't hand you my dick on a leash, so things could get weird fast, babe."

I froze, shivering, feeling moisture soak my panties. I wanted to hump his leg like a bitch in heat, desperate for anything to fill the emptiness inside me.

Instead I pulled away from him slowly. His hand slid free of my shorts and we stepped apart, eyes boring into each other.

"Fuck," Ruger muttered, running a hand through his hair. He looked away from me. The front of his pants bulged outward, his cock so hard I saw the thick head clearly outlined. I wondered what he'd do if I knelt down, pulling his pants low so I could run my tongue around the tip before sucking him deep into my mouth. It actually watered at the thought.

Desire speared me like a weapon. I sighed, licking my lips.

"I'm gonna get another beer," Ruger said harshly. I looked up from his cock to his face to find his eyes glued to my chest. Shit. I was still wearing the damned Barbie tank, which left nothing to the imagination. My suitcase sat in his car.

"Grab me one, too," I replied, my voice shaking.

"Sure that's a good idea?"

I looked at him and shook my head. His chest rose and fell too fast, his dark eyes almost fully dilated. He swallowed and I rubbed my hand against the top of my thigh, restless and hungry. The steady motion caught his eye and he swallowed again.

"No, but I want one anyway."

I walked unsteadily across the deck to a lounger and lay back on it, limp and full of need so intense I thought I might die. The sun had set, and the evening stars had started coming out somewhere along the line. *I should go back down to my little apartment.* I knew that. Instead I closed my eyes and thought about how much I wanted to reach down between my legs and rub my clit until I blew up right in front of him.

Something cold touched my cheek.

I opened my eyes to find Ruger standing over me, eyes intense. They slid slowly across my body. Impossibly, the bulge in his pants was larger. God, it'd be so easy to just reach out and take him into my hand, feel that hard length for myself. Or I could sit up and lean my head forward, letting my cheek touch him through the soft fabric. I couldn't take my eyes off it.

I rose until my face was only a few inches away from his crotch. Then I looked up at him, wondering if I'd lost my mind.

"Here's your beer," he said roughly, holding it out to me. I took it and wrapped my mouth around the neck for a drink, holding his gaze.

I hated him for being sober and in control.

"Jesus, Sophie . . ." he groaned. "Don't fuckin' look at me like that."

"Like what?" I asked him, catching a drip on the side with my tongue.

"Don't play stupid," he whispered. "If you don't stop I'm gonna fuck you. We'll both regret that tomorrow. You're drunk."

I tilted my head to the side, thoughtful.

"Are you?" I asked him.

"What?"

"Drunk?"

He shook his head slowly, sinking down to sit next to me. He leaned over, scenting my neck. We weren't touching at all, but just the warmth of his breath on my skin almost killed me. I took another drink of my beer, slow and deliberate.

His eyes burned a hole right through me.

"No," he whispered. "I'm not drunk."

"Then what's your excuse?" I asked softly. "Mine's alcohol. Whatever I do tonight, I can blame the beer. What excuse should we use for you?"

Ruger reached over and took the bottle from my hand, setting it on the deck.

"No more tonight," he said, his voice cracking. "You're done. We're done. We're not doing this. Got me?"

"Yeah," I said, forcing myself to think past the buzz. I knew he was right. Noah needed us both, and we had enough trouble getting along already. I was going to be living in his basement, for God's sake, and it wasn't like he hadn't been clear—he wanted to fuck me. No heart, no flowers, no dates, and definitely no commitments. At least I wasn't just a piece of furniture anymore.

"Can I ask you something?"

"What?" he replied. I swallowed.

"Is this a new thing for you?"

"I don't follow," he said, glancing at me. His eyes pierced mine, the warm night air hanging heavy between us.

"Wanting me," I said softly. "Is it a new thing for you? I mean, aside from . . . back then . . . I always assumed that was just a moment, you know? You always looked right through me."

"It's not a new thing."

We sat together, neither moving, frogs chirping all around us.

After a while he reached up and rubbed the back of his neck, like he had in the car.

"You still sore?"

He nodded. "Yeah, I kinked it somehow last night while I was driving. Stupid."

"Want me to rub it for you?" I asked him.

"No fuckin' way you're touching me," he said. "We covered that already. I'm not drunk, Soph. I won't fuck things up for Noah."

"We're not going to fuck up anything," I told him. "I'm getting sober now, it's okay. I took a massage class, though. I'm actually pretty good at it. Let me help you. You've done so much to help me, I feel like I owe you something."

"Not a good idea."

I rolled my eyes, and bumped his shoulder with mine.

"Chicken?" I asked, smiling at him.

"Jesus, you're annoying," he muttered, but he didn't protest when I crawled behind him. I ignored the screaming need between my legs as I knelt up and put my fingers on his shoulders. They were hard and strong, soft skin stretched over sleek muscles more than capable of supporting him while he pounded into my body.

Unfortunately, it was too dark for me to see much of his tattoos, which was a damned shame. Ruger wasn't shy about taking off his shirt, but I never got close enough to really scope them out.

I dug my fingers in and he groaned, head dropping forward. He wasn't kidding about being tight, either. Big knots snarled his neck and shoulders. After a few minutes of going at them with my fingers, I started using my elbows. Slowly I got his neck to relax and started moving down his back.

"Lay down on your stomach," I told him, sliding off the side of the lounger behind him. I flattened it. He didn't move.

"You really are chicken," I murmured. "I'm just going to give you a back rub, Ruger. Enjoy it for what it is, okay?"

He grunted and rolled onto his stomach. I leaned over him and went to work. Some of the knots just wouldn't give, so I decided to climb on top of him to get good leverage.

Was this stupid?

Of course. Did I care?

Not one drunken bit.

I straddled his butt, enjoying the feel of his hard body between my legs and his skin under my fingers. He smelled fresh and clean, but still utterly male. Drove me crazy. With every stroke of my hands I rode him, not getting quite enough stimulation to satisfy me, but enough that when I felt a light beading of sweat break out, it definitely wasn't from the effort of giving the massage.

At first he tensed, but slowly he gave in to it, each muscle group relaxing in turn. Finally my hands were tired and we were both limp. I lay down across his back, taking in his scent, the warm summer breeze just enough to keep me from overheating.

"Soph . . ." he said, his voice a warning.

"Don't, Ruger," I whispered. "It doesn't mean anything. Just let it be, all right?"

He sighed, and silence fell between us.

I was still frustrated, no question. But it was a strange, relaxed kind of sexual desire washing through me now. Night sounds surrounded us and I let myself enjoy the feel of Ruger's body under mine, wishing I really could have a man like this—strong, steady, and capable of protecting me from anything.

If Ruger were mine, I'd be safe. Always.

"It'll be okay, Sophie," he murmured softly, sounding half asleep. "I promise."

I didn't answer, because I didn't believe him. Instead I dozed off. The next thing I remembered was him lifting me and carrying me down to my bed.

CHAPTER FIVE

Ruger was wrong. It wasn't okay.

Things got weird.

So weird that he took off on me for nearly five days, leaving Sunday afternoon and not showing up again until Thursday. I had no idea where he went and didn't ask him about it when he came back. But it *had* to get less uncomfortable, right? Because you can only be all tense and strange around each other for so long . . .

At least Noah started school without any problems, which didn't really surprise me. He'd always been good at making new friends and tended to roll with whatever changes came along. Before Ruger left on his club run (I wasn't a hundred percent sure what "runs" were, but apparently this one involved being gone for five days), he'd handed me some money and suggested I wait until the next week to start job hunting. He wanted to explore work options with the club, and also thought I should focus on helping Noah adjust to his new situation.

I'd love to say I'm such a strong, independent woman that I told him to butt out, but it was actually a huge relief. I couldn't remember the last time I'd had a week off, and I loved it. I unpacked everything, sucked up the sun and got reacquainted with the area.

I also spent an afternoon with my old friend Kimber.

She invited me over for lunch on Tuesday. We'd stayed in touch through the years, and last summer I'd stayed with her and her new husband when we came to visit. Kimber had gone a little wild for a while after graduation. Then she met Ryan and settled down. He was some kind of software engineer and apparently did pretty well for himself, because she had one of those big houses popping up like mushrooms out on the Rathdrum Prairie. It was part of a development, not custom like Ruger's, but twice the size and pretty impressive.

She also had a pool.

"You want a margarita?" she asked, opening the door in a bikini, a brightly colored wrap, and sunglasses that would've made Paris Hilton jealous. I smirked, because some things never change.

"This early?"

"It's always happy hour when you have kids," she replied, shrugging. "Either that or it's sad hour, and that's not half as much fun."

We grinned at each other like total dorks.

"So, you want one or not?" she asked, dragging me through her grand entryway and down the hall to her kitchen. "Because I'm definitely having one. Ava was up all night teething. She *finally* fell asleep about fifteen minutes ago. If I'm lucky, I have two hours before she's up again. I need to make the most of it and pack in six weeks' worth of social life before you go."

"Okay," I told her. "But just one. I have to drive and pick up Noah later. I take it you're enjoying mommyhood?"

"Loving it," she replied, pouring me a drink in a brightly colored martini glass with a flamingo-shaped stem. "I can't believe how amazing Ava is. But it's crazy, too. I had no idea how much work they could be—I still can't believe you did this when you were seventeen. I couldn't even find my keys half the time back then, let alone keep track of a baby."

"Well, sometimes life brings us surprises," I replied, thinking back to those early days. After Noah, I'd gone to the alternative high school and lived with Ruger's mom. It hadn't been easy. "I couldn't give him up, so I figured it out. What doesn't kill us, and all that shit."

I waved my hand airily to illustrate the point.

Kimber burst out laughing, and it was just like high school again. God, I loved her. We made our way out to the backyard, sitting at a tile-topped table under a vine-draped pergola. Her backyard really was gorgeous. Totally different than Ruger's wild acreage . . . Kimber had a perfectly manicured little Garden of Eden in the suburbs.

"So, you're staying with Jesse Gray," she said, arching a brow. I laughed.

"I haven't heard him called Jesse since his mom died," I replied. "He goes by Ruger."

"Um, yeah," she said, eyes drifting away from mine as she sipped her drink thoughtfully. "I don't want to be negative, but is this a good thing? I thought you hated him. I mean, things got bad there before you left . . . It was an ugly time."

"Um, 'hate' is probably too strong a word for Ruger," I replied, taking a sip from my flamingo-themed glass. Ugh, way too much tequila. Yuck. She wasn't kidding about packing in weeks of social life. I set it back down, eyeing the yard speculatively. When she went inside, I'd dump it on a shrub or something.

Did tequila kill shrubs?

"I'd say our relationship is a little tense, though," I added. "He was kind of a jackass about me coming back to town, but I have to admit, it's a good move for us. Things weren't so great in Seattle."

Kimber made a soothing noise and waved her hand at me.

"You'll be glad you came back," she replied. "If nothing else, now you'll have me around to babysit for you. I promise—no drinking when I'm watching your kid. Scout's honor."

"They kicked you out of Scouts."

"Only the Girl Scouts," she mused. "Those boys always found room for me in their tents. Seriously, though, Noah's a great kid, and it's not like I get to go out and do anything these days anyway. Not that I mind—I've had my fun."

I snickered at that. She didn't even blush. I wasn't entirely sure she was joking about the scouts and their tents.

"Speaking of fun . . ." she said slowly, swirling her drink. "I need to tell you something."

I glanced over at her, and for the first time since I'd known her, Kimber looked embarrassed.

"What?" I asked, a little nervous.

Nothing embarrassed Kimber.

"I don't know how to say this, so I'm just going to spit it out," she replied, swallowing. "I slept with Ruger three years ago. It was a one-night thing, nothing special. I figured you should know, since I might want to come and hang out at your new place sometime. Full disclosure."

I gaped at her.

"*Why* did you sleep with Ruger?"

She cocked a brow at me, eyes knowing.

"Seriously?" she asked, and I flushed. Of course I knew *why*. "It was before Ryan, so it's not like I did something wrong. You were still living in Olympia and could hardly stand him long enough to let him see Noah. I thought I was in the clear."

I looked away from her, trying to process. The thought of her and Ruger felt wrong. In fact, it made me kind of angry. And that was ridiculous, because it wasn't like I had any business being upset. Not only that, it'd been three years ago. A full year after things fell to shit here, and not even Kimber knew all the details on that one . . .

Strong or not, I took a big gulp of my margarita, which blazed a nasty, fiery trail down my throat. My lungs spasmed in protest.

"You aren't planning to do it again, are you?" I asked once I stopped coughing. She burst out laughing and shook her head.

"Of course not!" Kimber sputtered. "For one, I'm *married.* Remember? You were in the wedding, dumbass . . . But even if I wasn't, he's not a return-trip kind of guy. I mean, I'd have done him again, because he's that good—trust me—but he's definitely not the type to stick around. He's fucked half of Idaho. It was fun, but I don't get off on being one of many."

"Do we have to talk about this?" I asked, squirming.

"No, not really," she said. "But I wanted you to know, just in case."

"Just in case what?"

"Well, just in case I come over. It seems weird not to tell you, now that I know you have a thing for him. I didn't know that when I fucked him, though. I swear. I thought you hated him as much as you hate Zach."

"I don't have a thing for him," I said quickly.

"Don't bother denying it," she replied lightly, giving a theatrical shudder. "I can see it in your face when you talk about him, and I get it. He's one of those guys you just want to shove down and lick all over. Which I did, actually. He's nasty in bed, too, never tried some of that shit before. Pierced dick. I shit you not."

My eyes widened and I took another gulp of my drink.

"Are you kidding?" I asked. "Does that mean—wait, no. *No.* I don't want to know."

She burst out laughing.

"The answer to your unasked question is *yes*," she said, leering comically. "But you need to stay away from him, babe. No kidding on that one."

I rolled my eyes. I wanted to be annoyed with Kimber, but you just couldn't. She was too sweet and crazy to get pissed at.

"I live with him," I said dryly. "I can't stay away."

Her smile faded.

"I guess that's my point," she said thoughtfully. "But you can keep your distance in other ways. You need to build your own life and cut out any fantasies of messing around with him, because it won't end well. If you guys fall into bed one night, you better be ready to wake up and clear out before the next chick shows up. And the next one and the next one and the one after that. That's just how he is."

"I know. Pisser, hmmm?"

"Well, it's not like you have to give up on sex," Kimber said. "Like I said, I'm stuck at home all the time anyway. Might as well watch Noah so you can go out and get some. You're hot—guys'll be crawling all over you. In fact, there's someone I want you to meet."

"I don't do setups," I told her.

"You will," she replied knowingly. "Trust me, when you see his picture you'll be all over him. His name is Josh, he works with Ryan, and he's loaded."

She turned on her phone, flipped around until she found what she wanted, then handed it over.

Damn. This guy really was hot, in a pretty, clean-cut lawyer kind of way.

"Okay," I told her.

She burst out laughing and I chugged the rest of the margarita. Ava squawked over the baby monitor and Kimber groaned.

"Fuck my life . . ."

As Kimber went inside to check on her, I pulled off my sarong and slid down into the pool, considering Kimber's cute friend. Unfortunately, when I tried to imagine him kissing me, I thought about sucking on Ruger's lip ring instead. Then I thought about sucking on other things, which wasn't productive at all.

What exactly did a pierced dick look like, anyway? And how would it feel inside?

I shivered.

Kimber finally got Ava settled and came back outside, jumping into the water with me.

"So, have you started job hunting yet?" she asked.

"Not yet," I replied. "Ruger wants to see if there's something I can do with the club. I'm on the fence about that. Not sure I want to get involved."

"Well, if your goal is to make good money, the best place to work is The Line."

"The strip club?" I asked, widening my eyes. Everyone knew about The Line, of course, but I'd never been there.

"Yup. Totally paid for my degree that way," she replied, leaning back into the water to wet her hair. I gaped as she came back up.

"You worked at a strip club? Stripping? *Seriously?*"

Kimber laughed.

"No, I worked there valet parking," she replied, rolling her eyes. "Yes, I stripped. Made really good money, too. I only had to work two nights a week. It kicked ass."

"But wasn't that kind of . . . icky?" I asked, intrigued. She shrugged.

"Define 'icky,'" she replied. "I mean, sometimes it was really fun. I liked dancing on the stage and all the flirting. The lap dances weren't quite as much fun, especially if the guys were old or something. But they aren't allowed to touch you. At least, not unless you go back into the VIP rooms. All kinds of things happen back there—but only stuff you decide to let happen. Nobody forces you to do anything."

I turned this information over in my brain, stunned.

"So did you?" I asked, knowing it was rude but completely incapable of *not* asking.

"What?"

"Go back in the VIP rooms?" I asked, unable to help myself. She giggled.

"Yeah, I did," she replied. "You don't have to, but that's where you earn the most money. Security keeps a pretty close eye on things. It's not dangerous or anything."

I stared at her. She stared back, smirking.

"Wow," I said finally. "I didn't know that."

"What? Are you going to get all judgy on me?" she asked. "Fuck that. I'm not ashamed. Ryan knows all about it, too. That's where I met him."

"And it didn't bother him?" I asked, even more startled.

"It would be pretty damned hypocritical if it did," she said, laughing. "First time he came in, he paid for me all night, and I gotta tell you, we had a damned fine time in that little room all by ourselves . . . I swear, I fell for him on the spot. He didn't like the idea of sharing me with any other guys, so I quit the next day. I didn't want to fuck things up between us, you know?"

"Wow," I said. "I know I keep saying that, but I'm just trying to wrap my head around this. I hate to be too nosy, but how much were you making?"

She leaned over and whispered in my ear.

"Holy shit!"

"No kidding, right?" she asked. "Now, I worked hard at it, took it seriously. And I didn't get into drugs. A lot of the girls blow their money on drugs and stupid shit. But the smart ones? They save their cash and retire early. I covered our wedding, our honeymoon, and the down payment on this house. Ava's got a college fund started, too."

"Damn," I murmured. "That's amazing."

Kimber laughed.

"Well, it's not a long-term career," she said. "But think about it. A regular job keeps you away from Noah forty hours a week, at least. Maybe more. You start stripping, you're only away from him two nights a week. What's better? A mom with a lily-white reputation, or one who's actually around to take care of her kid?"

"Hell of a good point," I answered, bemused.

"No shit," she replied. "And consider this—you start making good money, you'll have your own place in no time. I don't care how nice Ruger's house is. So long as he's living there, you're up shit creek."

Hard to argue with that.

PORTLAND, OREGON
RUGER

"I've never seen a town with so many damned strip clubs," Picnic muttered, sipping his beer. Ruger glanced over at his club president and shrugged. It was Wednesday afternoon, but they'd only been awake for a couple hours.

Last night Ruger had found a hot little blonde who'd done her best to make him forget all about his new roommate. Unfortunately, he'd fucked himself over by pretending she was Sophie the entire time he'd pounded her slick pussy.

He wasn't a hundred percent sure, but he might've called Soph's name when he came.

Shit, he needed to get a handle on this . . . But there was just something about the thought of her in his house, all available and at his mercy. It was too much power.

Ruger had never been one of the good guys.

He took a long, deep breath. This was a business trip, so time to pull his head out of his ass. He glanced over to the stage, where a nearly naked woman gyrated lifelessly around the pole. She could've been cleaning toilets for all the enthusiasm she showed.

"Too bad they're more interested in quantity than quality," Ruger said, nodding toward the stage. "Fire her ass, she worked at The Line."

Deke gave a snort of laughter. Ruger glanced at him, noting the humor didn't reach the Portland president's eyes. Man was dead inside, so far as he could tell. He'd heard that Deke was national's first choice for enforcement, and he had no trouble believing it. The former marine could probably pull off a hit in his sleep.

Good guy to have at your back in a fight.

"You bastards have it easy up there in Idaho," Deke said. "Fuckin' monopoly, so all the talent has to compete to work for you. We got more strip clubs here than anywhere else in the damned country, or so I hear. Market's saturated, and that means owners gotta take what they can get. Some of these places barely break even. Crazy-ass shit."

Ruger glanced around the room with new interest. Aside from their table, there couldn't have been more than six customers total. No, make that seven. Some lucky bastard was getting a hand job back in the far corner.

"So it's always this empty?" he asked. "That's fucked up. No wonder she isn't trying. Why bother?"

"Can't dance for shit, but at least she gives a hell of a blow job," Deke responded. "Try her out later if you like. Any of the girls, for that matter."

Deke glanced over at their waitress, jerking his chin toward their drinks. She carried over a tray of refills, smiling nervously. Ruger eyed her, considering Deke's offer. The girl wore a black leather bustier, a short, tight skirt, and black fishnets. Long, reddish-brown hair, sort of like Sophie's. And there his cock went again, getting all hard.

Yeah, this good-guy bullshit wasn't his gig at all.

Damn, but he'd wanted Soph in his bed a long time. Every inch of her hot little body was burned in his brain, starting that first night he'd seen her screwing Zach in his apartment, which officially classified him as one sick fuck. She'd been sixteen years old and scared shitless, and what'd his response been?

He'd jacked off in the damned shower while she hunted for her panties in his living room. Panties she'd never found, by the way, which he fucking well knew because he still had them. Pink and lacy, innocent as hell, and enough to get his ass thrown into jail back in those days.

Then he'd gone and really fucked things up four years ago, fucked them up so bad her entire life exploded. Not entirely his fault, but he still regretted how he'd handled Zach. Should've killed the cocksucker when he had the chance. Even with all his guilt and regret, though, one thing hadn't changed.

He *still* jacked off to those panties sometimes.

"Where the fuck is Hunter?" he asked irritably.

Deke narrowed his eyes.

"Like I give a shit?" he answered. "I'm not on board with this. We don't talk to Jacks. We hurt them. That's how it's done—there's a *system.*"

Toke, one of the younger Portland guys, nodded in agreement, his face grim. He'd insisted on being part of this meet. Gracie was his old lady these days. Between him and Deke, they were sitting on a fucking powder keg . . .

"We're talking to this one," Picnic said, his voice soft but unyielding. At forty-two, he was the oldest man at the table. He and Deke might have equal rank, but Pic had been around a long time, and when he spoke, men listened. Ruger knew he'd been talked about for national president, but the man wasn't interested. "Something's going on. I want to hear what this asshole has to say about it."

"Fuckin' simple," Deke replied. "Little bastards are movin' in on our territory. You know it, I know it. This shit needs to end."

Pic shook his head and leaned forward, pale blue eyes intense.

"Doesn't make sense, brother," he said. "Four guys living in a house in Portland . . . Two of them going to fucking school here, like they're citizens or something. Nomads. You seen them pull a goddamn thing these past nine months?"

Deke sighed, and shook his head.

"Like I said, doesn't add up," Pic continued. "We know they're our enemies. They know it, too. So why the fuck would they be here? Death wish?"

"Setting us up," Ruger suggested. "Trying to get us to relax? Either that or a mind fuck."

"Your situation in Seattle, they give you any shit about it?" Pic asked him, although Ruger knew he had the answer already.

"Nope," he replied. "Fuckwad was theirs to punish, no problem with that. Made our lives easier. Damned civil about it, too."

"Exactly, and you ever know a Devil's Jack to be polite?" Picnic continued. "Fuck, didn't think they knew how. These guys are young—different—and none of us has ever seen them before this year. Roseburg boys say there've been dustups in northern Cali. Something's happening in that club, and for once I think it might not be about screwing us over."

Deke slammed down a shot, then leaned back, arms crossed, face grim.

"They don't change," Toke muttered. "Doesn't matter what games they're playing, doesn't matter who's in charge, none of it. They're Jacks and they belong in the ground. Period. Every day they're livin' in my town, it eats at me. I want to end it."

"You got one-track minds, both of you," Horse said, pulling up a chair to join them. "I swear, we're goin' in fuckin' circles here. Slide just texted. Jacks are in the parking lot. Just the two of 'em, no sign of anyone else. Don't do anything crazy until we finish talking, okay?"

Toke nodded, eyes narrowed.

Shit, Ruger thought. They shouldn't have let him come along. Man hated the Devil's Jacks, and with good reason, but he was like a damned grenade without a pin.

The door opened, bright sunlight framing two figures Ruger recognized. Hunter and Skid—the same bastards who'd come up to collect their former brother in Seattle the weekend before. Both were big, although Hunter was the taller of the two. He was young, probably no more than twenty-four or twenty-five. Nomad, so he didn't have a home chapter. No official status, but the man carried himself with instinctive authority.

If the Jacks had a serious power-shift in progress, Ruger would bet a thousand bucks Hunter was at the center of it.

The music changed and a new girl strutted out onto the stage. Ms. Personality hopped on down, but she didn't bother coming over to their table trying to sell lap dances. She might not be enthusiastic about her job, but apparently she wasn't entirely stupid.

None of them stood as the Jacks approached. Ruger kicked a chair over to Hunter, who caught it with a smile that was anything but friendly. He flipped it backward, straddling it casually. Skid dropped down next to him.

"You ready to talk?" Hunter asked, looking between the men. "I'm Hunter, by the way. With the Devil's Jacks. Motorcycle club, may have heard of us? This is Skid."

Deke's eyes narrowed, and Ruger had to bite back a grin. He wasn't sure yet if Hunter was an idiot or not, but the kid had balls of fuckin' brass.

"Picnic," the Coeur d'Alene president said. "My brothers Deke, Horse, Toke, and Ruger. Deke's the president here in Portland.

Gotta say, he's a little hurt you haven't dropped by to introduce yourselves before now. You might not know this, but Portland belongs to the Reapers."

Hunter held up his hands, palms forward.

"No problems there," he said. "My rocker says Nomad, not trying to claim Oregon. Your town, your rules."

"You're breathing our air," Deke said, his voice cold. "Generally we charge for that. I think we discussed this with one of your boys last winter. Stayed with us for nearly a week, if I remember right."

Skid's eyes narrowed, but he kept his mouth shut. Hunter shrugged.

"These things happen. We get shit's not good between the Jacks and the Reapers," he said, his tone mild. "But we're here today because you helped us out. Been wantin' to meet up for a while now. This opened the door. We wanted to offer our thanks and talk to you about a truce. Asshole you handed over up in Seattle—he was a problem for us. Serious problem, more than you realize. Now the problem's gone. We appreciate the gesture, that's all."

"Really?" Deke asked. "Because we've got some problems, too. You truly appreciate the favor, we could use some help resolving those. You get me?"

Hunter's eyes darkened.

"Yeah, I get you," he replied. "That was a bad business—"

"No, that was my *niece*," Deke said, slamming his hand down on the table. "Cute kid. Never gonna have kids of her own, though, what with the way your boys ripped her up from the inside out. Spent a year on a fuckin' psych ward. Still scared to leave her house."

Toke grunted, pulling out his knife and laying it on the table. Hunter leaned forward, his face every bit as intense as Deke's. He ignored the knife.

"That problem's been solved," he said. "We offered proof."

"Proof wasn't good enough," Deke replied. "Dead is easy. They needed to suffer, and I needed to be the one making them suffer. You stole that from me."

Hunter glanced at his friend, then nodded to the waitress, gesturing for her to come over. She approached their group cautiously, clearly reading the tension.

"Another round for the table," Hunter told her. She scuttled off, and silence fell. The girl returned with the drinks, and Hunter picked up his beer, sipping it thoughtfully. Ruger joined him, wondering how this would play out. He'd stand by Deke and Toke—still his brothers, right or wrong—but attacking some kid who'd had nothing to do with the incident wouldn't accomplish much. Finally, Skid spoke.

"Things are changing with the Jacks," he said. "Lot of things in play. What happened to your niece? There's no excuse for that and no way we're trying to say it was okay. None of us were down with it, and we took care of the men involved. Only two were our brothers. The rest were hangarounds, and all of them are gone now."

"We should've brought them to you," Hunter added. "We get that now. At the time, we just took care of business, because your girl was the last straw in a much bigger, much uglier situation, so wrap your head around that. Figured we'd minimize your risk and haul out our own garbage. I can't travel back and fix what happened to her. Can't give you a shot at them, either. It's done. What I can do is try to move forward, make sure it never happens again. We're tired of this."

"Tired of what?" Picnic asked, his eyes narrowing.

"Tired of putting time and energy into fighting Reapers when we should be focused on more important things."

"Funny, you weren't feeling all peaceful last December," Horse put in. "My woman was in danger. I don't appreciate assholes like yourselves threatening my property."

Hunter sighed and leaned back in his chair, rubbing the bridge of his nose between his fingers.

"Times change," he said finally. "We all know that. Some of our guys, they're a little slow, clinging to the past. That was their play, and it was a fuckin' stupid one. But most of my brothers and me, we're looking to the future. Fighting you is a waste of time and energy. Used to be we were in the minority on that one. Now we're not, so I'm opening the door. This wasn't an easy meeting to arrange, but we all put down our guns and came here today. That's a start."

"I didn't put down my gun," Deke rumbled.

Hunter smiled, shaking his head.

"Jesus, you're a hardass," he told Deke. "Respect. But seein' as I'm still alive right now, I think my point stands. We're talking, not shooting. Gotta be a record."

"That's your play?" Picnic asked, openly skeptical. "You had some kind of revolution back home, so now you're here tryin' to make peace? Lemme guess, you think we should all just hug and make up, maybe swap some recipes, organize a potluck?"

Hunter laughed, his body language so relaxed it was almost insulting. Didn't he realize they could take him in a heartbeat?

Yeah, Ruger decided. He knew it.

He just didn't care, and a man who'd stopped caring was dangerous as fuck.

"Cut the shit," Ruger said suddenly. "What do you want?"

Hunter leaned forward and met his eyes, voice serious.

"I'm here because we've been losing territory and influence for years, and it's getting worse. We got boys coming up from the south, out of L.A., and they're looking to expand. We need to be fighting them, but we're fighting you instead. So far as I can tell, we're doing it out of habit like a bunch of damned monkeys who can't figure out something better to do," he added.

"Swattin' flies isn't habit, it's housekeeping," Deke rumbled. "Same with killin' Jacks."

Hunter shook his head.

"Tell me this," he said. "Your niece, that was some bad shit. But before her, Reapers killed three of our guys in Redding. Two of those guys had kids. You remember that?"

"Assuming it happened—which for the record, I don't acknowledge—it's probably because they attacked our guys the night before," Picnic said. "Preemptive self-defense."

"Your guys were down there to steal one of our shipments," Hunter said flatly. "And they burned down our clubhouse while they were at it. Why'd they do that?"

Picnic shrugged.

"Dunno. I wasn't in on that decision," Picnic admitted. "That was all Roseburg."

"Yet we're prepared to fight and kill each other over it," Hunter said. "And each time we strike back, it gets worse. Sooner or later we're gonna kill each other off completely, which is exactly what the gangs down south want. Our clubs, we got history between us, and it's not good. But we're the same kind—we know what it means to be brothers. Men like us, we live to ride, and ride to live. Fuck the world."

Ruger nodded, acknowledging the point.

"Now we're seeing boys movin' north, boys who aren't part of a brotherhood . . . and I mean *boys*—they got kids workin' the streets can't be more than ten years old," Hunter continued. "These *children* are takin' orders from generals who don't get their hands dirty, let alone throw down for them. They don't get to vote, they don't get to think, and they don't even know why they're fighting. They're a threat to our way of life, yours and mine. I'm tired of putting time and energy into worrying about Reapers when every time I turn around some high school dropout's takin' potshots at me. I just want to ride my fuckin' bike and get laid."

Ruger glanced at Picnic. His face was thoughtful, although his expression didn't give away a thing. Horse grunted, polishing off his drink.

"I'm not the only one who feels that way," Hunter said. "Lot of my brothers, we're tired of this war. Those same brothers are moving up in their chapters, thinking maybe it's time for us to be on the same side in this little game. It's about values and what we stand for. We're brothers and we ride, all the rest is details. These fuckers, though . . . Deep down inside, there's nothing there. We gotta stop them before it's too late. I can't do that if I'm fighting a war on two fronts."

"Enough," Deke growled. "You're a little fuckwad and you don't know jack. What's gone down between us, that shit doesn't go away just because you and your boyfriends decide you're scared of someone new moving in on your territory. You wanted a war with the Reapers and now you've got it. We're going to kill you. *All of you*. Might take a while. I'm patient."

"Deke—" Picnic said, his voice low and full of unmistakable command. "What they did to Gracie can't be fixed, brother. But the bastards paid and now they're gone. The more we fight, the more likely some other girl's gonna get hurt. I got two daughters. Peace between clubs isn't always a bad thing. Especially when the cartel's movin' in. I hear stories . . ."

"We know you got two daughters," Hunter told Picnic, eyes narrowing. "In fact, we know a hell of a lot more than you'd like. We know because there's guys in my club who think we should strike, think we can use the cartel to throw you off balance. They called the shots last December, but they aren't in control right now and I'd like to keep it that way. You got two choices here . . . First one is nut up and work with me to control this new threat. We pull that off, everyone goes home happily ever after, shittin' rainbows and dancin' with unicorns. Second choice is keep fighting with each other until they take us all out. You want that? Fine. I'm not scared to bring it. But consider this . . . You got daughters you care about. One's up in Bellingham, other's in Coeur d'Alene. Pretty girls, which I know 'cause I've seen 'em for myself. Recently."

"You leave my girls out of this," Picnic said, reaching for his gun. Ruger's hand flashed out, catching him.

"Hear him out," he murmured.

Hunter grinned, the expression feral.

"You *should* worry, old man," he continued. "Because I guarantee those cocksuckers down south won't care how pretty those girls are when they give the order to shoot them down in the street like dogs. Now me? I don't even own a fuckin' goldfish. At the end of the day, who's got more to lose here? You call me when you're ready to talk."

With that Hunter stood up, shoving away his chair. Deke flushed, but Picnic's face could've been carved from stone. Hunter thew a handful of bills on the table and walked out the door.

"He's fuckin' with us," Toke said. "Cartel's got fuck all to do with us up here. He's losing territory. That's not our problem."

"You really think they can hold out?" Ruger asked him. "Cartel's got a thousand kids ready and waitin' to die, every one of them so hungry for glory they'll shoot their own mothers. Jacks are tough bastards, but they'll be fucked if they can't shut them down before they get a foothold. We would be, too, and you know it. Those gangs exist for one reason—to make money. We let them take over, we'll lose our territory and our *freedom*. No fuckin' point in breathing without that. Not to mention the cartel doesn't care where they shit or who they kill. You want them here in Portland?"

"This is big," Picnic said slowly. "Bigger than we can decide here. We'll get the brothers together, make sure we're all on board. Take it from there."

"I'll never make peace with the Jacks," Toke muttered. "You want peace, you'll go through me to get it."

"That a threat?" Ruger asked. He respected the hell out of Toke, but it wasn't his decision to make. "I hate the thought of taking on a brother, but don't think I won't. We're in this together, Toke. That means we make the call as a group."

"You think you could take me?" Toke asked, cocking a brow.

"Only one way to find out," Ruger replied, meeting his gaze without flinching. "But I tell you one thing. We start fightin' with each other, the cartel wins. Keep your eyes on the prize, brother. We make peace with the Jacks, they're our buffer. That lets us put our energy into makin' money and gettin' laid. We give it a shot and it falls apart, least we'll pick up some good intel along the way. Make it easier to go after 'em, the time comes."

Toke took a deep breath, then let it out, visibly forcing himself to calm down.

"I'll never forgive them for what they did," he said. "Jesus, she's still so fucked up. You got no idea."

"You damned well shouldn't," Horse told him, voice serious. "What happened can't be undone, and the assholes who did it deserved to die. Good news is, they did. Think ahead. We turn the Jacks into allies, we'll own half the west coast with the Jacks as a line of defense between us and the cartel. That's somethin' we should consider."

"I'll settle for protecting my girls," Picnic muttered. "Fuckin' asshole knows where they are, maybe's even watching them. You know what that means?"

"Means nobody's safe," Horse said softly. "And he's damned right about one thing—in our world, we don't fuck with citizens, so long as they show respect. We keep our towns safe and control what gets in. I know the Jacks did your niece, Deke, but she got as much justice as they could give. The cartel, though . . . They're shootin' women and children, and they don't give a fuck who they kill so long as they get their money. No values. I'll take the Jacks over them anytime."

"*If* they're telling us the truth," Ruger said. "Remember—they lie. We need information."

"Time to call the brothers together," Pic said. "No help for it. You want to host, Deke?"

"Do it in Coeur d'Alene," the Portland president replied, shaking his head. "We got nothin' like the Armory. Whatever else the Jacks might be, they aren't magic. We meet at the Armory, we'll have space to talk. I'll start making calls."

CHAPTER SIX

SOPHIE

No girl should have to lose panties this expensive.

I felt almost wistful when I found them in Ruger's couch. Dark, rich purple silk, delicate lacy cutouts in the front. Whoever she was, she'd shelled out way too much money prettying up for a one-night stand with the man-whore.

I knew the pain of lost panties myself . . . On that less-than-spectacular night Noah had been conceived, I'd had to go without mine after we got kicked out of Ruger's apartment.

Sighing, I dropped the couch cushion I'd been vacuuming under. I'd made my first pass through Ruger's house doing surface cleaning. Now I was on to the deeper stuff, which meant hunting through the bowels of the furniture, among other things.

It was Thursday afternoon and the week had come together nicely. After my visit with Kimber, I'd gotten in touch with some of the girls from the club who'd left their cell-phone numbers. They were coming over on Friday night to meet me and hang out.

They sounded every bit as nice and thoughtful as I'd suspected, and I couldn't wait to put faces to names.

I'd also gotten to know the neighbor down the road, a woman in her late thirties named Elle. She'd been widowed a couple years back and now she lived alone. We met her Tuesday afternoon, when Noah and I went exploring and wandered onto her property.

She and I spent a couple hours sitting outside her house (she had one of the old, original farmhouses, which meant a kick-ass porch complete with swing and rockers), sipping iced tea, and shooting the shit. Elle really hit it off with Noah, too, and had already offered to babysit if I needed it. I got a great vibe off her, Noah adored her, and we'd been thrilled when she had us over for dinner on Wednesday.

Wednesday was also when I started cleaning Ruger's house.

This was partly out of boredom. I also felt guilty, because Ruger was a single man who clearly enjoyed his freedom, yet he'd brought us home anyway. This had to cramp his style. Not that I particularly liked the idea of him being completely free to indulge himself . . . I knew I couldn't have him, but it still bugged me to think of him with other women.

And I totally got how messed up that was.

Didn't change how I felt.

Anyway, I decided the best way to pay Ruger back was to become his unofficial housekeeper. He didn't plan to charge us any rent, but I wouldn't feel right if I wasn't earning my keep.

Which brought me to the pair of tiny purple panties lost in the couch.

Sadly, this was not the first piece of lingerie I'd found in the last twenty-four hours. They weren't all the same sizes, either—Ruger clearly appreciated variety among his many booty calls.

I picked up the panties with a pair of kitchen tongs and carried them into the laundry room. I didn't know who they belonged to, but I didn't think I should be tossing out anything I found, no matter how . . . used . . . it might be. I dropped the panties into one of the four plastic boxes I'd lined up across the top of the dryer.

The first held money. So far I'd found ninety-two dollars and twenty-three cents. Box two was condoms. I found stashes in almost every room. Some were definitely on purpose, and I left those in place. But I'd also found them in the pockets of stray pants, in the silverware drawer, on top of the bookshelf . . . I'd even found two in the pizza box on the coffee table. Chocolate-flavored ones. This led to a series of fantasies about pizza-themed sex, which squicked me out a bit.

Also made me sort of hungry.

That's when I decided I needed little boxes to put all this stuff in, so I could just close the lids and pretend they didn't exist. So far it was working pretty well. Box three held women's underwear, bras, and a single silk stocking. Box four was "other"—small, strange chunks of metal, random tools, a Buck knife, and two ticket stubs from a Spokane Indians game.

Weird pangs of jealousy aside, I wanted Ruger's house fresh, clean, and comfortable when he got home. It was the least I could do. I cleaned everywhere but his bedroom, although I did wade in just far enough to grab the worst of the laundry.

That night, Noah asked me when Uncle Ruger would be back. I had no idea what to tell him, and I wondered if living in his house could ever feel normal. Free rent was great, but Kimber was probably right. Ultimately, I needed my own place, where the couch cushions weren't full of strange underwear and the silverware drawer was condom-free.

The thudding of feet overhead woke me up around three o'clock early Friday morning. Ruger was home, I noted drowsily, and it sounded like he was throwing a party. Fortunately, my kid and I could sleep through anything, so five minutes later I was out again.

The next day, Noah and I did our best to stay quiet as we got ready and used our own door to leave the house. When I got back from dropping him at school, I had a near-miss with the house alarm, punching in the code twice before I got it right. Ruger's obsession with security was damned inconvenient at times . . .

I showered and straightened up our little apartment. By then it was almost ten and still no noise from upstairs. Maybe I dreamed the whole thing up? God knew, Ruger had a tendency to invade my dreams.

I slipped up the stairs softly, not wanting to wake him. I reached the top, turned toward the kitchen and swayed, completely shocked.

Apparently a hurricane had hit the house in the night.

Empty beer bottles covered every possible surface. The furniture had been shoved around, with one end of the love seat actually lifted up and resting on the back of the main couch. There were partially empty pizza boxes, spilled beer—and the most disturbing part of all?

A completely naked blonde chick sat at the breakfast bar, lighting a cigarette.

Seeing her hit me hard—I actually couldn't breathe for a second, and I felt dizzy. I knew Ruger slept around. I'd found the evidence myself, but somehow this finally brought it all home for me.

She was gorgeous and utterly unselfconscious. Naturally, I wore an old tank top and cutoffs, hair in a messy bun, and no makeup. I wanted to kill her. Dead. Strangle her on the spot for being a damned whore and being prettier than me and fucking my man.

I gave myself a mental smack.

I had no claim on Ruger. None. This was his house and he could do whatever he wanted in it, including this whore.

I didn't even *want* him, not really.

"So, you Ruger's property?" she asked me, eyes hostile, red-tipped talons tapping the bar idly.

"Um, I don't think I understand the question," I replied, torn between staring at her perky, jiggly boobs and watching the trail of smoke rise from her cigarette toward the ceiling. Once that smoky smell gets into a house, you never get it back out.

Yet another reason to hate the bitch.

"Simple yes or no," she said. "You belong to him? He patch you?"

"I have no idea what you're talking about," I said, glancing around the living room, growing pissier by the second, despite the fact that it was none of my business. This was going to take hours to clean and it sure as hell wouldn't be me doing it, I decided. Let the whore do it. Or Ruger himself—what a concept!

"That's a no . . ." she said slowly. "So why the hell are you here? Did he call you this morning? Seriously, if he wanted a three-way, he should've talked to me earlier. No offense, but I can do better."

She looked me up and down as she said this, judging every inch of my body.

"I think I should go back downstairs," I said with careful control. I turned to leave, but Ruger's voice stopped me.

"You still here?" he called. The blonde answered, voice all sweet like honey, eyes sparkling with possessive triumph.

"Sure thing, baby. You need me?"

Ruger strolled down the stairs and into the living room, wearing only a pair of unfastened jeans. I could tell this because they drooped low enough to leave very few secrets. Damn.

I knew Ruger was hot, but it seemed like I forgot just how hot whenever I didn't see him for a while, because it still shocked me. I could spend a year trying to describe him, but you still wouldn't fully appreciate his unique appeal until your panties spontaneously combusted the first time he smiled at you.

Or, in this case, when he walked through the living room wearing half-fastened jeans commando, eyes still sleepy.

My eyes caught on his chest, sliding down along the lines of his muscles. Oh, my . . . Perfect pecs, sculpted obliques and abs. They disappeared into the denim, which just barely rode his hips, ready to slip at any minute. I wanted to lick him all over.

Right after I killed him for fucking The Blonde Slut.

"Morning," he said, looking from me to TBS. I raised my hand and gave a little finger wave, wondering if the knife in the laundry room was well-balanced for throwing.

"Welcome back, Ruger," I said, trying not to sound like a jealous wife, because nothing crazy about that, right? "Have a nice trip? Noah missed you. I was just going downstairs. Have a great morning."

TBS smirked, taking my attempted retreat as a victory for her. Or that's what I imagined was behind her smirk. For all I knew, that could have been her thank-God-I'm-not-in-a-three-way-with-this-loser face.

Whatever it was, she could damned well shove it up her ass.

"No," Ruger said, staring at me intently. His eyes flicked down my figure, and no matter how hot the chick in the kitchen was, I could tell he still wanted me. His eyes were dark and needy like they'd been the other night. And all those years ago, too . . .

Nope, not going there, I reminded my brain. This situation's fucked up enough already.

"We need to talk. It's important," he told me. Then he glanced toward TBS. "We're done, time to go. Don't call."

Wow. That was cold.

I liked it.

"You seriously want *her* over *me*?" TBS demanded, looking between us, face genuinely confused.

"Sophie's my nephew's mom," Ruger said, voice going hard and flat. "One of her in dirty sweats is worth ten of you naked on your knees, so get the fuck out."

Oh, that was *sooo* cold. Maybe I didn't hate him quite so much, because he might be an asshole, but he was definitely being a bigger asshole to her than to me. Justice, for once.

"You're kind of a dick," TBS said, pouting.

"Ya think?" he asked, walking past us to open the fridge. Ruger pulled out a container of orange juice and chugged it without using a glass. He finished, wiped his mouth with the back of his hand, and slammed it down on the counter. Juice splashed, reminding me of the brand-new, giant-ass mess everywhere else.

A mess I wouldn't be cleaning. Enough of this.

I needed to retreat back downstairs, away from this bitch and Ruger, the world's biggest asshole. He ranked up there with the biggest pigs, too, based on what he'd accomplished in one night with his friends. I turned to the stairs but his hand caught my arm, tight and unyielding as a handcuff. He tugged me through the kitchen to the bar, pushing me into a seat.

"Stay," he ordered me, his eyes hard. Then he looked over at Blondie. "Go."

His tone didn't leave room for discussion, and she jumped up, scowling. Ruger strode quickly across the living room and up the stairs. Blondie followed him, then ran back down fast, her clothes flying over the balcony from the loft.

Five minutes later she was gone with a massive slam of the front door and Ruger was back in the kitchen making me all nervous. I wasn't quite sure what to say to him. I hated him for bringing her home. I was jealous of her, because she was hot and she'd felt his cock inside her last night, when all I'd gotten inside me was my vibrator. Hell, it wasn't even working right—some sort of loose connection. Half the time it wouldn't turn on and I didn't have money to buy a new one. How pathetic was that?

Too broke to buy a damn vibrator.

Maybe I should stand outside the Adam & Eve store holding a sign reading "Single Mom, Anything Helps" and a cup for change.

Ruger narrowed his eyes at me. He still hadn't buttoned his pants. Holy shit. I sincerely hoped I wasn't drooling.

"So, tonight the girls from your club are coming over," I told him, trying to find a safe place for my eyes. They skittered across the tribal tattoo on his pec and caught on his nipple ring. I flushed. Definitely not *there.* "I guess we're planning some sort of party for tomorrow at your club's armory? Do I want to know why your club has an armory?"

"It's an actual National Guard Armory," he said. "Club bought it when it got surplussed, years ago. It's got everything from a big kitchen and bar to rooms upstairs for people who need somewhere to crash for the night."

So. His clubhouse had beds. Why did this not surprise me?

I wanted to ask him why he hadn't fucked TBS there instead of bringing her home to me and Noah, but I couldn't think of a not-crazy way of doing it. Instead I decided to keep talking about my schedule.

"They had me line up a sleepover for Noah at my friend Kimber's house for tomorrow night," I said, eyes darting to his face. Not a flicker of recognition at her name. Good. "Anyway, they invited me and I promised you I'd give it a shot, so . . . I'll see you at the party?"

He cocked his head and studied me, utterly impossible to read. Silence stretched between us. I struggled not to start babbling just to fill the void.

"Bigger party than they think," he finally said, his voice low. It took me a minute to remember what we'd been talking about. Oh, yeah. Party planning. Armory. "Whole bunch of guys from all over coming in tonight and tomorrow. Not sure I want you there."

He shook his head slowly, tongue flicking out to slide along his lower lip, catching on the ring. I wanted to flick it with my tongue, too. Then I caught a glimpse of something else . . . Shit. His tongue was pierced. There was a hard, round ball right in the middle.

That hadn't been there four years ago. I would've remembered.

What would it feel like in my mouth . . . or lower? I'd never kissed a guy with a pierced tongue, let alone had one go down on me. I started tingling between my legs, which was *not* what I needed in that moment. Assholes this big shouldn't be so hot.

Hairy ears, I thought. *Pretend he has hairy ears.*

"You're a very frustrating person, Ruger," I said, torn between bitching at him for being such a giant whore and jumping over the counter, ripping off his pants, and riding his cock. Not the best way to handle the situation.

I knew this.

Really.

"You say I shouldn't judge the club," I added, trying to focus. "You say you want me to get to know everyone, and that Noah's life would be better if he had the club behind him. If that's true, why can't I go to one of their parties?"

"Because this one's gonna get pretty fuckin' wild. Not really a starter party," he said, unfolding his arms to brace them on the counter on either side of his body. I saw his biceps rippling under his full-sleeve tattoos. He had more ink across his shoulders, some kind of rounded slash things in addition to the pattern on his chest. There was another tat curling around his stomach from his hip. A panther disappearing down into his pants on one side.

Lucky cat.

I really, really wanted to see the rest of it.

"You said some shit the other night that we gotta deal with. Um, Sophie? I have a face, you know," he added, and my eyes jerked up from his stomach. I felt myself flush and he stayed silent, watching me with hooded eyes. He raised a hand and rubbed the back of his neck, biceps and triceps flexing nicely, then scratched at his stomach. The muscles between my legs took note, pulsing their approval.

"What do we have to deal with?" I asked, feeling my cheeks flush again.

"No friends with benefits for you," he told me without a trace of humor. "No fucking around, no kissing, or even fluttering your goddamned eyelashes at any guy in the club. That's the only way you'll be at the party. Or any club event."

I raised my brows at him and shook my head. No matter how uncomfortable this conversation might be, I needed to set some boundaries.

"That's stupid. I'm single. If I meet someone I like, it's my decision whether I flirt with them or kiss them or whatever. And you're one to talk—you just threw a naked chick out the door without even a thank-you for the road. Hypocrite much?"

"My house, my rules," he replied. "You go to that party, nothing happens. You're the Virgin fuckin' Mary, got me? Otherwise you stay home."

I thought about this, then straightened, placing my hands flat on the counter. Until that moment, I'd been on the fence about the party. I wanted to give the club a shot, but I'd been nervous about jumping in headfirst. Now? Now I'd show up at that damned Armory if it killed me. I'd flirt all over the place, too.

Fuck him and his whore.

I glared at him. He glared back. Neither of us blinked.

There's a lot Ruger and I refused to talk about, and God knew he could hide his thoughts from me. Now I couldn't even begin to follow his logic—he'd made it clear nothing would happen between us, so why the jealous boyfriend act?

"Why does it matter?" I asked finally. "Are your friends so dangerous that I'm not safe? Because you've spent a lot of time giving me shit for assuming they're dangerous criminals instead of giving them a shot. So it's either that or because you're jealous. That it? You don't want me but nobody else gets me, either? Would it be easier if you peed on me so they know I'm taken?"

"It'd be easier if you'd shut the fuck up," he said, eyes darkening.

"That's what you want from me? Silence?" I demanded, feeling my temper rise. "Call me stupid, but it seemed like you wanted a hell of a lot more the other night. You can't have it both ways, asshole. Either there's something between us or I'm a free agent."

Ruger pushed away from the counter, holding my gaze as he stalked across the kitchen.

"Oh, I *can* have it both ways," he said. "You shouldn't make assumptions about what I'm capable of, Soph. I'll be nice and give you a heads-up what's happening here. I want to fuck you."

He rounded the kitchen island, prowling like the big cat tattooed on his hip. The kitchen felt smaller and smaller. I was all too aware of his bare chest, black ink rippling as he moved, and just how tightly controlled he kept his strength. Perhaps direct confrontation had been a mistake . . .

"That's the thing about guys like me," he continued, his voice low and smooth, eyes boring right through mine. "We don't do what we're supposed to. We take what we want. And me? I *want* all kinds of things. First I want to tie you up in my bed with my belt. Then I want to cut off your clothes and fuck you in every hole you have. I also want to come on you and rub it into your skin and lick your pussy until you scream at me to stop because if you come one more time you'll die. Then I want to do it again. I want to *own* you, Sophie."

He stopped beside my stool, so close the heat of his body engulfed me. I couldn't even turn my head to look at him, frozen like a rabbit, his words turning over and over in my head. His scent surrounded me. I tried to breathe as he leaned in close, one arm braced on the counter, whispering in my ear.

"I want to own *every part* of you," he continued, his breath hot against my skin. "I *want* to throw you face-first across this counter, rip off those shorts, and fuck you hard and fast until my goddamned cock stops hurting and my balls don't feel like they're gonna explode. Because they've felt that way for a helluva long time, Soph, and I'm startin' to think it's not gonna go away unless I do something about it."

It took everything I had not to squeak in panic. Every part of my body tingled and I clenched my legs together tightly, putting pressure on my clit with every pulse of desire. Oh, that felt good. Not good enough, though, I needed more. My cheeks flushed and my breath came quick. I considered reaching down and shoving my hand into those half-fastened pants. Maybe discover for myself if Kimber had been telling the truth about his cock . . .

Ruger hadn't even touched me.

He *still* wasn't touching me. I bit back a moan.

"But that's probably not a real good idea," he added, his voice cooling as he pulled back. "We both know it. Not what Noah needs and a fuckin' tar pit for you and me, too. But your idea about hooking up with one of my brothers? That keeps runnin' through my head, Soph, and then I start thinking about shootin' people. I don't want to have to shoot anyone tomorrow, get me? Shitty way to end a party. Not to mention the prez might get frustrated, one of the local brothers loses it in public with the whole fuckin' club here for a meet."

Holy crap.

I nodded, chest tightening.

"So, all things considered, you might think about doing *exactly what I say* at that fuckin' party," he said, and while he phrased it like a suggestion, it was a straight-up order. "I get that you don't want someone like me in your bed, not as a keeper. Don't want things to get weirder than they are between us, either. But if you're gonna screw a biker, Soph, I'm the only one you get. I won't stand by and let you fuck one of my brothers."

"I can't believe you just said all that," I whispered. "That's wrong on so many levels. I don't even know where to start."

He considered me, eyes hard, voice cold.

"I don't care if it's wrong," he said. "That's the way it is. My house, my world, my rules. Tell me you understand and I'll let you go to the party."

"I'm an adult," I managed to say, although my voice shook. "You don't get to tell me what to do."

"And yet I'm doin' it," he returned, shrugging casually. "Do you really think I won't enforce this? I'll fuckin' enforce it, Soph. Don't test me."

"I haven't decided about the party," I whispered. "But I'm done with this conversation. I'm going back downstairs."

"No, you're not," he said, and that little, instinctive voice deep down inside me screaming to run finally won. I slid off the stool and made a break for the stairs. Big mistake, because Ruger caught me around the waist and lifted me up onto the kitchen bar, eyes blazing. Two seconds later he stepped in between my legs, one hand pulling me in tight and the other twisting through my hair, jerking my head back.

"Let me go," I whispered. He cocked his head, as if considering the idea, then slowly shook it.

"I can't," he said. Then his lips covered mine and a fuse blew in my brain.

CHAPTER SEVEN

It wasn't a polite kiss. It wasn't slow and seductive and deeply meaningful. This was an explosion of pent-up lust . . . Years' worth, to be honest. Ruger's chest was like a concrete wall, and I wrapped my legs around his waist without a thought. His hand tightened in my hair, tilting my head to the side, giving him better access. His tongue was thrust deep and without mercy. The little ball in the center teased me, reminding me that sex with him would be different than anything I'd felt before. His cock pushed into my stomach so hard it almost hurt.

Holy hell, I wished we weren't wearing so many clothes.

Ruger slid his hand into my tank, pulling his torso back just enough to cup my breast. His fingers found my nipple, tweaking it through the thin silk of my bra as I arched my back, desperate for more. He tore his mouth free, and we stared at each other, panting, mesmerized.

"We decided this is a bad idea," I reminded him rather desperately, wondering how he'd feel if I just leaned forward and sucked on his lip. I couldn't take my eyes off it, all dark red and glistening with a sheen of moisture from our kiss. "I'm not drunk today. No excuses."

"You said you wanted to get laid," he replied, pupils dark and full. "I'm here. It's already all screwed up between us, so why not make the most of it? Damage is done, we're totally fucked. I can't forget how you tasted the other night, or how you felt on top of me on that couch. I need inside you, Soph."

Oh, so tempting . . .

But could I keep messing around with Ruger and still live here? I'd lusted after him forever, and there was no question he wanted me. Then I thought about the woman who'd sat naked in this very kitchen just half an hour ago. The purple panties. The green bra . . . All in Ruger's house, which was supposed to be Noah's refuge.

Sleeping with Ruger was suicide.

I felt like banging my head against something hard, but only his chest was handy and getting closer to that expanse of bare skin was the last thing I needed.

"Bad idea," I said. His fingers rolled my nipple. His other hand lowered to brace my hips as he rubbed the rigid length of his cock against my clit. That slow back-and-forth would only get better once he slid inside me.

I felt all wound up inside, almost dizzy. I don't think I've ever wanted anything more than I wanted him in my body.

Except a decent life for Noah.

"If we do this, you can just move along afterward," I told him, closing my eyes. My sex clenched tight, desperate and empty. I tried to ignore it. "Who you sleep with is nothing to you, Ruger. But I'm different."

"You're the one who was talking friends with benefits," he murmured. "Why's your story changin' now? Scared?"

"Hell yes, I'm scared," I replied, opening my eyes again, searching his face. I saw no mercy or understanding there, just harsh, unyielding lust. "I live with you and I don't have anywhere else to go. I found three pairs of panties in your couch cushions yesterday, and none of them were the same size. I don't think I can sleep with you and then nod and smile while a parade of women passes through the house. Sounds like a pretty good reason not to do this."

"Why the hell were you looking through my couch cushions?" he asked, and his hips stilled.

I'd caught him off guard with that one.

"I cleaned your house," I replied. "Kind of a surprise-slash-thank-you-present. Your company last night pretty much took care of that, though."

"Jesus," he whispered, shaking his head slowly, hips starting to rock again. Oh, that was nice . . . His cock felt so good rubbing against my most sensitive spot. Could I come from just that, even with the fabric between us? "I'm sorry about that. I didn't even know they were coming over. Don't suppose that's much of an excuse."

I shrugged, unable to meet his gaze. I looked at his tattoos instead. Most of them were high quality, fanciful designs clearly put together by a true artist. He took his body art seriously, I realized. Ink wasn't just a whim. I'd bet he had a story for each one, and I wanted to hear those stories far more than was healthy.

Ruger eyed me thoughtfully, rubbing the tip of my nipple with his finger in a slow circle. Then he took my hand and slid it down between us, pressing it against the length of his hard cock, the backs of his own fingers brushing my clit. I gasped and squirmed. My grip tightened, shaping him through the stiff fabric of his jeans. Even through the denim, I could tell he was big and broad, much bigger than my vibrator. Was that hard bump near the tip his . . . ? I didn't even know what to call it. I wanted to see it—to see all of him—so badly I could've died. His knuckles framed my clit and I moaned.

Ruger's eyes darkened.

"You want this as much as I do," he said, voice soft. "It's not goin' away. We're just going to burn up higher and higher until one of us explodes and we get hurt. Let's end it now. I need inside you, Sophie."

"You *needed* to be inside your blonde last night," I replied quietly. "And look how that ended. You going to kick me and Noah out if things get awkward?"

"You're wrong about that," he replied.

"About kicking us out? It's not going to work, us sleeping together and you sleeping around. Some random guy I could just ditch, but I'm stuck with you."

"Wrong about needin' to be inside her last night," he corrected me. "I needed *you.* You're all I thought about while I was gone. Went to sleep every night with a stiff dick, woke up harder, didn't matter how much I jerked off or who I fucked. Riding home from Portland last night, I knew that if I came back into this house all dark and quiet, I'd go downstairs and find you. I'd crawl into your bed and stick my fingers into your pussy and open you up for me whether you wanted it or not. So I tried something else, because we decided we weren't going to screw around with each other. It didn't work."

My hand had started rubbing his dick through the rough fabric. It was hard to focus on his words, between that and his knuckles stroking my clit. They'd found a steady rhythm up and down, and my hips rolled into them ever so slightly, rebelling against all rational thought.

"Is that supposed to make me feel better?" I asked. "Because when I saw her, I wanted to kill her. And you. I don't have any right to feel that way."

"I don't have any right to put you off limits, either," he replied. "But I'm doin' it anyway. No fuckin' around with anyone at the club. Make that no fuckin' around, period. You're mine."

I lifted my hand and slid it down into his jeans, fingers tracing his naked cock. I found the metal bar piercing his glans—two hard, metal balls capped it, top and bottom. I touched it softly and he groaned.

"Imagine those deep inside you," he muttered, closing his eyes and as his hips spasmed. "First I'll rub them against your clit, and then they'll hit your G-spot the whole damned time I'm riding you. Un-fucking-believable, babe."

I tightened inside at the thought, nearly undone. I played with them a few seconds longer then moved lower, gripping his shaft firmly. He moaned and I tightened my fingers, almost angry because I wanted him so bad.

Ruger opened his eyes, giving me a lazy smile.

"You trying to hurt me?" he whispered. "Because you'll never be able to, babe. Squeeze me hard as you like. I get off on it. I'm stronger than you, which means in the end, I'll win. That's the way of the world."

"That's not fair," I replied softly. He leaned forward, resting his forehead against mine. His fingers pulled away from the front of my cutoffs to slip inside. I felt them lower, one on either side of my clit, fluttering and squeezing. His cock pulsed in my hand, hot and hard, the ball brushing lightly against the inside of my wrist.

"Life isn't fair," he whispered. "Sometimes you just have to make the most of what you've got."

"Would this be a one-time thing?" I asked, so tempted. Could I do it? Just give in for once, then go back to pretending it never happened?

"No idea," he replied, voice lowering, growing harsher. "Probably take more than once, gettin' out from under each other's skin. I've wanted you a long time, Soph. Never forgot how you tasted, not for one single fuckin' day in the last four years. Jesus, you were sweet."

My breath caught.

"And after it's over?"

"We move along," he replied. "I'll show you respect, you do the same for me. Won't bring any women here. Shouldn't have done it anyway, got beds at the club."

"But you'll move on," I said slowly, feeling something deep inside me tear apart. "And I'll just be another in your lineup, because that's what you do. You fuck women, and then you fuck them over."

"Better than fucking my hand," he said bluntly. "I've never pretended to be somethin' I'm not, babe. I'm not gonna settle down. I don't want to commit. I love my life the way it is. Most guys feel the same way—the difference between them and me is I'll never lie to you about it."

"That's why this is such a huge mistake," I told him, wishing it could be different. I hurt, and not just from frustrated desire. I'd always known this about him, but hearing him say it so bluntly . . . that got to me. "I should go downstairs right now and we'll forget it ever happened."

But my hand kept sliding up and down his cock, reaching up and catching on the metal as I found his pre-come, using it to ease my way back down. His fingers kept moving on my clit, rolling it as a shiver tore through me. My inner muscles clenched and I knew I had to be dripping wet by now.

"We'll stop soon," he said, rubbing his nose along mine oh-so-slowly. "Just one more taste."

Ruger's lips parted mine again, tongue plunging deep, filling my mouth the way I wanted him to fill my body. It was hard to focus on all the sensations—Ruger's hungry kiss, his fingers gliding along my clit. His hard cock in my hand, pulsing as those two metal balls taunted me. All of it blended into one big ball of aching, burning need. Then his fingers moved faster and I gave up everything but my own pleasure.

Tension built in me as he pulled his mouth free, tugging up my shirt. The cup of my bra came down and his mouth took my breast, sucking it in deep and hard, flicking the peak with his tongue. The hard metal tormented my nipple, the contrast between solid steel and hot flesh destroying my ability to think. Ruger's powerful body surrounded me. His fingers played me and I couldn't do anything but fall back into the incredible intensity of his touch on my clit.

I was close now, panting harshly.

Ruger's mouth still held my nipple trapped. He caught the other in his fingers, tugging and jerking everything all together. I whimpered, so close I could taste it but needing just a little more to go over the edge. Then he stopped teasing and pushed down against my clit, rough and demanding. My hips convulsed as I came, twisting on the counter shamelessly. Ruger covered my mouth with his once more, kissing me softly as the tremors ran through me, leaving me limp in his arms.

Then he lifted his head, meeting my eyes.

The hunger in his face was intense, more than I'd ever seen on a man. I'd stopped stroking him in the thick of things, but I still held his cock. He'd gotten thicker, and now I pumped his length hard. His fluid coated everything and my fingers slipped across his pierced head as he arched in my hand. We stayed like that, locking gazes, as I worked him faster and faster. After a minute his face darkened and his breath quickened.

Then he reached between us, pushing down his jeans and pulling his cock fully free, hand covering mine. He started jerking our joined hands up and down together, much rougher than I'd do on my own. The heel of my hand caught his pierced head each time, and he growled, primal and hungry.

"Let me fuck you, Sophie," Ruger gasped, his voice full of pain. I shook my head, closing my eyes because I didn't want him to see how close I was to giving in.

"No," I said, almost crying because it hurt so bad to say it. "I'm not going to screw you and then watch you with other women. I can't do it. I *know* myself, Ruger. Unless you can tell me right here, right now that you want to seriously try to make something together, I can't sleep with you. Let me finish this and then it's over."

He caught my hand, squeezing it tight around his cock and closed his eyes, shuddering. Then he pulled my hand away with visible pain and twisted it behind my back, jerking my body forward into his, transforming me from lover to prisoner so casually it terrified me.

"There's no lie here," Ruger said, voice grating. His face flushed dark red and his chest heaved, eyes burning. Every part of him was rock hard, from his chest crushing my breasts to the naked cock pressed into my belly. "No manipulation between us. It is what it is. But I'll give you the ride of your life, Soph. That I guarantee."

"The ride of my life?" I asked, the words hitting me like cold water, breaking through my fog of stupidity.

Holy hell. What was I doing?

I'd lost my fucking mind.

Ruger might be a great uncle, but I couldn't trust him for shit with my body, let alone my heart.

"Zach already gave me the ride of my life, Ruger," I said, making every word count. "I learned my lesson from him. Sex is short and it changes everything. That's something men like you can't begin to understand."

He jerked away from me, mouth tight and eyes hard, glaring at me.

"Jesus Christ, you're a bitch."

"I'm not a bitch," I replied, and it took everything I had to keep my voice steady. "I'm a *mother.* I can't afford to play games with you, Ruger. You'll break me, and that will break Noah."

"Un-fucking-believable," he muttered, slamming his hand next to me on the counter. I jumped, almost scared as he reached down to tuck himself back into his pants, visibly pained. He refused to step away or allow me any kind of escape, taking my shoulders in his big hands with a jerk.

"Nothin' is changed," he said, eyes burning with anger and frustrated need. My breath caught—Ruger had always been scary . . . But because there's something wrong with me, seeing him this angry turned me on, too. He leached the common sense right out of my body. "You go to that party, you keep your hands off. That's a fuckin' order. No flirtin', no makin' out, no touchin', *nothin'*. These aren't Boy Scouts, and they won't be happy if you start something you don't plan to finish. You're off bounds. We clear?"

"Crystal," I whispered. "I understand you completely."

"Thank fuck for that," he muttered, letting me go and stepping back. Finally. I took a deep breath, dizzy with relief. He ran a hand across his hair, glaring a hole through me. "Now get your ass out of my house. Go for a car ride, go shopping, whatever the fuck you want, but don't come back until you've picked Noah up from school. I'll be gone by then."

"Where are you going?"

"You seriously think that's any of your business?" he asked, raising his brows. "Because we aren't fuck buddies, you aren't my old lady, and I sure as fuck don't remember puttin' you in charge of my life."

"You don't owe me anything," I said. *But you don't get to control me, either,* I thought, way too chicken to say it out loud. "And I'm sorry. You aren't anything like Zach. I know that. But this isn't just about us, it's about Noah. He's not losing another home because we can't keep our pants on, Ruger."

"Have I ever done anything—*anything*—to hurt that child?" he asked.

"I don't think you'd do it on purpose."

"Get the fuck *out* before I change my mind, Sophie. Jesus."

I got the fuck out.

KIMBER: No fucking way!!!!! Ur fucking with me!!!!!! His dick in ur hand and u still said NO?!??

ME: I wish it was a joke. It happened, tho

KIMBER: Part of me thinks u made a lucky escape . . . Rest of me thinkgs u shud have fucked him

ME: That would make it all worse. You told me to stay awy from him, rmemember?

KIMBER: Um, it's worse already, dumbass, u blew it. Ur screwed and there's no out. Sex is just the symptom. This is about u guys being all twisted up with each other. He wants u way more than I thought

ME: No shit

KIMBER: U are so dens. This morning was gamechanger. Remember—I kno him. He's not like this with other women. I take back what I said about it being a bad idea. U should have sex. Mite as well get the fun if ur paying the price—it's already fucked up past the point of no return

ME: Thats the truth. Weirder every day. Harder every time I see him

KIMBER: HARDER!!!!! Love it <-;

ME: Perv

KIMBER: Ur just jealous of my pervy deliciousness. So I think maybe he WANTS u. Like, to keep

ME: Like a pet? I'm not a kitten

KIMBER: I WILL make pussy jokes if u don't pull your head out of ur ass. Serosly. Think about it

ME: Hate you. Even if he wnats me, he's stil gonna fuck around. Deal breaker

KIMBER: I know . . . We need a plan. We also need margaritas. Cures everythng. Come over tonight?

ME: Um, Im meeitng the girls from the club tonite. My place

KIMBER: What time

ME: 7

KIMBER: I'll bring mix and booze. Make sure u have ice

ME: Um . . .

KIMBER: Easier if u just give in now Soph. I'm coming over to figure this out. Rugers gonna fuck u sooner or later, so it's time to decide how to make him play nice. We can talk and then I'll tell u what to do

ME: I think he's got dibs on telling me what to do! Bossy asshole

KIMBER: Ha!

ME: Bitch

KIMBER: You love me. See you tonight <3

My eyeballs were going to explode.

Or maybe just pop out of my head?

I'd never tasted anything quite like the flaming shot prepared by my new best friend, Em. I nearly snorted it out my nose, but managed to hold on to token dignity as my throat ignited and my eyes watered. The circle of women around the deck table burst out cackling like a bunch of witches, so I flipped all of them off.

They laughed louder.

My morning encounter with Ruger might've been bizarre and tense and frustrating as all hell, but the evening had shaped up nicely. Four lady Reapers had arrived a little after seven—Maggs, Em, Marie, and Dancer. They brought pizza, beer, and a bunch of those tiny bottles of hard liquor, the kind you get on airplanes. I'd been a little overwhelmed at first, trying to keep everyone straight, but by now I'd figured them out.

Maggs was Bolt's old lady, and he was in prison. She looked very normal for a woman with a man in jail, and not "old" at all. I didn't think much of this whole "old lady" business, but the Reaper girls seemed to use it with pride. Maggs had shaggy, shoulder-length blonde hair full of wild curls. She was petite and perky and had such an infectious smile you couldn't help but smile back at her.

I really, really wanted to ask why her man was locked up, but managed to keep my mouth shut for once.

Dancer was tall and elegant, with bronzed skin and long, straight hair. Had to be part Indian, I decided. Coeur d'Alene Tribe? I didn't want to ask, but it seemed likely, since she'd grown up here. She was married to a guy called Bam Bam, and Horse was her half brother, born right after her mother married his father when she was two years old. Em was young, probably younger than me. She had the most amazing sky-blue eyes with dark rings around the edges of her irises. She was about my height and had brown hair pulled back in a messy bun. She was Picnic's daughter, whoever he was.

The last of the old ladies was Marie, a short girl with lots of long, brown, wavy hair and a bright, bubbly personality. She was with Horse, which I found hard to picture. He was huge—you'd think he'd break her or something. She wore an unusual engagement ring, a blue stone surrounded by sparkling diamonds. Apparently the wedding was at the end of the month. The big, intense biker I'd met in Seattle hardly seemed like the type to get hitched, but he was obviously ready to sign on the dotted line for Marie.

She made it clear I was invited to the wedding and her bachelorette party, the likes of which would put the Reaper men to shame.

Attendance was not optional.

When they'd rung the front doorbell on arrival, it was the first time I'd come back upstairs to see the ruins of the kitchen and living room. Surprisingly, Ruger had cleaned up quite a bit since that morning. The place didn't shine like before, but the bottles were gone and he'd put the love seat back on the floor. The women came through the door in a wave, all hugs and smiles and bags of food and drink. I showed them downstairs and introduced them to Noah, who'd spent the afternoon picking wildflowers in honor of our dinner together. My grubby little boy melted them instantly, of course.

"I have a son who's a year older than you and another who's a year younger," Dancer told him. "Maybe you can meet them sometime."

"Do they have Skylanders?" Noah asked, never shy. "If they have Skylanders, we should play at your house. Otherwise they should come here, because I want to show them the pond."

"Um, I'll talk to your mom and get it figured out," Dancer said.

Noah shrugged and took off outside again. He wasn't one for wasting time on useless conversation.

The only awkward moment was when Kimber arrived, shortly after I put Noah to bed. She marched down the stairs smiling brightly, but when they saw her, Maggs and Dancer got funny looks on their faces. Whatever they knew about her, Em and Marie clearly weren't aware of it.

"Hi, I'm Kimber," my friend said, setting a blender on the counter. She surveyed the room and crossed her arms, planting herself firmly. "Let's get this over with. I used to work at The Line and I screwed Ruger and a lot of other guys. Mostly customers, but a few from the club. Anything else we need to talk about, or does that about cover it?"

"Holy crap," Em said, eyes wide. "You make a hell of an entrance."

"It would've been better if I could carry the vodka and mix with me in one trip with the blender," Kimber replied seriously. "Now—you girls into huckleberry margaritas? I'm kind of a margarita artist, or so I've heard. We can hang out and have a great time and drink together if you like. Or you can take turns calling me a whore, which is a lot less fun for all of us, but still doable. Either way, I'm not leaving, so let's process and move on."

"You screw Bolt, Horse, or Bam Bam?" Em asked, clearly fascinated. The tension in the air suddenly grew heavy.

Kimber shook her head.

"Nope," she said. "Don't even know who Horse is. Met Bolt and Bam Bam a few times, but never got close to them. They're whipped—at least that's what I heard."

"Like the sound of that," Dancer murmured, a slow smile crossing her lips. "We'll just skip the whore thing, then?"

The tension broke, and Kimber demonstrated that she was, indeed, something of a margarita artist.

Now it was nearly midnight and we'd progressed past blender drinks. Kimber had been queen of the party girls in high school, and clearly she hadn't given up her title entirely.

"You have to understand," she said, her voice grave as we sat in a circle around Ruger's deck table. "I love being a mom. But I need to get *out* sometimes, you know? I had no idea their little bodies held so many fluids!"

Dancer started laughing so hard she almost fell out of her chair.

"Know the feeling," she gasped. "Sometimes it starts spraying out and out and out and you'd think they'd deflate or something!"

I gave Kimber a loud high five, happy she had a kid she loved and even happier mine was mostly past the spraying phase.

"That's why I'm not having babies anytime soon," Em declared. "Lose your freedom and your mind, apparently. You're pathetic, all of you."

"Gotta have sex first to have a kid," Marie said, waggling her eyebrows dramatically as she poked Em's shoulder. "I keep telling you, we need to just go out and get you laid. Get it over with, punch that V-card."

"If I get ten punches, do I get a free pizza?" Em asked her. "Seriously, I don't know why I'm waiting at this point."

"Well, don't bother waiting for Painter," Maggs said, rolling her eyes. "He's had his full patch for three months now. He hasn't manned up yet, it's not gonna happen."

Em frowned.

"It's not like that," she said, shaking her head. "I was into him, okay? Liked him a lot, actually. But he blew it. He cares more about not pissing off my dad than being with me."

"To be fair, your dad has a bit of a reputation," Dancer said, her voice dry. "He shot your last boyfriend. Thinking about that's gotta mess with a man's head."

I looked at Em with new interest, trying to remember who her dad was. Oh, yeah. Her dad was Picnic. *Picnic?* What kind of name was that? Almost as weird as Horse . . .

"What the hell is up with all these names?" I demanded abruptly, swaying in my seat. They all looked at me blankly. "Picnic? Bam Bam? Horse?!? Who names their baby Horse? And what the hell is Ruger all about? His name is Jesse, for God's sake. I met his mom and she *told me*."

They all burst out laughing.

"What's so funny?" I asked, feeling put out. It was a serious question.

"You thought they were real names!" Marie asked, losing it again. "It's funny because I know exactly how you feel. I asked the same question. Horse is a fucking ridiculous name, isn't it?"

I narrowed my eyes.

"Is that a trick question? I don't want to insult the guy you're marrying. Also, he's scary. He has a metal bat and likes to carry around duct tape. All he needs is black plastic garbage bags and he could be a serial killer."

I leaned forward and jabbed a finger to make my point.

"I know these things. I watch TV."

Marie snorted so hard margarita came out her nose.

"Horse's real name is Marcus," Dancer said, giggling and rolling her eyes. "He's my brother, by the way. Horse is just his road name—like a nickname, you know? Most of the guys have 'em. Girls, too. Dancer's my road name."

"What's your real name?"

"No comment," Dancer replied primly.

"Agrippina," Em declared proudly. "I shit you not."

Dancer blew a stream of frozen margarita at Em through her straw.

"Traitorous bitch."

"Are you fucking with us?" Kimber asked, looking between them. "Agrippina? After Agrippina the Younger or Agrippina the Elder?"

We all looked at her blankly.

"Mom had a thing for Roman history," Dancer said after a pause. I shook my head, trying to follow the conversation. The drinks weren't helping. Oh, yeah. Road names.

"So why is he called Horse?" I asked. Marie blushed bright red and looked away.

"Ha!" Dancer said, smacking the table for emphasis. "Horse says he's called that because he's hung like one. But I know the real reason. When he was a kid—like three, four years old maybe?—he used to carry around this little stuffed horsie all the time, slept with it and everything. One day he and I got in a fight and he started hitting me with it, over and over again. Mom took it away from him and gave it to me. He started following me around crying, 'Horsie, Horsie,' all the time, and it stuck."

Marie's eyes opened wide.

"Are you fucking serious?" she asked. Dancer nodded, her face full of the kind of evil glee only an older sister can express. "Holy shit, that's hysterical."

"His dad insisted it was because he had a big dick, right to the day he died," she continued. "But I swear to you—it's because of that stuffed animal of his. Don't let him fool you."

"Did you ever give it back to him?" Em asked breathlessly. Dancer shook her head.

"I still have it," she declared. "And I promise you this, Marie.

The day you marry his stupid ass, I'll give it to you. That'll keep him in his place."

We all lost it again. Kimber poured another round of margaritas from the king-sized pitcher she'd found in Ruger's kitchen. This party wasn't ending anytime soon.

"So are all the names like that?" I asked when I could speak. "I mean, shouldn't bikers have cool names, like Killer or Shark or Thor's Revenge?"

"*Thor's Revenge?*" Maggs asked, raising a brow. "Are you serious?"

"That's just silly," Em broke in. "Road names stick because something happens to make 'em stick. You know, a funny story or something stupid someone does. You earn them—just like any nickname."

"Emmy Lou Who, for example," Dancer said, blinking innocently. Em's eyes narrowed.

"Shut the fuck up, *Agrippina*."

"Seriously, they also serve a purpose," Maggs said. "If people don't know your real name, makes it harder for them to rat you out to the cops."

"So what's 'Ruger' all about?" I asked. "He's been called that forever."

"I have no idea," Dancer said, frowning. "You'll have to ask him—Ruger is a gun brand, that might be it. Picnic got his because he threw a guy through a picnic table."

"Speaking of . . ." Marie said. "We haven't finished talking about Em's situation. You need to get your dad to back off, babe. Nobody will date you so long as he keeps shooting your boyfriends."

"He didn't shoot him because he was dating me," Em snapped. "It was a hunting accident and he's fine. The fact that he was cheating on me is a total coincidence."

The women burst out laughing again, while Kimber and I stared.

"Go ahead and keep telling yourself that," Dancer murmured.

I made a mental note to learn this story as soon as possible.

"Let's talk about something else," Em declared. She looked around the table, searching for a new victim. Her eyes reached me, filling with sudden, unholy glee. "Like . . . hmmm . . . So tell us, Sophie. What's the scoop with you and Ruger? You guys fucking or what?"

Everyone—even Kimber—looked at me. Kimber stared, silently urging me to speak. I kept my mouth shut and shook my head.

"Shit, I have to do *everything*," she burst out. "Okay, here's the whole story."

Ten minutes later they knew far too much about me and Ruger, and I'd silently vowed never to tell Kimber anything again. Ever. Not even where I stored the toilet paper, because that's how untrustworthy she was.

"And he just tucked in his dick and walked away?" Em asked for the third time, clearly awed. "He didn't even start yelling or throwing shit?"

I shook my head. I should've been embarrassed, but I was a little too drunk to fully appreciate my humiliation. Stupid Kimber. Backstabbing bitch.

"He's a man-whore," Kimber declared, shrugging. "Who knows why guys like that do anything? Instead of wondering *why* he did it, we need to focus on the real problem. How do we get them into bed with each other?"

"No!" I said. *"I am not sleeping with him.* Didn't you get the whole point of the story? That would fuck things up for me and Noah living here."

"Don't be stupid, it's already fucked up," she told me. "I was all in favor of avoiding him, but then you crossed the Rubicon!"

"What the hell does that mean?" I asked.

"Means we need to adjust our plan of action. Avoidance is no longer an option."

"No, what the hell is a Rubicon?" I asked her. Kimber sighed heavily, clearly frustrated.

"It's the river that separates Cisalpine Gaul from Italy," she said. "It's where Roman generals used to leave their armies before returning home, as a sign they weren't a threat to the Roman Republic. Two thousand years ago, Julius Caesar had to make a decision whether to obey the Senate or bring his troops home with him, starting a civil war. His legions crossed the Rubicon, which led to the end of the Republic. Not officially, of course. Augustus was the first to acknowledge dicatorship openly. Fuckin' turning point in Western civilization, dumbass."

We all stared at her, eyes wide.

"Where the hell did you learn all that?" I asked her. Kimber rolled her eyes.

"College," she said. "I have a history minor. Christ, is there a law that strippers can't read or something? Now, please, focus. All of you."

"My mom would like you," Dancer said. "She would like you a *lot*."

Kimber shrugged.

"This whole situation is like a great big zit that needs popping," she continued. "The damage is already done—your face looks like shit and no concealer's gonna cover it. You might as well squeeze hard and get your money shot. You'll both feel better afterward."

"Ewwwww . . ."

"That is the least sexy thing I've ever heard anyone say about sex," Maggs announced. "For the first time in two years, I'm kind of glad Bolt's in jail, because there's no damned way I'd touch his cock tonight after that."

"I call it like I see it," Kimber declared. "Now, let's figure out the best way for Sophie to start screwing Ruger without letting him think he's won."

"Kimber," I growled, lunging toward her. I bumped the pitcher of huckleberry margaritas instead, which splashed across the table, dousing Maggs, Dancer, and Marie with sticky, sugary, boozey deliciousness.

Everyone burst out laughing again, and this time Dancer actually did fall off her chair, which made it even funnier.

"That's what you get for making fun of my historical analogies!" Kimber howled at us gleefully. "I am the QUEEN. You do what I tell you, bitches!"

"You're crazy," I announced, dipping a finger into the puddle on the table and tasting it. Sooo good. What a waste. "But you're right about one thing. I may be a petty, selfish person, but I don't want him to win. He *always* wins. I think you might be right about popping the zit, though."

"This is an important discussion," Maggs said solemnly, holding up a hand to halt us. "And as the senior old ladies present, Dancer and I will moderate it as soon as we get changed. Is it okay if we dig through your closet?"

"Sure," I said. "Here, let me come help you find something."

"No worries," Dancer said, giggling. "We'll find it. We know our way around the apartment already."

I smiled at her happily.

"Thanks again," I told them all. "I can't tell you how amazing it was to come here and find everything all fixed up. Noah loves his room, too."

"It's what we do," Maggs said. Marie grinned at me, then shivered, rubbing her arms up and down.

"This stuff is cold. Let's get changed," she said, and the three women took off down the outside stairs.

"I'm going to get some hot water to pour over this mess," I said, contemplating the Great Margarita Lake. "There's got to be something we can use in the kitchen."

We trooped into the house, and I rummaged through Ruger's kitchen cupboards until I found two big mixing bowls, which we used to pour hot water over the table. Then we flopped back in the chairs and Kimber made herself useful for once, asking the question that'd been eating at me all night.

"So, you really a virgin?"

"Mostly," Em said, rolling her eyes.

"Oooh, *mostly*," Kimber said, leaning forward, practically quivering with curiosity. "We'll get back to that in a minute. Now tell me what's up with the V-card. How old are you, anyway?"

"I'm twenty-two," Em said. She didn't seem to mind the questions at all. Kimber wasn't the only one with boundary issues. "And I'm a virgin because I haven't wanted to just do it with some random guy to get it over with. But every non-random guy I meet is scared of my dad. To be fair, he really *is* scary. My sister stands up to him, but it seems like I never can. Now I'm stuck at home, while she's loving life in Olympia. She's my *little* sister—still can't figure out how that happened."

"Have you always lived at home?" Kimber asked, her eyes wide with something like horror. "No wonder you're a virgin!"

"No, I lived in Seattle for my first semester of college," Em explained. "But I didn't really know what I wanted to be, and as soon as word about my dad got out, the guys stayed away from me. Didn't help that he showed up at my dorm one day and made a public announcement that any guy who tried to get me naked would lose his dick."

"Holy shit," I muttered, eyes wide. Kimber swallowed.

"That's hard-core," she admitted.

Em rolled her eyes and threw up her hands in disgust.

"That's my dad. Mom used to keep him under control, but she's been gone for a while now. He's the club president, so it's not like there's anyone to stand up to him."

"What about this Painter guy?" I asked. Em groaned and dropped her head to the table, banging it dramatically.

"Painter," she said. "Painter is a pain in my ass. He was a Reapers prospect until a few months ago. Got his patch now. He seems to like me, he's flirted with me, and he'll scare off other guys who come around me, yet when I tried to jump his bones in the dark he ran away like a fucking chicken. Every. Single. Time."

Kimber shook her head knowingly.

"Yup, scared of daddy," she said. "Lost cause, babe. You need to find someone else."

"Yeah, I know," Em said, her voice wistful. "I could kind of understand it back when he was a prospect, so I cut him some slack. Prospecting's hard work. But he's got his colors now. He needed to put up or shut up, so that's over."

"Damned straight," Kimber said, banging her fist down on the deck table. The whole thing rattled and we all jumped a little. "Let's go to Spokane next weekend, the three of us. The way I see it, Maggs, Marie, and Dancer have to rat you out, because they're part of the club. But me and Sophie? We're free agents. Let's get your card punched with someone disposable, and then work on finding you a man who's not a fucking pussy. This Painter guy is full of shit."

"Actually, I've been talking to someone online," Em admitted, flushing a little. "I really like him. A lot. We've been chatting for a couple months, but we just started calling each other sometimes. I'm pretty into him, but I kept hoping Painter—"

"Screw Painter," Kimber declared. "He's not a real man. Maybe your online guy isn't either, but we've got your back. See if he's available next week, let's get this thing done. We'll meet up in a public place. Get our own hotel rooms, so we can make sure you're safe."

Em's eyes grew bright. The whole idea seemed sort of half-cocked to me, and I frowned.

"Okay . . ." she said. "Wow, I can't believe we're going to do this. But what about Sophie? I don't think Ruger would want her going out like that."

Suddenly I didn't care how stupid it sounded. Ruger wasn't in charge. Fuck him. Nothing quite like flaming shots to give a girl courage.

"I'm in," I declared. "He doesn't tell me what to do."

"Seriously?" Em asked, peering at me in the darkness. "We'd really just go out and do this?"

"Why not? Ruger's not my boss. And Kimber needs to get out sometimes, too. We'll check this guy out and make a call for you about whether he's worthy. There's always more guys if he's not. Trust me, if Kimber can't find you a man, he doesn't exist. She's like a sexual bloodhound. Always has been."

"Damned straight," Kimber said without a trace of embarrassment. "I'll ask Ryan if he can watch Noah for you, Soph. He owes me. He gets to play poker every single week, and when I was pregnant I told him that if I was sober, he should be sober, too. He totally ignored me. Also, he bought me a minivan. A *fucking minivan.* What kind of man does that to a woman?"

I started giggling. Em joined me, and then all three of us were laughing, and I'm still not entirely sure why. We were still cackling like drunken hyenas when Marie, Dancer, and Maggs got back. They looked funny in my clothes, particularly Dancer, who was way too tall and more than a little too curvy. She'd found some yoga pants and an old T-shirt, both of which were extremely tight in critical areas.

"Bam is going to love this," she said, twirling for us and shaking her ass dramatically. "If he's home tonight. Anyone know the schedule?"

"Party tonight for the brothers coming in," Marie said. "Guess some kind of big club meeting is going down? Horse will be here in about an hour to give us rides home. Me and Maggs are throwing together breakfast tomorrow, if anyone wants to help. They've already lined up a pig to roast for the afternoon, so all we need to worry about is snacks and sides."

"I can do a Costco run in the morning," Dancer said. "Em, wanna come with?"

"Sure," she said. "Dad said they'll be done with church around four. You can come out anytime after that, Sophie."

"Church?" I asked, startled. Dancer snickered.

"That's what they call their meetings," she told me. "No idea why, just always been that way as long as anyone can remember. Nothing to do with us, though—club business. Don't worry about that. Your job is to have fun at the party."

"I'm not sure I'm going to the party," I said, losing some of my bravado. "After Ruger's little tantrum, I think it might better if I stayed home."

"Not happening," Dancer said firmly. "Whatever's between you two—and don't think we've forgotten, that conversation was interrupted *just* when it was getting interesting—needs to be resolved. Otherwise you'll kill each other at this rate. Going to the party is perfect."

"Why?"

"Because he'll either lose his shit or he won't," she replied. "I mean, some guy is going to talk to you at some point. Ruger loses it, we'll see some action and you'll get things figured out. He doesn't, you're off the hook and life can get back to normal. Either way, we'll be there to watch it all, and in the end, it's really all about us, right?"

"Um, this may shock you, but Ruger can be scary," I said. "I don't want him losing his shit. It's happened before and it wasn't nice."

"It'll be okay," Maggs assured me. "These things work out at the Armory, no worries there. Maybe a good fight will clear his head."

"I agree," Marie said. "Get it out in the open. If you're in front of the club, he'll have to claim you as his property or let you go. That's how it works."

"You don't find it even a little bit creepy to be called property?" I asked. They all burst out laughing again.

"It's a different world, Sophie," Marie said finally. "Trust me, I get how weird it sounds. When Horse first asked me to be his property, I dumped his ass. I didn't get it back then—it's like their own language. To bikers, being property means you're important, special. Being an old lady is an honor and they treat it with huge respect."

"Here's what I wonder," Kimber broke in. "I know a little about club life from working at The Line, but I've never figured this one out. If your whole identity depends on your relationship to a man, isn't that a little fucked up?"

Pretty good question.

"Maybe," Dancer admitted. "But I'm not too worried about it. My *identity* is all my own. Always has been, always will be. It's true that the club is for men and they usually call the shots when they're playing with their friends. At home, though? Not so much. Bam pisses me off, I'm not suffering from a shortage of ways to make him pay."

"Like what?"

Dancer smirked and raised a knowing brow.

"You really have to ask? Even the virgin girlie gets *that*."

"Shut up," Em groaned. "Don't you ever get tired of discussing my sex life?"

"No," the Reaper women chorused, and we all burst out laughing yet again.

"Here's the thing—it's up to you to decide what works and what's a deal breaker," Maggs said when the fit of giggles died down. "You lay it out for Ruger, Sophie. Either he's on board or not, but the most important part is that you stick to your guns. If it's a deal breaker, you're done with him. Do whatever it takes to draw the line. I'm serious. You may have to find somewhere else to live if that happens, but don't let him convince you there aren't options. There's always options."

"No, what she really needs to do is screw him and dump his ass," Em said, shivering with delicious glee. "He's hot, she should just nail him. Is he any good, Kimber?"

"Don't you dare," I warned my friend, holding up a hand to her face. "Mouth. Shut."

"Wait a minute! Party planning aside, we're forgetting an important part of why we're here," Marie said suddenly. She turned to me. "I can't believe we haven't talked about work, Sophie. Sex is just way more interesting. Has Ruger mentioned a job?"

"No," I said, more than ready for a change of subject. "I'm going to start looking on Monday. He said something about working for the club, but it seems a little weird to bring it up after this morning."

"I manage a coffee shop for a friend," Marie told me. Maggs, Em, and Dancer sobered, exchanging glances I couldn't quite read. "I could really use some help in the mornings, if you have a way to get Noah to school. You'd be done by the afternoon when he gets home."

"Um, I can look into it," I said, wondering if my neighbor would help get Noah on the bus for me. Or maybe they had one of those morning drop-off programs?

"I think she should be a stripper at The Line," Kimber piped up. Marie's eyes widened.

"No way," she said, her distaste visible. "That place is disgusting."

"It's a good way to earn money," Kimber insisted. "Perfect for a single mom. She could work two nights a week and be with Noah every day. How is that a bad thing?"

"Um, the part where she sucks some stranger's cock?" Marie asked. "I'll bet Ruger would just looove that."

"What?" I demanded. "I thought we were talking about dancing. No sucking cocks. Deal breaker!"

"We *are* talking about dancing," Kimber said, rolling her eyes. "Nobody makes you work the VIP rooms. Totally your choice. Or you could waitress. They don't make as much money, but they still do pretty well. Especially if you're nice to the dancers. They'll tip out if you treat them right."

"You do *not* want to work there," Marie insisted. "Seriously, most of those girls are whores. Not talking about you, Kimber, but the rest of them? You can't trust that place for shit."

"No, I was a whore," Kimber announced blithely. "If by 'whore' you mean I got guys off for money. Mostly hand jobs, but if he'd pay enough I'd go down on him. Now I own a gorgeous house, I have a degree, and I even started a college fund for my kid. I'd do it again in a heartbeat."

We all looked at her.

"Oh, seriously?" she asked, rolling her eyes. "You girls live in a *fucking motorcycle gang*. You really think you should judge me?"

"Club," Em said. "It's a motorcycle *club*. Being part of a club isn't a crime, you know."

"Whatever," Kimber replied, waving her hand. "I own my body. It's totally mine, and what I do with it is my business. I danced for guys, I touched them sometimes, and they gave me lots of money. How many women get groped every day by strangers? At least I got paid up front for it. I'd do it again, and I think Sophie should, too, if she really wants to provide for Noah."

"No way," I said, shaking my head.

"Working at The Line isn't a bad idea," Maggs said, surprising me. "I tended bar there and did pretty well. That's how I met Bolt."

"And did anyone bother you?" I asked. She shook her head.

"It's a controlled environment," she said. "Nobody gets in without security knowing. They keep an eye on everything. Even in the VIP rooms, security's always right outside the door. I was probably safer there than I am at home."

"Did you . . . I can't think of a better way to ask this, so I guess I'll just spit it out. Did you have to walk around naked?"

"No," she said, smirking. "Servers at The Line are like furniture from IKEA. Okay to look at, but not what you want to draw attention to. I wore a black bustier, a short black skirt, and dark tights. Blended right in."

"That doesn't sound too bad," I said. Marie scowled and shook her head, but Maggs grinned at me.

"I'll introduce you to the manager tomorrow," she said. "He'll be at the party. And you're coming—no negotiation. If you don't figure things out with Ruger, maybe you'll come home with a job."

CHAPTER EIGHT

RUGER

"Huge fuckin' mistake," Deke declared. He stood in the center of the Armory's second-story game room, surrounded by officers from almost every Reapers charter. Usually they had church downstairs, but there wasn't enough space for all the visiting brothers below. This group included both national and local chapter officers, and whatever decisions they made would be binding on the whole club.

"We can't trust them, we all know that," Deke continued. "What kind of dumbfuck sticks his head in a noose? We do this, we deserve everything we get."

Picnic sighed and shook his head. Ruger leaned against the wall behind him, wondering how much longer they'd be going over the same points. He wanted this over with, because he'd been wound up tighter than hell since yesterday morning.

Sophie tied him in fuckin' knots.

Not even a blow job from one of the club whores had helped. She'd barely gotten his pants open when he'd started thinking about

Sophie and Noah, and it was all over. Last night he'd been surrounded by thirty of his best friends and brothers, more booze than he could drink, and free pussy on tap, and he was still fuckin' bored. All he really wanted was to go home, read Noah a bedtime story, and then fuck Sophie's brains out.

Picnic shifted, the sound of his chair scraping pulling Ruger out of his thoughts.

They'd been at it for nearly two hours, and so far nobody had changed their positions on the truce. Most of the men wanted to give it a shot. Ruger agreed. He thought the Jacks were walking, talking bags of shit, but at least they were a known quantity. They understood the lifestyle, and all other issues aside, they were still bikers. He wasn't ready to throw down for a Devil's Jack, but backing off for the duration? That made sense.

Deke disagreed.

Strongly.

"Anyone else want to talk?" asked Shade. The big man with spiky blond hair and a nasty scar across his face was the national president, a position he'd held for less than a year. Ruger didn't know him well, but what he'd heard was good. Shade lived in Boise, although he'd made noises about moving farther north.

"I got somethin' to say," Duck announced, boosting his big body up off the couch. In his late sixties, Duck was the oldest member in Coeur d'Alene. One of the oldest members in the entire club, actually. He wasn't an officer, but nobody was stupid enough to tell him he couldn't talk. Ruger knew whatever he said could be the tipping point.

"I hate the Jacks. They're cocksuckers and assholes, we all know it. That's why it hurts me so much to admit this, but I think we should give the truce a shot."

Ruger cocked his head—hadn't seen that coming. A Vietnam vet and fighter from day one, Duck had never been the voice of peace.

"Here's the thing," Duck continued. "That little prick Hunter is onto something. We're the same kind of men where it counts. We know what life is really about, and that's the freedom to ride and live on our own terms. We joined this club because we don't give a shit about citizens and their rules. I've always taken what I wanted when I wanted it, no apologies. I live free. Any laws broken along the way are just collateral."

Brothers around the room murmured in agreement—even Deke.

"These kids moving in, though, they're not like us," Duck said, looking around, pinning each man with his eyes in turn. "*They're. Not. Like. Us.* They got no freedom and no reason to live, aside from making money. They wake up every morning plannin' to break the law, which means *the law rules their lives.* I'm not scared to fight, you all know that, but why fight when we can let the Jacks do it for us? Live to ride, ride to live. Not just words, brothers. Anything gets in the way of living and riding is a waste of my time, and that includes fighting the cartel."

Men all over the room voiced their approval. Deke shook his head, and Ruger knew him well enough to realize he was pissed. He'd been beat, and Deke wasn't used to losing. And Toke? He was practically vibrating, he was so pissed off. At least he kept his mouth shut—kid like that had no business speaking here.

"We're all gonna pay for this," the Portland president said. "But we've hashed it out. No reason to keep talking at this point. Let's vote and get it over with."

"Anyone got a problem with that?" Shade asked. Ruger shot a look at Toke, concerned. Nobody spoke up. "Okay, then. All in favor?"

A chorus of "ayes" echoed around the room, which held close to forty men.

"Opposed?"

Only six guys disagreed, four from Portland and two from Idaho Falls. No surprise, Toke was one of them. That was unfortunate, Ruger thought, given Hunter's location. Not that he gave two fucks about the man, but he liked him better than any other Jack he'd met. What he'd told them about the cartel added up—it was a big problem, one they'd have to deal with sooner or later. Ruger didn't want their shit in his territory, and neither did his brothers. Might as well let the Jacks be their cannon fodder.

"We gonna have a problem here?" Shade asked Deke bluntly.

"They keep out of our way, we won't have a problem," Deke said after a pause. "Right or wrong, we're Reapers. We stand together."

"Gonna hold you to that, brother," Shade replied.

"The girls have been workin' hard, putting together food for us," Picnic said, rising to address the room. "Pig won't be ready for another hour, but the kegs are tapped. Thanks to everyone for comin' up here. We always appreciate the company. Reapers forever, forever Reapers!"

"Reapers forever, forever Reapers!" echoed through the room, rattling the windows. Toke didn't look happy, but Ruger knew he'd do his part. Men stood to talk, some heading downstairs to the party, others standing in clumps.

"A word?" Picnic asked Ruger before he could escape. He stopped, turning to his president.

"What's up?" he asked.

"Em's pretty hungover this morning," Pic said, eyes speculative. "How about your girl?"

"Not my girl," Ruger grunted. "And no idea—didn't go home last night."

"Really?" Pic asked, raising a brow. "That 'cause you had business here or 'cause things are fucked up at the house? Em seems to think they're fucked up. That gonna be a problem for the club?"

"Em sure talks a lot," Ruger said, narrowing his eyes.

"Em still hasn't figured out she can't fool her daddy when she's drunk," Picnic said. "It's useful to me. She seems to think you're claiming this girl for your property. Says you told her she can't talk to any other guys. What's the story?"

"Not sure that's any of your business," Ruger replied, his tension growing. "Sophie knows the situation and so do I. That's enough."

"That's great, so long as we don't have any misunderstandings," Picnic said. "If she's yours, fine. She's not? Lot of guys here today, guys who aren't usually around. You can't explain the situation to me, how do you plan on explainin' it to them?"

"Won't be a problem," Ruger replied, his voice firm. "Made things clear to her and she knows what she needs to do."

Picnic eyed him thoughtfully.

"Send her home," he said. "Bring her around for a family party, start small. See how it goes. This is throwing her into the deep end and that's gonna backfire on you."

"Scare her off, you mean?" Ruger asked. "That might be best. I don't know what the hell I want with her—"

"You want to fuck her," Picnic said bluntly. "You can tell when your dick gets hard, did you know that? Probably tough for you to understand, seeing as most of the time you're just jacking off, but most men like to stick their cocks—"

"Shut the fuck up," Ruger said, wondering whether it'd be a bad move to punch out his president in front of so many witnesses. Probably. Might be worth it.

Picnic laughed.

"So you gonna send her home?" he asked. Ruger shook his head.

"I send her home, she wins," he said. Picnic raised a brow.

"What is this, junior high? You're the man, lay it out for her."

Ruger took a deep breath, forcing himself to think instead of just lashing out. He needed a good fight or something, some way to blow off the tension. There'd be boxing later. That would do it . . . hopefully.

"I lay it out, she wins," he admitted finally, scowling and running a hand through his hair. "That's the problem. She called me on my bullshit and I can't talk my way out of it. I make her leave, it's like I'm saying she was right about the club being dangerous and a bad influence for Noah. Not to mention making me look like a fuckin' pussy in the process, because I can't handle having her around."

"One, you're a dumbass," Picnic said. "Two, she's right. Club is dangerous for an unclaimed woman, particularly tonight."

"I get that," Ruger said. "That's why I'm gonna protect her. You got a cure for the dumbass thing? That part's kickin' my butt, gotta admit."

"Nope," Pic said, clapping a hand to Ruger's shoulder. "But I know something that'll make you feel better about the situation."

"What's that?"

"Pulled pork sandwich," Pic replied. "Beer. Then—if you're smart, which I'll admit is a stretch—you'll take your girl somewhere and fuck her 'til she can't walk straight. She may win, but who gives a damn, 'cause she'll be suckin' your cock for the foreseeable future. I find that works wonders."

"You're a fuckin' asshole."

"I get that a lot."

SOPHIE

I wasn't horribly hungover the next day, but I wasn't eager to start drinking again, either. This was probably just as well. Despite my alcohol-fueled tough talk, I really didn't want to make trouble at the party. I Googled the address, then drove out to the Armory early that evening, after I dropped off Noah with Kimber. She'd ended up spending the night on my couch, waking up more than a little worse for the wear.

I suspected she'd be in bed about five minutes after she got the kids down.

I was nervous driving out to the party. The Reapers' clubhouse was a couple miles off the highway, toward the end of an old state road. I passed a group of four motorcycles headed for the highway, ridden by men dressed a lot like Ruger. Tattoos, jeans, boots, and black leather jackets. Loaded saddlebags.

They didn't appear to be happy campers.

The building itself surprised me. I guess I hadn't expected the Armory description to be so literal, because this was an honest-to-God converted National Guard building. Three stories tall, walls built to withstand tanks, and an enclosed courtyard with a gate big enough to drive a large truck through.

There were quite a few people there already. Lots of guys, all of them wearing their distinctive colors. They had different states or towns on their lower patches, but the Reapers' symbol and name were the same.

Unsurprisingly, there were lots of motorcycles, but also quite a few cars, most of which had been parked in a gravel lot off to the side. A younger guy wearing a cut without very many patches waved me over in that direction, so I pulled in next to a little red Honda. Four girls who'd clearly been drinking for a while poured out. They were young, slutted up, and ready to party. Last night I'd noticed that the club women weren't afraid to show off their bodies—Dancer rocked a pair of jeans and backless top in a big way—but the Reapers' old ladies looked somehow more classy and confident than this bunch.

Maybe it was about the attitude? I got the impression these girls were on the prowl, and that they weren't necessarily planning to be too picky.

They ignored me entirely, giggling and taking shots of each other with their phones. I guess I didn't rate their attention, which was both depressing and a bit of a relief. Not that I cared how I looked—I'd gone with a basic T-shirt, my standard cutoffs and a pair of flip-flops. Despite my fight with Ruger yesterday morning (not to mention my margarita-fueled belligerence last night), I really did want to keep things low-key.

I wasn't sure what to expect at a Reapers party but I figured I'd be fine if I stuck with my girls.

I'd sent a text to Ruger letting him know I was coming. He'd replied with a reminder about our conversation, which almost convinced me to change into something sluttier just to spite him. Then I pulled my head out of my ass. Ruger losing his shit was not something I wanted see, no matter how satisfying it would be to defy him.

Defy him? Christ, how old was I?

I also texted Maggs, Em, Dancer, and Marie. They said to come straight through to the back, where they were setting up the food outside. They'd asked me to stop off and buy a bunch of extra chips, so I'd hit Walmart on the way.

Now I trailed behind the slut brigade, their big hair, loud makeup, and microscopic clothing providing plenty of cover as we walked toward the big gate in the courtyard. A couple of guys stood outside, obviously monitoring the entrance. The gaggle flirted with them and then passed on through. They probably thought I was a total hag in comparison, I realized glumly. A little lip gloss wouldn't have killed me. Apparently giant shopping bags full of chips counted for something, though, because the men welcomed me enthusiastically enough.

Sex appeal is great, but there's nothing quite like food to win a man's heart.

"I'm Ruger's almost-sister-in-law," I told one of the guys, who nodded me on through. I followed the narrow driveway that ran along the side of the building until I reached the main courtyard out back—a broad, open space that was a mixture of parking lot and grass. Loud music blasted through giant box speakers, and evergreen-covered mountains surrounded us on all sides. It really was a gorgeous place—much nicer than I'd expected.

A good-sized group of children darted through clumps of adults and took turns playing on a giant, clearly homemade swing set, complete with a fort at the top. There were men everywhere, far more men than women, although another group of girls followed me. I guessed the men had been there earlier and now the rest of the guests were arriving?

Ruger was nowhere to be seen. I spotted a row of long folding tables near the back wall of the building covered with a mismatched series of tablecloths. Off to one side stood a black-barreled BBQ smoker almost as big as my car, mounted on a trailer. Smoke drifted out and the scent of roasting pig filled the air.

"Sophie!" Marie called, waving me over toward one of the tables. I moved quickly toward her, trying not to stare at anyone, but it was hard. The guys were almost all at least a little scary-looking. I mean, some of them were regular enough, I guess, but somehow rougher. They had tanned skin and a disproportionate number of beards. Others were less normal-looking. I saw a lot of tattoos and piercings, and very few shirts, although they all seemed to be wearing their leather vests. All of them were Reapers and most seemed to be in a pretty good mood.

I also noticed a few of the little boys wearing their own tiny vests. Not real ones, but play ones clearly meant to copy their daddies'. Shit. Knowing my luck, Noah would be begging for one of those if he saw them. Good thing I hadn't brought him along.

"Want some help with the bags?" a man asked. I opened my mouth to refuse, then looked up and realized it was Horse. I smiled, relieved to recognize someone besides just the girls I'd met last night.

"Yeah, thanks," I said. "I met Marie. She's great."

"No shit," he replied, offering me a movie-star grin. Damn, but he was beautiful. "Worth every penny I paid for her."

That caught me short. I stopped, wondering if he could possibly be serious. He didn't look like he was joking.

"You coming?" he asked, glancing back at me. I pulled myself together and started walking again. What the hell had he meant by that?

"Sophie!" Em called, spotting me from behind one of the tables. She darted forward and gave me a big hug.

"I'm so glad we're going out next weekend," she whispered in my ear. "I talked to Liam this morning about meeting in real life, and he's all over it. Thank you so much!"

"That's fantastic!" I replied, pulling back to look at her. She was so pretty this afternoon, the excitement in her eyes bright and shining. "Just remember, we're going to stay safe. Don't tell him where you live or anything. We'll check him out, and if he's a creeper, we'll ditch his ass."

Em laughed.

"Actually, telling him my address would be perfectly safe," she answered. "Remember who I live with? Our house is a fortress. Which reminds me, I want to introduce you to my dad."

She took my hand and pulled me across the courtyard to the giant black BBQ. Several men stood around it drinking from red plastic cups. They turned as we walked up, openly checking me out. Clearly, subtlety wasn't a highly valued trait here at the Armory.

"This is my dad, Picnic," Em said, stepping forward to wrap her arm around the one standing closest to us. He pulled her close, offering her an indulgent smile. He was tall and fairly well-built. He shared her piercing light blue eyes and his hair was a couple months overdue for a trim. I could tell he was older by the faint lines around his eyes, but his hair held only a hint of gray at the temples. And his body? Nice. Em's dad was hot for an old guy.

Not that I'd tell her that—who wants to hear that their dad's hot?

The most compelling thing about Picnic, though, was his air of command, mixed with just a hint of menace. I would've known he was club president even without the patch on his cut to tell me.

No wonder guys were scared to ask her out.

"Dad, this is Sophie," Em continued. "She's Ruger's . . . Um, what are you, anyway?"

"I'm sort of his stepsister-in-law," I said, smiling awkwardly. "His stepbrother, Zach, is my son's father."

"He mentioned you were back in town," Picnic said. His face gave away nothing, and I couldn't tell if he was happy to meet me or annoyed I'd crashed their party.

"This is Slide and Gage," Em continued, nodding toward the other men.

"Nice to meet you," I said. Slide was a short, middle-aged guy with a bit of a gut and a beard that wasn't totally white, but close. He didn't actually look old enough for such white hair, so maybe he was just one of those guys whose hair changes early? He had a real Santa vibe going for him. Well, if Santa wore ripped jeans and carried a giant knife on his belt.

Gage was another hottie. He had dark hair, so dark it was almost black, and his skin held just enough color to make me think his ancestors hadn't all been of the milky-white variety. Latino or Indian, most likely. Because sometimes God is generous and kind, Gage wasn't wearing a shirt, offering me glimpses of his bare chest, which was every bit as ripped as Ruger's. He had fewer tattoos, though. His cut had a little patch under his name that said "Sgt. at Arms," which surprised me. I guess I hadn't expected bikers to have so many officers and such. It just seemed so . . . organized?

Not only that, they obviously had to pass some sort of minimum hotness test to join up.

"You Ruger's woman?" he asked, breaking the spell I'd fallen into. I blushed, hoping my pervy thoughts weren't totally written all over my face. The smirk on his face wasn't comforting.

"Um, no," I said, glancing over at Em. She grinned. "But he's letting us stay in his basement. I have a seven-year-old. Our old place in Seattle wasn't working out."

That was the understatement of the year, for sure.

"Where's the kid?" he asked, glancing around.

"He's with a sitter," I said. "This is my first club event, and I sort of wanted to check things out for myself before dragging him along."

Picnic raised a brow, and I realized I'd probably just insulted them. Great.

"Also, I hear the parties go pretty late," I added quickly. "I didn't want to have to leave just when things were getting fun. A friend offered to watch him, so here I am."

Em grinned at me and I gave a sigh of relief. Okay, apparently my quick save had actually worked.

"Well, you get bored, come and see me," Gage said, offering a slow smile. "I'd be happy to show you around, maybe even take you for a ride later."

"Um, thanks," I replied, Ruger's warning ringing through my head. Gage was cute, but despite the fact that I didn't acknowledge Ruger's right to give orders, I also didn't want to get into a huge fight with him. "Nice to meet you all. I'm gonna go find Marie and Dancer now. I want to make sure they don't need any help setting things up or something."

"I'll come with," Em said, popping up on her toes to give Picnic a quick kiss on the cheek. For all her whining about him, she obviously adored the man. I felt a twinge of jealousy. Even before they'd kicked me out, my parents were never the kind of people you'd just casually walk up to and kiss.

Nope, not in the Williams household. I'd been devastated when they said they'd have nothing to do with a daughter who was a whore, let alone her bastard. Now I realized I was way better off without them. Noah's circle might be small, but everyone in it loved him unconditionally, and they weren't afraid to show it.

My parents didn't deserve to meet their grandson.

We found Dancer, Marie, and Maggs arranging a mountain of food on the tables, laughing and smacking hands playfully as guys tried to steal bites before it was ready.

"Thanks for picking up the chips," Maggs said. I noticed all three women wore black leather vests.

"I thought you said only guys could be club members?" I asked, nodding toward them.

"Oh, these aren't club cuts," Dancer said. "Check it out."

She turned around and I saw a patch on the back that said "Property of Bam Bam," along with a Reapers symbol. My eyes widened.

"I didn't realize the property thing was so . . . literal . . ."

"The guys have their colors and we have ours," Maggs said. "Civilians don't get it, but all the patches mean something. The guys fly their colors because they're proud of the club, but their cuts tell stories, too. You can learn a lot about the guy by the patches he wears. It's like a language or something. Everyone knows where everyone else stands."

"The great thing about a property patch is that you're totally covered," Dancer added. "There's not a man here who's gonna touch me, no matter how drunk or stupid he gets by the end of the night. Not that I'm too worried here at our own clubhouse, but we go on runs where there are hundreds of riders, even thousands. Everyone who knows a damned thing about the MC world takes one look at this and they know not to fuck with me."

"Yeah," Em said. "You fuck with one Reaper's property, you better be ready to take down every guy in the club."

"Huh," I said, trying to sound noncommittal. I liked the idea of protection as much as anyone, but there was something very uncomfortable to me about a woman choosing to call herself property. Shades of Zach and how possessive he was, maybe. But Maggs and the others didn't seem too terribly oppressed, either.

I glanced around, taking in how many women were starting to fill the courtyard. Only a handful wore property patches.

"What about the rest of them?" I asked. Em shrugged.

"They're not important," she said bluntly. "Some of them are sweetbutts and club whores, which means they're around a lot—the guys share them. Some are just random girls looking for a walk on the wild side. But none of them really count, not compared to us. They're all fair game."

"Fair game?"

"Free pussy," Maggs said, her voice matter-of-fact. "They're just here to party, and if we're lucky, they'll help clean up. They give anyone shit, their asses are out the door. Good news is, they know their place. Half these girls work at The Line anyway."

"What about me?" I asked, unnerved. "I don't have a patch."

"That's why you'll stick with us," Dancer said, her voice serious. "Despite his general dickitude, Ruger's right about one thing. You really don't want to fuck around with the brothers. Don't flirt if you aren't interested in following through. And for fuck's sake, don't go off alone or into the Armory with anyone, particularly upstairs. There's some wild shit that happens up there. You don't want to be part of it, trust me."

"Jesus, you're gonna scare her," Em said, frowning. "Look at it this way—would you go to any party or bar without taking some basic safety precautions? Only take drinks you've poured yourself, or ones that we've given you. You ever been to a frat party? Think of it that way. Dad, Horse, Ruger, and Bam Bam are safe. Don't go off with someone you don't know, though. Stay in public areas. Use common sense and you'll be fine."

Oookay.

"Hey, the good news is I saw Buck earlier," Em added. "He

manages The Line. I'll introduce you at some point, you can ask him about waitressing. I'm definitely not on board with you stripping, but waitressing could be a pretty good gig."

"Would you work there?" I asked her. Em burst out laughing, joined by Maggs and Dancer.

"My dad would kill me before he let me work at The Line," she said when she finally caught her breath again. "Or maybe his head would just explode? He's still trying to convince me I shouldn't work at all. He'd love it if I just stayed home and kept house for him, maybe did some charity work on the side. He hasn't decided to join us in this century quite yet."

I thought about the tall, stern man I'd just met and had to smile. I could totally see him being overprotective like that.

"Doesn't he want grandkids some day?" I asked. "There's a middle step, you know."

"I don't think he's thought that far ahead," Em replied with a giggle.

The whistle of a firework shooting off cut through everything, and we all looked up to watch an explosion of red, white, and blue above the courtyard.

"Isn't that illegal?" I asked, eyes wide.

"Don't worry about it," Dancer told me. "We're so far out nobody gives a shit. And if they did, they'd just call the sheriff's department, and we've got a good relationship with him."

"The Reapers get along with the cops?" I asked, stunned.

"Not all of them," Dancer said. "But the sheriff is a pretty good guy. What a lot of people don't realize is that there's always gangs trying to move into the area. The sheriff can't begin to keep up with them. Even if he knows about them, he can't do shit without evidence. The Reapers help keep some of those problems under control, in our own special way. It's a mutually beneficial arrangement, no question. City cops are a different story, though. They hate us."

Another rocket shot up, this one exploding with a mighty flash and a bang. It wasn't dark yet, but the light was fading enough for it to mess with my vision. When I stopped blinking from the bright light, I saw Ruger watching me from across the courtyard.

"There he is," I muttered to Maggs. "I haven't seen him since we had our little blowup. You think I should go over?"

"Yeah," she said. "Gotta face him sooner or later. Remember what we talked about—you lay it out, and if he won't play, leave. You've got choices. Always."

CHAPTER NINE

Ruger's face was completely unreadable as I approached, and for one horrible moment I thought he might not talk to me.

"Hey," I said, feeling nervous. Seeing him should've pissed me off or maybe even scared me. My body didn't get the memo, though, because standing close to him mostly turned me on. I think his scent was a big part of it—nothing got to me like that hint of sweat and gun oil. He'd taken off his shirt, leaving only jeans, boots, and his cut. His tan told me he'd spent a lot of the summer that way.

Then I caught a glimpse of that panther tat disappearing down into his pants and I shit you not, it made me feel a little light-headed. All that blood rushing downward, you know?

"Hey," he said. I tilted my head up to look at his face, reminded once again just how much physically larger he was than me. "So, we gonna fuck around here or just get to the point?"

"Um . . . Not quite sure I follow," I admitted, still off balance.

What woman would seriously be able to pay attention, confronted with a body like that? Ruger grunted, exasperated.

"You gonna follow my rules tonight?" he asked. "If not, you need to get your ass in your car and leave."

"I'll follow the rules," I said slowly, eyes catching on his chin. He hadn't shaved that morning, leaving just enough stubble to make a light burn on a girl's skin. "On one condition."

He raised a brow, clearly skeptical.

"And what would that be?"

"You tell me why you're being so controlling," I said, laying it out. The girls had been right. Either he was with me or he wasn't, but one way or another I'd be taking charge of the situation. "Is it because you're jealous and you want me to yourself, or because the Reapers are too dangerous?"

He studied me for a moment, his face thoughtful. Then he seemed to come to some sort of decision.

"C'mon," he told me, and it wasn't an invitation. He grabbed my hand and dragged me almost roughly across the courtyard, toward the large shop built against the back wall. Enclosed on three sides, the front was open to the elements, almost like a supersized carport.

Inside the air was much cooler, and it gave a sense of privacy. One half of the building held bikes in varying states of repair, including several that seemed to be little more than frames. Counters lined the back, and every tool imaginable hung from the walls. There were also some larger pieces of power equipment, including a huge drill press, a grinding wheel, and others I couldn't begin to identify. A track had been mounted on the ceiling, with a rolling hoist hanging from it.

Filling the other side of the building were a panel truck and an old cargo van. The counters extended into that area, along with hooks for more tools. Ruger tugged me over between the van and the far wall. Despite the fact that the party continued a couple hundred feet away, we felt totally isolated. I thought about the warning I'd been given not to go off anywhere.

Did that apply to Ruger, too?

My gut instinct said I wasn't safe with him right now . . . Not physically unsafe, of course. He'd never hit me. But I was pretty damned sure I'd be sorry I'd come in here with him.

Not that he'd given me much of a choice.

Ruger raised his hands, framing my face and studying me closely. He licked his lips, drawing my eyes to that ring of his once more as he stepped forward into my space, pushing me toward the van. It threw me off balance, and I stumbled. Ruger reached down and grabbed my ass, boosting me up and bracing me against the vehicle, my sex pressed to his, my breasts flat against his chest. I reached around his neck and my legs gripped his waist for balance.

"You really want me to answer your question?" Ruger asked, his voice low and matter-of-fact. "Or you want to leave the party while you still can?"

I should leave.

I knew that. But his cock was already hard against me and every bit of blood in my body raced downward, away from my brain. Self-preservation gave way to raw lust.

"I want the answer," I whispered. Ruger smiled, and it wasn't a nice smile. It was hungry as hell and utterly merciless, just like him.

"I'm jealous as fuck," he said, his voice rough. "That's not really my thing, but it's the truth. I don't much like the idea of some other man touchin' your sweet ass, and if one of them tries to stick his cock into that pretty little cunt of yours, I'm gonna cut it off. And, Soph?"

I caught my breath.

"Yes?" I answered, a thousand thoughts running through my brain. How did I feel about this? What should I say? The girls told me to lay down the law and stick to my guns. The look in Ruger's eyes, though . . . That wasn't the face of a man who was interested in respecting my limits.

Who was I kidding? I couldn't even remember what those limits were supposed to be right now.

"I'm dead serious," he continued, leaning his head down, scenting me. I felt it like a bolt of electricity, all the way through my body, right down to my toes. "Another man touches you, I'll cut off his cock and feed it to him. That's not a threat, that's a promise. And you fuck someone? He's dead, Soph. Four years ago I made two serious mistakes. I didn't protect you from Zach—I'll regret that every day for the rest of my life. And then, because I felt guilty as fuck, I did the *right thing* and let you go."

I closed my eyes.

"I don't want to talk about it."

"News flash, Soph," he whispered. "It's about fuckin' time we talked about it, because it's hanging between us and I'm tired of pretending it didn't happen."

I started squirming, trying to twist free. Everything in me screamed to run, because he was about to take us to the bad place.

"Stop," Ruger ordered, his voice harsh. I kept squirming, so he pushed into me harder, forcing me to still. "We're gonna deal with it, Soph. Deal and move on, because things are gonna change for you now. My mistake wasn't touching you that night, and it sure as shit wasn't making you come. The mistake was doing it without taking out Zach first. If I'd known . . . why didn't you tell me?"

"I really, really don't want to talk about this," I hissed, trying to ignore his soft breath in my ear, the hard length of his cock pushing against me. My nipples were tight and my entire body screamed for me to open to him, but deep inside my brain lurked a cloud of darkness and fear that threatened to tear free with every word.

"I should've killed him for what he did to you," Ruger said, eyes full of frustrated regret. "But then he was in jail and I didn't want to do that to Mom, so I let him live. You left and I've hated myself ever since. I can't go back in time, but I sure as fuck won't make the same mistake twice. This time you're not gettin' away, Soph."

I took a deep breath, trying to calm my hormones enough to *think*. Then it hit me. I should tell him the truth. If that wasn't enough to convince him this was a lost cause, nothing would.

"It's my fault," I said, the familiar wave of self-disgust washing over me.

"Honey, Zach beatin' the shit out of you was *not* your fault," Ruger said, his voice like ice.

"No," I said, looking him right in the eye. "It was my fault, Ruger. I planned it. When you starting kissing me—touching me—I knew Zach was coming over. He'd texted me, wanted to make sure I had food ready when he got there. I *knew* he'd catch us. He was so jealous of you, Ruger. Drove him crazy. I knew if he caught us together, he'd lose it. I wanted him to hit me hard, because then I could make it end."

Ruger inhaled sharply.

"What the fuck are you talking about?"

"Zach had to leave bruises," I whispered. "I was so scared all the time, Ruger. I never knew what he'd do. Some days he was great and things were fine, like they were before Noah. Then I'd drop my guard and he'd turn on me. I tried calling the cops, but he never left marks, so they wouldn't do anything. He told me he'd kill me if I left him."

Ruger took a deep, ragged breath and his eyes went dark.

"When you came over that day, I saw my chance," I admitted, disgusted with myself. "This tension—lust, whatever the hell you want to call it—it was between us by then. I felt it every time I saw you. And you were so good with Noah, always coming around, fixing my car or mowing the yard for us. I'd bring you a drink and you'd look at me like you wanted to throw me down on the ground and fuck me until I screamed. You know what? I wanted you to do it. So I let it happen."

Ruger gave a dark, harsh laugh that had nothing to do with humor.

"Yeah, babe, I remember that part," he said. "Although we never did get to my happy ending, what with Zach comin' home. You seriously telling me that was planned?"

"I'm so sorry," I whispered, my eyes filling with tears. "I knew seeing us together would drive him crazy. I *knew* he'd lose it. Noah was safe at your mom's house. So I let him catch us and have his little pissing match with you. He took off, you took off, and I waited for him to come back and punish me, like always. But this time he was finally worked up enough to leave evidence—I made damned sure of it. I told him how much better you were than him. I told him I'd been fucking you all along. For a while I thought he might kill me, and you know what? It would've been worth it, just to make it end. You know the rest. He got arrested, I got my restraining order, and me and Noah were finally free."

Rugers eyes narrowed as emotion rippled across his face. Anger. Outrage. Disgust? For a second I thought he might actually hurt me, he seemed so angry.

No, I realized. That was the difference between Ruger and Zach. Both men had tempers, but Ruger? Ruger would never hurt me.

Never. No matter what.

"He beat the shit out of you," he whispered. "You almost *died*, Soph. Why didn't you tell me? I would've *fucking killed him* for you. You didn't have to let it get that bad. You should've told me the first time he hurt you. I can't believe this was happening and I was too fuckin' stupid to see it."

"Because he's your brother!" I said to him, tears running down my face. "Your mother *loved* him, Ruger. What he did to me almost destroyed her. If you'd lost it, if you'd gone after him, you'd be in jail right now and your mom would've died alone and miserable. What kind of hateful bitch would I be if I let that happen?"

"You could've gone to one of those places for women," he said, shaking his head. "I don't get it, Sophie."

I gave a harsh laugh.

"Damned straight you don't get it—it was his word against mine," I said, willing him to understand. "I had no evidence, nothing. Sure, I could go to a shelter, but he'd still have a right to visit with Noah, maybe fight me for custody. You think I'd risk my baby alone with Zach? Nobody could help me until he took it up a notch, so I made it happen. I'm not an idiot. A woman who's being controlled by a man can't get shit for help unless she's got *evidence*."

"Those weren't just bruises," Ruger said. "Three broken ribs and a punctured lung are *not* bruises. And why the fuck do you think I would've gone to jail, hmm? Look at me, Soph. Do you think I'm the kind of man to do time when I don't have to? He would've just disappeared. *Poof.* Problem solved. I dare you to look me in the eye and tell me there's one fuckin' reason that a man like Zachary Barrett should still be breathing, because I'm comin' up blank. I nearly had him taken out while he was locked up, but I figured a dead guy couldn't pay child support."

I gasped, eyes wide.

"You're serious?" I whispered.

"Yeah, Sophie," he said, sounding almost tired. "I'm fuckin' serious. Christ, I'm the first thing Noah saw in this world. I caught him with my own hands on the side of the road, babe, and then he opened those eyes and looked right at me. From day one, I can say with a clear conscious that there is nothin'—not a *fucking thing*—on this earth I wouldn't do to protect him or you. How long?"

"What?"

"How long was Zach hurtin' you before it all went down?"

I shook my head, looking away, trying to think.

"It wasn't big stuff," I said finally. "Not at first. He'd yell at me, make me feel like shit. Then he started doing it in front of Noah."

His entire body stiffened, his jaw clenching spasmodically. I stared at his chin and forged ahead.

"I had to do something, Ruger. I couldn't let my son grow up that way. And then you came over to help out with the water heater. I kept watching you and I died just a little bit inside, because I knew I was stuck with the wrong brother. Then you looked back at me and it all came together in my head."

"Fuck me," Ruger muttered, leaning his forehead down against mine. I was still wrapped around him, back against the van, enclosed in his arms and his scent. "You're just full of surprises, now aren't you?"

"Do you want me to move out of your basement?"

Ruger pulled back, frowning.

"I just told you I'll kill any man who touches you and you think I want you to leave?"

"That was before I told you what I did. I used you."

"Answer one question for me—total truth," he said slowly. I nodded. "Was it real? Yesterday, when I kissed you, when I sucked on your tits and fucked you with my hand? How about when I went down on you four years ago and you screamed my name? Before Zach found us and it all fell to shit. Was that fake?"

"No," I whispered. "Aside from Noah, that's the only part of those years I want to remember, because it was beautiful, Ruger. Whatever else happened, you gave me beautiful."

"Well, fuck me," he muttered. I felt his hands tightening on my butt, his hips tilting more firmly into mine, sending twinges of desire washing through me. I'd felt safe in his arms back then and I felt safe in them now.

That's when it hit me. I didn't just lust after Ruger.

I loved him. I had for years.

I tightened my arms around his neck, raising myself up to brush my lips across his. He didn't respond, so I brushed his lips again, sucking the lower one into my mouth and nibbling on it.

That set him off.

One of his hands came up, fingers twisting in my hair as he took my mouth in a long, hard kiss, tongue punishing me in a mixture of anger and desire. I couldn't blame him for whatever he might be thinking, because I'd used him and it was wrong. My arms tightened around his neck and I tried wiggling my hips, desperate for the friction of his cock against my clit. He stilled suddenly, pulling back and looking down at me, eyes burning intensely.

"Serious mistake, babe."

My eyes widened. My body ached for him, the rough leather of his cut torturing my nipples. Every part of me yearned for his touch, which explained why my brain wasn't working so well.

"There's a lot of ways I could interpret that," I said softly.

"You just admitted you're mine," he replied slowly. "I've been wonderin' if I could take you—whether I *should* take you. I keep thinkin' about Noah and whether it's right for him, but now I get none of it matters, because you're mine already. You've been mine for a hell of a long time and I just didn't realize it."

"I've worked hard to make my own life. I don't belong to anyone."

"How many men have you fucked?" he asked bluntly.

"Excuse me?"

"Answer the question," he demanded. "How many men have you fucked? How many dicks have been in your cunt?"

"That's none of—"

"Now would be a real good time to answer, babe," he said, grinding into me deliberately. "Seein' as I'm the one with the power here. This is my club. Whatever the fuck I do to you, they'll cover my ass. Don't push."

I caught my breath.

"You won't hurt me."

"No, I won't hurt you. Answer the fuckin' question."

"I've slept with three men," I said. "Zach, a guy in Olympia, and another guy in Seattle."

"And how was it?"

"What do you mean?"

"They make you come? You dump them or the other way around?"

"I dumped them," I said slowly.

"That's because you belonged to me," Ruger said, satisfaction filling his eyes. "We fucked around, wasted time, and you'll never know how sorry I am about Zach. But I'm done now. You're mine, Soph, and it's about time we figured that out. I'll let the club know and we'll be finished with this bullshit."

"Are you asking me to be your girlfriend?" I asked. "Because I don't think anything's changed. We can't afford to get involved and then have it go sour. Noah deserves better than that."

"I'm not askin' you anything," he said, deliberately grinding his hips against mine. I groaned out loud. What the hell was it about this man that tied me up in knots? Maybe I had some sort of primitive hardwiring running the show, attracting me to a man strong enough to care for my child . . .

"I'm tellin' you," he continued. "You're my property, babe. I'll take damned good care of you and Noah. You'll take care of me. But only one cock goes into that pussy of yours—mine—and that's the end of it. Got me?"

I blinked at him, confused.

"I thought you weren't looking to settle down?"

"I'm lookin' to take care of you and Noah," he said. "Neither of us wants to fuck up Noah's life. But you know what? I'm good for Noah. It's a fact. Boys need men in their lives and I love the crap out of him. We've been all twisted up in each other forever and now it's all out in the open anyway."

"I won't be your whore," I muttered. Ruger grunted, a touch of humor entering his eyes.

"Trust me, I don't put this much time and effort into whores," he said, his voice rueful. "Whores are nothing. You'll be my old lady, my property. I know this is all new to you, but it's a big fuckin' deal in my world."

I turned that over in my head, which was difficult, because he leaned down and started kissing my neck, boosting me higher so he could reach. Not his usual hard and brutal invasion . . . No, this was slow and seductive, and then he started sucking gently and I wanted to cry, it felt so good. I squirmed against him, my hips desperate for more stimulation, but he wouldn't give it to me. Instead he nibbled along my chin before finding new places on my neck to suck and nip.

I heard the music from the party in the background, the sounds of people laughing and talking, but here in the cool darkness of the shop it felt like our own separate world. Ruger surrounded me with his smell and strength and the sheer, vibrant energy that defined him as a man overwhelming my senses.

No one got to me like he did.

He pulled me away from the van, carrying me across the shop without pausing in his attentions to my neck. I found myself laid back on the counter behind the panel truck, Ruger's body covering my own. My hands clutching his head as he kissed down my throat, pausing every few seconds to suck, his fingers reaching between my legs to rub slowly up and down along the inside of my thigh.

I'd worn a black T-shirt with a V-neck, which proved no barrier to him at all. Ruger tugged the shirt up and flicked open the front clasp on my bra with disturbing speed. Then his mouth sucked in my nipple—the hard metal ball in his tongue almost painful—and my back arched up off the counter.

The hand between my legs unzipped my fly, and he lifted my

hips just enough to slide off my cutoffs and panties. I felt the cool metal of the counter on my bare ass as Ruger's roughened fingers rubbed up and down along my clit.

"Holy shit, that feels good," I muttered, trying to wrap my brain around everything he'd said. This wasn't the plan, not even a little bit. For one, I hadn't planned on unpacking and sharing all that old baggage about Zach. Not now, not *ever.* The girls had told me to confront Ruger directly, set out my requirements and then stand up for myself.

Instead he gave the orders and I melted like a damned puddle all over a dirty bench in a shop.

What if someone walked in on us?

I'd opened my mouth to protest when Ruger pulled away from my breast, shoving his fingers into me hard at the same time. He dropped to his knees, lips finding my clit, and my brain shorted out completely.

His tongue flicked over my most sensitive spot, teasing me with the unholy combination of his soft tongue and that hard metal ball. Throw in the steady suction of his mouth and it was nearly enough to send me over the edge. Then his finger pressed deep, finding that perfect spot on my inside wall, sending shudders racking through my body. He kept up a steady pressure, rubbing back and forth as his tongue drove me slowly insane.

Then Ruger pulled away long enough to say, "Play with your tits."

It didn't occur to me to argue.

I moaned and reached up, taking my nipples and rolling them between my fingers, pinching and tugging like he'd done the morning before. I'd held out against him then—I'd put Noah first, because any relationship between me and Ruger would be a disaster, and the fallout could leave us homeless again.

This time I wasn't strong enough to say no.

There's only so much self-control any woman can call upon

before she melts. Mine was officially used up. Those fingers of his, rubbing across my G-spot, placing a strange, terrible pressure on me from within . . . That flicking tongue with its hard little knob . . . The strength of his shoulders as they supported my draped knees . . .

I wanted to squirm and kick and push against him. Instead, Ruger took his free hand and held it down across my stomach, controlling me. He drew me to the brink three times, utterly sadistic, and I hated him when he pulled away to catch his breath. Then I heard voices in the distance and reality broke through my haze.

There were people around—lots of people.

People who could walk into this shop at any minute. It didn't even have a door. I opened my mouth to tell Ruger we needed to stop, but he chose that exact instant to suck me in again, hard, plunging his fingers deep. Instead of protesting, I felt my back arch as I exploded in a deep climax, trying my hardest not to scream, with mixed results.

Ruger stood up slowly between my legs, running his hands along my body, from my breasts to my thighs, eyes full of dark satisfaction. I lay there, almost dizzy as he leaned over and caught my hands. He pulled them tightly over my head, whipping out his belt and wrapping it quickly around my wrists, securing them to something behind me.

The whole process took about thirty seconds—Ruger was a little too proficient at tying someone up for my comfort. I tugged my wrists, realizing it wasn't just for show. He had me. Completely. My eyes widened. Ruger gave me a hard, feral smile as he unzipped his fly.

"Yeah, you're mine now," he muttered. "Don't come until I say you can."

I heard more voices, turning my head to look for them. Were they in the shop? I opened my mouth to protest, but Ruger reached up and put a finger over my mouth.

"Don't start with me, Soph," he said, his voice low and merciless. His hands reached down between us and then I felt the head of his cock rubbing up and down along my clit, slow and deadly. Holy shit. Kimber hadn't been lying—there was definitely something metal down there and it felt *fucking fantastic.*

Given that I'd already come, you'd think Ruger would be in rougher shape than me. Instead I found myself super-sensitized. If I'd thought his fingers felt good, they had nothing on his cock sliding along my clit. He teased me until I hovered right at the edge again, eyes fixed on the hoist hanging from the ceiling. Then he leaned down, sucking my nipple in so hard it almost hurt, and sensation burst through me. I tried to wiggle my sex against his cock, but he held me pinned and immobile.

"You don't come until I say," he repeated, letting my nipple slide free, giving it a quick lick. "We clear?"

I nodded.

"Look at me," Ruger demanded. I did, finding his face full of grim satisfaction. He slid his cock up and down my clit again, one, two, three times. I grew wetter with every pass and for the life of me I couldn't remember why I'd been against this.

Then he centered his cock on my opening and pushed it in.

CHAPTER TEN

RUGER

He slid his cock into Sophie's sweet pussy as slowly as possible, savoring every inch. She was fuckin' tight, like a clamp around his dick, the tug at his barbell making things just that much better. He could actually feel her heartbeat. If he didn't know for a fact she'd given birth to a child, he'd think she was a goddamned virgin—hot and swollen and perfect.

Maybe he should've felt guilty, taking her like this.

She was all worked up emotionally, and vulnerable as hell. Understandable. Her little confession about Zach had floored him. He still couldn't believe he'd been so blind, but he'd already decided one thing.

Next time he saw his stepbrother, he'd kill him.

As for Sophie . . . He'd fucked up by not keeping a closer eye on her and Zach, and fucked up even worse by letting the law step in to fix the problem. He hadn't been ready to admit Sophie was his responsibility four years ago, despite what'd happened between them at Noah's birth. He'd spent too long playing the good uncle, ignoring what he felt because he knew it wasn't the best thing for her. She deserved to be free, and who was he to take that away from her?

Well, fuck that.

He was a jealous asshole, and the thought of some other man's cock in her juicy little cunt . . . Picnic was right—he needed to claim her or let her go, and *that* sure as fuck wouldn't be happening. Ever. Sophie might not be ready for a property patch, but that didn't matter. He'd patched her a different way, with a ring of slowly purpling marks around her neck. His very own collar, branding her and declaring to the world that she had a man who owned her.

God, he loved the sight of her laid out on the bench, hands tied with his belt, tank and bra pushed high, boobs shaking every time he slammed home. Better than he'd ever imagined, and fuck, he'd spent a lot of time imagining her just like this. He tried to be careful, but when she started whimpering and convulsing around him it was too much. Ruger drove deep, loving the little scream she gave, blowing his self-control. Something primal and powerful broke free.

He grabbed her hips, digging his fingers into her ass. One hand slid closer to her rear and he thought, what the hell, sliding in his finger. She stiffened and shrieked, interior muscles convulsing around him so hard he had to stop and hold steady, trying not to explode on the spot.

That hadn't been a shriek of pain, thank fuck.

Sophie stared at him with wide eyes, panting so hard her tits practically danced. It was fucking hot. He'd remember this moment as long as he lived. Ruger started moving again, savoring the clench of her muscles with every stroke, wondering if it was possible to die from pleasure.

Seemed pretty likely, all things considered.

He used his finger deep inside, and his hand on her hip, to control her position. He knew from her gasp that he'd hit exactly right.

Now every stroke ground the rounded head of his barbell against her G-spot. Making a girl come while playing with her clit was fine, but he fuckin' loved the way it felt if he got them off from the inside.

He wanted that from Sophie—total convulsion, total submission. She stiffened and moaned. Fucking close.

"Okay, baby," he said, watching her face. She'd closed her eyes, head turned to the side, back arching as she strained toward him. He should've patched her years ago. What the fuck had he been thinking, missing out on this? "Blow around me, show me what that sweet pussy of yours can do."

In the background, Ruger heard voices, and knew some of the brothers had come into the shed. The thought of them seeing him like this, watching him brand Sophie, almost sent him over the edge. This wasn't just about fucking her—although fucking her definitely kicked ass. No, this was about claiming her once and for all, and the more people who saw it, the better.

Ruger slammed into her harder, loving the little grunting noises she made with every thrust. He knew she was close, damned close, so he pulled out just enough to center his cock head on her G-spot and started a series of hard, short, unrelenting strokes. She came with a scream, hips jerking and tits shaking. Her pussy felt like a damned vise, and that did it for him. Ruger pulled out at the last second, spraying his come across her stomach.

Perfect.

She'd never been more beautiful—at his mercy, covered in his seed, and marked so that any man who saw her would know she was fucking *owned*. He wanted to tattoo his name across her ass and keep her tied up like this all day, ready and waiting for his cock.

Somehow, he doubted she'd be on board with that. Ruger bit back a grin. Sophie opened her eyes and looked up at him, dazed.

"Wow," she whispered.

"No shit," Ruger replied, wondering if any man in history had ever felt half as satisfied as he did in that moment. Probably not. He dropped a hand down to her stomach, rubbing his come slowly up her body toward her nipples.

Yup, he was a pretty sick fuck, because even that turned him on.

Having an old lady wasn't half bad, he decided. Not half bad at all.

SOPHIE

Holy shit on a stick. That was . . . unprecedented.

Ruger had asked how many men I'd been with and I'd told him three. But compared to him? I wasn't sure the others even qualified. I'd never felt anything quite as good as what he'd just done to me. Not even close. Now he gazed down at me with lazy, hooded eyes, smug as all hell.

He deserved to be.

I grinned right back at him. Maybe this wasn't such a huge mistake.

"Damn, she squealed like a fuckin' pig," a man's voice said off to the right. I went from afterglow to pure horror in less than a second. Not only was I splayed on the counter, totally exposed, but my hands were tied up, too. I thrashed, trying to get free, hoping to hell they'd just heard me, rather than watched the whole show.

Ruger laughed, which was not an acceptable response. Not even a little.

"Fuck off," he said, turning toward the three men who'd come up next to the van. He didn't sound pissed, though. He sounded pretty damn pleased with himself. "This one's mine. Go screw your own girl."

The men laughed and wandered over to the far side of the shed to look at the motorcycles, as if they hadn't just seen me getting publicly plowed.

Oh. My. God.

"Ruger, pull down my shirt and let me go," I hissed. "Now."

He reached down and straightened my bra and T-shirt, then tucked his cock back into his pants. This wasn't cutting it—I wanted my arms free and my shorts on. Now. Instead, he leaned down over me, standing between my legs, elbows braced on either side of my body.

"Okay, we got things clear now?" he asked. I glared up at him.

"What the hell are you doing?" I hissed. "Jesus, Ruger, let me go. I need to get on my clothes. I can't believe they saw me like that."

"Like you've got anything they haven't seen before?" he asked, smirking. "You worry too much, Soph. These are bikers, they've seen people fucking. And it's a damned good thing they saw, too."

"How do you figure?"

"Because now they know you belong to me," he said. "I was so fuckin' worried about Noah, I didn't figure it out until today."

"Figure what out?"

"That this thing between us is already out there and it's already real. We can't make it go away. We're together and we'll make it work. Or we won't. Sex is the least of it, though. This goes way past sex."

Sudden hope hit me, then I shook my head, reminding myself not to be stupid. This was *Ruger.* I might love him, but I wasn't blind . . .

"Are you saying you care about me?" I asked skeptically. "Like, really care?"

"Well, yeah," he said, wrinkling his forehead. "I've always cared about you, Soph, no secret there. I mean, I fuckin' held you on the side of the road while you pushed out a baby. Don't wanna sound like a dick here, but the fact is not every guy would do that. Somethin' happened that night. We pretended it didn't for a long time. Now we're done pretending."

"You're a giant slut," I said flatly, hating the words even though they needed to be said. "I won't be with a guy who sleeps around, yet here we are at a party where some random couple *fucking in a shed* doesn't even hit the radar. You plan to keep it in your pants?"

His eyes were dark and cool, and I knew my answer before he even opened his mouth.

"I won't bring anyone home," he said. "Right now I can't imagine wanting to fuck anyone but you. But this life, it's about freedom. I became a Reaper so I could make my own rules. Not looking to put my dick on a chain and hand it off to some woman like it's a damned puppy or something."

Pain ripped through me, and I thought about what Maggs had told me.

Lay it out for him. Either he's on board or he's not.

Clearly, Ruger wasn't on board, which meant this was one big, fat dead end. My missing sense of self-preservation finally kicked back in. God, I was such an idiot.

"You gonna untie that belt or what?" I asked, forcing myself to detach. Ruger and Zach might be very different men, but they had one thing in common. They both saw me as a thing to own, a possession. Ruger narrowed his eyes.

"Don't get all pissy," he said. "I'm not saying I plan to sleep around, but I don't think—"

"Let me up, Ruger," I said, my voice soft. "I need to put on my clothes and get cleaned up. Then I want to go visit with my friends and pretend this didn't happen."

"This happened."

"Let me up."

He scowled at me, but he reached over and loosened the belt. The instant my hands came free I sat up, pushing at his big, stupid chest to get him out of my way. I hopped off the counter and grabbed my panties and shorts, sliding them on. Then I started walking away. I needed to find a bathroom, clean myself up. He hadn't even worn a fucking condom.

Shit. SHIT.

How stupid could I be? At least I was on the pill . . . No little brothers or sisters for Noah, thank God. Still, I'd need to get tested. *Idiot.* Thankfully, I knew he usually wore condoms—I'd certainly found enough of them around his house.

I'd talk to him about that later.

"Stop."

I ignored him.

"Sophie, I said to fuckin' stop," he said, his voice harder. One of the men across the shed glanced up, speculation in his eyes. Great. I guess giving the locals the first show wasn't enough. We were still on Ruger's turf, though, so I'd follow his rules. For now.

"What?"

"We're together now, you get that, right?" he asked. "I'm serious, Soph. You're my property."

"I'm my own property," I said slowly and clearly. Time to make a break before things got even worse. "I didn't plan for this to happen, but I have to give you credit. You're pretty good at getting a girl off. I enjoyed every second of it. And I think you're right about Noah, too. He needs a man in his life. But us actually screwing doesn't really change anything—we're not working out. That doesn't mean he needs to suffer. You guys keep doing your thing together. I won't get in your way."

"The situation is finally working for the first damned time."

I shook my head, resolute.

"Let me tell you what's going to happen in the next few days," I said. "I'm going to find a job, and then I'm going to find a cheap place to live. Get out of your hair."

"That's fuckin' bullshit."

"No," I replied. "That's reality. You want the freedom to sleep around. I'm not willing to give you that—I want more. Sounds like we have a fundamental difference of opinion here, and I'm not going to try to change you. But I'll tell you one thing, Ruger—I deserve to be with someone who gives a shit about me, as a person. Someone who values me enough not to fuck other women. *I'd rather be alone the rest of my life than settle for what you're offering*. Consider yourself a hell of a booty call, but that's it. We clear?"

With that I walked away from him, hoping I didn't look too much like I'd just gotten my brains screwed out.

Not that it really mattered.

As much as I hated to admit it, I probably wasn't going to be seeing any of these people again anyway. So far as I could tell, women were only part of the club when they were attached to a man, and I considered myself officially detached. I'd be collecting my purse and my keys from the food table and then I'd be getting the hell away from the Reapers MC for good.

Too bad about the girls. I really liked them a lot.

"Holy shit, what happened to you?" Maggs demanded. She looked me over and burst out laughing. "Ladies, check this one out."

I blushed, wishing I could disappear. So much for nobody guessing what I'd been up to.

"I see you and Ruger had your little discussion," Dancer said, peering closely at me. "What the hell is he, a damned vampire?"

"What do you mean?"

"You have hickies all over your neck," Em said, smirking. "Big ones. He did it on purpose—no way a person could do that by accident."

Fucking asshole.

"He is such a dick," I muttered.

"And this is news?" Marie asked. "They're all dicks. It's sort of a defining characteristic of men, babe. You know, that dangly thing between their legs?"

"I'm going home," I said. "I can't take this."

Maggs stopped laughing and put her hands on her hips.

"You are *so* not going home," she said. "Absolutely not. Wasn't this the plan? To figure out what he really wanted from you? Looks like he stepped up. Doesn't mean you can't stick around and have fun with your girls."

"Oh, I know what he wants from me," I muttered, feeling miserable. "He wants me to be his property."

The women all squealed, and Marie tried to give me a hug.

"That kicks ass!" Em said. I shook my head, and they sobered, confused.

"He told me that if I sleep with another guy he'll cut off his dick and feed it to him," I said. "And then he told me he wouldn't make any promises about not sleeping around himself. He did say he wouldn't bring anyone home, so I guess I'm supposed to feel good about that? Um, *no*."

"Ouch," Marie muttered. "That's not gonna work."

"Nope," Maggs replied. "Although I see where he gets it. Some of these guys, they fuck anything that moves. They have their old ladies at home, ass on the side, and everyone just pretends it's not happening."

"Why would anyone think that's okay?" I asked. "I don't get it."

"I don't get it, either," Marie said. "But it's not really my business, telling other people how to live. I know what I'd do to Horse, though. He'd be praying for death by the time I finished with him."

"He would be," Em added grimly. "Marie's real good with a gun."

"Yup, I'd shoot his dick right off, one inch at a time," she confirmed. "And trust me, he knows it."

"Well I don't care how other people live," I said. "If they want to let their men sleep around, that's their business. But I'll be damned if I'll put up with it. Not good enough for me, and no way I want Noah growing up thinking that's how you treat a woman.

Ruger can take his offer, stick it on a fork, and shove it up his ass. Now I need to find a job and somewhere to live, because I'm sure as hell not living with him any longer."

Maggs nodded, reaching into her back pocket and pulling out a tiny flask.

"It's medicinal," she said gravely. I twisted off the lid and took a quick sniff, which led to a sneezing fit.

"What the hell is that?"

"My own special mix," she said, waggling her eyebrows. "Trust me, it won't solve a thing, but you know what it will do?"

"What?"

"Distract you," she said. "You'll be too busy trying to put out the fire in your throat. Bottoms up!"

I took a swig. Damned if she wasn't right.

Four hours later, my throat still burned from Maggs' special medicine. I'd decided not to leave—the girls convinced me that I shouldn't let him win by running away.

Making sure Ruger didn't win was extremely high on my list of priorities.

The party was surprisingly fun. Maggs and I stuck together, seeing as both of us were man-free. She wore Bolt's property patch so guys left her alone. I wore a ring of hickies that darkened and grew nastier as the night progressed, which may or may not have served the same purpose. It would've been totally humiliating, except I'd already decided I didn't give a flying fuck about any of the Reapers or their sluts.

And there were a *lot* of sluts floating around, including Blondie from the kitchen. She gave me a nasty little one-finger wave. More showed up every minute, multiplying like rabbits. To be fair, most of them seemed like pretty nice people, but I was heavily invested in hating them.

I kept wondering which ones Ruger had fucked.

The old ladies—there were about ten total—were a different group entirely. I liked them a lot and was sorry I wouldn't be getting to know them better. Maggs and Marie must've spread the word about my situation, because nobody asked me any nosy questions. The girls kept me so busy I hardly had time to think about my humiliation.

I did learn a few interesting things, though.

For one, Maggs shared why Bolt was in jail. It was an ugly story. Apparently he'd been convicted of raping a girl who worked at The Line. We were sitting in a couple of camp chairs over by the playground, watching over the kids, when Maggs started talking about it so matter-of-factly that I thought I hadn't heard her right at first.

"Um . . ." I said, desperately searching for some kind of response. What do you say when someone tells you her man's in jail for rape?

"He didn't do it," she said, shrugging. "He got set up."

I looked away, wondering how a woman who seemed so smart could be so stupid. Who stays with a rapist? If he'd gone to prison, odds were good he'd done the crime.

"No," she said, taking my hand and squeezing it. "I can see what you're thinking. It's not like that. I was with him when it happened, hon."

"Didn't you tell the cops?" I asked, eyes wide.

"Of course," she replied. "But the girl ID'd him and there was another witness who said they got into a car together. They never tested the DNA, although we've got a lawyer working on that. He says it's just a matter of time before we get him out. It's not Bolt's DNA, but the state lab is so far behind it takes a fucking miracle to get them to lift a finger. The cops said I was lying to cover for him. Made me look like a criminal and a whore on the stand."

"Damn," I said. "That's horrible, Maggs."

"Tell me about it," she said, her face sober. "I love him so damned much. Bolt is a wonderful man. He's done some crazy-ass shit, but he's not a fucking rapist, you know? But being a biker's old lady? To the cops, that means you're nothing more than a club puppet. My testimony meant jack shit by the time they finished with me. He's up for parole in a year anyway, but I want his name *cleared*."

"Why haven't they processed the DNA?"

"Good question," she said. "New excuse every day. Fucking prosecutors."

Huh . . .

I didn't know where to put that, so I fell quiet. What I didn't do was get up or look away, because while I'd only met Maggs recently, I believed her. She wasn't stupid and she wasn't weak.

Scary to think the system could be so corrupt.

"They definitely screwed Bolt," Marie said, plopping down next to us. "But the local prosecutors aren't all bad. I got off on self-defense last year, after things went down with my brother."

I glanced over at her, curious, but she seemed lost in thought. That story could wait for another day, I decided. If we *had* another day. The girls were being supportive, but whether they'd be friends long-term was iffy. I got the impression that once you left the club, you were out . . . and I was out before I'd even gotten in.

We settled in to talk about other, happier things as the sky darkened. By nine, the kids were all gone and things started getting wilder. The music went up and women's shirts started coming off, none of which fazed my new friends. Then the guys started a big bonfire and broke out a fresh keg. Couples started disappearing into the darkness. I tried not to look too closely, afraid Ruger had already found someone new to screw. He was free to do whatever the hell he wanted. Didn't mean I needed to watch.

That seemed like my cue to leave, except I still hadn't talked to Buck about a job. The more I thought about working at The Line, the less realistic it seemed. Maybe I should just let it go . . . I mentioned this as I helped Marie, Maggs, and Em clean up the food tables. Dancer had taken her boys to her mom's house a while ago and hadn't gotten back yet.

"Why don't you talk to Buck and decide after that?" Maggs suggested, piling half-eaten bags of chips into a cardboard box. "I'll help you find him. Let's get this finished first, though. All this shit needs to go into the kitchen."

"Here, give me the box," Marie said, reaching for it. "Sophie, can you grab that other one?"

"Sure," I said, picking it up. Marie was really sweet—she'd spent half the night talking about her wedding, which was just three weeks away. She'd made it very clear that she wanted me to come, no matter what was up with Ruger.

Now I followed her into the Armory through a back door, leading past a set of bathrooms into the large kitchen area. It wasn't anything special—not a professional kitchen. Still big, though, like you'd find in a church. Three fridges, lots of counter space, and a big, round garbage can that had overflowed onto the floor.

We both stopped, staring at it.

"Jesus, I cannot believe what pigs these boys can be," she muttered. "Take the fucking garbage out when it's full. Doesn't take a genius."

"You think we can handle it?" I asked, considering the can. It was packed hard and looked heavy.

"Only one way to find out," she replied. We set down the food, stuffed in as much of the spilled garbage as possible, and then each grabbed a side. It wasn't easy, but we wrestled it out through the kitchen and into the main lounge of the Armory, which I hadn't seen yet.

"Holy shit," I said to Marie, eyes wide. The place was full of men drinking and women walking around all but naked. There was a bar with a naked chick giving body shots. My eyes skittered away only to land on another girl whose head bobbed up and down over a man's lap. He sat on a ratty couch, leaning back with his eyes closed, one hand wrapped tight in her hair.

"Just ignore it," Marie muttered, rolling her eyes. "Bunch of dumbasses. The Dumpster's out in the front, across from the parking lot. The geniuses who designed this place didn't put in many external doors. Built to be a fortress. Annoying as hell."

We lugged the garbage across the room, and I felt my cheeks burning. Then a man came up and grabbed the heavy can on my side.

"You girls should've asked for help," he said, smiling at me. He was kind of cute, I realized. A little older—probably in his thirties. He had a long beard, tattoos (they all had tattoos, I figured it must be in the bylaws or something), and he wore a cut with one of those little diamond 1% patches. His name read "D.C."

"Thanks," Marie said brightly. "Grab the door for us, will you, Soph?"

I opened the big main door leading out into the front parking lot. There were more guys out there, sort of standing around—the guys I'd seen earlier, who didn't have very many patches on their vests.

"Prospects, get your asses over here and take care of this garbage," D.C. yelled, and two of them jumped up to grab the can.

"It needs to go back in the kitchen when they're done," Marie told D.C.

"No prob, babe," he replied. "Who's your friend?"

Marie and I exchanged glances. I could tell she didn't want to introduce me, but neither of us wanted to be rude, either.

"I'm Sophie," I said, taking the pressure off her. "I'm just visiting. In fact, I'm heading out soon."

Marie opened her mouth to add something. Suddenly a giant man came up behind her, swinging her up and twirling her around before throwing her over his shoulder.

Horse.

"I need fucked, woman!" he declared, smacking her ass. Then he carried her back into the building as she shrieked in protest.

I suddenly found myself alone in the dark with D.C. and the prospects. None of the younger guys looked me in the eye, and I thought very hard about the warnings I'd been given earlier.

Yup—I was in the negative on every detail.

"Nice brands," he said. He reached up to trace the stupid hickies Ruger had given me. "You belong to someone?"

Now that was a loaded question.

"It's complicated," I replied, glancing around. I don't know what I was looking for. Kimber would know what to do at a time like this, I thought darkly. "I need to get back inside, find the girls. I'll just . . . go over there," I added, nodding toward the big gate in the wall to the side of the building. The gate I'd come in before. No way I would be walking back through that clubhouse by myself, not after what I'd seen in there.

"I'll take you," D.C. said, wrapping his arm around my shoulders and tucking me in tight next to his body. I smelled booze on his breath.

Shit. SHIT. *SHIT!*

"Hey there!" Em yelled, waving at me from the gate. I'd never been so happy to see someone in my life. She walked over to us, her smile bright and sweet. "Thanks for finding Sophie, D.C. I need to get her back now—Ruger's up next in the ring, and he'll be super pissed if she misses his fight. They live together, you know."

D.C. let me go and I ran over to Em. He frowned at me.

"Told you it was complicated," I said, my voice wavering. "Sorry?"

He snorted as he turned and walked back into the Armory, slamming the door behind him. The remaining guys looked everywhere but at me and Em.

"Jesus, I could kill Marie for leaving you with him," Em muttered, grabbing my arm and dragging me across the parking lot toward the gate. "At least she yelled at me to go get you as Horse carried her past. Never leave a sister behind, you know? That could've gotten ugly."

"Um, she didn't really have much choice," I said. "Horse just grabbed her and carried her off. It happened really fast."

"All Horse thinks about is sex," Em snapped, her voice heavy with a mixture of disgust and what sounded suspiciously like jealousy.

"At least Marie sent you out here," I said. "Would he have hurt me?"

"Probably not," she said, her voice smooth. "But odds are good he's drunk. You get a guy drunk enough, he doesn't always hear the word 'no.'"

"Does that happen?'

"Rape?" she asked, bluntly. I nodded.

"It's not supposed to," she said. "It's not like it's considered okay or anything, but I'm sure it's happened here. It happened in my college dorm, too. Anytime you put people together, some of them are going to do horrible things. And you get enough horny men drinking enough alcohol, it can lead to bad shit. I'll tell you one thing—I feel safer here than I have at some frat parties. Reaper parties might get wilder than college ones, but we have rules and trust me, they're enforced."

"And you grew up around this?" I asked. "Wasn't that . . . scary?"

"I grew up with twenty uncles," Em said, smiling brightly as we passed through the gate. She raised a hand to the guys standing there and they all waved back. Clearly, Em was loved. "All of them would've done anything for me. I had aunties all over, too, and a bunch of kids to play with—kids I'd known all my life. You saw how many children were here earlier, and they were all having a great time. Of course, we send them home before things get too crazy."

"And what age did you start staying later?" I asked. She rolled her eyes and shrugged.

"Dad told me to leave about half an hour ago," she admitted. "He doesn't want me to grow up. Not that any guy here would lay a finger on me. That's the thing—this is a family. Family takes care of each other."

"And all these women running around?" I asked. "That D.C. guy wasn't interested in me as family."

Her face fell, and she sighed.

"You aren't family," she said softly. "I mean, you're Ruger's family and you'll be treated with respect—D.C.'s not from around here, and he had no idea who you were—but if you're serious about not being Ruger's property, you'll never be a real part of the club."

"Would you hate me if I told you I don't want to be part of the club?"

"I get it," she said, sighing. "Believe me. I just wish it could be different for you guys. I wouldn't settle for what Ruger's offering either, though. No fucking way. You want to get out of here? My dad's gonna see me sooner or later, so I might as well bug out now."

"Yeah, I really do," I told her.

"Let's go watch a movie or something," she said. "You can come over to my place if you like. We have a killer home theater setup."

"Um, that sounds good," I replied, sort of surprised. "You know, it's funny. I don't think of a motorcycle club president as being the kind of guy who'd have a home theater."

"I'll bet you wouldn't think he'd have a virgin daughter, either," she said, regaining some of her humor. "Fuck this, let's go. Last time they had a party this big, I walked in on my dad screwing this chick I graduated with. It was disgusting."

• • •

Back out in the courtyard, a circle had formed beyond the bonfire. People cheered, yelled, and groaned every few seconds.

"What's that all about?" I asked, craning my neck.

"Fights," Em said shortly. "That's what happens when you have too many penises concentrated in one place. Oh, and I wasn't kidding when I said Ruger was up next—he's out there right now. For some reason they think it's fun to hit each other. Let's find Maggs. Maybe she'll come watch movies with us."

I laughed, then spotted Maggs. She stood near the fire, staring deep into the flames. I walked over to her but she didn't look up.

"You okay?"

She sighed and crossed her arms, frowning.

"Peachy," she said, rolling her eyes. "I'm just sick and fucking tired of being here without my man. The club's great and all, but it's not like having Bolt in my bed."

I wasn't quite sure what to do, so I hugged her. She hugged me back. I really wanted to stay friends with these women, despite the whole Ruger situation.

"Hey, you want to come and watch movies with me and Em?" I asked. "I'm sick of Ruger, Picnic says Em has to leave, and you're lonely. Sounds like God himself wants us to get out of here and eat some chocolate ice cream."

She snorted.

"Ice cream's no substitute for a man," she said wryly.

"We can have whipped cream on it," I said, waggling my eyebrows. "You can pretend you're licking it off him instead of the spoon."

"You're a dork," she replied, but she smiled.

"I know," I said cheerfully. "But I'm a dork who knows her refrigerated toppings, and that's mission-critical tonight. Let's go."

"I want you to meet Buck first," she said. "You need to ask him about a job."

I frowned. Did I really want to work at a strip club—especially one owned by the Reapers? Didn't seem like the best way to distance myself . . .

"You don't have to decide tonight," she said. "Just talk to him, and then we'll get back to what's really important—ice cream and chick flicks. A sad one, please, because I'm definitely in the mood for a good cry. Let's just talk to him, okay?"

"Not like you have anything to lose," Em added, coming up beside us. "Find Buck, then we'll ditch this place. I'm ready for a three-way with Ben and Jerry."

Maggs took my hand and pulled me toward the crowd surrounding the fighters, Em trailing us like a puppy. I couldn't see much of the fight, what with the wall of bikers cutting us off, but Maggs wormed her way through them like an expert. Soon we stood on the edge of the "ring," which was just a line traced in the dirt. She was looking around for Buck, but the sound of a fist hitting flesh caught my full attention.

Ruger stood in the center of the circle, naked to the waist, hands bare, expression hostile. He was facing off against a man I didn't know. He looked a little younger than Ruger, and based on the blood dripping down his face, Ruger was kicking his ass.

Em stumbled to a halt next to me.

"What the hell does Painter think he's doing?" she muttered. "I can't believe he's fighting Ruger. That's fucking stupid."

"Why?" I asked, eyes glued to the men circling each other. I could see the top half of Ruger's panther tattoo above his jeans. It really was perfect for him—every movement was lithe and smooth and utterly predatory.

"Ruger's really good," Em said shortly. "He'll slaughter Painter."

"Is that the one . . . ?"

"Yeah," she said, her voice grim. "That's him. The guy who won't put out for me. I hope Ruger kicks his ass."

Ruger chose that moment to plow his fist into Painter's stomach, and the crowd roared. Painter gasped but he stayed upright, recovering surprisingly fast, at least to my uneducated eye.

"He's over there," Maggs said, grabbing my arm again. I looked at her blankly.

"Who's over there?"

"Buck," she said. "You wanted to talk to him about a job, right?"

"Oh, yeah," I said, forcing myself to look away from the circling boxers. What kind of idiots fought like this on purpose? Maggs dragged me through the crowd some more, coming to a halt next to a big man watching the fight with his arms crossed. He didn't look too happy.

"Hey, Buck," Maggs said brightly. He glanced down at her and raised a brow. I swallowed.

"Um, we can do this a different time," I leaned in and whispered to Maggs. "He doesn't look like he's in a good mood."

"He's just like that," she said. "Right, Buck? You're always kind of a dick, aren't you?"

The big man actually smiled.

"And you're always kind of a bitch, but I like you anyway," he said. "You ready to ditch Bolt's ass and fuck a real man?"

"I think Jade might have a problem with that, and she's a helluva good shot."

This time the smile reached his eyes.

"That's the fuckin' truth," he said. "God, but she can be a bitch. Never boring. So who's this?"

"This is Sophie," she said, jerking me forward. From the ring I heard the crack of flesh hitting flesh, and saw Painter staggering in the corner of my eye. Ruger circled him like a cat playing with its food. I forced myself not to pay attention, focusing on Buck instead. Talking to him couldn't hurt.

"Sophie's looking for a job," Maggs added.

"Dancing?" he asked, raising a brow. His eyes crawled down my figure, assessing me closely in a new way—all business now.

"I want to waitress," I said. "I've waited tables in bars before. Never a strip club, but I'm a hard worker. I hear it's a good place to work."

He studied me, face thoughtful.

"You belong to anyone?"

Maggs and I looked at each other, and I shook my head.

"Not really," I answered.

"What the fuck's that supposed to mean?"

"She—"

"Shut up, Maggs," he said, although his tone wasn't mean. "She can't talk for herself, she's got no place in my bar. So what's the story, you belong to someone or not?"

There was a sudden flurry of activity between the fighters, a series of fast blows that I couldn't quite follow in my peripheral vision. Based on the crowd's reaction, things were getting interesting.

"You this slow takin' drink orders?" Buck asked. "'Cause I don't need a slow waitress."

"Sorry," I said, gathering myself. "Ruger is my son's uncle."

"He give you that ring around your neck?"

"Um, yeah," I said, grimacing. "And I live with him. Nothing between us, though. I just really need a job."

Buck eyed me speculatively, then glanced at Maggs. She smirked and rolled her eyes. Buck nodded slowly, then leaned over to the man next to him.

"Hundred bucks on Painter?"

The man stared at him, brows raising.

"You fuckin' insane?"

"Nope," Buck said. "We got a bet?"

"Sure, I'll take your money. Kid's almost finished."

Buck turned back to me.

"Show me your tits," he said.

My eyes widened.

"I'm not looking to dance," I said quickly. "Just wait tables."

"Yeah, I get that," he replied. "But I need to make sure you'll fill out the uniform right. You can leave your bra, but lift that shirt if you want a job."

I glanced at Maggs, who nodded reassuringly.

"Don't worry," she said, bright eyes darting between me, Buck, and the men fighting. "You need a decent rack to waitress at The Line. Go ahead, nobody will care."

I took a deep breath, reached down, and pulled up my shirt all the way.

Two seconds later I heard a huge crash. Suddenly Ruger was between me and Buck, fist slamming into his face. Buck went down and Ruger followed, pounding him brutally.

I screamed as Maggs jerked me to the side, both of us ducking our heads and huddling together. Three guys jumped on Ruger, pulling him off Buck. He fought against them, cussing and growling. Picnic appeared, followed by Gage, who carried a bat.

"Shut the fuck up, everyone," Picnic yelled. "Ruger, pull your shit together! You're out of the ring, you forfeit. Now stop thinkin' with your dick, jackass."

"Let me go," Ruger growled.

"You gonna pull your shit together?" Gage asked. Ruger nodded tightly and the guys let him go. Gage reached down to Buck, giving him a hand up. "We got a problem here?"

Buck spat out some blood and grinned, the bright red outlining his teeth horrifically and dripping down his chin. He looked like a serial killer.

"It's all good," he said, licking his lips. "Asshole just won a bet for me. Too fuckin' easy."

Then he glanced at me, still crouched next to Maggs, utterly stunned.

"No job," he said. "Got enough bitch drama at the bar already.

At a fight, though? Perfect. Ruger always wins, fuckin' beautiful moment. Thanks, sweetheart."

"Um, okay," I said quickly. "I think I'd do better working somewhere else anyway."

Ruger glared at me, chest heaving, his entire body covered with a sheen of sweat.

"You asked him for a job?" he demanded, grabbing my arm and jerking me through the crowd. I tried to break away, but he didn't even notice.

"Let me go!"

Ruger dragged me over to the courtyard wall and pinned me up against it, putting a hand on either side of my head as he got down into my face.

"What part of this is so fuckin' complicated?" he asked, as angry as I'd ever seen him. Well, almost . . . "You don't just go around flashing your tits. It's not a difficult concept, Sophie."

"Maggs said he needed to check me out for the waitress job," I told him quickly. "She said it wasn't personal, not a big deal at all."

Ruger's eyes darkened.

"When a man asks to see a woman's tits, it's *always* personal," he said slowly and clearly. "And yours belong to me. No fuckin' way I'm letting you work at The Line. And keep your damned shirt on. Christ, it's like I'm talkin' to myself half the time."

"No worries," I said, not bothering to argue. Pointless. "I've had enough of this club, I'm leaving. Em and I plan to watch movies and eat ice cream."

Ruger stilled, then reached out and brushed my hair behind my ear, his touch gentle. I felt myself relax a little. Maybe he wasn't as angry as I'd thought. Then his fingers slid deeper into my hair and his eyes hardened.

His hand tightened painfully as he jerked my mouth into his. His tongue stabbed deep into my mouth, possessive and dominant. His other hand caught my arm, jerking my body forward into his as he twisted it up and behind me. One knee shoved between my legs, and he slanted his head, taking everything he wanted and more.

My body loved it, the faithless bitch.

The fight had left him sweaty all over, sending out pheromones so strong it's a wonder I could still stand upright. I wanted to wrap my arms around him but he held me too tight, controlling every move.

I was starting to sense a pattern with Mr. Don't-Come-Until-I-Tell-You.

Finally he pulled away, both of us gasping for breath. He still held me tight, completely incapable of movement even if I'd wanted to get away, which I didn't. My brain had checked out a while back. His hips ground into me, cock more than ready to finish things off.

"You belong to me," he said, voice harsh.

"Ruger—" I started, but a sudden, loud, feminine scream tore through the air.

Ruger dropped me and spun around, covering me with his body as he scoped out the situation. The screaming continued, and then I heard a roar of masculine rage. In the dim firelight I saw a man tear across the courtyard, with about ten more guys chasing him. He hit the far wall, jumped high and caught the top with his hands, pulling himself over.

"Holy shit," I muttered.

"Stay out of the way," Ruger said, turning to me. His eyes were deadly serious, and for once I had every intention of doing exactly what he said. "I'll send one of the girls over, then you get the fuck outta here. Walk to your cars together. Got me?"

"Shouldn't we call the cops?" I asked as the screaming died down. Now I heard crying and angry shouting. "Someone's hurt. What the hell is going on?"

"No idea what happened," Ruger replied. "We'll get help, no worries. But don't call the cops. We handle things ourselves, within the club. Do what I say for once and wait for me to send someone over. Then go home and stay there. I can't deal with this and worry about you, too."

I nodded and he kissed me hard, then ran off toward the Armory gate. In the distance I heard bikes roar to life and then a gunshot. I slid down the wall and sat, knees drawn up tight against my chest, and did my best to obey Ruger perfectly.

Maggs came over ten minutes later. Her face was grim and she had streaks of blood on her arm. I stood and threw my arms around her, clutching her tight.

"What happened?" I whispered.

"Fucking Toke," she muttered. "There's some sort of club shit going down. They voted on it today, supposed to be a done deal, but Toke—he's out of Portland—had a few too many beers and decided there should be a recount. He started fighting with Deke and pulled a goddamned knife, waving it around like a jackass."

"Who was screaming?" I asked. I pulled away and looked down at her arm. "You're all bloody. Who got hurt?"

Her eyes hardened.

"Em," she said. "Cocksucker caught Em with his knife."

Shock hit me and I felt myself sway.

"Did anyone call an ambulance?" I asked, glancing around the courtyard. Beyond the fire I saw someone sitting on the ground, surrounded by women.

"She's fine, thank God," Maggs said, her voice harsh and angry. "It's not a bad cut at all. We've got a guy who'll give her a few stitches, keep the whole thing off the radar."

"What about that gunshot?"

"Pic wasn't too happy about his baby girl getting cut," she said, which I figured was a bit of an understatement. "Had to be him. Toke took off, right over the wall, and I'll bet he's setting a new land-speed record right now. If he's smart, he won't stop 'til he hits

Mexico. Em's a special girl, everyone loves her. Not to mention pulling on his own president. This is more than a fight—it's club business. Toke just stepped in a giant, steaming pile of shit."

I shivered.

"Let's go," Maggs said. "They want all the girls cleared out. Marie and Dancer'll stick with Em, but the rest of us are no longer welcome. We need to stay out of the way. Hell, at this rate we'll be posting bail . . . Be sure to sleep with your phone tonight."

"You serious?" I asked, eyes wide.

"If Pic catches Toke, shit'll get ugly," she said. "But don't worry—our boys are smart. They'll keep the situation under control."

"And the bail thing? That was a joke, right?"

"Just keep your phone close, okay?"

Holy hell.

CHAPTER ELEVEN

My hands shook so hard I had trouble getting the keys into the ignition. Maggs offered to follow me home but I wanted to go by myself. I had a lot to think about and I didn't feel like company. Clearly, Ruger and I had different definitions of what normal, appropriate behavior looked like.

For one, I felt that long-term relationships should be monogamous. He felt they should be monogamous for me and open for him. Another issue? My parties usually wound down when people ran out of food and got tired.

His occasionally ended with stabbings and high-speed chases.

And last, but certainly not least, I tended to think sex should be private. He liked rubbing his sperm on my stomach in front of his friends after branding me with hickies.

I needed to move out.

Immediately. No more messing around.

The more I thought about what had happened, the angrier I got.

Em could've been killed. I might already have a fucking STD, seeing as I screwed the King of the Man-whores—condom-free—in a damned shed, because I'm classy like that. Oh, and what's-his-name might've raped me in the darkness, just because I'd had the nerve to take out the trash when it needed emptying.

What the hell was wrong with these people?

Two hours after pulling into Ruger's driveway, I'd nearly finished packing up our stuff. We'd only been at his house for a week, so it wasn't exactly hard. I just threw shit into boxes and then hauled them out to my car. I could probably get it all in one trip, seeing as Noah was still at Kimber's. I'd call her first thing in the morning and ask if she could put us up for a couple of days.

Fuck Ruger. Fuck his beautiful house and fuck the Reapers. Fuck their motorcycles, too. I hoped they all got food poisoning at one of their damned pig roasts.

I'd already finished packing my clothes, the living room, and the bathroom by the time I heard Ruger's bike pulling into the driveway. Well, wasn't *that* just craptastic . . . I'd planned to be gone before he got home, but if he wanted a fight, I'd give him one. I might not have my life entirely together, but I was pretty sure about one thing—parties that ended with stabbings weren't part of the long-term plan.

Neither was being tied to a man in prison, working as a stripper, or worrying about whether or not I was safe without a goddamned brand across my back like a fucking cow.

I'd started throwing Noah's clothes into the suitcase when Ruger's boots thudded down the stairs. He paused in my kitchen and I heard the sound of water filling a glass. So, now it wasn't good enough for him to put me in danger and invade my privacy? He had to get my glasses dirty, too? I threw Noah's stuffed dragon, Puff, into the case with a disgusted thud.

Wait.

Why the fuck should I care where he got water?

I wouldn't be here to wash the damned dishes. Wasn't my house. The ridiculousness of the night, the horrible way the party ended, packing to move God-knew-where at three in the morning—it all hit me at once. I grabbed Puff and slid down next to the bed, laughing at my own craziness.

Why had I ever, for even a second, thought we could live in Ruger's basement?

I laughed as Ruger walked down the hall. I laughed as he came in the room, and I kept laughing when he knelt down in front of me. I ignored the waves of frustrated anger rolling off him because I just didn't give a damn. He reached out and caught my chin, forcing me to look into his eyes. They cut through me accusingly—like he had the right to an opinion?

I stopped laughing and gave him my most evil smile.

"What the hell is going on here?" he asked.

"I'm packing," I told him, holding up the dragon for him to see. "We're leaving. I'm not your whore and Noah's not your son. Your club is insane and I don't want a damned thing to do with any of you."

"Do you remember when I said coming to the party was a bad idea?" he asked me, raising a brow.

"Yeah, I remember that," I snapped. "But you know what would've really driven the point home? Mentioning that when your parties get wild, girls get stabbed . . . Because I'm pretty sure we didn't cover that part. I would've remembered, Ruger."

"She'll get her justice," he said, eyes darkening. "Toke will pay. Deke and Picnic are on it."

"Um, hate to break it to you, but Em doesn't need *justice*," I pointed out, voice heavy with sarcasm. "She needs to *not get cut with a knife in the first place*. Women are finicky that way—we like *not* getting cut."

"It was a horrible accident," he said slowly. "And despite whatever crazy shit you're imagining, it's not something that's ever happened before."

"You're telling me with a straight face that you never have fights at your clubhouse?"

"No," he said, speaking slowly and clearly. "I'm telling you that they don't usually involve innocent women. Two men want to fight, that's their business."

"And what about women who aren't so innocent?" I asked. "Where do you draw the line on that one? Do you like to hit girls, Ruger? Is that okay in your stupid club?"

The air changed between us, growing cold. Oh, that got to him . . . A whole new level of angry rolled into the room between us, and I suddenly realized taunting him might not be such a great idea.

"Don't talk about the club like that," he said, face like stone. "Show respect if you want to be treated with respect. And you know what? Damned straight I'd hit a woman, if she hit me first. I'm not a knight in shining fucking armor, Sophie. What part of this don't you get? I've been honest with you all along, no bullshit. And yeah, a woman who attacks a man deserves what she gets. She wants to act like a man, she can damned well fight like one."

"And that doesn't bother you?" I asked him. He shook his head.

"Not a bit. You want equality, babe? That's equality."

"Yeah, you're practically a feminist," I muttered. "Em wasn't fighting, Ruger. She'll have a scar the rest of her life. And how is it women have equality when it comes to taking a hit but the rest of the time they're just some guy's *property*?"

"Stop talking shit about things you don't understand," he growled. "'Property' is a term of respect. It's part of our culture. You start judging us for that, you better start judging every woman who changes her name the day she gets married, because it's the same damned thing."

He stopped, running a hand through his hair, clearly frustrated. "When you're someone's property, you're a woman the brothers will die to protect," he continued, his voice softening. "They'll die to protect your kid, too. Don't turn that kind of loyalty into something ugly because you don't like the words we use. Dancer, Marie, Maggs? They're proud to be property, because they know what it means. Nobody forcing them to do anything."

I swallowed, processing that.

"So tell me this," I asked. "Why did Horse tell me that Marie's 'worth every penny he paid for her'? Because that sounded a little fucked up, and I don't think he was joking."

"You're at the clubhouse for less than a day and you've already heard about that?" he muttered, almost to himself. "Jesus. A little fuckin' discretion would be nice."

"Yup, don't want to scare away the new girls with reality, do we?"

"Don't worry about it," he replied. "Marie and Horse are fine, and they're getting married next month, so I think it's a moot point."

"Holy shit, did he really buy her?" I asked, eyes widening. "Ruger, that's—I don't even have words for that!"

"Good, maybe you'll shut up," he said. "If you're interested, I have an update on Em for you. You know, your friend you're so worried about? Maybe a little more important than lecturing me about women's rights, ya think?"

I froze, shamed. Ruger was right. I'd been more focused on fighting with him than on Em. How shitty was that?

"Yeah, I'd like to hear how she's doing," I said. I tossed Puff to the side and rose to my feet. He stepped forward into my space, doing that intimidation thing he was so good at. "So how is she?"

"She's fine," he said after a long pause. "It wasn't much of a cut. About three inches long and not deep at all. We got a friend of the club who came by, gave her some stitches to make sure she stays all pretty when it heals. Antibiotics, just to be careful. Last I saw her, she was high as a kite on oxy and singing some kid song about kittens and mittens. Picnic's not feelin' quite so festive, gotta admit."

"That's good news," I replied, staring at his chest blankly. He really was way too close. "I got a text from Maggs an hour ago, but I wasn't sure if she was downplaying things or not. I don't like your parties, Ruger."

"First part wasn't half bad," he said slowly, a knowing smile stealing across his face. "You know, in the shed?"

He reached out and touched my neck lightly, then wrapped his fingers around it.

"My marks look good," he continued. "Might keep 'em on you long term, haven't decided yet. But you need to learn not to flirt with other guys, babe. You're claimed now."

"One, take your damned hand off me, because *I am not claimed*," I said. He ignored me. "And two, I didn't flirt with anyone!"

"You flashed your tits at the whole damned club," he said. His hand tightened ever so slightly on my neck. Not hard enough to hurt—just enough to show he could.

Oh, I didn't like *that* at all . . .

"Take. Your. Fucking. Hand. Off. Me," I growled. This time he did, but at the same time he pushed me forward with his body, unbalancing me. I fell back on Noah's bed, almost hitting my head against the wall. Before I could roll away, Ruger dropped down over me, trapping me just as surely as he had back in my Seattle apartment.

"I was wearing a bra and Maggs told me to do it," I hissed, not bothering to fight him. That'd probably just turn him on. Perv. "She said he needed to check me out if I wanted to waitress at The Line. I need a damned job, Ruger. Didn't seem like a big deal. Half the women there weren't even wearing shirts. It's not like I took off my bra."

"You're a fuckin' idiot," he snapped. "Of course Buck checks out potential waitresses . . . at the club. During business hours. He did that to piss me off and get me out of the ring. He played you to win a bet, Soph—he'd never hire you without my permission, anyway."

"Why did Maggs say it was okay, then?" I demanded. Damn, he was heavy. He smelled good, too, which I hated. Predictably, my body wasn't listening to my brain again, because I had the urge to spread my legs and wrap them around his waist.

"Fuck if I know, but she did it on purpose," he growled. "Might want to ask her about that. She set you up, and that means she set me up. I'll have words with her later."

I narrowed my eyes.

"You leave Maggs alone," I said, glaring. "If someone needs to 'have words' with her, it'll be me. If you and Horse had a problem, would you want me involved?"

"Jesus, you're a pain in the ass," he said.

"And you're a disgusting pig man. No respect for me at all—"

"I respect you," he said, frowning. I snorted.

"Yeah, I'll bet you fuck all the women you respect in public? And what the hell was that shit about coming on my stomach? I'm not a damned porn star, Ruger—I'm *still* all sticky and disgusting. Kinda hard to clean up in a Porta-John."

"This house has three showers, babe. Not my fault you haven't taken one yet. I *like* the idea of me all over you, so no rush on that."

"I was busy packing! I wanted to get out of here before you got home, asshole!"

"Yeah, I see that," he muttered. He leaned down, his face so close our lips almost brushed. "You're not moving out, babe. You're mine. We covered this. Done deal."

"Oh, I'm definitely moving out," I told him. "Not even you can think this is healthy, Ruger."

He smiled at me with the eyes of a predator.

"I don't care if it's healthy," he whispered. "Whole damned world's unhealthy. You think all those people living in giant houses on the lake have happy, pretty, perfect lives? You think those bitches aren't backstabbing each other while their husbands fuck interns on their lunch breaks?"

I shook my head.

"My friend Kimber's not like that. Her life's nice and normal and not crazy at all."

"Then she's one in a thousand," he replied. "Because I swear to you, sometimes the nastiest shit happens behind the prettiest doors, while everyone laughs and smiles and pretends everything's okay. Here's the thing about my world. We're fucked up. We own it. We take care of business and move on. In twenty years those 'healthy' people you're so jealous of will *still* be backstabbing each other, and their kids will, too."

"I'll take my chances," I said.

Ruger scowled and pushed himself up abruptly. Then he grabbed me and threw me over his shoulder like a sack of wheat. I squawked as he carried me out of the room and up the stairs to his loft, kicking and punching him the entire time. Didn't do a bit of good. I don't know what I expected—maybe that he'd throw me down on the bed and ravish me, like a movie or something. He didn't. Instead he carried me into his big bathroom, dumped me in the shower and turned on the faucet.

"What the hell are you doing!" I shrieked as cold water hit me, still fully clothed. Ruger grabbed the shower hose and started spraying me down with it.

"I'm showin' you *respect*," he yelled back at me. "So sorry I got you all messy earlier. Just doing my best to make this relationship *healthy* and *clean*, because that's so fuckin' important to you. Aren't I a fuckin' prince?"

"I hate you!" I screamed, lunging for the hose. He laughed and sprayed my face. I lashed out and slipped. In a flash, Ruger caught me, then pulled me tight into his body. I found myself looking up at him, my wet clothes soaking both of us, one of his arms wrapped around my waist and his other hand tight in my hair.

We glared at each other.

"Jesus, you fuck with my head," he said roughly. "My cock gets hard just thinkin' about you. You're in my dreams every night. I wake up in the morning and all I think about is you in my house, you and Noah finally mine. *My family*. It's even better than ridin' my bike. I'm crazy for you, Soph."

I shook my head, stunned. I didn't believe him. I couldn't afford to.

"You're just saying that to control me," I whispered, not sure whether I was talking to myself or him.

"Fuck me, you just don't get it, do you?"

He took my mouth in a fast, hard kiss and I fought him for about two seconds. Then I gave in, because my body recognized him, needed him. Suddenly there were too many clothes between us. Our hands scrambled and I discovered that water-logged jeans—even cutoff ones—must be the least convenient thing on earth to wear when you need quick access.

Still, I managed to get them down and kicked away just as he grabbed my waist, spun me around and leaned me against the counter. I looked up to see him in the mirror, face flushed red with need, eyes capturing mine as he slammed his cock deep inside. It filled me fast and hard, stretching me until it bordered on pain. I gasped, the sound a mix of pleasure and pain.

I've never felt anything better in my life.

"Fuckin' crazy for you," he muttered, fingers digging into my skin. "Always have been."

"Ruger . . ."

Then he took me, forcing me to brace myself with both hands as he pounded me from behind. One hand steadied my hips while the other reached around to my clit. That piercing of his slid along my G-spot, the hard little knobs of metal on the top and bottom of his cock head carrying me to a whole new level of sensation. My orgasm hit with agonizing speed and I screamed, pulsing around him.

Ruger thrust three more times and then he came, too, hot seed spurting.

Shit. We'd forgotten the condom again.

He pulled out of me slowly and we looked at each other in the mirror, our chests heaving. He was fully clothed and I still wore my T-shirt. My hair was sopping wet and scraggly, and eye makeup ran down my face.

I was a hot mess without the "hot" part.

"Do you have any diseases?" I asked, my brain valiantly fighting for control. He shook his head, still watching me in the mirror.

"I always use a condom," he said. "Never fuck a girl without one, actually."

"Fucked me without one twice," I said, my voice dry. "Wanna rethink your answer?"

He offered a smug smile.

"I know you're on the pill," he said. "So pregnancy's not the issue. Also know you're clean. You're my woman, so why shouldn't I feel you around me? And I swear to you, babe. I have never, ever fucked anyone without protection before. I even donated blood about two weeks ago—all clear."

"That's a relief," I said, straightening. I looked around for my panties and shorts. They'd landed near the toilet, dripping water everywhere.

"How do you know I'm on the pill?" I asked, reaching for a towel to wrap around myself.

"Found 'em in your purse," he said without a hint of shame. I looked up, startled.

"Why were you in my purse?" I asked, not pleased.

"To get your phone," he replied, tucking himself back into his pants. "I wanted to set up the GPS on it."

I stopped cold.

"You have GPS tracking my phone?" I asked, incredulous.

"What the hell is wrong with you? You want to chip me like a dog, too?"

"I want to be able to find you if there's an emergency," he said, his face growing serious. "I know it sounds paranoid, but we had a real bad situation last winter . . . Marie and Horse would be dead right now if I hadn't had GPS on her. Nearly died as it was. Now I do it for all the girls in the club. Don't worry, I don't spy on you or anything. But it'll be there if you ever get in trouble."

"I don't even know where to start," I said, closing my eyes. I was exhausted, I realized. No wonder my brain wouldn't kick in and tell me what to do.

"Let's go to bed," he said. "I'm tired. You're tired."

"I'll sleep downstairs," I told him, clutching the towel as I reached for my clothes.

"You'll sleep up here with me," he replied. "You can fight me on it and lose, which is more work for both of us, or you can just give in. Gonna end the same either way."

I looked at him and knew he was right. I'd set him straight later—right now I needed rest.

"Can I borrow something to wear?" I asked, trying not to yawn. "I'm too tired to go get dry stuff."

"I'd rather you sleep naked."

"I'd rather you go fuck yourself, but seeing as that's not an option, can I borrow something to wear?"

He smiled at me.

"Knock yourself out. Shirts are in the top drawer, underwear in the second one down."

I left the bathroom and looked around to find his dresser. Sure enough, the top drawer held a variety of T-shirts. I found one with a Reapers symbol on it and pulled it out. Then I moved down to the next drawer. Most of his stuff was black or gray, but a flash of pink in the back caught my eye.

What the hell?

I pulled out a pair of silky, pink panties.

"Jesus, Ruger," I said. "Is there anywhere in this house women don't leave their lingerie? It's like a damned Victoria's Secret in here!"

I turned to him, holding the panties out with two fingers, disgusted. He cocked his head and gave me a strange smile.

"Those are yours, actually," he said slowly. "You left them behind."

"What are you talking about?"

"That first night," he said. "With Zach. You left them in my apartment. Had 'em ever since."

I froze, and studied them more closely. It'd been a long time, but they did look familiar. I'd been so sad to lose them, because I'd bought them special . . .

"I can't decide if that's just a little bit creepy or really, super creepy," I said finally, glancing over at him. He shrugged, eyes holding mine steady.

"You asked me the other night if wanting you was a new thing," he said, his face free of mockery for once. "It's not a new thing, babe. Not a new thing at all."

I woke suddenly, wondering where the hell I was. A strong, masculine arm lay across my stomach, pinning me down. A vaulted cedar ceiling rose overhead. I turned to see Ruger lying facedown next to me, and it all came back in a rush.

I needed to get out of here before he woke up and started in on his you're-my-woman-and-I-own-you bullshit. I couldn't afford to play around anymore—Noah had been through enough already.

Lifting his arm cautiously, I rolled out of bed and turned to look at his sleeping form. Ruger's back was half covered by the sheet, and for the first time I had the chance to study his ink in full light.

His perfectly sculpted body wasn't just sexy. It was literally a work of art. His arms were a mass of patterns and designs so intricate I had trouble following them, but dominating his right bicep was a picture of what had to be Noah's Ark. The animals marching away from it were fantastical, dragons and demons and snakes, but the Ark itself was unmistakable.

My breath caught. How had I never noticed that before?

He shifted in his sleep, the sheet slipping lower. I couldn't allow myself much time . . . I wanted to leave before he woke up and we started fighting. Given our track record, I'd have sex with him again if that happened. My clit perked up and sent an urgent memo to my brain endorsing that option. Screwing a man-whore had one advantage—he certainly knew what he was doing.

As for the pink panties I wore? I didn't know what to think about that. It should've grossed me out, but it mostly just turned me on. All those years I'd been lusting after him, and he'd been lusting after me, too. Not enough to stay faithful, of course. But he'd still wanted me.

My nipples joined my clit in petitioning for another round.

I ignored both of them.

Nothing had changed. The party, Em, all the reasons I should avoid the Reapers. Ruger and I simply couldn't be together. But for a few minutes, while he still slept, I let myself study the incredibly sexy man who'd been an unofficial father to my son. Across the top of his back was a broad, curved banner of ink matching the patch on his cut that said "Reapers." Their symbol—the Reaper himself—covered the center, and I saw just a hint of the bottom rocker, which I knew would say "Idaho."

Strange as it sounds, the combination of his club colors and the Ark illustrated Ruger's contradictions perfectly.

Strange spots covered his shoulders, and along his side I saw just a hint of the panther's claw reaching around from his hip.

He shifted and I froze, reality crashing back down.

I needed to get out or we'd have another fight. Realistically, we'd have another fight regardless, but a little break would be nice. I went downstairs and found my phone, checking the time. Seven in the morning. It took me less than thirty minutes to finish the last of my packing. Then I carried everything out to the car, loaded it, and climbed in.

I turned the key in the ignition, feeling sad and just a little wistful.

Things would turn out, I told myself firmly. I was doing the right thing. As if to prove my point, the sun was already high and bright. Birds were singing like in some stupid Disney movie. I turned out of the driveway onto the road and saw Elle, Ruger's neighbor, walking along with her dog. She smiled as she saw me, waving me down. I pulled over.

Elle's eyes flicked over the car, noting the presence of boxes and the lack of a child.

"Trouble in paradise?" she asked dryly.

I smiled ruefully and shrugged.

"You could say that," I replied. "Ruger and I live in different worlds. I realized it doesn't matter how cheap the rent is, staying isn't going to work."

"Do you have a plan?" she asked, and it wasn't one of those questions that's actually a passive-aggressive accusation in disguise. My mother had been the master of those . . . I could tell Elle was genuinely concerned.

"Not really," I said. "But I guess that's okay. Every time I make plans they fall apart anyway. Noah's with my friend Kimber, and she's got a spare room. I'm sure she'll put us up until I pull something together."

"I see," she replied, pursing her lips thoughtfully. She glanced over at Ruger's house, then cocked her head at me. "Why don't you come over and have some breakfast? There's something I'd like to talk to you about."

That startled me.

"Um, I don't want to sound rude, but I'm sort of trying to get out of here before Ruger wakes up," I told her. "He's not going to be too happy about this."

"He'll get over it," she said, that dry tone back in her voice. "He may be a big, bad biker, but he's still just a man, and men are notoriously stupid. You can't see my house from the road and he probably won't come looking for you there, anyway. I have a shotgun if he does. I also have caramel rolls."

My mouth dropped. Hadn't seen that one coming.

"Okay," I replied, suitably impressed.

Half an hour later we sat at her kitchen table, eating sweet rolls and discussing my crazy life. Somehow, she managed to bring out the humor in the situation, making things seem less scary. I wanted to be Elle when I grew up, I decided. She was smart, funny, cynical, and pretty sexy for a woman pushing forty.

"So, you've got a bit of a problem," she said finally, the queen of understatement. "You're smart to move out. I agree with you one hundred percent."

"Really?" I asked. "Because I think Maggs set me up last night. She's trying to push us together, I know it."

"Well, there's together and there's fucking," Elle said, delicately slicing a cantaloupe wedge.

"It kind of freaks me out when you do that," I admitted.

"Do what? Eat melon? Orange fruits and vegetables are extremely healthy, Sophie."

I giggled and shook my head.

"No, act all ladylike and then cuss like a sailor."

"My late husband was in the navy," she said, smiling softly. "And I assure you, his language would make your motorcycle club friends cry like little girls. Ruger actually reminds me of him in a way. So wild and violent, but contained, too."

"Do you miss him?" I asked softly.

"Of course," she replied, her tone sharpening. "You can't help but miss a man like that. But here's the thing, Sophie. I gave up everything for him. We moved every couple of years, so I had trouble making close friends. I thought about having a child, but I didn't want to raise one by myself and I knew he'd be gone half the time. Then he went and died on me and now I'm all alone. Sometimes I hate him for that."

I didn't quite know what to say, so I took another bite of my roll. Elle sipped her tea and then sat back in her chair, looking at me very seriously.

"I did something very stupid when I was your age," she said. "I let a man make the decisions for me. I have no idea if you and Ruger belong together, but you need space to figure things out. You can't let yourself be dependent on someone unless you can truly trust him."

"I trust Ruger," I said slowly. "I trust him with Noah, at least. I also trust him not to change, which is sort of the problem."

"Men rarely do," she agreed. "Although it's possible, I suppose. As I said before, I think I may have a solution for you. Did you know there's an apartment in my barn?"

"Your barn?" I asked, blankly. I looked out the window toward the wooden structure behind the house. "I didn't know you used the barn."

"I don't," she said. "This farm belonged to my great-aunt, and she had part of the barn converted to an apartment for my cousin. He was developmentally delayed. She wouldn't let them put him in a home, but he couldn't live on his own. The apartment gave him some freedom and independence, but also kept him safe. He passed two years ago and it's been empty ever since. I'm sure it needs cleaning, but I'd like to offer it to you and Noah."

"Are you serious?" I asked. She nodded.

"Of course," she said. "I wouldn't have offered it otherwise. It's not being used and I like both of you. Noah deserves a decent place to stay, and it's definitely better than crashing on someone's couch.

Only one bedroom, but you don't need to live there forever. It's furnished. Just until you get back on your feet."

"What are you looking for in terms of rent?" I asked cautiously.

She thought for a moment.

"I was hoping you could help me with the yard work," she said. "I've been having trouble keeping up with it lately."

I met her eyes across the table and neither of us said anything for a long moment.

"You're a very nice person," I whispered.

"So are you," she replied quietly. "I have no idea whether things will work out between you and Ruger, but this way Noah can stay in the same school and still be within walking distance."

"You think it's a good idea for me to be this close to him?" I asked bluntly.

"Good luck finding somewhere he can't follow you," she replied wryly. "It hardly matters how far you go. Like I said—I have a shotgun. The barn has a good lock. Between the two I think you'll do all right. Would you like to go and take a look?"

"I'd love that."

ME: Thanks again for watching Noah this weeknd. All moved in now, still cant believe Elle had this place just sitting here. Good luck for me!!!!

KIMBER: No prob. So . . . have u seen HIM yet?

ME: Who? :->

KIMBER: Don't be a dumbass. Thats Rugerss job. Did he freak?

ME: Thats the creepy part. He didn't

KIMBER: Seriosly?

ME: No. He texted and asked me if I was ok. I said yes. He asked where I was

KIMBER: U tell him?

ME: Yes. He'd figure it out anyway

KIMBER: Huh . . . thats weird. After what happeed Sat night, that's a total turn around. I expected him to come chase u down and drag you back—you know, like a cavman or something

ME: I know. I was expectign more too. Makes me nervous

KIMBER: Ha! U WANTED him to be pissed!

ME: No . . . maybe? Its stupid. I have a job interview tomorrow afternoon. Recpetionist at a dental clinic. Right near the school

KIMBER: Woooot wooot!!!!! Dont change the subject

ME: Hey! I need a job more than I need to talk about Ruger

KIMBER: This is about ME, babe. I need gossip. U owe me. Iwatched ur kid AND I got you drunk. Entertain me

CHAPTER TWELVE

"Sophie, I'm so sorry, but Dr. Blake is still running late. Can you stick around a little longer, or should I see if he can reschedule? I hate to pressure you, but he's really hoping to make a decision tonight, and you're the last interview . . . We're pretty desperate."

"No problem," I said, smiling brightly at the flustered hygienist behind the counter. It was a big fucking problem. Noah would be out of school in an hour and I needed to be there to pick him up. But I also needed to be able to buy food to feed him, too, and after the first three months this job came with health care and sick leave . . . not to mention dental. I hadn't had my teeth checked in four years.

"Are you sure?" asked the hygienist. Her name was Katy Jordan, and for the past hour I'd been sitting in the waiting room, watching her juggle patients and the phone. Apparently their old receptionist left without giving notice because of a family emergency, the temp was a no-show, and the doctor's assistant had gone home at ten that morning throwing up. A mother with two kids sat next to me, obviously impatient. She'd been waiting nearly forty minutes for her appointment to start and things were getting tense.

"I'll make a quick phone call," I told her.

"Sounds great," she said. "Mrs. Summers? Are you ready?"

The woman beside me stood and coralled her children, herding them into the back. I stepped outside the office, which was in a low-lying, mixed-medical building. Kind of like a mini-mall for doctors, although classier, with fancy landscaping, cedar siding, and covered walkways.

I tried Elle first. No answer. I tried Kimber, too. Nothing. I called the school to see if he could go to the after-school program for a day, only to learn he needed to be formally enrolled to participate, something I'd have to do in person, at the district office.

That left me with the girls from the club or Ruger . . . and the girls from the club weren't authorized to pick him up at the school. I could change that, of course. All I had to do was fill out some paperwork at the school office.

In person.

That left Ruger.

I hadn't had any communication with him since Sunday morning, aside from that one text asking if I was okay. I punched his number and waited. The phone rang long enough, I thought I'd get voice mail. Shit . . . Then he answered.

"Yeah?"

He didn't sound particularly friendly or welcoming. More like the old Ruger, the one who looked through me like I was furniture. I suppose that's what I wanted. It didn't feel good.

"Um, hey," I said. "I'm really sorry to do this, but I have a favor to ask. For Noah."

"Yeah, you always have favors to ask," he said, his voice almost a growl. "Yet I still answer the damned phone when you call. Tryin' to figure out why."

"Are you working this afternoon?"

"Yup."

"Any chance you could duck out long enough to pick up Noah at school? They keep moving back my job interview. If I have to leave, I'm probably going to lose my shot here."

He sighed.

"Yeah, I can move things around here," he said. "How late do you think you'll be?"

I paused, hating every second of this.

"I don't know," I finally said. "At this rate, it might be toward the end of the day. I need to meet with the doctor. He had some sort of emergency earlier and now they're running behind. He's just trying to fit me in between patients at this point."

"Okay, I'll take the rest of the day off, bring him back to my place."

"Thanks, Ruger."

"It's what I do," he said, hanging up. I looked down at the phone, wondering how such a great guy could be such an asshole slut at the same time.

Then I pasted my "Hire me, I'm friendly and competent!" smile back on and returned to the waiting room.

By four thirty I still hadn't done my interview. I'd pretty much given up on it, because there'd been a second emergency. A high school girl knocked out half her front teeth during soccer practice. She'd been hysterical when her coach rushed her in, bloody towels pressed to her face. The other patients watched in fascinated horror as Dr. Blake himself came out to fetch her, bustling her back into the treatment room.

Forty-five minutes later he reappeared.

"We're going to have to reschedule everyone," he announced to the room, looking exhausted. "I'm so sorry. I don't have anyone here to help you right now. We'll need to call you tomorrow."

There were several frustrated sighs, but it wasn't like people could complain, given the circumstances. Dr. Blake's eyes caught on me. He was a handsome man, although older than me. Probably in his late thirties or early forties?

"Are you one of my patients?" he asked. "I don't recognize you."

"I'm Sophie Williams," I answered, straightening the scarf I'd tied around my neck. "I'm applying for the job as your receptionist. I'm guessing that interview isn't going to happen today?"

The phone started ringing. Again. Then the door opened and a UPS deliveryman came in, followed by a woman with three children.

"Hey, Dr. Blake!" she said. "We're all ready for our checkups. How are you doing?"

"Great," the doctor replied, offering her a pained look. "But we've had a little complication in the scheduling today. This is our new receptionist, Sophie. She'll take care of you."

Just like that, I had a job.

I felt proud of myself when I turned the car down Ruger's drive that night. I'd jumped right in at work, and while I didn't know how to use the scheduling program, I still managed to look up the last two patients for the afternoon and call them to cancel. I'd also handled the phone and even talked to a potential new patient. I still needed to fill out paperwork, but Dr. Blake had been thrilled.

Just having an income source changed everything . . . The fact that it came with benefits, sick leave, and vacation? Amazing.

I'd never had a job with paid vacation before.

Of course, that good feeling ebbed as I pulled up to the house. I hadn't seen Ruger since I'd snuck out of his room three days ago. I wasn't sure what I'd expected from him. But I'd expected *something*. This silent acceptance of what I'd done, after what a huge deal he'd made about "owning" me? That made me very nervous.

Making matters worse, he'd saved my ass this afternoon. Again. That meant I owed him even more than before—just one more complication to our already twisted relationship.

I knocked on the door but nobody answered. I'd texted him around four thirty to give him an update and he'd replied that they'd gone fishing, so I walked around the side of the house to his deck and made myself comfortable at the table to wait. Well, as comfortable as I could, given our recent interactions. I still had my key, but using it felt wrong under the circumstances. It was a little after six already. I hoped he'd be back soon. Noah needed dinner and a bath before bed.

Ten minutes later I saw them walking up toward the house across the meadow from the pond, the big man and little boy looking like something out of a country-living postcard. Ruger carried the fishing gear and Noah bobbed along next to him like a puppy, holding a string of three tiny little fish.

"Mom!" he yelled, spotting me. He took off running toward the house and I met him at the bottom of the steps. He jumped at me and then I was holding him as the fish slapped against my side in all their slimy glory.

Ewww . . .

"Mom, I got *three fish*," he told me, eyes wide with excitement. "Unce Ruger and I went to the pond and we even got to dig up some worms and they were really, really squirmy!"

"Wow, that sounds like fun," I told him, wondering if I'd be able to get the fish smell out of my interview outfit. I couldn't get upset about it, though—not with him so happy. Sometimes I forgot just how much I loved my little boy, because seeing him again after a long day apart nearly made my heart explode.

"I have good news, too," I told him, smiling big.

"What?"

"Mama got a job!" I said. "I'm going to be working at a dentist's office right by your school. I'll be able to drop you off every day, and then I'll pick you up from the after-school program. No more working at night! What do you think of that?"

"That's fuckin' great, Mom!" he said, eyes bright.

"Noah! Do we use that word?"

His face fell and he shook his head.

"I'm sorry," he said. "Uncle Ruger told me not to say it in front of you."

Ruger set the fishing gear down under the deck and I turned to him.

"Noah says you told him not to curse in front of me?" I asked, raising a brow.

"Long story," he replied. "And I'm not gonna get into it with you, so you can either let it go and enjoy some grilled fish with us for dinner or get all worked up. Result will be the same."

I glared at him as Noah started wiggling to get down. I let him go and he held the string of fish up, so proud he practically glowed.

"Uncle Ruger and I are going to cook dinner," he declared. "We're eating my fish. You can share!"

I glanced down at the three tiny little rainbow trout, smaller than could possibly be legal. Then I looked up at Ruger, questioning.

He shrugged.

"I've got some salmon marinating in the fridge," he said. "I'll grill it with corn."

"I brought Noah his favorite macaroni and cheese," I replied. "Want me to cook that up while you get the grill going?"

"Sounds great."

Dinner was a little awkward, but not as bad as you'd think, under the circumstances. I'd busied myself doing the macaroni and prepping the veggies while Ruger and Noah cleaned the fish. I wouldn't have trusted Noah with a knife, but Ruger guided him carefully, explaining each step as he slit the fish open, gutted them, and then rinsed them out. We wrapped everything in foil and threw it on the grill while Noah ran off to play and I set the table.

"So, you got the job today?" he asked, leaning back against the railing, a casual eye on the food. It was almost like things hadn't blown up between us over the weekend. Okay. I could work with that. Denial had always been an excellent strategy for me.

"Yup," I said. "It's a good one. They do full benefits after three months and I'll have a week of vacation starting next year. Thanks again for grabbing Noah."

"No problem," he said, shrugging. "It's not like he's hard to be around, if you can get him off the whole Skylanders thing. He ever get tired of that?"

"No," I said. I saw a spark of humor in his eyes and I smiled back. At least we had Noah between us, I realized, no matter how fucked up everything else was.

"You've done a hell of a good job with him," Ruger said. "I want you to know that."

"Thanks," I said, startled. "What brought that on? I thought you were pissed at me?"

Shit, did I just say that out loud? Why did I have to go and stir things up, right when we were starting to get along? He didn't jump all over me, though. Instead he just gave me a slow smile, which was strangely worse.

"You'll figure it out," he said.

Crap.

He stepped over and rotated the corn while I studied him, suspicious. He stayed quiet, pulling out his phone and checking his messages. Yup, definitely worse. At least when we fought I knew where we stood.

On the bright side, Noah's little trout were pretty tasty—all three bites. He turned down salmon to eat SpongeBob-shaped macaroni and cheese, no huge surprise there. Ruger startled me by bringing out a bottle of sparkling cider to celebrate my new job. Noah was ecstatic, drinking half the juice by himself out of a real wine glass. I have to admit, I was touched. After dinner we cleared the dishes while Noah took off again, with a stern warning that we'd be heading home in ten minutes.

"You start work tomorrow?" Ruger asked as I loaded the dishwasher.

"Nine on the dot," I replied, feeling a little rush of excitement. "It's perfect. I can't believe how things worked out. Thanks again for helping today—you have no idea how much it meant to me."

"I note you didn't follow up on the job at The Line," he said, cocking a brow. I frowned and looked away.

"Um, I wasn't really serious about that anyway," I said. "I don't want to work for the club."

"Yeah, you made your feelings about the club clear," he said. My mood deflated a little. "I've got something for you."

"That's a loaded statement," I replied, my voice flat. He smirked, and I felt better. It wasn't an angry smirk.

"Dirty mind, Soph?" he asked. "Seriously, this is important. Come on into the living room."

I followed him, then sat in a chair. He sat on the couch, then patted the seat next to him. I shook my head. He held up a thick, business-sized envelope.

"You don't get your surprise if you don't come over here."

"What makes you think I'll want it?"

"Oh, you'll want it," he said, clearly pleased with himself. I got up and walked over to him slowly. He grabbed my hand, pulling me down and across his lap. I gave a token struggle, but he handed me the envelope and curiosity took over, so I let him win.

Also, it felt kind of nice to sit on his lap. Yeah, I know. Stupid. But I'm only human.

I opened the envelope and saw cash. A very large wad of cash.

My eyes opened wide and I pulled it out, shocked. I didn't count it, but it seemed to be all hundred-dollar bills . . . there had to be three or four thousand dollars in here.

"What the hell is this?" I asked, looking at him. He gave me a grim smile.

"Child support."

"Holy shit!" I gasped. "How did you get this out of Zach?"

"It's from Mom's estate," Ruger said. "I paid him out and then he paid you out. In exchange, he gets to keep living. Everybody wins."

I turned to look at him, shocked.

"Are you serious?" I asked. Our faces were about two inches apart, and his eyes flicked to my lips. I licked them nervously and felt something stir under my butt. His arms came around my waist, holding me loosely, and my nipples hardened.

Damn it.

"Pretty hard to get more serious," he told me. "Old friend tracked down Zach for me in North Dakota and I rode over there Sunday afternoon, got back early this morning. We had words. Then we went to the bank. I didn't give him the promise to let him live in writing—that's just a little side incentive. I'll revoke it if he ever gets within ten miles of you or Noah again. Mom would've wanted this anyway. She never stopped loving him, but she sure as shit stopped trusting him."

I swallowed. I wasn't sure I wanted to know the details . . . But I couldn't feel sorry for Zach. He'd earned everything he got and then some.

"How much money is in here?" I asked, flipping through the wad of cash.

"Not all of it," he said. "That's just last year's. The rest is in transit. Dealing with that much cash gets complicated. Needs to be cleaned up a bit, and then we'll find a way to get it to you that won't leave an ugly trail. The trade-off is, we agreed on your current monthly rate, and it's not like you can take him to court to ask for more if he gets a great job or something."

"I couldn't even get him to pay what he owed already," I said. "Health and Welfare won't do shit, either. I don't think upward adjustments were on the table."

"Sort of what I figured," he replied. "So I'm real glad you got a job, but you won't be living paycheck to paycheck anymore."

"That's amazing," I whispered, looking back down at the envelope. "I have to ask . . . Is it going to come back on me and Noah? Am I going to get arrested?"

"You're good," he said. "That's not enough cash to catch any IRS attention, and Horse is working on getting the rest of it to you all safe and legal. He's a damned good accountant, and he'll work with our lawyer. Fuckin' shark. If Zach ever tries to cause trouble about it, you call me and I'll make him go away."

His arms tightened around me, hinting at his strength, and I shivered.

"This is another case of you doing my dirty work for me, isn't it?" I asked softly.

"It's Noah's money," Ruger said, his face serious. "This isn't about you, Sophie. It's about Zach taking care of his son—and it's not like it even came out of his pocket. That insurance settlement came out of nowhere. Noah has a right to this money, and my mom would shit if she knew Zach was starving you guys out. I fixed the problem. Don't think about it anymore, just use the money to take care of our boy, okay?"

I nodded my head, leaning my head against his chest. He kissed the top of my head and rubbed up and down my back.

"So Horse is an accountant?" I asked after a minute. "I find that hard to picture."

"I'd just as soon you not picture Horse at all," he muttered, and I smiled.

"Thank you," I whispered. I'd never seen that much money in my life. Hell, at this rate we'd have the fancy macaroni and cheese all the time! And the rest? If I saved it, I'd be able to pay for Noah's college.

My kid would go to college. I felt tears well up in my eyes, which bugged me because I hated crying.

"If you really want to thank me, give me a blow job," Ruger said, his voice light. I straightened up and smacked his shoulder, and he burst out laughing.

"Why do you have to say things like that?"

"You were getting all soft and sweet," he said. "And when you get like that I really want to fuck you. But Noah's right outside and this is shit timing. Riling you up takes care of that soft and sweet crap."

"You're impossible," I told him, trying to get up. He held me down, though, and riling me up clearly wasn't making him less interested in sex. The evidence under my ass was getting harder by the second.

"How about this," he said. "One kiss. Give me one kiss and we'll call it even."

"No," I told him. "You're up to something. You can't let me win, can you?"

Ruger grinned at me.

"Yeah, you're right," he said. "I'm up to something. And I'm never going to let you win, so you might as well give up now."

With that his lips came down over mine in another of those kisses that destroyed my ability to think. He explored my mouth softly and I explored right back, wishing like hell that Noah was with a babysitter. Heroin. The man was pure heroin. *Heroin kills people,* my brain screamed. My body flipped off my brain and kept kissing Ruger. Finally he let my lips go and pulled back, smiling and looking smug as hell.

"Like I said, might as well give up, Soph," he said. "Sooner or later I'm gonna win this little game of ours."

I sat up slowly, shaking my head. How did he do that to me? I wanted him so bad I couldn't see straight, and he turned it off, just like that. Noah ran up across the deck and looked at us through the window, pressing his mouth wide open against it and making a blowfish face. Then he started laughing wildly and ran off again.

Okay. That turned it off.

"You want to keep your own place for a while," Ruger said, touching my cheek softly. "I'll try to understand that. It's all happening fast and that's scary. But you're still mine, Soph. Don't think for one minute I've forgotten that or changed my mind."

"You planning to keep your dick in your pants at the club?" I asked bluntly.

"I'm not planning *not* to keep it in my pants," he said slowly. "But I've told you—I'm not a one-woman man. I won't lie to you or make promises I'm not sure I can keep."

"And there we have it," I replied, shaking my head. "Fuck off, Ruger. I'm going home."

RUGER: What time do you get off work?

ME: 5. Why

RUGER: Want to come over and check your place out for security

ME: No

RUGER: You haven't figured this out yet? I'm going to do it. Rather do it when it's convenient for you but happens either way. What time? I'll bring pizza

ME: We get home around 6. Noah likes his pizza plain

RUGER: Plain? Like nothing?????

ME: Plain. Be happy. Used to be he wouldnt let them put sauce on it

RUGER: Plain it is. See you at 6

ME: He's invading my space

KIMBER: ?????

ME: Ruger. He's invadng my space. Coming over tonight to check out security on new place. Bribing us with pizza

KIMBER: Control freak much? What's security

ME: He likes my apartments to have alarms. Checks for bad windows and locks. Deadbolts.That kind of thing

KIMBER: thats sweet tho! He wants u safe

ME: He's the biggest danger

KIMBER: Be happy. U have a hot guy coming over and he's bringing dinner. Women have killed for less

ME: Whose side you on?

KIMBER: Mine. Haven't u figured this out yet?

ME: Bitch

KIMBER: Ho

ME: At least I don't drive a minivan

KIMBER: See if I make YOU margaritas again! LOW BLOW!!!!!!

ME: <3

"You don't have to spend a lot of money to keep a place safe," Ruger told Noah, his voice serious. They crouched together as Ruger installed a new deadbolt on our exterior door. We had two—one leading outside and the other leading into the rest of the barn, which was pretty cool in its own right. Among other things, it had a loft complete with mounds of old hay for Noah to jump in. Even better, there were stairs leading up to it and a railing, safety features I assumed they put in for Elle's cousin.

"If you have empty pop cans, you can make an alarm by stacking them in front of your door," Ruger said. "The goal is to make noise, so that you know if someone tries to come in. Most bad guys will run away if there's noise. That's why I put those little alarms on the windows. If you ever see a bad guy, don't be quiet. Start screaming. And don't yell help—yell 'Call the cops!' as loud as you can, okay?"

"You're going to scare him," I said from the couch, debating whether I should eat the last slice of pizza. Between Ruger and Noah, it'd disappeared pretty fast.

"You scared, Noah?" Ruger asked.

"Nope," Noah said. "Ruger's smart. He's teaching me all kinds of safety stuff. He says you need to stop texting on your phone when you walk places, Mom, and pay attention to the people around you. He also says there's this little stick you need to start carrying around. It's called a cuburtron."

"Kubaton," Ruger corrected, looking over at me. "It's a little baton for your keychain. Very effective, very safe. You should come take the self-defense class at the shop, Sophie."

"I don't need a self-defense class," I said, rolling my eyes. "I have my own personal stalker to protect me already. It's almost Noah's bedtime—you planning to go home at some point?"

"After I finish up," he said. "Bath time, kiddo."

Noah did the obligatory whining and begging to stay up, but his heart wasn't in it. Bath went fast, with Ruger finishing the lock just as Noah got out.

"Will you do my story tonight?" he asked Ruger.

"Sure thing, little man," Ruger said. "What are we reading?"

"Magic Tree House," Noah replied. "I can read it by myself, but I like it when you do it."

I picked up the small living room as Ruger read to Noah. We had a futon for a couch, which was where I slept. Normally I'd start setting it up by now, but I didn't want to give Ruger ideas. After half an hour, he came back out, closing Noah's door behind him softly.

"Kid's out," he said. "Fell asleep halfway through the chapter. I think he's doin' great, but he's been through a lot lately."

"Thanks for your help," I said awkwardly.

"Here're your new keys," he said, tossing them toward me. "I replaced all the locks, so you'll need to give a set to Elle. Her old ones won't work."

"Um, that's great," I said.

"Can I have Noah for a while on Friday afternoon?" he asked. "I'm headin' out on a run this weekend. Might not be back for four or five days."

"Sure," I said. "I need him by seven, though."

"Sounds good," he said. He crossed his arms and leaned against the wall casually. "So how long are we gonna do this?"

"Do what?"

He raised a hand and gestured around the little apartment.

"Have you and Noah live here when you could be over at my house."

"This is nice," I protested. "It's clean, it's safe, and I don't need to worry about the landlord attacking me in the night. It's not happening between us, Ruger. Not. Happening."

He didn't respond, and I watched him warily. He was up to something . . . I could *smell* it. Suddenly he pushed off from the wall and walked over, catching me around the waist. Then he threw me over his shoulder, just like he'd done that weekend.

"No!" I yelled. "You don't get to haul me off whenever you don't get your way!"

He smacked my ass.

"Shut up," he said. "You'll wake up Noah. If he comes out here, he'll see you like this, and then you can figure out how to explain it to him. If he asks me, I'll tell him the truth. Mommy's been a bad girl and she needs a spanking."

"You asshole," I hissed, kicking and smacking his back as hard as I could. Maybe I *should* take one of those kube-thingie classes. I could've shoved it up his big, dumb ass as he carried me out of the apartment and into the barn.

Ruger ignored my struggles, which pissed me off even more.

He carried me through the barn and up the stairs to the hayloft. I sensed a pattern. At least there wasn't a bathroom up here, so no cold water spray. Small comfort. He dropped me down on a pile of straw so hard I lost my breath, looming tall as he unbuckled his belt and ripped it through the loops on his jeans. Then he folded it between his hands and snapped it. I glared at him, scuttling backward across the hay like a crab.

"I need to tie you up again?" he asked.

"We aren't doing this," I declared, even though my brain had already started the familiar shutdown his presence seemed to cause. God, I loved how he smelled. Not to mention the feel of his cock deep down inside . . . those little metal knobs made a hell of a difference. "Go to hell, Ruger."

"Fuck no. We are definitely doing this," he said. "Maybe I can fuck some sense into you. Words obviously don't work."

With that he pulled off his shirt and tossed it aside. I glared at him as he opened his fly and pulled off his jeans without another word. He knelt forward in the hay and caught my hands, pinning them on either side of my head. His head lowered as he scented me, kissing the fading bruises on my neck, nibbling and sucking like he'd done at the party.

Damned distracting. Shit, that felt good.

"They're fading," he said, pulling away just enough to meet my eyes. I didn't like his expression, not at all. "Maybe I'll give you some new ones. What do you think?"

"I think you're a raging asshole."

Ruger laughed.

"Yeah, well I think you're a bitch, but my cock likes you, so we'll figure something out."

He caught my mouth again, but this time the kiss wasn't hard and brutal. Nope, he changed tactics, because now his lips whispered over mine, nipping and sucking, drawing them apart gently as I tried to ignore him. Then he tugged my hands together over my head, freeing a hand to slide down between us. His fingers drifted across my stomach before reaching the top of the yoga pants I'd put on when I got home.

He starting pulling them down, and I realized this was it.

Ruger was about to win again, because Ruger always won, and I always let him because my body wanted him more than my brain hated him. I raised my hips, making it easier for him to take off my pants, which was just another nail in my fucking coffin. Then his fingers slid into me and I shuddered.

The damage was done already anyway, I justified. What difference would it really make? When he finally stopped kissing me, we stared at each other, panting. His fingers stroked down below, grazing my clit, and I twisted, wanting more.

"Jesus, you piss me off," he murmured. "Good thing your cunt's so fucking hot."

"Don't call it that."

His lip twitched.

"Good thing your vagina's so gosh-darned hot," he whispered. "Because I really, really want to stick my penis in it and have repeated sexual intercourse, bringing us to a mutually satisfactory culmination of our desires. How's that sound?"

"Almost dirtier," I said, mouth quirking. Fucking ridiculous. All of it. I wanted to kill him and screw him and scream at him, so now he made jokes? I almost laughed, but his fingers rubbed right up against my G-spot while his thumb played with my clit. I couldn't figure out how he made me so wet, so fast, every single time.

"Oh, it's dirtier," he told me, nuzzling me again, tugging on my ear with his teeth. "If I let go of your hands, are you gonna try to get away?"

I considered the question seriously.

"No," I admitted. "But this is a one-time deal. We're never having sex again after this time."

Ruger gave me that lazy panther smile of his and didn't answer. He did let me go, though, and I reached up, pushing him over and back down into the hay. Then I straddled him. I had one shot at this, I realized. One last chance to play with Ruger's body. What should I do with it?

I went for his nipple ring, sucking it deep into my mouth as he groaned, hands twisting into my hair.

"That's good, Soph," he whispered. "But could you grab my dick while you're at it? All I can think about, it's fuckin' killing me."

I reached down and found him, hard steel bound in silk. I trailed my fingers over the head of his cock, catching the barbell, brushing back and forth.

"Holy fuck," he groaned. "Too much, babe. Just the shaft for now, okay?"

His hand covered mine, showing me exactly how he wanted it—slow and deep, with a bit of a twist that should've been painful. I remembered he liked it rough so I didn't hold back, and soon his hips arched under me.

That's when I gave his nipple a final flick and started working my mouth down his stomach. Ruger wasn't like some guy in a magazine ad. He had a model's perfect abs, but he also had just enough hair to remind me I was dealing with a real man, not some prefabbed fantasy of clean, waxed sexuality. I rubbed my chin against the dip of his navel, savoring the power I held over him before going lower.

Some girls love giving head.

I've never been one of them, so I didn't have a lot of experience to work with. What I did have was a hell of an imagination, and I'd been thinking about taking his cock into my mouth since that first night on his deck. I remembered sitting there, seeing him outlined in front of me through the thin flannel of his lounge pants, wanting to touch him more than anything.

Now I could.

Ruger tilted his head up, one arm folded back and under his neck, watching with hooded eyes as I rubbed the head gently against my cheek, considering my next move. I reached out my tongue and flicked the notch at the bottom of his glans. Then I swirled it around the little metal knob.

Ruger's breath hissed and I felt a surge of pure, feminine power.

I licked it again, playing with his piercing before sucking him in hard. The metal post was weird, but it wasn't like I planned to deep-throat him, so it didn't matter. I started bobbing my head up, working him with my hand at the same time. His fingers burrowed deep into my hair, guiding me.

"You're killing me, Soph," he muttered, groaning. "Stop. I'm gonna come if you don't stop."

I liked that idea. For once it would be nice to see Jesse "Ruger" Gray lose control. But just when I'd decided to make it happen, his fingers tightened in my hair, dragging my mouth away from his cock.

"Ride me," he ordered.

Oh, I could work with that . . .

I climbed over him, reaching down to guide him into my body. Even though I was probably wetter than I'd ever been in my life, taking his full length went slowly. From this angle I felt every inch of him, stretching me so wide it almost hurt. I stopped several times to let myself adjust, his eyes boring into me the whole while. When I finally had all of him I stilled, catching my breath.

Ruger still watched me, his face full of need and intensity and desire. He leaned up on one elbow, the flex of his stomach muscles almost painful against my oversensitized clit. He reached out and caught a strand of my hair, tucking it behind my ear, and then cupped my cheek, his face almost tender.

I closed my eyes.

Angry Ruger? Fine. Horny Ruger? I'd gotten used to that, too. But Ruger as a gentle lover? I didn't have room for that in my head, not if I wanted to survive and move forward with my life. I started rocking back and forth on him, the movement ever-so-slight but almost painfully pleasurable. His hand dropped from my face to my hip, urging me to go faster, so I did.

It didn't take long to bring him back to the edge. At some point I leaned forward on his chest for leverage, digging my nails into his pecs, which seemed to turn him on even more. Ruger liked a touch of pain, I decided, so I did my best to crush him with my inner muscles.

I'm generous that way.

I was close to coming myself when he lost patience, rolling me over and taking control again. He grabbed my legs, shoving them up and over his shoulders. Then he pounded me hard until I screamed out my orgasm.

Ruger followed right behind, and when he came, he called out my name.

I fell asleep with him wrapped around me, both of us on our sides, one of his hands resting lightly against my stomach. He'd gone downstairs and grabbed a blanket, covering the hay and creating a nest for us.

At some point I woke to find Ruger's hand between my legs, slowly stroking me as I drifted. He rolled me to my stomach, spread my legs, and slid into my body gently and carefully. I sighed, the delicious pressure building and exploding with a subtlety I'd never experienced before.

Then he wrapped himself around me again and I drifted back into sleep. I woke up when my cell rang at six the next morning, finding myself alone on my futon, surrounded by his smell. I didn't recognize the name and the caller hung up. Fucking wrong number.

I rolled to my side and saw the empty pizza box, still sitting on the coffee table.

Damn. What the hell was I supposed to do with a situation like this? Insane. All of it.

CHAPTER THIRTEEN

"God, I love dancing," Kimber said, sucking on a cigarette. It was just shy of midnight on Friday, and we stood on the sidewalk outside a club in downtown Spokane. I had a nice buzz going.

"My feet are gonna hurt so bad, but totally worth it," I agreed, swaying a little. I felt my cheeks flush, which was funny, so I started laughing. Kimber shook her head at me.

"I can't take you anywhere," she said gravely. "Lightweight. Where the hell did Em go? I want to check out this guy of hers. I thought the deal was we'd look him over and decide whether he's worth her time. She's cheating."

"No shit. Bitch. I hate her."

"Yeah, me, too," Kimber replied, stabbing the air with her smoke for emphasis. "How am I supposed to live the single life vicariously if I don't get any details?"

I shook my head and shrugged mournfully.

"I'm doing my part. I tell you everything."

"And don't think I don't appreciate it," she said, tearing up slightly. We gave each other a drunken hug.

We'd hit the first bar around ten, and by ten thirty Em had disappeared to meet her online hottie, Liam. She was supposed to bring him inside to meet us, but they snuck off to a bar down the street instead. I would've suspected kidnapping and murder by eleven thirty, when we moved on to the next club, but she'd been sending us regular text messages that made it clear she was enjoying her evening.

Long story short—Liam was gorgeous, we'd get to meet him in a while, she was definitely going to sleep with him, and she was pretty sure he could handle her dad. Apparently Liam was Em's perfect man.

She promised not to leave the other bar without us, so we called it good.

"Hopefully they're in some corner booth making out," I said glumly.

"Not too much," Kimber said darkly. "If she fucks him before I give my approval, she's losing her margarita privileges."

Talking about making out reminded me of Ruger, and thinking of Ruger made me want to drink more. I still couldn't believe I'd fucked him. Again. I couldn't shake the man. Thank God we didn't need to be back in Coeur d'Alene until noon, because I had a lot more alcohol to drink. Kimber's husband was definitely taking one for the team tonight, watching both kids. I needed to bake him cookies or something . . .

"Is it creepy that I want to bake for your husband?" I asked her. She burst out laughing and I started laughing, too, and then my phone buzzed.

EM: I want to go back to the hotel. He's defintely THE ONE

I read it and squeed, handing the phone over to Kimber. She started thumb-typing furiously.

KIMBER: Dont u dare! We have to chck him out frist. Ur NOT follwing the plan

EM: Yu'll meet him in a minut come down to Mick's and we can head from there. We'll wait outside

I yanked my phone back and glared at Kimber.

"That's mine! I get to yell at her first."

"We can't yell at her in front of Internet Hottie!" she told me. "That's a cockblock. We'll yell at her tomorrow."

I considered this.

"Okay," I said. "But I still call dibs on first yelling once we ditch his ass."

She sighed and rolled her eyes.

"Whatever."

We didn't see them outside Mick's. It was a tiny hole-in-the-wall place we almost missed because it was next to a good-sized club with a long line. I texted Em and got no response.

"She's probably just peeing or something," Kimber said, eyeing a group of collegey-looking guys standing in a clump on the sidewalk. They eyed her back and she smiled.

"Hey!" I hissed. "Married, remember?"

She laughed.

"I'm just looking, don't be so uptight. I promise not to touch, okay?"

My phone buzzed.

EM: Heading out

We stood on the sidewalk for another five minutes. Nothing. I started getting a little nervous. I texted again. No reply.

Another ten minutes passed and I'd had enough. This didn't feel right.

"I'm gonna go check on her," I told Kimber. She'd lost interest in the college boys when they'd come over and tried to pick us up. They'd been pretty to look at, but not exactly brilliant conversationalists.

She nodded, concern on her face.

"I'll wait out here," she said, looking up and down the street. "Just in case they show up."

"I don't want you outside by yourself," I replied. She jerked her chin toward the bouncer at the club next door.

"I'll be fine," she said. "Anything happens, I'll scream for him. Go find our girl."

"All right," I said, my voice grim. "But when I find her, we're kicking her ass. This isn't cool."

The place was small and dark—just a tiny, narrow little bar, way rougher than I expected. No wonder the college boys stayed outside. The men in here would crumple them up and throw them away like used . . . um . . . something. Straw wrappers? No, something worse. I shook my head, foggy from the booze. *Focus*. There were more men than women, and most kept their eyes on their drinks. My quickly sinking opinion of Liam went down another notch. What kind of guy took a girl to a place like this?

We shouldn't have let Em out of our sight, I realized.

I didn't find her in the main bar so I wandered to the back, where a long hallway led past some grotty-looking bathrooms and an office. It ended with a fire door that had been propped open with a brick.

I texted Kimber.

ME: Any sign of them?

KIMBER: No this is bllshit

ME: Not in bar. I'll look in the ally then com back

I stepped up to the fire door cautiously. Would Em really go out there with a guy she didn't know? Except she probably felt like she *did* know him. They'd been calling each other for a while now. Hell, I'd gone on dates with guys I'd only met a few times. Still . . . I pushed the door open and peeked outside to find a tall, dark-haired man in faded jeans and motorcycle boots leaning against the side of a battered cargo van.

He smiled at me like a shark and winked.

Oh my God. I recognized him. It was one of the guys from that other club, the Devil's Jacks. The ones who'd come to my apartment in Seattle.

Hunter.

What was he doing here? Holy shit . . . Coincidence?

Or were Hunter and Liam the *same person*?

I opened my mouth to scream when someone shoved me from behind, knocking me out into the alley. I stumbled and nearly fell. Then Hunter's arms caught me, swooping me up and carrying me toward the back of the van. I shrieked as loud as I could—kicking and fighting as he tossed me in—but the pounding music from the club next door almost guaranteed nobody heard me. Em lay on the floor, arms cuffed behind her back, a bandana gagging her mouth. Her legs were tied tight with what looked like white clothesline.

Hunter climbed in after me, wrestling me down and wrenching away my phone. Within seconds my own mouth was gagged and he'd closed another set of cuffs around my wrists. I lay facedown on the floor, eyes wide and staring at Em, who stared right back at me. I felt someone else climb in and heard a door slam, and the engine roared to life.

Hunter spoke, his voice cool and detached.

"Sorry, girls. Hopefully this won't get too ugly and you'll get to go home soon."

The van started moving.

RUGER

His beer had gotten warm.

For once, there wasn't a party at the clubhouse or a barbecue or anything happening, which was a fucking shame because all he could think about was Sophie out dancing in Spokane with her slut of a best friend. He should be focusing on his trip to Portland tomorrow, but he really couldn't bring himself to give a damn.

Jesus, he'd nearly shit his pants when he realized who she was going out with tonight. Kimber's stage name had been Stormie, and the bitch was famous for having a mouth like a vacuum. Even he'd taken her home one night . . . It'd been okay, but not worth breaking his no-repeats rule.

Now he wondered if she'd been filling Sophie's head with stories about him all along. Also explained why she'd been interested in working at The Line—Kimber had made a goddamned fortune there, one of their most popular dancers.

She'd been an even bigger hit in the VIP rooms.

He'd considered simply physically stopping Sophie from going, but figured that would do him more harm than good in the long run. She'd been dodging him since their night in the hayloft and he'd let it go. The first week of a new job was stressful, so he'd given her a break. This ladies' night thing had caught him off guard. He'd only found out because Noah had a big mouth.

Kid was full of all kinds of useful information.

Picnic walked into the main lounge with a girl trailing him. She looked about sixteen, although Ruger knew she had to be older. No jailbait in the Armory—that was trouble they sure as fuck didn't need. Pic wore the look of man who'd gotten well laid, and he sent her on her way with a smack on the ass. Then he walked over to Ruger.

"What's with you?" he asked, dropping into one of the mismatched chairs across from the couch.

"I'm bored," Ruger said, rubbing the back of his neck. "And apparently I'm getting old, because my neck hurts from sitting at my bench today, taking care of that special order."

"You're fuckin' pathetic," Pic said.

"That's the truth."

"I hear your girl moved out."

"Yeah, we can talk about something else now."

Picnic laughed shortly.

"First Horse and now you," he said. "Whole damned place is turnin' up pussy-whipped."

"Fuck off, asshole," Ruger replied. "The only reason I'm sitting here right now instead of fuckin' her face is I'm not willing to hand her my cock on a leash. And you should talk. Screwing kids younger than your daughter? Creeps me out, thinkin' of your old ass doing a chick like that."

"At least I got laid tonight," Pic answered mildly. "Unlike some."

His phone rang. He pulled it out and looked at the ID.

"It's Em," he said shortly, standing and ambling across the room. Then Pic froze, his body language screaming tension. Thirty seconds later, Ruger's phone rang.

Sophie.

"You better not be—" he started, but she cut him off.

"Shut up and listen," she said, her voice tight. Ruger sat up. "Those guys you met in Seattle? The Devil's Jacks? They've got me and Em. We're in Spokane and they—"

He heard her scream as someone grabbed the phone. Adrenaline slammed through him, taking him from relaxed to ready for action in a heartbeat. Instead of acting on it, he forced himself to stay calm and listen with everything he had. They'd need every clue they could to find Sophie . . . and Em? What the fuck? Jesus, Em should know better than to go out without giving Pic a heads-up. How had Em gotten mixed up in this?

"Ruger," a man said. "This is Skid. From Seattle. We got a bit of a problem."

"You're dead," Ruger replied, his voice flat, and he meant it. Out of the corner of his eye, he saw Picnic grab a bar stool and smash it against the wall. Horse was on his feet, pushing a trio of girls out the door as Painter grabbed a sawed-off shotgun from behind the bar.

Slide wandered in from the bathroom and glanced around, brows rising.

"Yeah, we'll talk about my death later," Skid said, sounding bored. "Listen up. Your boy in Portland—Toke—he went apeshit on two of our brothers a coupla hours ago. Just broke into the damned house and started shooting. There's cops everywhere, a couple of bitches who saw it all go down, total clusterfuck. Girls are talkin' to the cops, too, just to make things perfect. Docs are working on one guy right now, no idea if he'll make it. Toke dragged the other off."

"You're full of shit," Ruger said. Toke might be a wild card but he wouldn't ignore a vote by the full club.

"Process later," Skid snapped. "It's time for you to get your boy under control and our man back to us. Safe. Until then, we'll take good care of—what's her name again? Sophie? We'll take good care of sweet little Sophie for you. She'll be just fine once we clear this up. Our boy goes down? Her prospects don't look so good. Got a real nice ass. Might tap it before I shoot her. Got me?"

He hung up.

"Fuck," Ruger muttered, kicking over the coffee table as he stood up. Pic yelled as Horse and Bam Bam held him back. Ruger ignored the drama, striding down the hall, past the office, and into the large workshop where he did his special projects. He flipped open his laptop and pulled up the tracker, narrowing his search.

There they were—Sophie's and Em's phones were near the river, downtown Spokane. They'd be in the water soon. By the time he could get there, the Jacks would be in the wind, along with their girls.

Goddamnit. Ruger turned and punched the wall, smashing through the sheetrock. Sharp pain hit, helping him focus. He pulled an unregistered .38 semi-automatic out of his bench drawer and shoved it into his ankle holster, then grabbed extra clips. Then he turned and went back down the hall to find Picnic and the others arguing over what they should do. Pic wanted to ride now—Horse, Bam Bam, and Duck all wanted to take the time to make a plan, which Ruger knew needed to happen. Couldn't do shit in Spokane until they had more info.

Toke had lost the vote but he'd won the battle.

The Reapers and the Devil's Jacks were going to war.

SOPHIE

I don't know how long we rode in the back of the van. It felt like forever. Then I heard the sound of a garage door opening. We pulled in and it shut behind us. Hunter and the driver stepped out of the van, coming around to open the back doors.

Hard hands—not Hunter's—grabbed my ankles, pulling me out roughly. My cheek scraped, and if the kidnapping hadn't fully sobered me, the pain finished the trick. He half carried, half dragged me into the house. Then he dropped me down on the couch and I struggled to sit up. Hunter set Em down next to me, far more gently. He stepped back and joined his friend. Guy number two was Skid—the other Devil's Jack I'd met in Seattle. They stood over us, faces grim, and I knew we were well and truly fucked.

My stomach twisted and I thought about Noah. Would I ever see him again?

"Here's the situation," Hunter said, his cold gray eyes flicking back and forth between us. Could he actually be Em's Internet guy?

She hadn't been lying. He really was hot—even better-looking than I remembered.

Too bad he was a goddamned sociopath.

Or maybe he'd done something to Liam. For all I knew, Em's online boyfriend was lying dead in the alley. Shit.

"You're here as leverage. One of the Reapers down in Portland—Toke—made a real bad call tonight. He went to our house and started shooting, no warning, no provocation. He took a hostage when he left. One of our brothers is down and a second is probably getting tortured to death right now, so you'll have to excuse us for being a little abrupt about this whole thing. Your daddy," he nodded toward Em, "is gonna do what it takes to get our guy back for us. That happens, you go home."

She glared at him, eyes full of betrayal. He leaned forward and pulled off her gag, whispering something in her ear. Em jerked away from him.

"You're dead, Liam," she said, her voice utterly serious. So that was one mystery solved . . . Poor Em. My heart hurt for her.

"My dad is going to kill you," she continued. "Let us go now and I'll try to talk him out of it. Otherwise it'll be too late. I'm serious. He. Will. Kill. You."

Hunter shook his head.

"Sorry, babe," he replied. "I get that you're scared and pissed, but I'm not going to let a brother die just because some Reaper had a tantrum."

"Fuck you."

He glanced at Skid, who shrugged. Hunter sighed, rubbing a hand over his face, looking tired.

"Okay, let's go upstairs," he said. He glanced at me. "We'll take your gag off, but either of you starts screaming we'll just have to put them back on. We're in the middle of nowhere, so it's not like you're gonna get anywhere if you do. You two control how ugly this gets. Got me?"

With that, he pulled out a Leatherman multi-tool and cut the rope on Em's feet. Then he started on mine. I heard a clicking noise and looked up to find Skid pointing a small, square pistol at us.

"You cause trouble, I'll shoot you," he said. "Hunter's nice. I'm not."

I swallowed.

Hunter pulled me to my feet and I rocked nervously, trying to get circulation back. It was hard to balance with my hands cuffed behind my back. He helped Em up and then they marched us up the flight of stairs off to one side of the living room.

The house's second story was pretty typical, with a small landing at the top. Looked like there were three bedrooms, along with the bathroom, reminding me that I needed to pee in a big way. Hunter took Em's arm and pulled her into a room on the right, kicking the door shut behind them.

"Over there," Skid said, pointing to the door next to it. I walked in to find a queen-sized bed with a very plain wrought-iron frame, a battered dresser, and an old desk. There was a small window, which looked like it'd been painted shut. I wondered how hard it would be to get it open. If I did, could I manage a drop back down to the ground?

"Stand next to the bed, facing away from me," Skid said.

Oh, shit . . . The bed took on a whole new meaning. I did what he said, my body bracing for the worst. Was Skid about to rape me? Would Hunter rape Em? He'd obviously been cultivating some sort of relationship with her. Was it all about the club, or was there something more?

Em was a very pretty girl. A girl who deserved better.

I trembled as Skid came up behind me, feeling the heat of his body and hoping to hell I wasn't his type. I felt his hands touch mine, then he popped open one of the cuffs.

"Lie down," he said, his voice unreadable. Should I fight him, or just close my eyes and take it? I wanted to live a lot more than I wanted to fight. I'd let him do it and just hope it ended fast.

I laid down on my back, focusing on the ceiling, blinking rapidly.

"Put your hands up over your head."

I raised my arms as he leaned over me. He paused, looking me over, and I saw his eyes catch on the swell of my breasts. I bit the side of my cheek, trying not to break down and start begging. I didn't want to give him that power over me. He reached down, catching my hands, and I felt a tug on the cuffs as he threaded the chain through the wrought iron. Then he snapped the second cuff back on me.

Skid stood back up and walked over to the window, looking outside, crossing his arms. My breath caught. Was that it? Was I safe for now? He glanced back toward me, thoughtful.

"The guy Toke took is my brother," he said. "Not just my club brother—my half brother. Only family I have. Believe me when I tell you I'll do anything to get him back. Don't think being a woman protects you. *Nothing* will protect you. Got me?"

I nodded.

"Good girl," he said. "Keep it up and maybe you'll live."

He turned and walked out.

I lay there forever, needing to pee so bad it hurt. I supposed I should've asked Skid to take me to the bathroom before he locked me down. Sooner or later I'd wet the bed. I didn't care. I'd rather piss myself than call for Skid to come back and help me. Then I heard a scream and the sound of something shattering against the wall my room shared with Em's.

I forgot all about my bathroom situation.

"You cocksucking bastard!" Em shrieked. I held my breath as I heard another thump. Oh, God. Was she fighting with him? Was he raping her? Her voice was full of pain and I felt sick to my stomach, because whatever was going on over there wasn't good. The noise died down. I lay in the dark, counting the seconds. How had something this crazy happened to someone as normal and boring as me?

Goddamn Reapers.

Ruger's stupid fucking club. First Em got stabbed and now we'd been kidnapped. It was like some horrible virus, creeping in and destroying everything it touched without warning.

If I got out of this alive, I was never touching Ruger again.

I couldn't be with a Reaper, no matter how much I wanted him. I couldn't allow *this* to be a part of my life. It couldn't be part of Noah's life, either. If Ruger wanted to see my son, he'd damned well leave the club out of it.

As for me? I was done with him. Well and truly done. I knew it in my gut and in my bones—any man whose reality included women getting kidnapped wasn't good enough for me. He wasn't right, no matter how he made me feel.

Period.

I closed my eyes tight as Em screamed again.

I woke with a start as the bed dipped.

Where was I?

I heard Em's voice and it all came back.

"You okay?" she asked. I opened my eyes to find her sitting next to me. I studied her, looking for signs of abuse or crying.

She didn't look like a rape victim, though. She looked pissed as hell. If anything, she was prettier than usual, her cheeks full of color and her hair wild and free. Early morning light filtered in through the window. Hunter stood in the door, eyeing both of us, face unreadable. I couldn't believe I'd actually fallen asleep.

"I need the bathroom," I said, my voice hoarse. God, I felt hungover.

"Can she go to the fucking bathroom?" Em asked Hunter, her voice cold.

"Yeah," he said, walking toward me. She stood and moved out of his way, putting as much distance between them as possible. I tried not to flinch as he unlocked me, rolling away as quickly as I could despite my aching muscles.

"C'mon," Hunter said. "Both of you."

Em took my hand and we walked out of the room together, her fingers squeezing mine. I wanted to ask if she was all right, find out what had happened. No way I was going to talk in front of him, though.

We turned into the small bathroom, which didn't have a window. Em shut the door behind us, pausing long enough in the doorway to glare at Hunter in some kind of silent battle. Then the door shut.

I rushed over to the toilet, incredibly relieved.

"Oh my God," I whispered, looking over at her. She ran her hands through her hair, then crossed her arms and rubbed up and down. "How are you? Did he hurt you?"

"My pride? Definitely," she said, eyes snapping. "Not physically. I can't believe this. Seriously—I can't believe how stupid I was. I actually invited him to come and meet me. I made it so easy. *Idiot.*"

I didn't reply, washing my hands as we swapped places, then cupping them to take a drink. My mouth was all cottony.

"Do you have any idea what's going to happen to us?" I asked. "Skid scares the crap out of me."

"Did he hurt you?" she asked, her voice sharp.

"No."

"That's good. This is a pretty fucked-up situation," she said. "Toke—he's the one who cut me at the party—he's gone off his rocker. This shooting thing makes no sense to me at all, but if it really happened, we're screwed. Nobody knows where Toke is, not even Deke, and he's Toke's president. They've all been looking for him since the party. Cutting me was *not* okay, and Dad wants to make sure he pays for it."

"Shit," I muttered. "So your dad couldn't give them this Toke guy, even if he wanted to?"

"I don't think so," she said slowly. "I mean, he's really protective of me. When Toke hurt me like that, Dad lost it. If Dad could find him, he'd be found already. We're pretty fucked here, Sophie."

"Do you think they'll hurt us?"

She considered the question.

"Liam won't," she replied. "I mean, he won't hurt me. I don't think he'll hurt you, either."

I cocked my head at her.

"You do realize he was lying to you all along, right? Just because you liked him doesn't mean you can trust him, Em."

"Oh, I know that," she said quickly, then shook her head ruefully. "Believe me, I'm well aware that I'm the fuckwit who got us into this."

"You're not a fuckwit," I said forcefully. "He's a liar and he's good at it. Not your fault that he targeted you."

It was the Reapers' fault, but I figured rubbing it in wouldn't be particularly helpful.

"Doesn't matter," she said. "But I'm serious—I really don't think he'll hurt me. I'm more worried about Skid."

"It's his brother they've got," I told her. "His real brother. I think he *wanted* to hurt me."

"You guys okay in there?" Hunter called through the door.

"We're fine," Em snapped, startling me. "Give us a fucking minute, asshole!"

My eyes went wide.

"That was pretty bitchy," I hissed. "Do you think that's smart? Maybe I'm reading the situation wrong here, but don't we want him in a good mood?"

She snorted sarcastically.

"Fuck that," she replied. "I'm a Reaper and I'll be damned if I'll suck up to some Devil's Jack dickwad."

"Well I'm *not* a Reaper," I said quietly. "And I'd just as soon not die here and leave Noah an orphan, so don't piss him off."

She looked chastened.

"Sorry. I guess I have my dad's temper."

"Too bad you don't have your dad's gun."

"No shit, right? And I'm the good girl in the family. You should see my sister."

"You have one minute," Hunter called through the door. "Then I'm coming in."

Em washed her hands and we left the bathroom. I avoided making eye contact with Hunter, who stood back and jerked his head toward "my" bedroom.

"Go in and lie down on the bed," he said. "Both of you."

We did what he said—although I could see it killed Em to obey—and two minutes later he had us both cuffed to the bedstead. Thankfully, he only did one wrist each, which was way more comfortable than Skid's method.

"I'll bring you some food," Hunter said, tracing a finger across Em's cheek.

She glared at him. "I'm gonna buy a bright red dress to wear to your funeral, *Liam*."

"Yeah?" he replied, eyes narrowing. "Make sure it's short and shows off your tits."

"I hate you," she hissed.

"Keep tellin' yourself that."

He walked out, slamming the door behind him. I bit my tongue, wondering what the hell *that* was all about.

"Don't worry," Em said after an awkward pause. "We'll find our way out of this. We'll escape somehow. Either that or the guys will find us."

"Do you have any ideas?" I asked, wondering what the hell was going on between them. "Did he tell you anything, give you any hints or clues about where we are?"

"No."

I waited for her to say more. She didn't, and that worried me even more.

"So what *did* you do all night?" I asked slowly. Em ignored the question.

"I wonder if one of them will leave at some point," she murmured. "If we wait until there's just one in the house, I'll bet the two of us could take him. Or even if we distracted him, at least one of us could get away. Go for help."

"Do you think we're really out in the middle of nowhere?" I asked. "Have you seen outside?"

"Haven't seen outside, but we barely drove long enough to get out of the city," she said. "There may not be any houses next door, but there has to be something within walking distance. We just need to find a way out of these handcuffs. If we can find a paperclip or a pin or something, I can pick the lock."

"Really?" I asked, impressed. "Where did you learn that?"

"You'd be surprised at all the things I know," she said, her voice dry. "Dad believes in being prepared."

The door opened and Hunter came in balancing two paper plates. He had a couple bottles of water clutched under his arm and I suddenly realized how hungry and thirsty I was. My stomach growled. He set everything on top of the little dresser in the corner. Then he walked over and unlocked the handcuffs.

"You've got ten minutes," he said.

We got up and grabbed the food. It was just plain peanut butter and jelly sandwiches, along with some chips, but it tasted as good as any meal I've ever had.

"In a minute, we're going to call your dad," Hunter said to Em. "Let him know you're alive, and find out if he's made any progress."

Em glared at him darkly, chewing her food. He sighed, grabbing the chair from the desk and pulling it out.

"You want to sit?" he asked. She shook her head. Hunter spun the chair around and straddled it himself, his face blank. His eyes never strayed from Em's face. Once we finished eating, he nodded toward the bed.

"Lie down again," he said. We did. Hunter started with me, locking down my right wrist. Then he walked around the bed to do the same to Em's left. As he leaned over her, I saw her free hand snake quickly around to his back jeans pocket, lifting something. In an instant she tucked it under her body.

Hunter froze.

Shit, did he feel that?

We needed a distraction. Now. I bit down on my tongue viciously, then shrieked and started spitting blood at him as hard as I could.

"Jesus Christ!" he yelled, jumping away from the bed like it was on fire. Em dove right in.

"Oh my God, are you all right?" she yelled. "Hunter, you need to get her to a doctor!"

I stopped spitting, choking on the blood. Ughh . . .

"I'm tho thorry," I mumbled, trying to look embarrassed and shocked. "I bith my tongue and ith thcared me."

Hunter looked at the gobs of blood and spit on his arm with disgust, then glared at me.

"You're fucking kidding me," he said. "What the fuck's wrong with you? Shit, you got any diseases?"

"No, I don't hath any ditheatheth," I snapped. Or rather, I tried to snap, which backfired on me because my tongue was swelling so rapidly that I bit it again. "Owth!"

Hunter shook his head, and Em looked at me with wide, concerned eyes. Behind them, I saw laughter dancing.

"Drive me fuckin' crazy," Hunter muttered. "I'll get you a piece of ice to suck on. Jesus, that's fucking disgusting."

He left the room, slamming the door, and Em almost lost it.

"That was brilliant," she whispered. "Seriously brilliant. I got his Leatherman. I should be able to get us out of the cuffs with it."

"We're thucky he didn'th do both handth. Thkid did."

"Oh, that sucks," she said, wrinkling her nose at me. "Let me guess, did you have an itch on your ass or something all night?"

"No, thank fukth," I replied. Shit, my tongue *really* hurt. "When will you thry to pick the lockth?"

"When I think he'll be gone for a while," she said. She grabbed the Leatherman, then rolled over and crawled up the bed on her elbows, reaching down between the iron bars to tuck it in somewhere.

"It's between the mattress and the box spring," she said. "In case you need it."

I frowned—if I needed it, she'd be gone, and the implications of that weren't good.

Hunter returned, holding a paper napkin. I sat up awkwardly as he handed it to me, scooting back against the headboard. It held an ice cube, which I popped into my mouth as Em joined me.

My throbbing tongue started feeling better immediately, thank God.

"We're going to call your dad again," Hunter told Em. "I'll let you talk to him for a minute, then I'll see where the situation's headed."

"What about Sophie?" she asked. "Ruger will want to talk to her."

"Ruger can fuck himself," Hunter replied. Em glanced at me, and I realized she wanted more distraction. I wasn't sure why, but I'd follow her lead. I spat out the bloody ice into my hand awkwardly.

"Pleathe?" I whined, drooling. "My boy—Noah—he'th got a prethcription he needth, Ruger doethn't know where it ith. Let me talk to him for two minuteth. Pleathe."

He looked at me and narrowed his eyes.

"You're full of shit."

"You want a seven-year-old kid to die?" Em said, her voice cold. "Not enough to kill two women, now you're gonna take out a little boy, too? You're a hell of a man, *Liam*."

Hunter sighed.

"Do you ever shut up?" he asked. He pulled a cell out of his pocket, one of those cheap little flip phones you buy at grocery stores, watching us as he dialed. He put it on speaker.

"Yeah?" Ruger said, his voice full of restrained tension. Hunter nodded at me.

"It's Thophie," I said quickly. "I'm here with Hunter and Em, they're lithening."

Hunter's eyes narrowed and he snapped the phone shut.

"No fucking games," he said. "You're done."

I nodded and stuck the ice back into my mouth. At least Ruger knew I was still alive . . . I'd decided I was done with him last night, but he'd gotten me into this mess, so he could damned well get me back out before I cut him off for good.

"Calling your dad now," Hunter said to Em, dialing again. "Be a good girl, Emmy Lou—or did you need another lesson?"

Em flushed, looking away. My eyebrows rose. We heard the phone ringing through the speaker, and then it picked up.

"Picnic," Em's dad said, his voice cold.

"Hey, Daddy," Em said. "We're okay for now."

"What the fuck's wrong with Sophie?" Picnic asked. "Ruger says she wasn't talking right."

"She bit her tongue," Em said quickly. "Don't worry, she's fine. But you need to get us out of here."

"We know, baby," he replied, and his voice softened ever so slightly. "We're working on it."

"That's enough, girls," Hunter said, pulling away the phone. He clicked off the speaker and put it to his ear as he walked out of the room.

Em scooted closer to me, lifting her free arm to wrap it around my neck. I leaned against her, taking comfort from the fact that at least we weren't alone. The swelling in my tongue had gone down, too, which was a relief.

"We need to get ourselves out of this," she told me. "Like I said—Toke's AWOL. After he cut me, there's nothing he could have done to make things right with dad. If they could find Toke, they would've by now."

"How should we do it?" I muttered around the last of the ice.

"We should wait until there's just one guy here," she said. "Sooner or later, they'll have to go get groceries or something. That's when we'll move. I've thought about it a lot, and I think attacking is too dangerous, unless you've got some sort of secret ninja skills I don't know about. Great job with the whole spitting blood thing, by the way. I'm impressed."

"We all have to do our part," I said, feeling pleased with myself. "You're not half bad as a pickpocket."

"Had to pay for college somehow," she replied piously. "I don't believe in student loans."

"You're a nutjob."

"Probably," she said, mustering a grin. "But everything I have, I own free and clear."

"Yeah, me, too," I said. "Couldn't get a credit card to save my life. Apparently unemployed single moms are a bad risk."

"Speaking of, I have Hunter's now," she said, grinning. "I lifted his wallet while you were talking on the phone with Ruger. No idea if it'll be useful, but it's better than nothing."

I sobered.

"Okay, first thing—you need to stop picking his pocket," I told her. "He's gonna figure it out. He almost did when you got the knife."

"Yeah, you're probably right about that one," she said, sighing. "So here's my thought. I want to split up. More chance that one of us will get away and bring help. We wait until one of the guys leaves, then I'll go out the front of the house and you'll go out the back. Whoever's left can't chase us both. Hell, maybe we'll get lucky and he won't even notice us leaving."

"What if Hunter and Skid aren't the only guys here?"

"Well, then I guess they'll probably catch us again," she said seriously. "It's a risk, because they'll punish us. This isn't a game. But we can't just sit here and hope this all works out—realistically, it's not gonna be easy for the club to find us."

"I thought you said Hunter wouldn't hurt you?" I asked.

"I don't think he will," she said. "But Skid's different. Dad will find us sooner or later, but I'd just as soon we're alive when it happens. I don't want to get dumped in a ditch somewhere just because Toke's an idiot."

My breath caught.

"I don't want to get dumped in a ditch, either."

"So we just won't get caught," she told me, offering a grin. "Should be easy, right?"

"Did I mention you're a nutjob?"

"I get it from my dad."

CHAPTER FOURTEEN

RUGER

"I wish I had more to tell you," Kimber said. She looked like a raccoon, her eyes completely surrounded by tear-streaked, black makeup. She sat at a table in the Armory, obviously exhausted from her long night. Ruger still couldn't quite believe he'd actually fucked this woman. On purpose.

Sure, she had a great body, but compared to Sophie she was nothing. Not even on his dick's radar.

"You did the best you could," Horse said. It'd taken them a while to find Kimber because she'd gone on a rampage looking for Sophie and Em. When they'd finally caught up to her, she'd been holding four men hostage in the corner of Mick's bar with a canister of pepper spray in one hand and her phone in the other. She'd been filming them, demanding that they tell her everything they knew "for the record."

Thank fuck she didn't have a gun with her.

"I tried," she said. "I never should've let her go in by herself. The whole thing was a terrible idea. You'll never know how sorry I am. I hope you can believe that."

Picnic grunted, obviously unimpressed, but he managed to keep his mouth shut.

"It's good you weren't with her," Bam Bam said, his voice soothing. "If you were, we'd have three hostages instead of two. Not only that, you're not one of us, so they might consider you dead weight. This is better."

"You gonna be okay watching Noah until we get this fixed?" Ruger asked abruptly.

"Yes," she said, looking up and meeting his gaze. "I'll take care of him like he's my own. You don't need to worry about that."

"Okay," he told her. "I'll come over and see him if I can. I'm not going to let myself get distracted from finding Sophie, though. You need a gun?"

"Oh, I've got a gun," she replied, her voice dark.

"I'll walk you out," Painter said, his expression cold. Something in him had changed, Ruger realized. He'd always been a good man, but he wore a new sense of purpose this morning. Maybe this would motivate him to pull his shit together. He'd always assumed Painter and Em would end up together. Clearly she'd gotten tired of waiting. Fucking Internet dating . . . might as well paint a bright red target on her head.

Ruger was seeing things pretty clearly this morning himself. He needed Sophie back, safe and sound. Needed her more than his own life. He didn't give a flying fuck about any other woman. If he'd pulled his head out of his ass earlier, this wouldn't have happened, because she'd have been safe at home with him, in his bed.

Once he got her back, he'd never let her go again.

Never.

She wanted commitment? He'd tattoo her fucking name on his forehead if he had to. Whatever it took to keep her safe.

"Any news from the boys in Portland?" Duck asked.

"Not so far," Picnic replied. "They think Toke might have the Jack—goes by Clutch—out to the coast. They're looking for him, but don't exactly have a lot of leads."

"How's the one he shot?"

"Critical but stable, whatever the fuck that means," Pic said. "Guess that's something to be thankful for. Okay, let's get going on this. We got two hours before our meet with Hunter. Thoughts?"

"Let me handle this one," Duck said, crossing his arms. "You're too involved, and that means your brain won't be working. You and Ruger should stay here."

"No fuckin' way," Picnic said, shaking his head. "I'm the president. This is my job."

"You're a father and you're running on fumes," Duck replied. "You do this and fuck it up, your girl dies. You really believe you can look this fuckwad in the eye and play nice? 'Cause I don't think you can. Be smart and let me handle it. You don't want me, have Horse do it, or Bam Bam. We're your brothers for a reason. We've got your back."

Picnic shook his head again, face tense. He'd started methodically loading spare magazines for his new gun, which he'd been test-firing earlier. Ruger knew he planned to kill Hunter with that same gun, because they'd spent close to an hour together, carefully choosing just the right weapon to do it.

Something untraceable, with a small enough caliber to do slow, steady damage for a long, long time without ending the bastard's life too quickly.

"Ruger, you need to stay back, too," Horse said. Ruger glanced up at him and shook his head.

"Nope," he said. "I'm going. Nonnegotiable. I don't need to be lead, but I'll be there."

Horse and Duck exchanged looks.

"Okay, new plan," Duck said. "I'll be lead, you guys come along but keep back. We can't let him fuck with you—he gets you worked up, you do something stupid, he wins. Got me?"

"Got it," Pic said. "Just so long as you remember—in the end, he's mine."

"Ours," Ruger corrected. "Him and his friend."

"And Toke?" Bam Bam asked. "Thoughts on him?"

"Let him answer to the brothers," Ruger said. "We voted, we made a decision for the club. He ignored that. Fucker needs to pay."

SOPHIE

"He's going to go meet with Dad," Em said, finally speaking.

Earlier Hunter had come and taken her away, only returning her about ten minutes ago. She'd been gone with him for what felt like an eternity. Realistically, it probably hadn't been more than an hour. When she'd first come back she'd kept pretty quiet. Now she lay with me on the bed again, me cuffed by my right wrist and Em cuffed by her left.

"Why?" I asked.

"I think he's trying to save the situation," she said, her voice sounding a little mournful. "I think he actually cares about me, Soph."

I widened my eyes.

"You can't be serious," I said. "He wants to screw you—I get that, he's a guy and you're hot. But a man who cares about a woman doesn't kidnap her."

"Ask Marie about that," she said, sounding uncomfortable. "Horse totally kidnapped her. Now they're getting married."

That shut me up for a minute.

"Do I want to know the whole story?" I asked finally.

"It's not going to make you feel any better."

Motorcycle pipes roared outside the house and we heard the sound of someone riding away.

"That's Hunter leaving," she said. "If I get away and Dad finds out I'm safe, he'll kill him for sure."

"Don't," I said, looking over at her. She seemed downcast, thoughtful. Shit, we couldn't afford this. "Don't you dare have second thoughts. This guy is dangerous and we're going to get seriously hurt if we stay here. We're going to escape. In fact, we're going to escape soon."

"I know," she said. "I just wish—"

"I don't want to hear it."

We gave it an hour, or at least we thought it was about an hour. We wanted to be sure Hunter was far away before we tried our escape. Em opened the knife and popped out a tiny, thin flat-head screwdriver. Five minutes later we were out of the cuffs and taking turns peeking out the window. Hunter hadn't lied. We appeared to be in the middle of nowhere, surrounded by scruffy shrubs, open ground, and the occasional pine tree.

Only the van sat outside, no more bikes, which hopefully meant we'd only be dealing with Skid. Even so, there wasn't a lot of ground cover.

"If he chases us we don't have a chance," I said, my voice grim.

"He won't chase us," she replied. "Here's what we'll do. We're going to sneak downstairs. We'll figure out where he is, then you go out one side of the house and I'll go out the other. I can see a back door from here."

"And if he sees us?"

"Whoever he sees has to slow him down long enough for the other one to get away and find help," she told me. "No matter what it takes. And I'm going to be the one going closest to him."

"Why?" I asked, startled. "Not that I want any extra risk, but—"

"Because you have a kid," she said. "All other issues aside, Noah needs you and nobody needs me."

"Your family, the whole club, they all need you," I protested.

"You know I'm right," she said. "Don't even try to be noble here or something. If only one of us gets out, it's you. Let's not fight about it, okay?"

I took a deep breath and then nodded because she was right. Noah was more important than the rest of us put together.

"Okay, but promise me something," I said. "You need to seriously try to get away. Don't let yourself get caught or something just because you want to keep Hunter safe."

She looked back outside, and for a moment I thought she might argue. How much had Hunter fucked with her head, anyway?

"I'm serious. I'll start screaming right now and let him know we've got that knife if you don't promise me you'll do your best to get away."

"I'll do my best," she said. "If we get free, we could always give him time to get back before calling Dad, you know. It's not like it's all or nothing. I'm not stupid."

I kept my mouth shut. If I got away and found a phone, Hunter was toast.

"I suppose there's no time like the present, hmm?" I asked.

"Might as well go now," she said. "I'll keep the knife, unless you know how to use it?"

"You mean to fight?" I asked, startled. She nodded. "Um, no. I didn't take knife-fighting class in school. You can keep it."

"Okay, let's do this thing," Em said, using a very fine Arnold Schwarzenegger voice. Unfortunately, it was going to take more than a silly voice to make me feel badass. We bumped fists, opened the bedroom door, and started creeping across the floor. I was terrified we'd make it squeak, but fortunately it seemed solid enough.

She eased the bedroom door open, and from downstairs I heard the sound of a game playing on the TV.

"I'll go down the stairs first," Em whispered. "Then I'll wave you on. Be ready to go whatever direction I point you, based on where I see him. If I point back at the bedroom, go up and get yourself back into your handcuff, okay? If I wave you on, that's it. We'll only get one shot, so don't fuck it up. I'm counting on you to send help for me if I have to distract him."

"I can do it," I told her, hoping it was the truth. "Let's both get out, though, okay?"

"Oh, one more thing, and this is important," she said.

"What?"

"If you find a phone, call my dad or Ruger," she said. "Don't call the cops."

I stared at her.

"Are you fucking kidding me?"

"No," she said, her voice serious. "I'm not kidding at all. This is club business—if we get the cops involved, things will get much worse, and it'll happen fast, too."

"No," I said flatly. "If I get out of here I'm calling nine one one as fast as I can."

"Then we're not going," she replied. My eyes widened.

"Are you serious?"

"Absolutely," she replied. "You call the cops, Dad or Ruger might wind up in jail before this ends."

"How do you figure?"

"You think I was joking when I said Dad would kill Hunter?" she asked slowly. "This isn't a game. I'll try to convince him not to. I'll hope to hell it doesn't happen. But Hunter going to jail for this won't protect him, and if Dad takes him out, I don't want to lose him, too."

"Jesus," I muttered, shocked. "I don't know what to say."

"Say you won't call the cops," she replied. "If you're in the position to make a call, you'll already be safe. I have the right to make the decision for myself, though."

I thought about it for a second.

"Okay," I whispered. I didn't like it, but I'd do it.

She nodded, then started down the stairs very slowly. This would be the hardest part, because we needed to pass through the living room to go anywhere else in the house. He was probably in there, because that's where the TV was. I pictured the layout in my head—he'd be facing away, and I didn't remember seeing any mirrors on the walls.

Just a little luck and we'd pull it off.

Em looked up at me, lifted a finger to her mouth and then waved me down. I crept from step to step, trying to stay completely silent, while still moving fast enough so that we wouldn't lose our opportunity. Skid came into view as I reached the bottom of the stairwell. He sat on the couch, back to us, playing some sort of game that involved shooting at things.

Luckily, it also seemed to involve a lot of loud noises and blowing things up.

Em touched my hand and I looked at her. She pointed at her chest, then toward the front door. Then she pointed at me and toward the back of the house. She held up three fingers, then counted down with them, two, one—go.

I slipped past her, walking quickly but silently toward the back of the house. Within seconds I passed out of the living room, through a dining room, and into a kitchen. I found the back door. It was locked, of course, but all I had to do was open the deadbolt. No special security or anything.

They really *hadn't* been planning to kidnap us, I realized. Even I knew that when you plan a kidnapping, you prep a place for your prisoners.

So far so good.

I eased the back door open, and then Skid shouted behind me. I heard Em shriek at him and then a loud, crashing noise. I took off out the door, running as fast as I could in a wide circle around the house.

There was a long gravel driveway, and since we'd already been discovered, I followed it, listening for vehicles or gunfire. I didn't hear anything other than that first loud outburst. My heart pounded and my brain shut down—would Skid really kill Em? I ran hard, adrenaline powering my legs.

Then I heard a gunshot.

Fuck.

RUGER

Hunter had set up the meet in Spirit Lake, but Ruger got a text halfway there sending them to Rathdrum instead. The Devil's Jack waited for them in a bar that clearly stated "No Colors" outside the door, forcing them to take off their cuts before going inside.

Dick. Balls of brass, though.

They walked in to find him sitting in the back, nursing a beer. Picnic started forward, but Bam Bam caught his arm, pulling him back.

"Don't," he said, his voice low. Picnic nodded tightly as Duck took lead instead.

"Your girls are doing just fine," Hunter said as the men sat down, and Ruger realized he wasn't nearly as relaxed as he pretended. His eyes were like ice, and he looked almost feral. That wildness made Ruger damned uncomfortable. Man like that might do anything—no predicting his actions. "I'm planning to keep it that way, so long as you do your part. Where are we on that? You got news for me on your boy?"

"No, we got shit," Duck said, his voice calm and matter-of-fact. "Here's what you need to know. Toke—"

"Toke slashed Em with a knife," Hunter said. "I saw the damage. He's out of control, and not just with us. Am I right?"

"How did you see that?" Picnic demanded. "Why the fuck was her shirt off?"

"Shut up," Hunter said. Picnic lurched to his feet, but Horse caught him, pushing him back down.

"Not now, Pic," Horse murmured. "Hold it back."

"Why was her shirt off?" Picnic repeated. Ruger felt his own temper rise, but he kept his mouth shut and his eyes open.

"I think a better question is, why she did she get cut in the first place?" Hunter asked, his voice full of carefully leashed anger. "Or maybe, why was she meeting a strange man in a bar without any kind of backup? You fucked up, old man, and I've got her now. Looks like she needs someone new to protect her anyway."

Fuck me, Ruger thought. *He's got a thing for Em.*

"Let's get back on track," Duck said, his tone smooth and dangerous, which wasn't like Duck at all. Usually he had a big mouth and a short temper, but the crisis seemed to have brought out something more calculating in him. He'd told them stories about Vietnam, about patrols in the backcountry and sneaking behind enemy lines, but Ruger had always thought he was full of shit.

Now he wasn't so sure.

"We can't give you what you want," Duck told Hunter. "Believe me, we want to. We've been looking for him all week. And this shit—this goes against our whole club. We voted on the truce and the decision was made. He'll answer for that to the national officers. But don't go hurting two innocent girls trying to force us to do something impossible. I promise you, either of them gets a scratch and your life will end. Got me?"

Hunter sat back in his chair, studying each man in turn.

"You seriously expect me to believe you can't track down your own man?" he asked, cocking his head. "Sounds like the Reapers got some problems of their own."

"That may be," Horse said. "But it's a fact—we can't tell you where he is. I can't make you believe that, but no matter what you do to Em and Sophie, it doesn't change reality. We've had guys looking for him all week."

"Let me guess, his brothers in Portland? Deke?" Hunter asked sarcastically. "Because they'll cover his ass."

"Not just Deke," Horse replied. "And trust me, they want his ass as much as you do. This isn't just about you—he broke faith with all of us. We voted. We made a truce."

"Seriously, Hunter. We know jack shit about Toke," Ruger said, somehow staying calm and matter-of-fact, despite the fact he wanted to jump over the table and cut the prick's heart out. "I think you get we're lookin' at a war starting, right here, right now. Toke's out of control and we all know it. Whatever happens to him, he brought on himself. But you takin' our girls? That's different. When we come after you, we'll bring the whole damned club with us."

"Em and Sophie are safe," Hunter said. "And I promise they'll stay that way, at least for now. But you aren't getting them back."

"How 'bout giving us one?" Duck asked. "Sophie's got a kid. Send her back."

Picnic stiffened, but he kept his mouth shut. This wasn't part of the plan. Ruger saw where Duck was going with it, though. One was better than none, and if Hunter had a thing for Em, he'd be motivated to protect her. Not only that, Em would definitely want Sophie back with Noah. Ruger glanced over at Pic and saw understanding written on his face.

Fuck . . . He couldn't even imagine what Picnic was going through right now. It was bad enough they had Sophie. If somebody tried to take away Noah, he'd lose his shit all over the place. Rain goddamn hellfire on them.

"What'll you give me if I let her go?" Hunter asked. "I want something to take back to my club."

"How about a hostage?" Painter said suddenly. "They've got one of your brothers—you take one of ours and let both girls go."

Hunter gave a short laugh.

"Fuck that," he said. "Your ugly asses aren't worth shit to me. We want a Reaper, we'll pick one up in Portland."

He leaned forward, his eyes intense.

"I want peace," Hunter continued. "Even with all this, I still want peace. Nothing in our situation has changed, and if you're tellin' me Toke is rogue, give me something to take to my club and maybe we can still save the truce."

He pulled out his phone, glancing down at it.

"Back in five," Hunter said. He stood and walked away, holding it to his ear.

"This is a waste of time," Picnic said. "Deke was right—no point making peace with these fuckwads."

Ruger nodded, and he heard his brothers murmur agreement. The entire club needed to reevaluate their decision, no question. Didn't excuse Toke going rogue, but Ruger understood his motivations.

Hunter hung up his phone and turned back toward them. Almost immediately it rang again and he answered, studying their table the entire time. While his face stayed carefully blank, Ruger caught a hint of something wild in his eyes.

Then the Devil's Jack hung up the phone once more and walked toward them.

"Good news and bad," he said slowly. Ruger tensed.

"What's that?" Duck asked.

"Clutch is alive," he said. "At least for now. We don't have much information on him yet. They took him to the hospital. That's the good."

"And the bad?" said Picnic.

"It was cops that found him and Toke," Hunter replied. "Someone heard something and called it in. They caught Toke hiding in a hotel, our guy chained up in the bathroom. The girls who were in our house when he attacked are cooperating, so the cops have witnesses. They'll put Toke in protective custody. Out of our reach, for now. The brothers won't be happy about that."

"You gonna give us back Sophie and Em?" Ruger asked.

The question hung heavy between them as Hunter leaned back and took another drink, face blank.

"Yes," he said. "I'm doin' it to prove we're serious about the truce. Toke's situation still isn't resolved. But I'm willing to accept he wasn't acting on behalf of the Reapers, pull that out of the equation."

Ruger felt the band around his chest loosen for the first time since he'd gotten that panicked call from Sophie.

"When?" Picnic asked.

"Soon," Hunter replied. "But I'm getting out of here alive first, I think. I'm sure you'll see my concern?"

Duck snorted, almost a laugh.

"Yeah, I'd be concerned in your place, too," he said. "We won't forget this. Not sure that truce is gonna last after this little adventure."

"Me neither," Hunter admitted. "I'll do my best. Hope you will, too. Skid'll let the girls go once I give him the word. Won't happen until I'm sure I'm safe, so you start trailing me, your girls stay locked up longer."

"Understood," Picnic said. "Make it fast."

"One more thing," Duck said. "The Toke situation—you got any pull with those witnesses? We'd like to handle this within the club as much as possible. Toke'll keep his mouth shut, sure your boys will, too."

Hunter shrugged.

"We'll see what happens."

"Right," Duck said. "Keep Em and Sophie safe, got me? Otherwise I'll personally skin you and use it to make lamp shades for the Armory."

SOPHIE

Sometimes your brain tells you to do something and you know it's wrong.

My brain told me to run faster when I heard Skid's gun go off, to follow Em's plan like a good little girl. I was supposed to get out and get help. No turning back. My son needed me . . . We *agreed* on it.

Not only that, saving Em was Picnic and Ruger's job.

This wasn't my fight.

But somehow I knew—in my gut and in my soul—that if I kept running, Skid would kill Em. Maybe he already had.

I couldn't leave her behind.

So I stopped running and turned back toward the house, creeping up on it as quickly as I could, taking cover underneath a window on the living-room side. I listened for a second, hearing the muffled sound of Skid's voice. Em answered him, her tone pleading. I figured that meant he was distracted, so I popped up for a quick peek.

Em lay on the floor, pressing against the outside of her left thigh with both hands. Bright red blood seeped between her fingers. Skid stood over her, gun pointed and ready, and the look on his face wasn't friendly. This guy would be happy to kill her.

Fuck.

I looked around frantically, trying to think of a plan. I needed to stop him, and I needed to do it in a way that wouldn't end with someone dead. I crawled quickly around the side of the house, where the open front porch held two wooden chairs and a small table. I tried peeking in the front window to see what was happening, but shades covered it.

Then I heard Em scream.

No more time.

I grabbed one of the chairs, pleased to find that it was solid wood and had a nice heft. Then I rang the doorbell and waited, holding my chair ready.

"Who's out there?" Skid called.

I stayed quiet—I mean, what the hell was I supposed to say? *Please come out so I can hit you?* Using my elbow, I rang the bell again. My muscles started to burn from holding the chair. *Hurry up, asshole.*

"Fuck off!" Skid yelled. Em must've done something to mess with him because I heard a crashing noise. I rang the bell five or six times in a row with my elbow like an annoying kid.

Skid threw the door open.

I clocked him hard in the face with the chair. He staggered and the gun went off, thankfully missing me. I ignored the ringing in my ears and swung the chair around and hit him again. He shuddered, then lunged toward me, blood running down his face from his smashed nose. I screamed as he grabbed the chair by its legs, jerking it away and raising it high.

Then Em was on him from behind.

She attacked like a rabid ferret, arms tightening around his neck as she bit and scratched and kicked. He lurched forward and I joined in, grabbing the second chair and swinging it at his knees. He gave a high scream as he pitched forward off the porch, Em riding him down into the dirt. I jumped after them, landing between his legs and kicking him in the crotch over and over again. Hopefully there wouldn't be any little Skidlets in his future to carry on the family legacy.

Skid screamed like a baby the whole time.

And Em? I couldn't tell if she was laughing or crying.

• • •

Ten minutes later, we'd handcuffed Skid's bruised, bleeding body to a porch pillar. He'd passed out from the pain, which was probably a good thing. I didn't want to look into his evil eyes or listen to whatever bullshit he might spew.

Now I sat in one of the porch chairs, his confiscated gun carefully braced against my leg, cocked and ready to shoot. I didn't want to kill him, but I'd do it if I had to. I didn't doubt that for a second.

Em hobbled out of the house, her leg bandaged in strips of sheet from the bedroom. Thankfully, the bullet had just lightly grazed her thigh. Still, her face was white and drawn from the pain.

Despite it all, she managed a small smile, holding up a cell phone in triumph.

"Dumbass has Google maps installed," she said. "I know exactly where we are. I'm calling Dad to come and get us."

She dialed.

"Hey, Dad? It's me. We're okay. Could use a ride, though."

Her eyes flickered toward Skid as Picnic's muffled voice burst out of the phone.

"No, it's all good," she answered. "But you might want to bring the van. We may need some cargo space."

She gave them directions and hung up.

"They'll be here in about twenty minutes," Em told me. "They sounded pretty happy to hear from us."

"Was Hunter with them?" I asked. As soon as the question left my mouth, I regretted it. Did I really want the answer? Em swallowed and looked away.

"No," she said. "The meet was already over. I guess we missed him by maybe five minutes. He's got good luck."

I raised a brow, but kept my mouth shut. Em dropped the phone to the ground, then stomped on it, and I heard the crunch of glass and plastic.

"What the hell?" I asked, startled. "Why'd you do that?"

"GPS," she said shortly. "I don't want the Devil's Jacks tracing us with it, and we can't leave it here."

"What if we need it again?"

"We won't," she said. "Dad and Ruger will find us. Don't worry. By tomorrow it'll be like this never happened. In fact, I don't want to talk about it and I don't want to think about it. Got me?"

"Got you," I said, narrowing my eyes. Em grabbed the second chair and dragged it over toward me, sitting down.

"Want me to take the gun for a while?"

"Thanks," I said, handing it over. It was surprisingly heavy, and after the first few minutes my hand had started cramping. I stretched my fingers, looking out across the long gravel driveway into the trees.

"No offense," I said slowly. "But that was the shittiest girls' night out ever."

Em gave a short, startled snort of laughter.

"Ya think?"

CHAPTER FIFTEEN

RUGER

They crested the small rise overlooking the house and Picnic slowed, raising a hand for the others to stop.

Ruger pulled up next to him.

Holy fuck.

"That's my girl," Picnic said, his voice full of pride. "Goddamn, did something right with her."

"Both our girls," Ruger muttered. He felt his chest unclenching, a ball of tension he hadn't even realized was there letting go. "Shit, didn't know she had it in her."

Em and Sophie sat on the front porch like two neighbors visiting over sweet tea, except Em held a gun trained steady on Skid. His mangled, bloody form lay in the dirt, arms stretched up behind him and wrapped around the porch pole.

"Think she killed him?" Ruger asked.

"Hope not," Picnic replied. "Bad enough already, without her having to live with that. Not to mention messy as fuck for us to clean up."

"That's the truth," Ruger replied.

"It's Dad, we're here for you!" Picnic yelled down, waving at her. Em kept her eyes on Skid and her gun didn't waver.

"Glad you came," she called back. "I could really use some help."

"He the only one?" Pic asked.

"Hunter left a couple hours ago," she shouted. "It was only the two of them."

They rode slowly down the hill toward the house. Ruger studied Sophie carefully as he parked his bike, but he couldn't see any signs of serious harm. She looked exhausted, her eyes darkened with smudged makeup, but that was all. Em seemed worse off—her face was pale and a bruise was starting to form on her cheek. White, bloodied strips of fabric had been tied around her leg.

"Stay where you are, girls," Pic said shortly as he dismounted his ride. Ruger did the same, following him over to the man on the ground.

Skid was in rough shape. He wasn't moving, and Ruger saw trickles of blood seeping from his nose and mouth. More soaked the dirt, although he couldn't see where it was coming from. Ruger approached the man carefully, kneeling down to check his pulse.

Still alive. The beat was faint but steady.

"He's not dead," he said. "What's the plan?"

Picnic rolled Skid with a foot. Now they saw the wound—he had a gaping gash on the back of his head.

"He's been bleeding, but not too bad," Em said. "Don't know if he's passed out from a head injury or from shock. Sophie kicked his nuts to hell and back."

Ruger felt an instinctive shrinking in his own nether region and glanced up at Sophie. She gazed down at them, her face as smooth as a sphinx's.

Perfectly calm. Way too calm. *Shock,* Ruger figured.

Picnic stepped up to his daughter and held out his hand for the gun. She gave it to him, and he wrapped an arm around her shoulders, pulling her in close.

Ruger looked to Sophie again and she turned away. Then he heard the crunch of footsteps in the driveway behind him.

"How we gonna play this?" Bam Bam asked, eyeing Skid. Ruger glanced over at his president, wondering the same thing. Would they put the bastard in the ground or not?

"Not in front of the girls," Picnic said, squeezing Em tight. "Ruger, you and Painter take them, get them safe. Call the medic. He can meet you at the clubhouse. We'll clean up here."

Em shook her head, growing tense.

"Don't kill him," she said. "You do that, there's going to be even more fighting."

"This is about the club, Em," Picnic replied softly. She glanced down at Skid, then leaned up on her toes, whispering in her father's ear.

Picnic stiffened.

Em pulled away, eyes clearly pleading.

He shook his head at her and she crossed her arms, taking a step back. *Interesting.* Picnic narrowed his eyes, and the two stared at each other for long seconds. Then Picnic sighed.

"Okay, we'll take him with us and dump him somewhere he'll be found," he said. "See if you can find something to bandage him up with, Bam."

Ruger looked down at Skid. Intellectually, he knew letting him live was probably a good idea. All other issues aside, Em and Sophie didn't need that kind of baggage.

He still wanted the fucker dead, though.

They could always take him out later. If they did it right, the girls would never know.

SOPHIE

I didn't know how to feel as I rode home with Ruger, exhausted and drained from the adrenaline. We'd separated from the rest of the club, which broke into different groups going different places. He'd wanted me to get checked out by a friend of the club who was an EMT, but I insisted I was fine.

Which I was. Physically.

But now that it was over, I was so furious with Ruger that I wanted to scream and hit and kick his big, dumb ass for getting me into this shit. I also wanted him to hold me and make me feel safe again, which was ridiculous.

I'd never be safe around him.

More than anything, though, I wanted to get back to Noah. I wanted to hold him tight and make sure we never, ever had to worry about something like this happening again. Different plans kept running through my head, including changing my name and moving to a different state entirely. But I had a good job now, one that might actually let us get ahead.

I just needed a wall between me and Ruger. I'd draw the line—him on his side and me on mine, with no crossover. If I did that, we'd be fine.

But even angry with him, it felt right and safe to lean against his back as we drove, arms wrapped tight around his stomach. Every inch of Ruger was strong and solid. The leather of his cut lay under my cheek, broken by the embroidered fabric of his Reapers patches. His stomach was made of hard muscle that rippled under my fingers every time he leaned to take a curve.

For now—just for the next twenty minutes—I'd let myself touch him, savor his presence.

Then we'd go our separate ways.

• • •

When we finally pulled around the back of Elle's barn to the little gravel parking area in front of my new apartment, I dropped my arms and let him go. I didn't let myself feel sad.

I tried not to let myself feel *anything.*

He swung off the bike and took my hand, leading me over to the door, which was a good thing. I felt like I was trapped in a dream, everything distant and surreal.

"Crap," I muttered, looking at the lock. "I don't have my keys. They're in my purse, and I have no idea what happened to it, or my phone."

"They might find your purse at the house," Ruger said. "Your phone is gone. I'll get you a new one tomorrow."

He let me go and turned back to his bike, digging through one of the saddlebags to pull out a small black leather pouch. When he came back and opened it, I saw a collection of strange little tools.

"Lock picks," he said shortly.

"So this is just another part of your life?" I asked, numb. "You just go around, ready and waiting to break into places?"

He glanced up at me and opened his mouth to speak. Something in my face must have caught his attention, because his expression softened.

"Babe, I'm a locksmith, used to be my job," he said, his voice gentle. "Locksmith, gunsmith—if it's made of metal and has tiny little parts, I like working with it. When I was a kid I built shit out of Legos; now I have big-boy toys. For a while I worked full-time doing lockout calls. Sometimes it's not about scary stuff, okay?"

I nodded, but I wasn't sure if I believed him.

"Whatever," I murmured. The door clicked open and I walked in, looking around. Everything was just like I'd left it the day before. Normal. All normal. It could almost have been a dream.

"You need to get cleaned up," he said. "I'll call Kimber and tell her to bring Noah home in an hour or so. I don't want him freaking out."

"Was he worried about me?" I asked, walking over to get a drink of water. I considered offering him one, and then didn't, because *fuck Ruger.* The little surge of anger was good—made me feel less numb.

"I'm sure he was," he replied. "Kimber's been with him the whole time, though. They've been watching movies and shit. I talked to him for about five minutes this morning but I haven't seen him. I was focused on getting you back."

I turned to look at him, so big he seemed to fill my tiny living room.

"Soph, we need to talk," he said slowly, looking almost nervous. "I need you to tell me everything that happened. Did they . . . hurt . . . you?"

I snorted.

"Um, yeah, they hurt me," I said, reaching up to touch my bruised cheek. "They threw me in a van, tied me up, and held me prisoner while threatening to kill me because of some bullshit with your club that I don't understand or care about. So yeah, that part kind of sucked. Thanks for asking."

"Did they rape you?" he asked bluntly. I shook my head. His face softened with relief, and he walked toward me. I held my hand up flat, halting him.

Limits. Time to set them.

"Ruger, we've been playing around, and it's over," I said, focusing my eyes on his chest. His 1% patch taunted me, reminding me exactly why this had to happen. "I know I've said that before, but everything's changed now. It doesn't matter how you make me feel or how nice you are. Your club is dangerous, and I don't want anything to do with any of you. Noah and I, we can't afford that."

He stilled.

"I can see why you might feel that way—" he started to say, but I cut him off.

"No, you really can't," I said. "You didn't spend the night handcuffed to a bed, wondering if you'd get raped or murdered. You didn't hear your friend screaming in the dark, or hear a gunshot when you tried to escape. We could have *died*, Ruger . . . So here's the way it's going to be from now on. I'll let you see Noah once a week. We'll make the plans in advance. You'll keep him away from your club and you won't talk to him about motorcycles. You won't wear your damned colors and you won't do anything that could ever lead to any kind of danger. You'll call me to make arrangements and you'll pick him up and drop him off when and where I tell you."

His eyes hardened and his jaw clenched. I felt his anger and frustration in the air around me like a tangible thing, which was actually kind of funny because I didn't give a flying fuck what he thought of my plans.

Not anymore.

"You'll follow my rules," I continued. "Or I'll never let Noah see you again. Believe me, I'll do it. In fact, I'd like to do it right now, but I know how much he loves you and it would be devastating to him. So we'll try this out, and if it works, great. It doesn't work or I feel like he's in danger? You're gone."

"You can't do that," he said. He started toward me again. I stood my ground as he closed in, doing that domination thing, getting into my space. I stared up at him, his chest about three inches from my chin, and I didn't care how big and scary he was.

I didn't care about anything.

"I'm his mother. You have no rights. None. I let you see him because I'm a nice person, and I can stop being nice at any time. Do *not* fuck with me, Ruger."

He reached up and touched my face lightly, running his finger across my cheek. It sent shivers down my back, and just like that I wanted him.

"I won't fuck around," he said. "Just so you know. I nearly lost you. I won't risk that again. I told you before I'd never be a one-woman man, but I was wrong."

I looked in his face, studying his eyes. He meant it. I thought about lying in bed with him . . . I wanted to give in. I wanted *him*.

It didn't matter.

"Too late," I said, and I meant it. "I'm done with you, and I'm fucking serious. Get. Out. Of. My. House."

He held my gaze, then the miracle happened.

Ruger listened.

He backed away, turned, and walked out of the house. I heard his bike roar to life outside and then the sound of him riding away.

I'd done it. I'd finally managed to put Ruger in his place. Unfortunately, I was too tired to enjoy it.

MONDAY

KIMBER: How u doing?

ME: Ok. Noah's still kind of clingy. You did a good job but he was still scared. Thank you so much for taking care of him. Im so glad he was safe

KIMBER: That's what friends do—u wud do it for me. I've been thinkng about u . . . U want to get together, maybe talk?

ME: No. Just want to lay low for a while

WEDNESDAY

MARIE: Hey Sophie! Me and Maggs and Dancer want to hang out tomorrow night . . . Want to join us?

ME: Thanks but probably not. You have fun

MARIE: Okay. How are you?

ME: Im fine
MARIE: You talked to Em?
ME: No. She ok?
MARIE: Not sure. She wont tell me anything. I'm worried . . . Did anythng happen we should know about? I mean, while you guys were . . . wherever? Maybe we can get together and talk
ME: Im fine, just want to stick to myself and Noah for a while. Em and I werent together the whole time. If you want to know more, you need to get it from her
MARIE: Okay. We're worried about you too . . . How are things
ME: Fine. I just want space
MARIE: I get that. But please call if you need us ((hugs))

THURSDAY

DANCER: Hey. how goes it? Maybe we could let the kids play this afternoon?
ME: Um, we're pretty busy right now.
DANCER: Know how that goes . . . Did you remember Maries bachelorette party? Its a week from Friday. We have a sitter, she offered to watch Noah too
ME: Not sure I'll maek it. I'll find my own sitter
DANCER: Okay. Don't hide out too long

FRIDAY

KIMBER: This is bullshit. I get ur pissed at Ruger and Reapers but I'm not one of them, u can't freeze me out. You guys come over tonight or I'm sending Ryan to get u
ME; Noah and I are watching movies at home

KIMBER: No. Ur coming to my house. We're having a party. I need backup!!! NO Reapers. Nromal people. Kids too. U and Noah be here at six or I will come and get you. Not fucking around.

ME: Your a pushy bitch

KIMBER: Ya think? Get ur ass here or I'll come for u. No excuses. Bring swimsuits and a dessert

My brand-new iPhone said it was five fifty-six when we pulled up to Kimber's house. Ruger had dropped it off the previous Sunday, the day after my little adventure with Em. I wanted to tell him to go to hell, but I needed a phone, and I figured he could afford it better than I could. I didn't feel guilty about it, either. It was his fault I'd gotten kidnapped in the first place, so I might as well blame him for drowning my phone.

I didn't let him into the house. Noah wanted to go to his house and I told him no. Then I shut the door in Ruger's face.

Now it was Friday night and I'd caved to Kimber's ultimatum, because I knew she was serious when she said they'd come and get me. I held a plate of brownies in one hand and a bag of swim gear in the other, and when Kimber's husband, Ryan, opened the door, I had to smile. He wore neon-green swim trunks and a purple Hawaiian-print shirt. On his head was an orange cowboy hat, and he held a Super Soaker in one hand.

Coming here had been a good idea, I realized.

"Welcome to the party," he said, smiling at me broadly.

"Nice look," I said, eyeing his outfit.

"Hey, it takes a very confident man to pull something like this off," he said without an ounce of shame.

"Did you lose a bet?" I asked, smirking.

"As a matter of fact, he did," said another man, coming over to stand next to Ryan. He had longish, scruffy brown hair and a great smile, and the look in his eyes said he appreciated my appearance. He also held a Super Soaker, although he wore perfectly normal trunks and a T-shirt that said "Code Monkey Like You."

I'd seen his picture before—this was the guy Kimber had wanted to set me up with.

"Ryan and I had a little programming challenge at work, and I kicked his ass. Hi, I'm Josh. Nice to meet you."

"Nice to meet you, too," I said, glancing down at my full hands helplessly. "Um, sorry, I'd offer to shake your hand, but . . ."

He laughed, and then his eyes widened almost comically as he saw the brownies.

"Let me help you with those," he said, reaching out to grab the treats. "And who is this?"

"I'm Noah," my boy announced. "Do you have any more of those Soakers, Ryan?"

"I have a whole box out back," Ryan replied. "You want to come pick one out? We have a bunch of kids out there. I'll bet they'd love to play with you."

"Mom?" He looked up at me, eyes pleading.

"Go ahead," I said, feeling almost carefree. Kimber was right. I *had* needed to get out, and coming to a nice, suburban party like this was just what I needed. No Reapers, no kidnappings, nothing bad at all.

I could do this.

Noah took off through the house, followed by Ryan. Josh looked down at me, offering a friendly smile.

"So, once we get this stuff settled, could I get you a drink?"

"Sure," I said. "So tell me, how long have you and Ryan worked together?"

Three hours later I was feeling pretty good about life. Josh turned out to be a great guy, spending a good chunk of the night hanging out with me, but not so much that it felt weird. Ryan grilled burgers and hot dogs, the kids played in the pool, and Kimber's blender ran almost constantly, churning out margaritas in every imaginable flavor. I stuck with iced tea and laughed so hard I nearly cried when Ryan caught her and threw her into the pool.

The mob of kids kept growing, and I met so many people I couldn't begin to keep them all straight. Most were from Kimber's neighborhood or Ryan's work—sleek, polished yoga moms and their slightly dorky husbands who worked as accountants and IT professionals. Nothing like the Reapers' party.

The first time I'd met Ryan, I didn't understand him and Kimber together. He was so geeky and she was so wild and cool—but they balanced each other out perfectly. I was holding Ava and sitting by the pool after eating when Josh came over and flopped into a chair next to me.

"So," he said, grinning at me. "I've got a question for you."

"What's that?" I asked.

"You and Noah want to hit Chuck E. Cheese's for dinner tomorrow?" he said. "I know it's not the most romantic setting, but I've got this theory about skee-ball that needs testing, and I figured he'd be an excellent assistant."

I burst out laughing.

"Are you insane? Chuck E. Cheese's on a Saturday night is crazy. I bet you wouldn't last an hour."

His eyes brightened.

"Is that a challenge?" he asked. "You sure you're up to it?"

"You're too funny," I said, shaking my head.

"Funny enough to get a date with you tomorrow?" he said, offering a sly smile. "I'd go for the brooding, manly thing and try to be all mysterious, but I've never really been able to pull it off."

I sobered, thinking of Ruger. The two men couldn't have been more different, that was for sure.

"Um, I'm not really looking for a boyfriend," I said slowly.

"And I'll be honest—you bring a seven-year-old on a date, you're probably not gonna get some at the end."

He shrugged.

"It's just an evening," he said. "No big deal. Besides that, I've got a deep, dark secret to share with you."

He leaned toward me, waving me in close. I shifted, balancing Ava as he spoke in my ear.

"I really do have an amazing skee-ball theory," he said, his voice grave and serious. "It needs experimentation. You'd be doing me a huge favor."

I started laughing again, pulling away.

"Does that line actually work for you?" I asked. He smiled at me.

"I don't know, does it?"

I thought about Ruger, how he made me feel and compared it to this man. Josh didn't give me chills when I felt his breath against my ear, but he was nice to look at and seemed fun and friendly. And how much trouble could we get into on a date at a kiddie pizza place, anyway?

"Okay," I said, feeling proud of myself. I'd move past Ruger—this was the perfect first step. "That would be fun. But just friendly. I'm really not looking to get serious with anyone."

"Don't worry about it," he replied, grinning at me. "We'll just go and have some fun—and Ryan can vouch for me. I'm not an undercover supervillian, no dark secrets, nothing. What you see is what you get."

I started to reply, but a thick stream of water suddenly hit the side of my head, drenching me as Ava shrieked. I look up to see Noah running away with a small pack of boys, screeching in triumph. Little shit . . .

"I need to go dry off," I told Josh.

"Want me to go defend your honor?" he asked, holding up his Soaker.

"Yeah, you do that."

He stood and saluted me, eyes dancing with laughter, then tore off after the mob of children shooting each other and running around the grass.

I found Ryan by the grill. He held a beer in one hand and a pair of tongs in the other, and as he shifted them to take Ava, he smiled at me.

"You know, Josh's a real good guy," he said. "I've known him a couple of years."

"Um, he seems nice," I replied awkwardly. Ryan laughed.

"Don't worry—no pressure," he said. "Just wanted to let you know he's not a serial killer."

"Good to know," I said. "Thanks for having me over. Thanks for everything, actually."

"No problem," he said. "Kimber thinks you're the shit. You know, it's not that easy for her to find friends, despite what you'd think. You're special to her."

That startled me.

"Kimber's always had more friends than anyone," I said, laughing.

His face sobered and he shook his head. "No, she's always got more people at her parties than anyone. There's a big difference."

I didn't know what to say. Ryan shrugged, and smiled again.

"Go get dried off," he added. "We've got sparklers for the kids once it's totally dark. I'll need help, and Kimber's useless after three margaritas."

I smiled hesitantly and walked inside. Off to the left was a family room, with the kitchen and a breakfast bar off to the right. My sandal caught on the doorway, pulling the strap loose, so I dropped down to fix it just inside the entry.

"Jesus, did you see what Ryan's wearing?" I heard a woman say in the kitchen.

"I know," said another. "And Kimber's not much better. Could that bikini be smaller? You know she's a giant slut, right? She used to be a stripper. I just hope they leave before Ava hits school. I don't want Kaitlyn in her class."

"No kidding. That's why I moved to this neighborhood—I wanted all our neighbors to be normal, not trashy. And her friend . . . God, she must've been, what, ten years old when she had her kid?"

"I saw her skanking all over Josh. Disgusting."

My phone buzzed, and I pulled it out of my pocket to find a text from Marie.

Hey. I know things are weird, but I really hope you'll come to my bachelorette party next weekend. We're all hanging out tonight and thinking about how much more fun it would be with you here! xoxo

"So, my pedicure girl moved to a new salon. All Vietnamese, and I hate how they talk to each other without speaking in English. So rude!" said the woman in the kitchen.

"You're sooo right. I *never* leave a tip when they do that. They should be speaking English if they're going to live here . . ."

I stood up and walked through the kitchen, piercing each of the women in turn with a sweet smile. Bitches. How dare they gossip about Kimber, in her own house? I couldn't believe they'd get drunk on her booze while ripping her apart like that.

At least nobody was whipping out knives.

Not metal ones, anyway.

I wanted to go home.

"You got it, bud," Josh said, watching intensely as Noah lined up his shot at the skee-ball machine. I had to laugh. Josh had been joking about his theory . . . mostly. The man really did love the game. It turned out Noah loved it, too, so things had worked out pretty well.

We'd been at Chuck E. Cheese's for nearly three hours, and I'd had a blast. Josh was easy to be around. He didn't stress me out and he didn't scare me. We'd eaten dinner, and to give him credit, he ate the nasty pizza they served without a single snide comment (not even I could pull that off). Then he bought Noah more tokens than he'd ever seen before and we'd hit the games.

Now it was almost nine and I knew we needed to get Noah out soon or things could get ugly. I touched Josh's arm, catching his attention. He turned and grinned at me, looking like a big, happy puppy.

"We need to head home," I said, nodding toward my son. "He's tired. Don't want to push him too hard."

"Understood," Josh replied. He put an arm around my shoulders and pulled me close, giving me a squeeze. "You've got a good kid there."

I smiled, because I knew he was right. Also because I liked his arm around my shoulder. Josh didn't make my heart explode like Ruger did, but he had a good sense of humor and was fun to be around. That had to count for something.

We fed all of the tickets we'd won (and it seemed like thousands of them) into the chomping machines, which caused Noah intense delight. Then we spent another twenty minutes at the prize counter as he agonized over which tiny plastic rings or erasers to pick.

The sun had set when we finally walked outside. The pizza place was in one of those strip malls with free-standing restaurants in the parking lot. I looked over at the steak house longingly, still a little hungry—I'd only managed to choke down half a slice. Josh bumped my shoulder.

"Maybe next time we can get a grown-up meal," he said.

"Is that your way of asking me out again?" I asked, coming to a stop next to my car. Noah bounced around next to me happily, playing with his new treasures. I looked up at Josh and smiled. He smiled back, and I was struck by how cute he was. Geeky cute, like Ryan.

I could do a lot worse.

"Depends on what the answer would be," he replied, reaching up to tuck a strand of hair behind my ear. "I hate getting shot down."

"I don't think you'd get shot down," I said. He leaned forward and kissed me lightly on the lips. It was nice—not hot and intense, but pleasant.

"Uncle Ruger!" Noah yelled, and I felt him take off running. I pulled away from Ryan instantly, my mommy radar fully engaged. I bolted after him, shouting his name and yelling at him to stop. He ignored me, jumping into Ruger's arms where he stood on the sidewalk outside the steak house.

Several other guys from the club were with him.

"Noah, you can't run off like that!" I said, catching Noah's chin so his eyes had to meet mine. "You could get killed. You know better—you're a big boy now."

"I'm sorry," he said instantly. "I forgot. I got excited. I wanted to show Uncle Ruger my prizes."

Shit, I'd been so worried about Noah, I wasn't even thinking about Ruger. I looked up to find him staring across the lot.

"Who's your friend?" he asked, jerking his chin toward Josh, who gave us a halfhearted wave.

"That's Josh," I said defiantly. "He's a friend of Kimber's husband. They work together."

"He took us to Chuck E. Cheese's and we played tons of games and I got all kinds of prizes but I didn't have enough tickets to get what I really wanted so he said maybe we could come back another time and I said yes," Noah told him breathlessly. "He's pretty cool, Ruger."

Ruger's eyes hardened, and he set Noah down.

"Stay here, kid," he said. Then he stepped out across the parking lot, obviously planning to intercept Josh. Fuck.

"Stay," I said to Noah, then glanced up at Bam Bam. "Will you make sure he doesn't run off?"

Dancer's husband gave a quick nod, but his eyes weren't exactly friendly.

Great.

I scurried off toward Ruger and Josh.

"Hey," I said, looking between them. Ruger's face was like stone, his eyes glinting with possessive menace. Josh looked confused and a little uncertain. "Josh, this is Noah's uncle, Ruger. Ruger, this is my friend Josh. We were just leaving. Sorry about Noah bothering you."

"Noah never bothers me," Ruger said, cocking his head at Josh, who tried to offer him a smile.

"He's a great kid," Josh said. "You must be proud of him."

"Yup," Ruger said to him. "You need to go now. Probably be best if you don't call Sophie again."

Josh's eyes widened.

"Go fuck yourself, Ruger," I snapped. Josh glanced over at me, looking nervous. "Josh, please ignore him. He's leaving."

"Nope, I'm not leaving," Ruger said pointedly. "And I won't be leaving. You're not welcome here. Don't know what Sophie's told you, but she's taken."

"That's not true," I said quickly. Josh looked between us, swallowing.

"You need a hand, Ruger?" Horse called from the sidewalk. He offered Josh a wolfish smile.

"Not with this asshole," Ruger replied, holding Josh's eyes steadily. Josh broke, looking away.

"Um, I gotta get going," he said, offering me a quick, sheepish smile. Then he turned and walked away very quickly.

I stared, dumbfounded.

"Looks like your new boyfriend scares easy," Ruger murmured. "Didn't even make sure you were safe with me. Wouldn't want a man like that at my back. Of course, I don't need to worry about backup. My brothers are there for me, no matter what."

He took my shoulders and turned me toward the steak house. I saw Horse, Bam Bam, Duck, and Slide standing around my son. Bam held Noah's shoulder protectively. Ruger leaned down behind me, speaking softly in my ear as his fingers squeezed my shoulders.

"Look at that," he said. "You know them, so you know Noah couldn't be safer. But your buddy Josh? He knows shit about those guys. That didn't stop him from walking away to cover his own ass while they had your son. Hell of a man you've found."

I swallowed, because I knew he was right.

So Josh wouldn't be getting a second date if he bothered to call. Probably a moot point, because I had a feeling he wouldn't.

"You need to stay out of my life," I told Ruger, watching Noah carefully show off his prizes, offering Horse one of his precious rings. Horse accepted it, sliding it a quarter of the way down his pinkie.

Noah glowed with pride.

"Yeah, I'll get right on that," Ruger said. "Don't take Noah out with a guy like that again. You'll send him the wrong message."

"None of your business."

"It'll always be my business."

"You don't get to win every single time," I told him seriously. "Just because you say something, that doesn't mean it's true."

"Just 'cause I say it doesn't mean I'm wrong, either."

I glared at him, then marched over and collected Noah, trying not to grit my teeth. I took him home and put him to bed, feeling bitchy the entire time.

When I fell asleep that night, it wasn't Josh I was dreaming of. Nope, stupid Ruger. Again.

Even in my dreams he won.

CHAPTER SIXTEEN

SUNDAY

KIMBER: Josh won't tell Ryan anyting about ur date. Did somethig go wrong?

ME: Ruger

KIMBER: ???

ME: We had a great time then Ruger showed up. Pretty sure I'll never hear from Josh again

KIMBER: Jesus Ruger. Stalk much?!?!???

ME: No it wasn't like that. He was having dinner with the guys we ran into him in the parking lot. He had a little bullshit talk with Josh then Josh ran off. I realize he doesn't know us very well but he didnt even make sure Noah and I were safe when he left. Epic fail all around

KIMBER: Pisser. Josh loses margarita privileges. Hate wimps

ME: Meh . . .

KIMBER: So u talk to Ruger at all?

ME: Nope. Fuck him

KIMBER: Gotcha. Hey u going to the bachelorette party? Marie invited me and I wnat to go, but it would be wiered without u

ME: Can't decide. Like her and would love it, but . . . you know . . .

KIMBER: Yup, I get it. Keep me posted

MONDAY

RUGER: Can I pick Noah up after school? Got a thing I want to take him to

ME: What kind of thing?

RUGER: Got a friend who races, his car is down at the track. Said Noah could have a ride

ME: Is it safe???

RUGER: Safe as any car. He'll go slow

ME: Biker friend?

RUGER: No. No colors, no Reapers. Don't agree with you on that, but I'm giving you time

ME: I dont need time. I need you gone

RUGER: Can I take him or not?

ME: Okay. Home by 6?

RUGER: 7 work? I'll get him dinner

ME: Sounds good. No games, tho. Drop him off and leave

RUGER: I hear you. No games

WEDNESDAY

DANCER: So you coming to party or not? Marie really wants you there.

ME: Um . . .

DANCER: Please come. I know things are shit with you and Ruger. I don't care, neither does Marie. We'd love to have you there.

ME: Okay. Dont want to stay out too late tho. I have work on Friday

DANCER: No prob. Even a few hours would be great for Marie. Kimber, too? She's fun. Um, coul dyou ask her to bring her blender, too? Starting at my place before hitting bars . . .

ME: Dork :p

DANCER: Not dorky to know what you want ;)

ME: Guess not. I'll see if Elle can watch Noah

DANCER: You can share our sitter if you need to

ME: Rather have him closer to home. More likely to sleep. Oour lives have been crazy lately and he has school tomorrow

DANCER: See you tomorrow night <3

ME: Sounds good

THURSDAY

KIMBER: Can't believe she's having the party on a thursday. Sucks, Ryan has to work tomorrow. Hangover and baby don't mix!!!!!!!!!!

ME: You don't have to drink, you know.

KIMBER: Shut the fuck up. Ur not drinking?

ME: No—work in morning.

KIMBER: You preggo or something?

ME: Oh, you're funny

KIMBER: :-> So u know why a thursday?

ME: Marie said she's got a thing with her mom this weekend. Spa or something

KIMBER: Jealous. We should do that

ME: Right after I win the lottery

KIMBER: Hmmm . . . ur gonna have to start buying tickets

ME: Why don't you buy for both of us?

KIMBER: So long as I get to drink for both of us, I'm down with that! SMOOCHES

"Fuck!" Marie screamed, spinning around. "I lost my veil!"

She stood up in the limo's open sunroof. It was just after midnight, and we'd decided to cruise down along the Coeur d'Alene lake before hitting our final destination, a karaoke bar.

About an hour ago, Marie had declared she wanted—no, *needed*—to sing "Pour Some Sugar on Me" before the night ended. It'd been playing when she and Horse met, and apparently the world would end if we didn't sing it again tonight.

We knew this because she'd been very clear: The existence of the world literally depended on successful completion of this karaoke mission.

As one of the most sober women in the limo, I'd been assigned to make sure we didn't get distracted and forget. Seeing as I wasn't one hundred percent sober, I'd carefully written this on my inner arm with a pen as a reminder.

Now I stood next to her, watching in horror as the little white scrap of tulle she wore on her head flew through the air toward Painter, who followed us on his bike. Holy shit. Would it make him crash?

Apparently a drifting veil wasn't a serious road hazard to a bike going twenty-five miles an hour, because he avoided it easily enough. The prospect following him—one I'd seen at the Armory party but hadn't met—pulled off to go fetch it.

Nice.

"That's good service," I told Marie. She started giggling, and then she fell down into the limo, officially drunk off her ass.

I popped back down, too.

Dancer lay back across one of the seats, laughing so hard she was crying. Maggs had her shirt up, flashing her boobs while Kimber took a picture. Wasn't sure I wanted the whole story on that one. A woman I'd just met named Darcy was pouring champagne in that very slow, very deliberate way drunk people have. Unfortunately she'd forgotten the glass.

I hoped whoever arranged the rental had coverage for that kind of thing.

A woman with short, curly, reddish-blonde hair sat giggling in the corner. Back when she could still speak in full sentences, Marie had introduced her as Cookie. She used to live in Coeur d'Alene but had moved, and now Marie managed the coffee shop she still owned in town.

Em and I looked at each other and she rolled her eyes.

I'd decided not to drink too much because I had work in the morning, but I was still in a pretty good mood. Definitely planning on a cab ride home. Em, though . . . She had a haunted look in her eyes that bothered me. No wonder the girls had been worried about her—something was obviously wrong.

"So why don't they just go home?" I asked Em, scooting over to sit next to her.

"Who?"

"Painter and the other guy, Banks."

"Banks will stick with us all night," she said quietly. "He's supposed to keep an eye on us, make sure we make it home safe. I guess Painter's just along for the ride—maybe he's worried after what went down with Hunter and Skid."

"He was watching you while you were dancing," I said. "He may not have seemed interested before, but he's definitely interested now."

"I could give a fuck," she replied, her voice flat. "Painter,

Hunter . . . men in general. I think I'm swearing off them entirely. Too bad I can't just flip a switch and go lesbian."

"Pretty sure it doesn't work that way," I said, sighing. "Men really are a giant pain in the ass, aren't they?"

"Speaking of, how's Ruger?" she asked. "I hear you're fighting with each other."

"Um, that seems a bit strong," I said. "I'd say we're just not talking much, which is what I wanted. No offense, but after what happened, I don't think I want anything to do with the club."

She sighed.

"I can understand that," she replied. "You didn't exactly get a good intro. I know it probably doesn't seem this way, but they're actually really good guys. It's not like this shit happens all the time."

The car swayed, and Dancer crashed into us.

"You are boring!" she yelled in our faces. "We're having a good time here. If you don't sing me something good at the bar, I'm making you ride with Painter."

Um, no. I would rather have my eyes poked out than do karaoke.

I didn't say that, though. I just smiled politely and decided this was a sign—I'd call a cab after Marie sang her song. I had to be up in six hours, so that was probably for the best anyway. At least I didn't have to worry about Noah—Elle had taken him, offering to keep him overnight and get him ready for school the next day. That was a huge help.

"Oh my God!" Maggs squealed suddenly. We all froze. "We haven't done presents yet!"

"Presents!" Marie yelled, clapping her hands. "I love presents!"

Maggs lurched down to the front of the limo and pulled back a big basket full of unopened packages and envelopes. She grabbed one at random, throwing it to Marie.

"Who's it from?" Darcy asked. Marie tried to focus on the writing, then shook her head.

"Can't tell," she said. "They have really, really messy handwriting."

"Here," I said. "Let me look."

She handed it over.

"The tag was printed off a computer," I said, snorting. "It's not even a fancy script or something. You're too drunk to read. Oh, and it's from Cookie."

Marie pouted.

"It's not my fault you guys bought all those shots," she said. "It's not like I could let them go to waste! That's just wrong."

Darcy nodded sagely.

"She's right—if you throw away booze at your bachelorette party, the marriage is doomed."

"You say that about everything," I accused. "*The marriage is doomed* if she doesn't order the steak *and* the shrimp. *The marriage is doomed* if she doesn't dance with at least ten guys. *The marriage is doomed* if she doesn't tell us how big Horse's dick really is. How can all of that be true?"

"I know these things," she declared. "Am I right, ladies?"

"Hell yes," Dancer chimed in. "Darcy knows her shit. If she says the marriage is doomed if Marie doesn't drink enough, it's time to start pouring shots down her throat!"

"Right now it's time to open presents!" Maggs yelled. "Ladies, we need to focus. The marriage is doomed if she doesn't get these open before we hit the karaoke bar!"

"Shit," Marie said, her eyes opening wide in panic. She ripped into the bag, peeked down inside, and started giggling madly. Then she pulled out a giant double-headed jelly dildo in swirling colors.

"Oh, Cookie," she said, sighing. "It's beautiful! How did you know?"

We all burst out laughing, and Maggs grabbed another present. This one was from Darcy, and I shit you not, it was a giant, strap-on cock.

"That's so you can put Horse in his place," she told Marie. "That man's ego needs controlling, and that's a great tool to do it with."

"I love it," Marie whispered. "Oh, I cannot wait to try this."

"You think he'd actually let you use it on him?" I asked. She started giggling.

"I think just the sight of it will make his head explode," she said. "It's all about creating the right kind of romantic mood, you know?"

Em got her a beautifully illustrated Kama Sutra, Dancer got her a thong that said "Support Your Local Reapers MC" on it (along with a little Reaper's skull), I got her sensual massage oils, and Kimber got her some sort of electronic thing that we all just looked at, trying to figure out what the hell it was.

"Read the instructions," Kimber said. "Trust me, you turn this baby on, you're gonna love it."

Marie tilted it, obviously confused, and I tried to figure out where it would even fit on a person's body.

I really, really wanted a look at those directions, but when we looked for them, nobody could find them in the piles of tissue paper cluttering the limo.

We pulled up to the karaoke bar right as she finished. It was quarter to one, which gave us about an hour before last call. Because the marriage would be doomed if she didn't have more shots, Marie had more shots. Then she got up and sang her Def Leppard song and we all joined her for the chorus.

Maggs took over the mike to sing "White Wedding," and then Marie realized the marriage was definitely doomed if she didn't text Horse a picture of her modeling her new panties, so we all tripped back out to the limo.

That's when I decided to call it a night—it was my understanding that when the bar closed, they'd all be heading back to the Armory to join up with the guys. The girls didn't want me to leave, but seeing Ruger wasn't exactly one of my goals for the evening. Ten minutes later the cab pulled up and I gave him my address. I guess I'd had more to drink than I realized, because the next thing I knew, we'd pulled into Elle's driveway.

"Wake up," the driver said. "This where I drop you?"

I looked around, trying to clear my head. I wasn't drunk, but I wasn't totally sober, either.

"Um, yeah," I said. "Just pull around the house, okay?"

He did, and I fumbled in my purse for money. I gave it to him and stepped out, digging for the keys. I'd forgotten to turn on the outside light, which didn't help. Or maybe it was just burned out . . . I usually left it on all the time.

The driver must've been a nice guy, because he waited until I got the front door open before he pulled away. Too bad he hadn't waited a minute longer—when I flipped on the light I nearly had a heart attack.

Zach sat in the center of the couch.

"About time you got back," he said pleasantly, arms crossed over his chest. "Let me guess, you're drunk? Some mother you've turned out to be, Sophie. You're nothing but a fucking slut, you know that?"

Seeing him hit me like a physical blow.

I mean that—if someone had punched me in the stomach, it couldn't have hurt worse. I couldn't breathe, and I had to grab the wall to stay upright. That's the thing that nobody tells you as a girl, when they warn you about guys like Zach. You hear about women getting "abused," but that's such a sterile word for what Zach did to me. He didn't "abuse" me. He hurt me, owned me, trained me . . .

Broke me.

It's like hitting a dog with a rolled-up newspaper. You do it enough times, the dog will cringe whenever it sees the roll. Obedience becomes instinct, and in that second I felt it all come back to me.

Zach's bitch. That's all I was.

"You can't be here," I said feebly, wondering how just *seeing* him could make me feel so weak. "The restraining order says you can't be here. You're supposed to be hundreds of miles away. How did you get in?"

"I picked the lock, you stupid cunt," he replied. "Ruger taught me when we were kids. That and how to hotwire a car. Only fuckin' thing he ever did for me . . ."

He stood and walked over to me, a nasty gleam in his eye. He'd gotten bigger, I realized. Not taller, of course, and not fat, either. Zach must've started lifting weights, because those were some serious muscles. Steroid-sized muscles. He flexed them as he walked toward me, grinning as he read the fear in my face. He'd always had little-man syndrome.

My brain screamed at me to run, but my body wouldn't obey. I was strong during the kidnapping. I'd run from Skid, but then I turned around and fought him.

Why didn't I do that now?

I couldn't. My body wouldn't move.

Instead I just watched Zach, terrified, as he came up and cupped my face in his hands, fingers holding me just a little too tight.

"You're looking good," he said, licking his lips. He leaned forward and kissed me. Not a nice kiss—no, this one was meant to punish. I locked my jaw and kept my lips closed until he reached up and grabbed my hair, pulling it back sharply. "Open your fucking mouth, bitch."

I obeyed, because I knew pulling hair was the least of what he could do. He kissed me for an eternity, tongue stabbing into mine painfully. His mouth tasted stale and nasty, like he hadn't brushed his teeth in a year. I couldn't get any air and tears built up in my eyes.

Finally, he pulled away.

"Cunt still sweet as that mouth?" he asked. I didn't respond and he yanked my hair again. "Answer me, bitch!"

"I don't know," I whimpered. I should try to knee him. I should fight or kick or bite or something, but seeing Zach made me feel like a helpless little girl. He knew it, too. I could tell by the gleam of satisfaction in his eyes. Zach was a bully. How I hadn't recognized it from the start I'll never know, but I could sure as shit see it now.

"I hear you're fucking Ruger again," Zach whispered, face turning ugly. "I hear you're sucking his cock all over town, and that you're fucking his whole club, too. Is that true, slut?"

"No," I whimpered. "No, it's not true."

"What's not true?" he asked, mouth twisting into a smile. "Not true you're fucking Ruger, or not true that you're fucking his club? Because they don't just steal a man's inheritance for shits and giggles, babe. They don't do *anything* for free. You gotta tell me just how big a whore you are. Otherwise I won't know how much punishment you need."

"I'm not fucking anyone," I said. Zach burst out laughing. Seriously laughing, so hard he actually let me go and used the heel of one hand to press against his eyes, wiping away the tears.

"Let's try this again," he said when he finally stopped. "Who are you fucking? You belong to me, bitch. If you don't tell me the truth, I'll start breaking fingers."

He reached down and caught my hand between his, gripping my right index finger, bending it sharply backward.

I panicked, wishing I could get myself to *think*. My mind was numb, old survival instincts taking over.

Get it over with.

Do what he says.

Maybe he'll show mercy if you're a good girl . . .

"I had sex with Ruger," I said quickly. Then I closed my eyes, bracing for whatever might happen next. There's no preparing for something like that, though. Not really. I waited for my bone to snap, so it came as a complete surprise when he punched me in the stomach instead. I doubled over, gasping for breath. Holy *shit* that hurt.

Zach burst out laughing.

"You're too fuckin' easy."

Silly of me, I realized, clutching my stomach and praying he'd stop at just one hit. Zach never did what I expected him to do. You couldn't plan, couldn't get ready, nothing like that. He was like a tornado—suddenly there, spewing evil without warning.

Zach's laughter died.

"Hell of long drive to get here. I'm tired and hungry," he said. "So you're gonna make me something to eat. Then we'll talk some more about who you're sleeping with. Don't want to leave out any juicy details, do we?"

I dug through the fridge, trying to figure out what to cook him. My stomach ached, although I didn't feel like he'd broken any ribs. Yet. We didn't have a lot of food, but I could fix some eggs and toast. Zach had always loved breakfast for dinner.

"It was fucking stupid of you to come back to Coeur d'Alene," Zach said conversationally. He sat at the small table between the living room and kitchen, watching me and picking at his fingernails. "You couldn't just keep your legs shut, could you? I'll never let him have you. *Never.* Thought I'd made that clear?"

I didn't answer. No matter what I said, it would set him off. I remembered that much from before. Zach had always liked lecturing me during punishments, and if I didn't listen, the punishment got much, much worse. I just had to hunker down and push through. Sooner or later he'd get tired or bored and then it would stop.

At least for a while.

I'd never be truly free from him, though. I'd thought I could change my life.

Stupid, stupid, *stupid.*

"I've told you a thousand times about Ruger, but you still don't listen," he continued. "You never get it through your head, do you? I guess sluts like you can't control themselves . . . You need to be trained, like dogs. Bitches. Do you want me to train you?"

I took a deep breath, then let it out, closing my eyes tight. I knew what the next step was. Our little dance was well-choreographed.

"Yes, Zach," I whispered, feeling my soul tuck down deep inside, hiding from what was coming. If I drew far enough away from reality, it wouldn't hurt as bad when he started really hitting me. "I want you to train me."

"Good girl," he murmured, sounding almost human.

I knelt down and opened the drawer under the oven, looking for something to cook the eggs in. I had a small, non-stick frying pan I usually used. There was also a large, cast-iron skillet that I'd found when I moved into the apartment.

I'd never cooked with it—cast iron always seemed sort of strange and scary to me.

Huh.

Why should I be afraid of using a fucking pan? Because it was different than what I was used to? But changing how you do anything is difficult.

I could do it, though.

I could use that pan.

Almost in a dream, I reached down and picked up the skillet. How hard would it be . . . ? Harder than a man's fists against your flesh? Harder than cracked ribs, blackened eyes—your baby screaming for an hour because Mommy can't get off the floor to pick him up?

Changing how you react to a man hurting you is hard.

But it can be done.

The pan was heavy. Really heavy. My arms were strong, though. I'd been carrying Noah for years—this was nothing in comparison. I stood up and set the skillet on the stove, reaching over and turning on the burner.

"I think we need to get something clear," Zach said. He leaned back in his chair, grinning at me, all pleased with himself. Only seconds had passed as I found the skillet, but everything had changed. I felt my soul uncurling from its hiding place.

"You sent me to jail," Zach continued. "That was a very, very bad thing to do. I'll admit it threw me for a while. I let you get away with it. Then you stole my money, and that's more than a man can take. You try to fight me, I'll kill you. In fact, I won't just kill you, I'll kill Noah. Never did like that little shit."

Another gut punch. He hadn't used his fists this time. He didn't need to.

I looked down at the slowly heating skillet.

"Maybe I'll just make him disappear," he muttered. "Just take his little ass and dump him somewhere. You'll never find him again, always wonder if he's dead or alive. Maybe if you're really good, I'll tell you where the body is for his eighteenth birthday . . ."

I turned to grab eggs out of the fridge, glancing toward Zach. He was looking down at one of his hands, forming a fist over and over, flexing the muscles in his arm. I set the egg carton on the counter. Then I reached for a bowl to mix them in—he liked them scrambled, a mixture of full eggs and egg whites for extra protein. I started cracking them, the hard white shells looking like little skulls.

They broke open so easily.

I flicked another glance at him. He was still gazing down at his fingers, flexing and fisting.

Getting ready to hit me again.

"I'm gonna fuck you in the ass, I think," he said casually. "Make you beg for it. I've missed that about you, the way you beg."

My chest tightened, but I didn't let myself react to his words. I just picked up a towel and wrapped it around the hot pan's metal handle. Then I took a deep breath and thought of Noah, of what his little face would look like after Zach finished with him. Nope. Not gonna happen.

You can do this, I told myself, and I knew I was right. I could.

I lifted the pan, took three steps toward Zach and raised it high, bringing it down on his head with all my strength.

He never saw it coming.

Then I hit him a second time, just to be sure. And a third.

The smell of scorched meat filled the kitchen.

I smiled.

RUGER

He felt his phone vibrate, and he seriously considered just ignoring it.

It was nearly three thirty in the morning, and the girls had arrived at the Armory an hour ago. He'd never seen Marie so drunk. She wore a little white veil on her head and a white sash that said "Bride" across her chest, and she was carrying around some weird electronic vibrating thing like a trophy. Maggs said it was a sex toy, but damned if Ruger could figure out what it was for.

Horse was drunk, too, although not as bad as Marie. He'd carried his bride-to-be off not long after she arrived. They were upstairs now. That was the last they'd seen of them, although Dancer was trying to convince the girls that they needed to go and rescue Marie. That kept setting them off cackling like a bunch of damned witches.

Ruger pulled out his phone and saw Sophie's name. Fuck. Now what? He was trying to give her space, but it was fucking hard to pretend everything was fine while he waited. He missed her. The Jacks had taken her away from him for less than a day, but those hours had nearly killed him.

He needed her back. He needed her back *now*. Wasn't sure how much more of this he could take.

"Hey, Soph," he said, stepping out the door into the night air. It was almost October, but it was still warm out. A perfect Indian summer night.

"Ruger," she said, and her voice sounded strange. "Um, I have a problem."

"What is it?"

"I don't think I can tell you over the phone. Would—do you think you could come over? I mean, I know you're at the party . . . are you safe to drive, do you think?"

Double fuck. Something was really wrong. Her voice all but screamed it.

"Yeah, I'm good to drive," he said, and thankfully he was. Hadn't been in the mood to drink—too many thoughts running through his head. He heard her breath catch. "Should I bring anyone with me?"

"Um, we should probably be discreet," she said slowly. "I'm in some trouble here, Ruger. I don't know what to do."

"Are you hurt?" he asked quickly.

"I don't think so," she replied. "That's not really the worst of it . . . Ruger, I've done something bad. I think you should come over right now. I need you to tell me what to do. I know I keep asking you to stay out of my life, but I was wrong about that. I can't do this on my own."

"Okay, babe. I'll be right there."

He pulled up to her place twenty minutes later. She sat outside on the little stoop, arms wrapped tight around her knees. She looked impossibly brittle, like she'd explode into a thousand pieces if he touched her. Little red dots spotted her face.

Blood spatter. Fuck.

"What's up, Soph?" Ruger asked, crouching down. She looked at him with blank eyes. "Did you fall down or something?"

"No," she said quietly. "Zach punched my stomach and threatened to kill Noah, so I killed him instead."

Ruger froze.

"Excuse me?" he asked carefully, wondering if he'd hallucinated what she'd just said.

"Zach punched my stomach and threatened to kill Noah, so I killed him," she repeated, meeting his gaze. "He was mad at me because he'd heard I was sleeping with you. He's always been crazy jealous, you know that. I don't know what set him off, but he must've been spying on me somehow, because he knew exactly how to find me. He was inside the apartment, waiting, when I got home from the karaoke bar. He kissed me, and then he started asking questions and punched me. He said he was going to kill Noah and I knew he meant it, so I hit him over the head with a cast-iron skillet until he died."

Ruger swallowed. He didn't feel sorry for Zach, but this was one hell of a clusterfuck.

"Are you sure he's dead?"

She nodded slowly.

"I kept hitting him, just to make sure," she replied, far too calmly. "I checked his pulse. He's definitely dead. I'm hoping you'll tell me what to do next. I finally did my own dirty work, Ruger, but I don't know how to finish it."

Damn it. He shouldn't have left her alone. Should've come to check on her when she didn't show up with the rest of the girls . . . Fuck giving her space.

"Okay," he said. "Where's Noah?"

"Spending the night with Elle," Sophie said. "She'll get him ready for school in the morning. I'll pick him up and take him on the way to work."

Well, that was something.

"I'm going to go inside, check things out," he said. "That okay with you?"

"Sure," she murmured. "No problem. I'll just stay out here, I think?"

"That sounds good," he told her, reaching out and cupping her cheek. She leaned her head into his touch, eyes starting to water. Then he stood up and stepped past her, opening the door.

Fuck. Double fuck . . .

Zach was on the floor, his hair matted with blood. A pool of it surrounded him. A horrible stench filled the air, a mixture of burned meat and scorched hair.

The pan lay next to Zach's corpse, more blood crusting the sides. It'd splattered behind him, too. That would take some serious cleaning. New linoleum for sure, and they might even need to replace the floorboards underneath, he mused.

Ruger checked Zach's pulse just to be sure, but Sophie was right. His stepbrother was definitely dead. This was a mess, a big mess, and cleaning it up wouldn't be pretty.

He was proud of her, though.

She'd defended herself when it counted, and ultimately this was Ruger's fault. He should've killed Zach four years ago. Then he should have killed him when he'd collected the child support. Fucking weak of him.

He'd held off because of Noah.

Didn't want to kill the boy's father. Didn't want to do that to his own mother, either. She'd loved Zach, for reasons Ruger had never understood. So he'd given Zach another pass, leaving his woman to finish the job.

Fucking idiot.

Ruger pulled out his phone and dialed Pic.

"It's Ruger," he said. "I'm out at Soph's place. Could use some help here, it's delicate. Anyone up for it? Probably gonna need a van . . ."

"How delicate?" Picnic asked. He hadn't been drinking much, either, thank fuck. Neither of them had quite relaxed since the kidnapping, and that vigilance might save Sophie's ass now.

"About as delicate as it gets," Ruger said slowly. "We should talk in person."

"Gotcha," Pic replied, hanging up. Ruger went back outside and found Sophie still sitting on the porch. He sat down behind her, wrapping his arms around her body, legs surrounding hers as he pulled her close. She shivered.

"Hey, Soph," he whispered, nuzzling her neck. She leaned back into him and he realized she was crying softly, tears rolling down her face.

Good. Crying was better than that creepy calm she'd had earlier.

"I'm really sorry, Ruger," she told him. "I keep calling you in to fix things, always making you do the hard stuff. First Miranda, now this. I should've called the cops . . ."

"No fucking way," he said. "That's a mess we don't need. You might get off on self-defense, you might not. Not after you kept hitting him. He was just sitting when you attacked, right? He wasn't about to hit you or something?"

"Not really," Sophie replied. "He was looking at his hands and I was supposed to be cooking eggs."

"You did what you had to do," Ruger said, hoping she believed him. "He chose this—he threatened your son, Soph. You had to protect him. That's what mothers do."

She nodded her head.

"I know," she replied. "He said he'd kill all of us and I knew he meant it. The restraining order didn't do shit. Going to jail only stopped him for a while . . . What if he hurt Noah next time? I wasn't willing to take that chance."

"We'll clean this up for you," he replied, resting his cheek on her head. God, he loved how she smelled, although for once his dick had the grace to stay down. "Hopefully nobody knew he was coming here. He'll just disappear. If the cops ever come looking, we'll say I did it, okay?"

"You can't—" she tried to protest, but he cut her off.

"I'm not planning on it," Ruger said. "Trust me, prison isn't on my bucket list. We play things right, it won't be an issue. He wasn't here, it never happened. But if the shit hits the fan, you'll do what I tell you, what the club lawyer tells you. Got me?"

"I just feel so bad dragging you into it."

"We're a family," he whispered. "We take care of each other. That's the way it works, babe. You protected yourself and Noah, now I'll protect you. My brothers'll cover my ass, and we'll all make it through just fine."

"We are a family, aren't we?" she whispered.

"Always."

She nodded her head slowly, and he squeezed her tight. They sat together quietly, waiting for Picnic, listening to the frogs and crickets singing in the background.

CHAPTER SEVENTEEN

SOPHIE

Ruger, Picnic, and Painter took care of Zach.

They made him disappear, along with the frying pan, my clothes, and every other piece of evidence in the house.

Erasing a human life shouldn't be so easy.

Ruger had me take a shower, then I crawled into Noah's bed and tried to sleep. Even if my mind hadn't been racing, I hurt too bad to get any rest. I'd have a hell of a bruise. At least it wouldn't show anywhere. The sun was already rising when I heard him come back and turn on the shower. Twenty minutes later he padded into the bedroom and lay down next to me, pulling me into his arms.

I turned and burrowed into him, holding him tight.

"Thank you," I whispered fiercely, and I meant it. Not just for tonight, but for everything. "Thank you for always being here for me."

"It's what I do," he whispered back. His hand came up and ran through my hair softly, soothing me.

"I was wrong," I said.

"Hmmm?"

"I was wrong about you," I continued. "I kept saying I didn't want anything to do with you, that the club does horrible things. But I'm the one doing horrible things."

"You survived," he replied, and his voice didn't waver. "You protected your son. That's not horrible."

"When I called you, you could've told me to fuck off," I replied. "I had no right to drag you into this. Now you're an accomplice."

"Babe, it's over," he said. "Let it be over. I'll come by in a couple of days, put some new flooring in the kitchen, throw on some paint. Then it's done. We don't need to talk about it, okay? In fact, we *shouldn't* talk about it."

"Okay," I whispered. "What about us? I feel like this changes things."

"We don't need to figure it out right now, Soph," he said. "Try to sleep. You've got to be up in an hour for work. It's going to be a long, tiring day, and you've got to get through it. On the bright side, if anyone asks why you look like shit, you can say you're hungover. Plenty of witnesses to that, thank fuck."

"Wish I could call in sick," I said. "I suppose calling in with a hangover this early into the job isn't such a good idea, hmm?"

"Probably not," he said. He kissed the top of my head. "Like I said, we don't have to figure things out right now, but I'm going to stay with you for a while. I don't want you alone."

It didn't occur to me to argue. I really, really didn't want to be alone. I'd never believed in ghosts, but I was pretty sure Zach planned to haunt me.

Probably for the rest of my life.

A week later we still hadn't talked things through.

Ruger moved us back to his house the Saturday after I killed

Zach, and this time I didn't argue with him. He put me back in my old room, and while we spent almost every evening together, he never did more than give me a quick kiss good night.

I appreciated that more than I knew how to say.

Things had changed between us in a profound way, something I think we both knew. All our fighting and nitpicking seemed so silly now. So did my endless agonizing about whether or not I should be with him. Once a man disposes of a body for you, the moral high ground has been lost.

Nothing says "commitment" like accessory to murder.

Sooner or later we'd be together. I just wasn't ready yet, and surprisingly, Ruger was patient. We both worried that yet another move would upset Noah, but he took it in stride—apparently he'd never considered Elle's place as anything more than an extended sleepover anyway.

Elle just gave a Cheshire cat smile when I told her we'd be moving.

Apparently life goes on, even after you kill someone.

Marie and Horse had their rehearsal dinner the following Friday night. I wasn't originally invited to it. No reason I would be, considering I wasn't in the wedding party or a member of the family. Ruger was Horse's best man, though, so he had to be there. Apparently in his eyes, and in those of the club, we were officially a couple now, so Noah and I were invited, too.

It felt good to be included.

The wedding itself would be taking place out at the Armory, which seemed odd to me at first. They weren't getting married in the building or courtyard itself, though. Out beyond the wall was a large meadow where people camped out for club functions. It backed into a grove of old-growth trees, forming a natural canopy that was perfect for a wedding. There were already tents set up along the edges, but the center and back were marked off with neon-orange ribbon that outlined an area for the ceremony.

I offered to watch the kids during the rehearsal, including Dancer's two boys. We hit the play area inside the courtyard, and they all ran around like wild animals, shrieking and jumping off the swing set. The rehearsal dinner was in the courtyard, too, so I found myself helping the caterer set up while we waited. She was a friend of the club named Candace, and she had a wicked sense of humor.

I also met Marie's mom, Lacey Benson, and her stepdad, John.

Lacey was . . . different.

She looked a lot like Marie. In fact, she could've been Marie's sister, at least at first glance. But where Marie's hair was wild and free, Lacey's was in one of those styles you just know takes an expensive hair cut, double-processing, and a shitload of product to look so natural and perfect. Marie didn't usually wear makeup. Lacey's was flawless, and her clothes never seemed to wrinkle. She was the portrait of a stylish matron, except for the smell of cigarette smoke wafting around her.

She was poised, stunning, and utterly batshit crazy.

The crazy wasn't subtle, either.

She had a manic energy that couldn't be contained, and she hovered around Marie like a hummingbird, obviously overjoyed for her daughter. Just watching her was exhausting.

I learned that Candace was more than a nice person—she might possibly be a saint. No matter how many times Lacey made her rearrange everything, she did it with a nod and a gracious smile. This was a step beyond impressive, because Marie's mother rearranged things seven times.

Then she rearranged an eighth, this time while people were actually serving.

After dinner, Lacey stood up and gave a long and rambling toast, telling us stories I was pretty sure Marie didn't appreciate. We heard about how she didn't like to wear clothes when she was a toddler, and was always stripping down in the grocery store. We heard about the time she'd decided to ride the neighbor's goat . . . wearing spurs.

We also heard about when Lacey first met Horse, which led to an interesting side-ramble about jail, cops, anger management, her husband, and engagement guns.

Clearly feeling outdone, Horse's mother got into the spirit and we learned he'd refused to pee inside the house for the first five years of his life, something his father had found hysterically funny and encouraged.

Dancer's toast put both of them to shame, though. She stood in front of everyone and called Marie up for a special presentation. Then she pulled out the little stuffed horse she'd told us about the first night we'd met, along with a small bedazzled harness and matching leash.

Maggs and Em supplemented it with a tiny, toy-sized Harley for the horse to ride.

Marie laughed so hard she almost choked on her champagne. Horse smiled grimly, wrapping an arm around Dancer's neck and squeezing her shoulder in an almost-hug. It transitioned to a necklock and prolonged noogie. She screamed and cried and kicked, but he didn't let her go until she admitted she'd made the whole thing up, which none of us believed for a minute.

Noah and I left around nine, just as things were starting to get interesting. Guests had been arriving all day, camping out behind the Armory, and they joined the party once the official dinner events had ended. I was exhausted and my whole body ached, so I was happy to leave. I still had bruises, although thankfully no broken ribs this time. I collapsed into bed alone, wishing Ruger was with me.

The morning of the wedding dawned warm and perfect.

They'd taken a risk, planning an outdoor event in early October.

It paid off, because there are few things more beautiful than fall in northern Idaho. The evergreen-covered hills were spotted with bright yellow and orange patches. The air had a sharp feel that made me think of that first burst of flavor when you bite into a honeycrisp apple.

It took all I had to keep Noah inside while I got ready. I knew he'd be filthy by the end of the day, but I wanted to at least start things out with him clean. Ruger hadn't come home last night. I assumed he'd been partying with Horse all night, and I wondered about what they'd been doing . . .

There had been tons of people at the party last night, and a lot of them were female. He'd told me after the kidnapping that he didn't want anyone else but me, that he'd be faithful.

He'd even given me a soft kiss good night when he'd walked us to the car.

But I wasn't quite sure what our new arrangement was supposed to be, or where the limits stood. We still hadn't talked about it. We weren't having sex. Did that mean he'd been sleeping with someone else? Multiple someone elses?

Thinking about it made me feel sick.

I could just ask him. There were things he wouldn't tell me, but I didn't think he'd lie. I just wasn't sure I wanted to hear the answer.

I pulled up to the Armory about an hour and a half before the ceremony was supposed to start. There were cars everywhere, and bikes, too. The girls had been busy that morning decorating. I saw Painter as I pulled up, and he raised a hand in a friendly wave. I walked around the Armory and let Noah join the pack of children running wild out there, because the courtyard was off bounds. They were busy setting up the reception in there.

Picnic leaned back against the wall, watching the kids with a thoughtful look on his face. Then he saw me and waved me over.

"How you doing?" he asked. I shrugged.

"Pretty good, I guess," I said. Looking everywhere but his face,

I managed to choke out something I'd meant to say the night before. "Thanks for helping me. I mean, last weekend."

"No worries, never happened," he said, cocking his head and studying my face. "But I've been meaning to talk to you."

"Sure," I agreed, because I owed him in a big way.

"Do you know what happened between Em and Hunter?" he asked bluntly. "She's not herself, and she won't say shit to me. That's not normal—she's always been *my* girl, the one who'd tell me everything. Not her sister. Now she's closed off."

I sighed and looked into his face. His blue eyes held concern, and I saw how much it hurt him to ask.

"I don't know," I said. "She was alone with him the first night, and then again for an hour the next day. She never told me what happened, but I don't think he raped her, if that's what you're after. She didn't seem like a victim. Em was pissed at him—really pissed. That's about all I can tell you."

"More'n she's said so far," he replied. His mouth tightened. "She's upstairs with Marie. You might as well go up, too. They're like a bunch of fuckin' harpies. I tried to go up and talk to Em earlier and they wouldn't let me in the room."

"I need to keep an eye on Noah."

Picnic glanced toward the pack of kids running through the grass.

"He's not goin' anywhere," he said. "Plenty of adults out here already. You should be with Marie."

"I don't even know her that well," I protested. "I feel kind of strange . . ."

"Honey, you're in this club as deep as any of us at this point," he replied, his voice commanding. "Hard to get much deeper. Might as well have some of the fun, too."

He smiled and I found myself struck once again at how handsome he was for an old guy.

"Okay, I'll go see how they're doing."

"Have fun," he told me. "And keep an eye on Em. If you can think of any way for me to help her, let me know."

"Of course."

I found Marie up on the third floor in one of the bedrooms.

Maggs had discovered me in the kitchen and recruited me to help her haul up beer. Apparently Marie had decided that marrying Horse completely sober wasn't the world's greatest idea. As her girlfriends, we were required to join her, because that's what friends do.

Let it never be said I've abandoned someone in their time of need.

We lugged the beer up the stairs, Maggs telling me that she'd never seen Marie more beautiful . . . or more stressed out. I heard her yelling before we reached the room, something about being a grown-up and wanting to make her own decisions. I swung the door open and dropped the beer on the floor with a clanking of bottles.

Marie stood in the center of the room, wearing a gorgeous white dress—very classic-looking, with a sweetheart neckline, a narrow waist to show off her figure, and a sweeping gown. Her brown hair was pinned up, cascading down in a riot of curls, and she wore flowers woven through it. No veil.

I guess she'd gotten her fill of white tulle during the limo ride.

"I love you!" she yelled when she saw me, although I wasn't sure she even noticed who I was. Nope, she zoned in on the beer, grabbing one and popping the top off using her engagement ring as a church key. She chugged almost the entire bottle, then set it down and turned to face her mother defiantly.

"My daughter is not wearing black leather for her wedding," Lacey proclaimed, waving the offending item in her hand—Marie's vest with her "Property of Horse" patch.

"Horse wants me to wear it," Marie snapped. "It's important to him."

"It doesn't go with your dress," Lacey snapped back. "It's ridiculous. This is your day—you should look like a princess!"

"If it's my day, why can't I decide what I wear?" Marie asked, her voice rising. Lacey's eyes narrowed.

"Because I'm your mother and I know what you really want!" she yelled. "Fuck, I need a smoke."

"I don't want my dress to smell like smoke," Marie shouted back. "And I want *my day* to be about *me*! Give me my fucking property patch!"

"No!" Lacey hissed. She looked around frantically, then spotted a pair of florist's scissors on the counter. Snatching them up, she held them to the vest menacingly. "Stay back, or the patch gets it!"

We all froze.

"What if you take the patch off the vest and put it on the dress?" I suggested suddenly, inspired by the scissors. "That way you can still wear it, but the vest won't ruin the lines of the dress for the pictures."

"You can't pull off the patch," Cookie declared. "That'd be like divorcing Horse. But we could make a copy of it and pin that on her."

Silence fell across the room as Marie and her mother fought a silent battle with their eyes.

Lacey's nostrils flared.

"I could live with that," Marie said slowly. We all swiveled toward Lacey. She nodded slowly.

"I'm willing to accept it."

They glared at each other a moment longer. Lacey held out the vest slowly and Marie snatched it back. Dancer grabbed the vest and took off downstairs, presumably in search of the copier.

"I'm gonna go smoke and do some of my *peace affirmations*," Lacey said slowly, spearing us with her eyes, one by one. "When I come back, the patch will be on the dress in such a way that it's not visible from the front, for the pictures. If I see it from the front, we'll have a problem and no peace affirmation on Earth will be enough to save your asses. We have an understanding?"

She swept out of the room and Marie growled.

"I need another beer."

I handed her one quickly, then grabbed one for myself. Holy shit, and I'd thought her mom was crazy last night . . .

Marie pounded her drink as Dancer reappeared, panting. She held a color copy of the patch up triumphantly.

"Where do you want it?" she asked Marie. "We'll have to tape it on the dress right before you head down the aisle."

"I want it on my butt," Marie said, just as I'd taken a drink. "So my mother has to look at it the whole damned ceremony."

I couldn't help myself. I started giggling, which I tried to cover with a cough, forgetting I had a mouth full of beer. I ended up snorting it out my nose, and then everyone lost it. Dancer was actually crying when she finally stopped, and we all took a moment to poke at our eyes with tissues, trying to fix our makeup. Then she turned to Marie.

"I like the idea of it back there," she said, biting back another laugh. "I know it'll piss off your mom, and that's great. But it'll also send a nice message to Horse . . ."

Marie's eyes widened.

"Oh, you're right," she whispered. "Let's do it."

And that's how Marie ended up getting married to Horse with a property patch on her ass.

We all walked Marie downstairs, and then Dancer and Em bustled her off to wherever she planned to hide until things got started. I collected Noah and we wandered around back to the meadow, which had been transformed since the night before.

There were twice as many tents now, probably more than a hundred. They'd set up a little wooden pulpit at the front, and chairs had been laid out in neat rows on either side of the aisle, just like any outdoor wedding.

But this wasn't just any wedding. It was a Reaper wedding, and apparently they liked to add their own twist to the ceremony. All the guys had parked their bikes in two neat, diagonal rows on either side of the center, forming a path of shining chrome for Marie to walk through.

I had to admit, it looked cool.

As Ruger's . . . *whatever* . . . I had a place reserved for me up front, right next to Maggs, Cookie, and Darcy. We sat for about ten minutes, Noah squirming, while we waited for things to get started. Then the sound system crackled to life and the minister asked everyone to find their seats.

Horse and Ruger stepped out from the trees, coming around front to stand and wait. Both wore black jeans and bright white button-up shirts. They also wore their colors. The minister wore a vest, too, although he wasn't a Reaper.

"Chaplain from Spokane," Maggs whispered to me. "He's done stuff for the club before. Good guy."

I nodded, then we all turned to watch as Pachelbel's Canon started wafting through the meadow. The first to come down the aisle was a very little girl I didn't recognize, carrying a basket of flower petals that she scattered as she walked. Dancer's two boys followed as ring bearers. Marie's mom and stepdad were next, and then I heard the roar of a motorcycle across the meadow.

I craned my neck to see Picnic riding slowly toward the group with Marie on the back of his bike. My eyes widened, delighted. Maggs giggled and leaned over.

"We didn't tell her mom about that part . . ."

I glanced quickly to the front to see Lacey's eyes narrowed and suspicious. John wrapped an arm around her shoulders and whispered something in her ear. She glared at him, then shrugged and rolled her eyes. Apparently she knew when she'd been beaten.

Picnic came to a stop at the end of the aisle, where Em and Dancer—as bridesmaids—waited to help Marie off the bike and fix her dress. Then the two women walked down the aisle before her, side by side. We all rose as Picnic held out his arm to Marie, then slowly escorted her toward Horse.

That's when the people in the back started laughing.

Everyone around us looked confused, and I glanced up to find Horse frowning. He leaned over toward Ruger, murmuring something to him. The waves of laughter kept growing as Marie moved forward, and then I was able to see the patch—"Property of Horse"—proudly displayed on her rear end, as promised.

Picnic stopped at the end, stepping back as Horse came to collect Marie. She whispered something to him, and he looked around behind her to see the patch. His face split in a huge grin and I glanced over to see Lacey biting her lip, trying not to laugh. She winked at Marie, silently acknowledging that her daughter had won, and the ceremony started.

I don't remember all the details. It went fast. I kept looking up to find Ruger watching me, his face serious. I did note two very interesting facts, though. The first was that Horse's full name was Marcus Antonius Caesar McDonnell, God help him.

The second was that Marie didn't promise to obey.

Good girl.

Then the minister pronounced them husband and wife, and Horse swept Marie up into a kiss that I was pretty sure could get a woman pregnant. Def Leppard's "Pour Some Sugar on Me" burst through the speakers and Horse all but carried her back down the aisle as everyone cheered—and bikers cheer *loud*.

Ruger walked Dancer back down the aisle, and Em walked by herself.

"They left the second spot for Bolt," Maggs said to me, her eyes misty. "They always leave a spot for Bolt. They're waiting for him to come home."

I glanced over at Cookie, whose face had gone pale.

"Are you all right?" I asked. She gave me a tight smile.

"Excuse me, I need to go check on Silvie," she said. I must've looked blank, because she explained. "The flower girl. She's my daughter."

"Oh, she's beautiful," I said, but Cookie was already up and moving.

I'd noticed a few things since I started getting to know the Reapers.

They were fiercely loyal to each other. They seemed to talk in code sometimes, and they had their own rules and ways of doing things. They didn't like cops and they knew how to get rid of bodies. The Reapers didn't really shine, though, until you'd seen them party.

Give them a marriage to celebrate and a pyramid of kegs?

The place blew up.

Marie's mom definitely knew how to throw a reception, too. They'd gone with casual, and I entered the courtyard to find it transformed into something that wasn't quite elegant, but was definitely fun. There were lights everywhere, music blasting, and enough food for two armies.

Best of all? There was child care.

Yup, she'd hired the entire staff of a local day care center to come in and set up a children's area, complete with games, prizes, face painting, and a genuine fucking pony to ride on. The kids even had their own little buffet where they could put together hot dogs and hamburgers.

Noah lost interest in me immediately.

"Wow, this is amazing," I said to Maggs as he took off running. "I didn't realize Marie came from money."

"Marie comes from a trailer," Maggs replied, laughing. "But

her stepdaddy's trying to make up for lost time, and he's loaded. What Lacey wants, Lacey gets. Today she wants a pony."

"No shit," I said.

Then Ruger's arms came around me and he leaned down into me, scenting my hair.

"Hey," he whispered in my ear. I melted. Maggs rolled her eyes as I turned in his arms.

"Hey," I whispered back. Then I put my hands on his shoulders and lifted up on my toes to kiss him. We'd been doing this a lot the past week. Soft, sweet, quick kisses that let me show my feelings without things getting too intense.

This time it wasn't soft and sweet.

I guess watching Horse and Marie had inspired Ruger, because he kissed me fast and hard, just like he used to. Then he pulled away and looked down at me, his face serious.

"We okay?" he asked.

"Yeah, we're okay," I said, smiling up at him. "I missed you."

"I missed you, too. One part of you in particular. Let's get re-acquainted."

I blushed as he took my arm and half walked me, half dragged me across the courtyard. I stumbled, catching his drift but not on board with his timing.

"Where are we going?" I demanded. "We're going to miss everything!"

"Horse already said the party can wait until he's fucked his bride, and he's a smart man," Ruger muttered, pausing next to a table to grab a backpack. Then I realized where we were headed.

"No," I said, jerking and tugging against his hand. "Not the shed. I'm not going back into that shed."

"No prob," Ruger replied, changing direction without a pause. Now we headed toward the back of the Armory. I saw Dancer as we passed, and she was laughing and pointing at me.

Some friend.

Then we were in the stairwell, climbing back up to the third floor. Ruger spotted an open door to one of the rooms, and we walked in to find a woman on her knees, giving some man I'd never seen before a blow job.

"Need a blanket," Ruger said to him, pulling one off the bed. The guy nodded, and then we were back out again before I could burst into embarrassed flames. Ruger took me up one more flight through a door that opened onto the roof. It was wide and open, with big parapets ringing the edges. There was a bit of a slope, but not much. We were essentially out in the open.

"This isn't much better than the shed," I said, and Ruger turned to me, raising his brows.

"Are you fucking serious?" he asked. "I find the one place within a mile that we can have privacy and you're gonna bitch about it? Besides, it's tradition. Guys take girls up here all the time. Hell, Horse proposed to Marie on a roof."

I frowned.

"I guess it's okay," I said.

"Well that's a relief," he muttered, flinging the blanket down flat. Then his hands were tangling in my hair and his mouth covered mine.

I don't quite remember how I wound up on the bottom. I certainly don't remember what happened to my panties, although I sort of suspected Ruger stole them. He seemed to have a bit of a panty thing going on.

What I do remember is trying not to scream and failing when his mouth sucked my clit in deep. I also remember when he plunged into me, stretching me open wide and reminding me that I wasn't just crazy about him because he took good care of Noah.

Holy shit, the man had skills.

We took a break after that first round of reunion sex, relocating into the shade behind the little shed housing the stairwell. Ruger lay back and made a little nest for me in his arm, and I snuggled in close. He'd lost his clothes along the way, and I figured if being totally naked out in the open didn't bother him, I might as well enjoy the view.

I leaned up on one arm and started kissing his chest.

"That's nice," he said, his voice hoarse. "Jesus, I've missed touching you."

"I've missed you, too," I said. The tribal tat on his pec called to me, so I started tracing it with my tongue. I loved how he tasted, just a little salty and all male. I loved how hard his muscles were, too, and deep down inside I had to admit I loved the fact that he'd do anything for me.

Anything.

I dropped lower to find the ring in his nipple, flicking it with my tongue.

"Think it's time to talk yet?" he asked.

I let the ring go reluctantly.

"Yeah, probably," I said, looking up at him. "We should probably get us—whatever we're going to be—figured out."

"Let's make it official," he said. "I want you to be my old lady, pretty sure you know that. You up for that?"

"I think so," I said slowly. "Were you serious about being faithful? I mean, after you came to get me, when Em and I were with the Devil's Jacks? Were you serious about not sleeping around? Because that's still a deal breaker for me."

"Totally serious," Ruger replied. He looked me right in the eye. "I haven't slept with anyone else, babe. Not since I fucked you in the shed. I'll admit, I thought about it, but they weren't you. Just wasn't feelin' it."

I caught my breath.

"Then why did you keep telling me you couldn't make any

promises?" I asked, startled. "I thought you were screwing girls left and right the whole time."

"Always told you I wouldn't lie," he said. "Didn't want to make a promise I couldn't keep. But shit, Soph, when I thought I might lose you? It all got real clear, real fast. I don't give a flying fuck about anyone else, babe. I love you. Think I've loved you from the first, when I found you and Zach on my couch. Spent a lot of time trying to talk myself out of it, but it's not goin' away."

I blinked rapidly. He loved me. Ruger *loved* me. I guess I'd known that for a while now—you don't take care of someone the way he'd taken care of me and Noah if you don't love them.

Hearing the words was still nice.

"I love you, too," I replied, feeling suddenly shy. "I think I have for a long time. You were always there for me."

"That's what you do when you're crazy about someone," he said, giving me a little grin. "Trust me, I wasn't helping you move, putting alarms on your windows, all that shit, outta the goodness of my heart, babe. Not running a fuckin' charity here."

I gave a little laugh. His gaze was so intense, I couldn't meet it any longer. I looked at his shoulder instead, and for the first time I really studied the tattoos there. There was a series of round dots, each trailing off a bit, almost like a line of comets.

"What are those?" I asked.

"What?"

"The tattoos on your shoulders. I've been trying to figure them out for a while now. They don't look like anything."

He lifted, leaning back on his elbows, and gave me a serious look.

"Sit on my hips," he said. I raised a brow.

"You ready for seconds already?" I asked. "Or trying to dodge the question? Let me guess, you got drunk and now you can't remember what they are?"

He shook his head slowly.

"Oh, I remember," he said. "Go ahead, sit on me. Want to show you something."

I looked at him suspiciously, but threw my leg over his hips. His cock rested right against my opening and I felt a flush of desire run through me. He wasn't the only one ready for more.

"Now put your hands on my shoulders," he said.

"What?"

"Put your hands on my shoulders."

I did. Then it hit me.

"Holy shit, you're such a pig!" I said, stunned. "What kind of asshole has fingerprints on his shoulders? God, are the women you screw so stupid they need a guide so they don't fall off?"

His eyes widened, and then he started laughing. I ripped my hands away, glaring at him. I tried to get off, but he sat up and held my waist tight. Then he stopped laughing and smiled at me.

"First, some of them probably were that stupid," he admitted. "But those are your fingerprints, babe."

I looked at him blankly.

"You probably wouldn't remember, but that night you had Noah?" he said. "You hunkered down on the side of the road and held my shoulders while you pushed him out."

I realized what Ruger was saying, and I reached up, laying my fingers on the tattoos again. They fit perfectly.

"I don't even know how to explain that night to you," he said. "It was so intense, Soph. I had no idea what we were doing. I've never watched anything like it, never felt anything even close. You worked so hard to bring him to life. All I could do was hold you, hoping I didn't fuck something up. You squeezed my shoulders so hard they hurt for days. You dug in your nails, you left bruises, the works. Christ, you were strong."

I thought back to that night, remembering how I'd crouched on the side of the road. The pain. The fear.

The joy of holding Noah for the first time.

"I'm sorry," I said softly. "I didn't mean to hurt you."

He snorted at me and grinned.

"You didn't hurt me, babe," he said. "You marked me. Big difference. That night was the most important thing that's ever happened in my life. Holding you, catching Noah—it changed me forever. I didn't want to forget. So when the bruises started to fade, I went and got them inked, so I couldn't."

"Damn," I said, touching the spots lightly with my fingertips. "I think that's the sweetest thing I've ever heard."

I felt him harden under me, and he smirked.

"Sweet enough to get me laid again?" he asked. "Because I've told the story to women before, and it works every fuckin' time. Can't get their pants off fast enough after that. Hate to think you're the one girl who can hold out, considering it's about you."

I started laughing, and then he rolled me over, pinning my hands over my head. My laughter faded as his cock found my opening.

"Love you, babe," he said, sliding slowly into me. "Promise. I'll always be here for you."

"I know," I whispered back to him. "You always have been. I love you, too, Ruger. And I swear, you tell that story to any more girls, I'll cut that ink right off you."

"Noted," he said with a grin.

I reached up and kissed him as he hit bottom, slowly working in and out of me, grazing my clit with every stroke. I lifted my legs to wrap them around his waist, closing my eyes against the sun and letting the sensation of his thick cock spreading me soak through my entire being.

I loved this man.

I loved how he held me, loved how he cared for my son, and loved how he always fixed whatever fucked up, horrible things went wrong in my life.

As he rocked into me gently, I could hear the guests partying down in the courtyard, music drifting upward as people shouted and cheered and made the most of what had to be one of the last warm days of the year. Maggs was down there, and Em and Picnic and Dancer and Bam Bam . . . It wasn't just Ruger, I realized. All of them had helped me, even when I'd judged them for being Reapers.

But the Reapers were part of Ruger, and Ruger was part of me.

He hit particularly deep, and I started laughing.

"What the fuck?" he grunted without pausing.

"You're a part of me," I said, giggling.

He paused, raising a brow. Then he rotated his hips slowly and deliberately, making me gasp.

"Damned straight," he said, smirking. I grabbed his butt, urging him to start moving again, and he didn't complain. Within seconds I'd forgotten about the party below and focused on the sensations building inside. He moved faster, plunging into me, scooting my butt across the blanket with the force of his thrusts.

"Shit, I'm close," I muttered.

Ruger grunted, then pulled out of me abruptly, rolling to his back and gasping for air.

"What the fuck?" I demanded.

"Want to give you something," he said, his voice tight. I sat up and glared at him.

"No. You have the world's shittiest timing."

He laughed, although there was definitely a note of strain in the sound. He shook his head, sitting up and leaning over to dig through the backpack he'd brought up with us. Then he pulled it out. A black leather vest.

A vest that said "Property of Ruger."

My mouth dropped open, and I took a deep breath.

"Ruger—"

"Listen to me first," he said, eyes intent on my face. "You're not from my world, so you don't know exactly what wearing a vest like this means."

"Okay . . ." I said slowly, although I couldn't imagine anything he'd say that would make me comfortable with it.

"You look at this and see the word 'property,'" he said. "But what it really means is you're my woman, and I want everyone to know it. I live in a harsh world, babe. A world where bad shit happens, you've seen that for yourself. But no matter what goes down, my brothers have my back. This vest means you're one of us. Those aren't just words, Sophie. We're a tribe, and every Reaper in the club—men you don't even know—would die to protect a woman wearing this vest. They'd do it because they're my brothers, and because it means more than any ring ever could in our world."

"I don't understand . . ." I murmured, trying to wrap my head around his words.

"When a man takes a woman as his property, it's not about owning her," he continued, eyes searching my face. "It's about *trusting* her. This is my life I'm handing you, Sophie. Not just my life—my brothers' lives, too. It means I'm responsible for everything you do. You fuck up, I'll pay. You need help, we're there. You're the only woman I've ever met that I'd consider giving that kind of power to. Hell, I'm not just considering it, I'm desperate for you to take it. I want you to wear my patch, Soph. Will you?"

I sighed, then reached for the leather. It was warm from the sun, and I ran my fingers along it, feeling the strength of the stitching. It had been made to last, no question. I'd be able to wear it for years. Maybe even a lifetime.

I looked at Ruger, with his strong hands that had caught my son at birth, and his smile that left me breathless. I knew my answer. No need to make it too easy for him, though . . .

"Can I ask one thing?"

"Of course," he said, and I thought I heard a hint of anxiety in his voice.

"Was it really necessary to stop right in the middle of sex to have this conversation? I was almost to the good part."

He laughed, then shook his head.

"I made myself a promise," he said, looking almost sheepish.

"And that was?"

"I promised myself the next time I fucked you, you'd be wearing my patch. I got distracted, though. You got really nice tits, babe."

"You already screwed me once up here," I said, trying to keep a straight face. "Why didn't you just finish up?"

"Because I'm a dumbass," he said, shrugging. "I don't know. I realized you'd be exploding around me soon, squeezing my cock like the world was gonna end, and I wanted you to wear my patch when you did it. Just sort of came to me."

I held it up, considering it thoughtfully. Might as well torture him a bit, seeing as he'd left me hanging.

"Looks like a nice vest," I said slowly. "Are you sure you're ready for this?"

"Yeah, Sophie, I'm fuckin' sure," he replied, rolling his eyes. "So what's it gonna be? Either you wear it and put us both out of our misery, or we both go home in pain and horny as hell. Because I'm serious. No patch, no dick."

"Okay," I said.

"Seriously?"

"Yeah, seriously," I replied. "Don't look so surprised. You got a really nice dick, babe."

I put on the vest, savoring the look in his eyes as he watched. It chafed my nipples a little, and I bit back a laugh. Maybe Marie could give me some pointers on dealing with that . . . Then he pulled me up and over his body, lifting me just enough to slide the pierced dick in question deep inside. I braced my arms on his chest and leaned down, rocking slowly as I studied his face.

"So what do you think?" I whispered.

"Like how it looks on you, Soph," he said, smiling up at me. "Great view. Of course, wouldn't mind seeing it from the back. You up for some reverse cowgirl action?"

"First get the job done like this," I muttered. "Then we'll talk about getting creative."

Ruger smiled and reached down between us, finding my clit with his fingers.

"That a promise?" he asked.

"Hell yeah."

EPILOGUE

FIVE YEARS LATER
RUGER

"I'm gonna stick it in now."

Sophie's voice was soft and smooth, with just a hint of laughter.

Ruger smelled her special scent and felt a shot to his groin, the same as every time he'd seen her since that first night in his apartment. She was so beautiful he could die, and he still couldn't believe she was truly his.

But why the *fuck* she thought this was a good idea he couldn't fathom. She was moving too fast. They weren't ready, he needed her to slow down, to really think about how this would change things between them. Being part of the club had opened her eyes, but there should be limits, too.

He scowled, catching her hand and stopping her mid-motion.

"Why can't you just stay with me? It's always worked between us. I don't get why I'm not enough for you."

Sophie rolled her eyes.

"Christ, Ruger, tone back the caveman for once," she muttered.

"You know I've wanted to try it for a while now, and it's not like it's my first time. It's not going to change anything between you and me, babe. But I *need* this. You want me to be happy, you *always* say you want me to be happy. Sometimes that means giving up a little, taking the next step. Let me be in charge for once."

Ruger closed his eyes for a second, taking in a deep breath. Then he opened them again and gazed at the woman he loved more than anything. She grinned at him, and holy crap, he loved that grin.

"Sorry, babe," he said, leaning forward to give her a quick peck on those soft, perfect lips of hers. He had to trust her. Ruger forced himself to pull away, taking two steps back, gravel crunching under his heels.

"Ready?" she asked. He nodded tightly.

"Okay, then I'm gonna stick it in. Promise you won't panic?"

Ruger rolled his eyes.

"I wouldn't panic. I'm not a fuckin' baby, Soph. Jesus."

She didn't reply, but her eyes said it all, and Ruger felt a smile creep across his face.

"All right," he admitted, holding his hands up in surrender. "You win. I'm a big whiny baby and I just can't handle the thought of you doing anything fun without me. I never want you to have fun, I just want you barefoot and pregnant in the kitch—"

"Oh, shut up," she said, laughing. "Now I'm really doing it, and you're just going to have to deal with it. Stand back. I wouldn't want my big, bad biker man getting hit by gravel or something."

With that she slid the key into the ignition, and the red-and-black Harley softail roared to life. The look on her face was pure delight, and Ruger had to admit that the sight of her on the bike was fucking hot. He couldn't decide if he wanted her wearing more leather for protection on the road or less, because damn, she looked good when—

He cut off that thought. He needed to focus on his woman's safety, not her boobs.

"Be careful!" he yelled. Sophie laughed as she rolled down the driveway, then gave a shriek of delight when she hit the road and tore off.

Goddamnit.

"I'm gonna fuckin' kill Horse," Ruger muttered. He hated this. *Hated* it. "Kill him and that fuckin' bitch of his . . . always full of great ideas. She doesn't need her own goddamn bike."

"You shouldn't talk like that around Faith," Noah said, standing next to him. "She starts dropping F-bombs at preschool, Mom'll shit bricks."

The kid was twelve going on thirty, and in the past year he'd started shooting up into lanky adolescence. He was already getting phone calls from girls, which gave Sophie fits. Ruger was just happy Noah took after his mom in both looks and brains. Faith sat perched on Noah's shoulders, watching Ruger with big eyes, same as her mother's. She gave him a heart-wrenchingly beautiful smile, then opened her mouth and spoke solemnly.

"Fuckin' kiw Howse," she said.

Ruger sighed, then reached for his daughter, who climbed up him like a little spider monkey. He stuck his nose into her neck, smelling her sweet, not-quite-still-a-baby scent.

"You can't win this one," Noah said. "You know sooner or later Faith's gonna say something where Mom can hear."

"I'll just say she's copying you," Ruger said, narrowing his eyes. Noah laughed.

"You taught me in the first place."

"You're a little shit sometimes."

"Yeah, but I'm a little shit who's willing to throw you a lifeline," Noah replied thoughtfully. "If she says it in front of Mom, I'll say it's my fault if you pay me."

"How much?"

"Twenty bucks a pop."

"You got a deal."

SOPHIE

The bike roared under me and the wind danced across my face.

I loved it. I'd been practicing for a while, mostly out at Marie's place. She'd gotten her own bike a year ago. I'd never get tired of riding behind Ruger, but I loved being on my own, too. In fact, I'd spent six months trying to convince Ruger I should get my own ride.

Stupid man was positive I'd kill myself.

Problem was, deep down inside, Ruger was sexist as shit. Actually, it wasn't that deep—he'd always been pretty up front about it. But when he'd decided it was time for Noah to start learning on a little dirt bike, I'd had enough.

It was okay for my twelve-year-old son to ride, but not me?

Bullshit.

So earlier that week I'd announced I was buying a bike, and that he could either help me pick one out or live with what I got on my own. That lit a fire under his ass, and earlier today a friend of his delivered my pretty little Harley. Ruger didn't like it, but at least he knew it was a decent bike in good condition.

Still, I paid for it with my own money. I wanted it to be *my* bike. Not that we really had "mine" or "his" after we got married, but he insisted that I keep part of my paycheck in a separate account. I'd never said anything about it, but somehow Ruger knew—instinctively—that I needed to feel like I could take care of myself.

Having my own money helped with that.

I planned to use most of it for school for the kids, but every once in a while I treated us to something special. I'd taken him to Hawaii for our second anniversary, which had been a good investment, because I'd come home with Faith as a souvenir. I'd wondered if having a baby in the house would distance Ruger and Noah, but if anything they'd gotten closer. Every day Noah turned into more of a young man, and Ruger was a big part of that.

After a few minutes, I reached the end of the road and considered whether or not to turn back. I hadn't really put the bike through her paces—and she was definitely a *she*, I felt like we were sisters already—but I knew this was killing Ruger.

I smiled, feeling just a little evil.

Part of me wanted to just take off, feel the freedom and let him dangle for a while. It'd piss him off, but seriously . . . angry sex with my man was pretty damned good. I toyed with the idea, but turned the bike around and headed back toward the house instead.

Baby steps.

No need to scare him too much in one day, after all.

Best to save something for tomorrow, just in case he got out of line.

Printed in the United States
by Baker & Taylor Publisher Services